This book should be returned to any Lancashire County Council Library on or before the date shown

- 1 APR 2021

1 7

Lancashire County Council Library Service,
County Hall Complex,
2nd floor Christ Church Precinct,
Preston, PR1 0LD

www.lancashire.gov.uk/libraries

THE SHEIKH'S MARRIAGE PROCLAMATION

ANNIE WEST

THE BILLIONAIRE'S CINDERELLA HOUSEKEEPER

MIRANDA LEE

MILLS & BOON

First Published in Great Britain 2021
by Mills & Boon, an imprint of HarperCollins*Publishers*
1 London Bridge Street, London, SE1 9GF

The Sheikh's Marriage Proclamation © 2021 Annie West

The Billionaire's Cinderella Housekeeper © 2021 Miranda Lee

ISBN: 978-0-263-28234-4

Printed and bound in Spain
by CPI, Barcelona

THE SHEIKH'S MARRIAGE PROCLAMATION

ANNIE WEST

This one is for Erica Venning.
Thanks for being so positive and enthusiastic!

CHAPTER ONE

THE TRUCK STOPPED and Tara's pulse quickened. This was the part she feared. The dangerous part.

She could barely believe she was doing this, breaking the law, trying to enter a country illegally.

Escaping a country. That was more to the point.

She shuddered, thinking of her fate if she stayed in Dhalkur.

Any qualms about putting herself into the hands of a man she barely knew in order to escape faded compared to that.

The alternative, to remain in her mother's country, at Fuad's mercy, was impossible. Nausea swirled through her stomach and the stifling heat made her skin prickle.

Fear clawed at her. It made her ribs contract around her lungs and shortened her breath. Though perhaps the latter was also because of her tight cocoon, wedged in the back of the truck. It was early but the desert heat was rising.

There was a jolt, as if the driver climbed down or someone climbed aboard. Then the engine started and they rolled forward.

They'd passed the border.

Relief seared Tara's lungs as she sucked in a great gulp of air. As much as she could, anyway. There was precious little space and very little air, but she couldn't let herself think of that. She couldn't get claustrophobic now. Yunis would stop the truck once they were out of sight of the border and help her out of this confined space. All she had to do was keep calm and wait.

That took everything she had. The last month had been the worst of her life and now it had turned into a nightmare. Grief still ate away at her, making the world seem dull and grey. Everything except Fuad. *Him* she saw in Technicolor. And wished she didn't.

She never wanted to see him again. Her cousin had grown from a spiteful, sadistic boy into a ruthless, grasping man, ready to flatten anyone who stood between him and what he wanted.

Like Tara.

She shivered again, telling herself that soon she'd be free. The truck would stop and Yunis would let her out. Yunis, who'd known her mother years before and who took this enormous risk to help Tara. When she was safely away she'd find a way to repay him.

Tara yawned, tired despite the danger. Heat and lack of oxygen took their toll.

Soon they'd stop, and when they did…

She woke to panic and darkness. Heat pressed down on her, stifling. She couldn't move, her arms and legs were trapped. She couldn't see. She couldn't hear either. It was as if she were bound and weighted. Totally disorientated, she couldn't even tell which way was up.

Tara was about to scream when memory hit. The truck. The border. Yunis's offer to hide her in a delivery of merchandise he was taking into Nahrat.

She'd fallen asleep, that was all. She almost sobbed her relief.

Had she been this unbearably hot before? In the close darkness her overheated skin itched and her hair clung damply. How long had she been here?

There was a resonant thump as the back of the truck opened. Were those voices?

Instantly she closed her mouth on the words forming on her lips. Yunis was heading to the capital of Nahrat but promised to set her down somewhere quiet. The plan didn't involve other people.

Yet there they were again, male voices, muffled because of the way she was concealed and by the blood beating in her ears.

Where were they? Who were they? Had she made a mistake trusting the man who'd been her mother's friend?

Heart in mouth, she felt movement. Someone tugged at the bundle that concealed her. Masculine voices and a huff of laughter, and then, with a lurching sway that made her glad she'd had no time for breakfast, she was upended over something that might have been a shoulder.

Tara bit her lip, tasting blood, as she suppressed a cry of shock and discomfort. Fully awake now, unable to move, all she could do was stay silent and hope the change of plan didn't mean Fuad had found her.

Acid bit her belly at the idea of facing Fuad again.

Or the possibility of Yunis delivering her somewhere else. To ruthless men who'd have a use for Fuad's female cousin that she didn't want to think about.

Raif waited till he was alone then rose from the gilded seat at the centre of the marble dais. He stretched mightily, lifting his shoulders to ease the kinks there.

Despite his discomfort, his weekly public hearing of appeals was one centuries-old tradition he had no intention of changing. It was important people felt they had the ear of their Sheikh.

Today's session had started with a land dispute that had simmered for several generations, and which would try the wisdom of Solomon. From there he'd heard of an alleged dowry theft, issues with planning and electoral zone changes, and an accusation of impropriety against a government official.

Raif was particularly concerned by the allegation against the official. He administered funds for community-based projects and if true—

The doors opened and the palace chamberlain entered, bowing. He gestured to a tall man who carried something long over his shoulder. Even from here Raif saw the stranger was sweating, his breathing heavy and his eyes wide. Was his burden so heavy or was he nervous? The royal audience chamber was designed to impress visitors with its regal opulence.

'Quickly.' The chamberlain chivvied the man. 'Don't keep His Majesty waiting.'

Another bow and the chamberlain approached the royal dais. 'Sir, you asked to be informed when the gift for your aunt arrived.' He gestured towards the man slowly making his way across the floor of intricately inlaid stone. 'One of my staff happened to be at the border when the shipment came through, and ensured it was brought here immediately. I thought you'd want to view it to ensure it meets with your approval.'

Raif nodded. His chamberlain was a good man but sometimes too officious, eager to micromanage. He wouldn't be surprised if the palace official who'd happened to be at the border had been ordered to wait for the shipment. As if the delivery needed a special escort!

He transferred his attention to the stranger, who, with a huff of effort, carefully placed his burden on the floor. Then he bowed, keeping his head low.

'You may rise.'

Even then the newcomer seemed reluctant, straightening but staring in the direction of Raif's feet.

'Open the wrapping, so His Majesty can see.' The chamberlain stepped towards the package but instantly the stranger intercepted the movement, as if guarding his consignment.

'No!' He turned and for the first time met Raif's eyes. The skin drew tight at the back of Raif's neck. That look spoke of urgency, desperation even. 'If it pleases Your Majesty. You need to see this in private.' He looked over his shoulder towards the guard on the door.

Curious, Raif surveyed the stranger. 'Why is that?'

The man's mouth worked as if trying out and rejecting several responses. His hands twisted together. 'Please, Your Majesty. It's important. This is only for your eyes.'

Even the chamberlain looked surprised. 'Come now.' He started forward, as if to take matters into his own hands, but once more the stranger blocked the attempt.

'And you are?' Raif's voice cut across their altercation.

'Yunis, Your Majesty. I'm head of the Dhalkuri Royal Guild of—'

'I know who you are.' His aunt had sung this man's praises, which was why Raif had commissioned this gift for her from his workshop. 'I look forward to seeing what you've brought.'

Not merely because he wanted something special for his aunt, but because Raif's interest was piqued. His aunt hadn't only praised his work, but also his character.

'Please, Your Majesty.' Another, lingering look over his shoulder then Yunis placed a hand on his heart. 'I swear I mean no harm.'

Curiouser and curiouser. With an abrupt nod Raif dismissed the guard, who stepped out and closed the door behind him.

'Your Majesty!' the chamberlain expostulated.

Raif ignored him. Yunis wouldn't have been able to enter the palace if armed. Besides, Raif's aunt had vouched for him.

'Open it,' he ordered.

Yunis shot the chamberlain a last, disapproving stare then knelt and untied the strips of fabric binding the cylinder. He murmured something beneath his breath that Raif couldn't catch, then slowly, as carefully as if it were made of spun gold threaded with precious jewels, he unwrapped the parcel.

A tasselled edge of pale gold caught the light, as if giving flesh to Raif's imaginings. Now Yunis unrolled more, shuffling further away as the long carpet was revealed. Golds mixed with the pale colours of the desert sands, contrasting with indigo blues and deep purples.

His aunt would love it. The colours were her favourites and not usually chosen by traditional weavers. Raif could see the piece was beautifully made. Yet why the demand for privacy? Why take so long to unroll it?

The chamberlain obviously thought the same thing. Before Yunis could stop him he grabbed one side and yanked. The carpet unspooled with a thud and an unexpected flurry and Raif found himself staring down at bare limbs, a tangle of dark hair and huge, staring eyes.

The chamberlain jumped back, exclaiming. Yunis froze.

And still Raif stared.

She, for it was undoubtedly a she, wore a dress the colour of ripe raspberries. Or half wore it, for there seemed to be a lot of glowing golden flesh on display. Shapely calves and smooth thighs. Her breasts rose and fell beneath their scant crimson covering as she sucked in huge gasps of air. And still those eyes stared back at him.

Raif felt the impact of that stare somewhere near the base of his spine and deeper, in his gut.

Finally, a slender arm lifted and she pushed back the swathe of long hair to reveal a flushed face.

She was beautiful, or close to it.

Perhaps it was the ripe mouth that made her look so ravishing. She had full lips, slightly downturned at the corners. That should have made her appear disgruntled but instead created a sultry look.

Raif felt another phantom jab to his belly.

The flush mantling her cheeks, throat and the upper

slopes of her breasts, the tumble of dark hair and her breath-lessness inevitably made Raif think of bed. Of bed and passion.

'Cleopatra, I presume?'

The voice suited him. It trawled dark, deep and danger-ous through her middle, like a velvet ribbon wound around metal.

For there was definitely steel in that voice. She saw it too in those hooded eyes, hawk-like in their intensity. In the arrogant angle of his jaw and the black eyebrow that snaked up his forehead in an expression of enquiry mixed with derision.

Already tall, he towered above her from a raised plat-form, making her feel tiny and insignificant, sprawled be-fore him. His formal robes, pristine white and trimmed with gold, contrasted with her bedraggled state. His folded arms spoke of authority tinged with impatience.

He was magnificent.

And he knew it.

Feminine instinct, old as the ages, told her this man un-derstood the aura of power and unadulterated masculinity he projected. Knew and revelled in it.

Or simply took it for granted.

Blinking, still catching her breath, half dazed from dis-comfort and lack of oxygen, she took too long to understand the Cleopatra reference. Then it struck her. Cleopatra sup-posedly had herself smuggled into Julius Caesar's quarters wrapped in a carpet, then famously proceeded to seduce him.

Shock stabbed her, and a rising tide of mortification.

Tara groped with unsteady fingers at the tie of her wrap-around dress, only to discover the bow undone and the dress gaping.

With a gasp of horror she fumbled, searching for the

loose ends, hampered by hands that were too slow and a heaving stomach that threatened to embarrass her totally.

She heard voices, Yunis's perhaps, but couldn't take them in, overcome by the twin needs to cover her body and stop herself from retching. The long journey, stifling and overheated, left her prey to welling nausea.

Beyond the fringe of the carpet she saw intricate designs of semi-precious stones set into the marble floor. She lifted her head again and had an impression of enormous space. A domed, glittering ceiling above a room empty but for the podium where *he* stood.

The setting confirmed her fears. In that first instant facing him she'd been too befuddled and sick to do more than drink in his presence. Now the truth smacked her in the face.

This was no ordinary room. As the man surveying her so imperiously was no ordinary man.

Tara knew that austere, handsome face. Anyone with an interest in current affairs would recognise it.

Yunis hadn't sold her to some human trafficker. He'd brought her to the Sheikh of Nahrat.

Appalled, she felt her rebellious stomach lurch and her skin prickle.

She'd made it over the border but she wasn't safe. Bad enough to be discovered as an illegal alien sneaking into his country. But that would be nothing compared with her fate if he discovered who she was and decided to return her to her cousin.

Sick to the depths of her curdling stomach, Tara grasped her dress tight around herself and tottered to her feet, pushing her shoulders back and setting her jaw.

'Your Majesty.' She couldn't manage a curtsey, much less a bow, so she simply dipped her head and focused on staying upright despite the wobbling knees and whirling nausea.

'That was quite a performance.'

Impossible to gauge his mood from his words. Was he being sarcastic? She didn't lift her head to find out. Instead Tara swallowed hard, telling herself she would not be ill. She would *not*!

'Your name?'

Slowly she raised her eyes, hoping that this time he wouldn't look quite so indomitable. Tara wasn't sure she had the energy to deal with indomitable at the moment.

It was a vain hope. Sheikh Raif ibn Ansar of Nahrat looked more unmovable and keen-eyed than before.

'Tara, Your Majesty.' She drew a deep breath and mentally crossed her fingers. It was unlikely her surname would mean anything to him. 'Tara Michaels.'

'And the meaning of this exhibition, Ms Michaels?' His eyes narrowed on her. 'I admit it's a novel entrance but it lacks…dignity.' He didn't appear to move yet suddenly he looked even more imposing. 'Despite what some believe, I have no interest in women falling at my feet, literally or otherwise.'

His stare didn't leave her face but that didn't stop her searing blush, as if he'd raked that sharp gaze across her whole body.

Because something about his scrutiny made her inescapably aware of herself as a woman and him as a man.

Or because he'd already looked and found her wanting?

Then there was his outrageous assumption she'd *planned* this humiliating scene.

As if any sane woman would have herself unrolled at his feet like some…offering! She'd bet that old story about Cleopatra had been invented by a man. A man with a salacious mind.

Indignation sputtered to life.

'If you please, Your Majesty.' Yunis stepped forward to stand beside her. 'It was a mistake. This wasn't meant to happen.' He turned to Tara, his weathered features creased with worry. 'I was met at the border. I had no chance to stop and let you out before reaching the palace.'

'People smuggling,' said another voice, and a rotund little man moved into Tara's line of vision. 'I'll call the guard and have them locked up.'

At the words, Tara's strength crumbled. The thought of being locked up again, on top of what she'd been through! Her knees folded but Yunis grabbed her elbow, holding her steady.

'There's no need for that,' said the Sheikh. 'I'll interview them myself. You may go. And you will keep this to yourself until I decide what action to take.'

Tara barely heard the little man leave. But she did hear the firm tread of the Sheikh's feet as he stepped from the dais and crossed the floor.

'Are you ill?'

Tara struggled to straighten her spine and lock her knees. 'Motion sickness,' she muttered. 'There was no air in there and it got so hot.'

For long, silent seconds the Sheikh regarded her. He was close enough for her to see that his eyes were so dark they seemed black. The effect was arresting.

The need to meet his scrutiny, not to waver or look away, helped her fight her uneasy stomach and shaky limbs.

'Come,' he said finally. He turned and left the room, not bothering to see if they followed.

Twenty minutes later, Tara sat in a luxuriously appointed sitting room. Her chair was so comfortable she wanted to curl up in it and rest her weary head. She hadn't slept last night and the day had been fraught.

She'd half expected to be led to a bare interrogation cell. Instead, a smiling woman had brought a jug of iced water and a plate of biscuits.

Now Tara's nausea had receded, all she wanted was to leave. Except the Sheikh had taken Yunis with him and Tara couldn't leave without making sure Yunis was okay. It was her fault he was in this mess.

She would have searched for him except for the guard standing to attention outside the room.

So she contented herself with resting her head against the soft upholstery and closing her eyes, recruiting her strength.

She wasn't sure what woke her. Not a sound, but perhaps the sensation of being watched.

Tara opened her eyes and discovered she wasn't alone.

Fathomless dark eyes surveyed her. Sheikh Raif of Nahrat didn't even blink as he sat there, watching her.

Hurriedly Tara unfolded her legs, which had been tucked up beneath her, and sat straighter, feet to the floor. Tentatively she felt with her toes for her discarded sandals then gave up. So she was barefoot. He'd already seen her with her dress half undone. What were bare feet after that?

Swiftly checking the neckline of her dress hadn't gaped as she slept, Tara folded her hands primly in her lap. 'Where's Yunis?'

'You don't need to worry about him.'

'I don't?' Her head seemed thick and slow to work. 'You've released him? He's free?'

The Sheikh tapped the fingers of one hand on the arm of his chair. 'Of course not. He broke the law, smuggling you over the border. The rest of his consignment is being examined. Who knows what else he's smuggled in?'

Tara shook her head. 'It's not like that. He's not really a smuggler.'

'Not *really*?' He looked sceptical.

'It's *true*! He brought me in as a favour.'

'That's hardly an excuse for people smuggling. It's a serious offence. If he has no respect for our borders he may have committed other offences too. He'll be treated accordingly.'

The Sheikh looked so severe that Tara's heart dipped. She sat forward onto the edge of her seat, hands clasped.

'What have you done with him?'

Nahrat was reputedly a progressive country with modern laws. But recent contact with Fuad had proved how little the law meant when a powerful, merciless man chose to ignore it. Was Yunis facing more than interrogation? Horrified, she shot to her feet.

'Have you hurt him?'

The Sheikh sat back in his seat. 'Would it matter if I had?'

Horror crawled up Tara's spine and filled her mouth. She felt the blood drain to her toes.

'Of course it matters! Torture is wrong, as well as illegal.'

She dragged in a shaky breath but kept her gaze fixed on that enigmatic stare. She'd thought those dark eyes sexy. Now they seemed full of threat. 'Truly, he's a decent man. He's never done this before. He saw I was desperate and offered me a chance to escape. He was trying to help.'

The Sheikh nodded. 'So he says. He's currently waiting, unharmed, while his story is verified.'

Tara felt herself deflate like a punctured balloon. She landed back on the chair with a thump, her pounding heart at odds with her suddenly boneless body.

'Why did you let me think you'd hurt him?'

'That was purely your imagination, Ms Michaels. And a very vivid one it is.' He paused, and when he spoke again it was with the harsh ring of authority. Or was it annoyance? 'I uphold the law in my country, which means even wrongdoers receive a fair hearing.'

Tara noted the frown lines creasing his forehead and the now flat line of his mouth.

Had she bruised his pride with her question? Surely not. He'd deliberately toyed with her, making her worry. To unsettle her?

She'd spent too much time recently with Fuad. Her cousin stopped at nothing to get what he wanted and didn't shy from causing pain. In fact, he seemed to thrive on it. Had she wrongly tarred the Sheikh with the same brush?

'Tell me the truth, Ms Michaels.'

'I am!' Sitting straight, she fixed him with what she hoped was a calm look, when inside she felt anything but calm.

She'd escaped Fuad's clutches but if this man sent her back across the border there'd be no second chance to escape. She couldn't afford to go back. The question was, how much could she share with this man? How much could she trust him?

'I'm a British citizen and—'

'Congratulations. You speak our language well.'

'I...' How much to reveal? 'My mother was from Dhalkur and I was born there. I lived there till I was eight.'

'And you've come back to visit your family?'

Tara hesitated. This was unsafe territory. If he discovered who her cousin was, he'd feel obliged to return her.

'My mother is dead, Your Majesty.' Her throat turned scratchy and she found herself swallowing convulsively. A month wasn't long enough to adjust to the loss.

She looked down at her hands, saw them clenched, bone-white with tension, and made them relax. When she looked up the Sheikh's gaze was unreadable.

'There was nothing to keep me in Dhalkur. I want to go home. But I...lost my passport—'

'And your luggage?'

'Sorry?'

'My staff inform me no baggage was found in the truck. You were travelling light, Ms Michaels.'

Because if she'd been seen walking down into the courtyard with a suitcase she'd most definitely have been stopped. But she couldn't say that.

Tara forced herself to shrug. 'I was in a hurry. I have to get back to London quickly and Yunis offered to help me. He's an old friend of my mother's, from years ago.' That much was true, at least.

'So, instead of going to the authorities and reporting the loss of your passport, you chose to break the law, and incite your accomplice to do the same, by crossing the border illegally.'

His face was calm but his voice was stern, like a judge pronouncing sentence.

'Surely you can do better than that, Ms Michaels.' His mouth lifted at one corner in a cold smile that made her shiver. 'Or should I call you Princess Tara?'

CHAPTER TWO

TARA'S BREATH ESCAPED in a whoosh of defeat. Her shoulders sagged and she slumped back against the sumptuous upholstery.

This was it, then. No chance to escape now.

Despair cut through her. A chill blast of fear iced her bones at the idea of going back. She shivered and would have crossed her arms against the sudden cold except this eagle-eyed man would notice.

He noticed everything, she was sure.

There was no surprise on his features, not even satisfaction that he'd guessed right.

'You knew! All this time you knew and you didn't say anything.' That stiffened her backbone.

He shrugged, his wide shoulders rising with nonchalant ease. 'I was waiting for you to tell me.'

As if she had any reason to trust him. For all she knew he was a friend of Fuad's.

'*Is* Yunis okay? Will you release him now you have me?'

Something changed in that hard, handsome face. For a second it looked as if she'd surprised him. Yet how could that be? He was the one who'd walked into the room knowing her identity.

'You make it sound as if I *want* to have you.'

Tara blinked. Was there a chance he'd simply let her go? But she was clutching at straws. Even if he wasn't a friend of her cousin's, as leader of a neighbouring country he'd feel obliged to return her to Fuad. He wouldn't want to fracture relations for the sake of a woman he didn't even know.

'Please, at least let him go. Yunis was trying to do a good deed, that's all.'

'Yunis again?' This time his frown was more than a

slight twitch across his forehead. 'Does he mean that much to you? What is he? A lover?'

'Of course not!' How had he made that leap? 'He's old enough to be my father!' She met the Sheikh's sceptical gaze and shook her head. 'He's an old friend of my mother's,' she reiterated. 'They knew each other before she married. He helped me for her sake.'

For long seconds there was silence, then finally he inclined his head. 'Fortunately, your Yunis is also a trusted acquaintance of my aunt. After questioning him it was obvious he's not in the habit of smuggling. He'll be released with a warning.'

Tara's heart thundered with relief. It was enough, almost, to counteract indignation at the way this man had manipulated her. 'Thank you. He's a good man. I'd hate to see him punished for this.'

She'd bear punishment enough for two when she was taken back across the border.

'Is it possible, do you think…? Could you *not* mention his name when you talk to the authorities in Dhalkur?' Because even if the Sheikh of Nahrat refused to press charges, Fuad would make Yunis pay and his methods were likely to be ones Tara preferred not to think about.

'I'll consider it.' He paused. 'Depending on how straight you are with me, Princess.'

Tara stiffened. 'Don't. Please. I'm not a princess.'

Ebony eyebrows rose. 'You're the niece of the ruling Sheikh of Dhalkur.'

Tara hiked her chin up. 'But I'm not royal. I wasn't raised in the palace and I can't inherit the throne. My father was British.' The law in Dhalkur decreed that only men could lead the nation. Just as well. She couldn't imagine herself in that role.

'Yet some would say your lineage is more royal than your cousin Fuad's.'

Something inside her stalled. Was it possible Fuad, and by extension this man, saw her as a threat to Fuad's rule?

Her neck tingled with a presentiment of fear. She'd thought her fate bad enough, when trapped in Dhalkur, but if Fuad saw her as a rival, rather than a convenient tool to be exploited...

'Fuad is my uncle's eldest son. When my uncle dies Fuad will become Sheikh of Dhalkur.' That wouldn't be far off, given how poorly her uncle seemed.

The man before her inclined his head. 'That's certainly what Prince Fuad wants.'

His gaze dropped, surveying her from head to bare feet. Tara had to work not to twitch her toes in embarrassment. She wished she were wearing something classy and sophisticated. Something more than a cotton wraparound dress.

Sheikh Raif ibn Ansar didn't look at her the way Fuad did. There was nothing obviously sexual in that stare. Yet suddenly she was aware that they were alone together. That he was the most overtly masculine man she'd ever met. And that he made her aware of her femininity even now, when disaster crowded in on her.

'Your blood tie to the crown is stronger than his.' His voice, deep and musing, sounded far too appealing.

Tara's fingernails bit into the silk upholstery of her chair. There *had* apparently been muttered protests about Fuad inheriting the throne. The complaints were about his character and ability to lead the nation but not, as far as she knew, about the fact that his father, the current Sheikh, had been adopted by Tara's grandfather.

'People say that *yours* is the truly royal bloodline,' her interrogator murmured.

'No! My uncle was legally adopted and became my grandfather's heir. The royal council accepted it.'

Her mother had privately revealed that Tara's grandfather, the old Sheikh, had been so heartbroken when his first wife died that he'd refused to remarry to father a male heir, even though his daughter couldn't inherit the throne. In the end, bowing to pressure, he'd married his best friend's widow, adopting her son as his. The marriage and adoption were legal. But, according to her mother, the marriage was never consummated because the Sheikh couldn't bring himself to sleep with a woman other than his first wife.

Tara had thought the secret story terribly romantic. Like her parents falling in love at first meeting.

The fact remained that Tara's grandfather had gone to enormous lengths to secure the royal succession. She had no intention of becoming a pawn for those who tried to complicate it now. Especially as she had no desire to remain in Dhalkur.

'My home and my life are in Britain,' she said crisply. 'The current, legitimate Sheikh has two sons. Either could inherit the throne.'

Yet it was Fuad, the eldest, who was most likely to ascend the throne. Especially as his brother Salim was away overseas. Knowing Fuad, he'd try to keep Salim away till after the coronation.

Then there was his plan to use Tara, and especially the inheritance she hadn't known about till a week ago, to boost his position. Her stomach churned whenever she thought about it, a reaction that had nothing to do with her long, uncomfortable journey.

'So, *Ms Michaels*.' Tara felt her tension unravel a little now that the Sheikh had dropped the title that was so foreign to her. 'If you lost your passport, why not report it and get a new one?'

She met that obsidian-dark stare and knew she should have an answer ready. Yet the stresses of the day had sapped her inventive powers. She'd never had reason to lie in the past and it didn't come easily now.

'I...'

'Yes?' Elbows on the arms of his chair, he steepled his hands beneath his chin, as if waiting to consider her answer.

Did he have any idea how daunting he was? With his piercing gaze and the low, coaxing voice that encouraged the sharing of secrets yet barely concealed what she guessed was razor-sharp intelligence.

This man would see through any fumbling lie she proffered.

'Are you a friend of my cousin?'

'Why?' His expression didn't alter yet Tara *felt* the difference in him. As if suddenly he was on high alert.

'I'm curious.' Tara kept her gaze steady and her chin up, as if a quiver of nerves wasn't racketing through her taut body.

'You think that's sufficient reason to pry into personal matters?'

Tara was about to retort that he was prying into her life, but the situation wasn't the same. She was the one who'd sneaked into his country, his very palace, breaking who knew how many laws.

When she didn't reply he lifted his shoulders. 'I know your uncle and both your cousins. I wouldn't say I'm a friend of Fuad.'

Her shoulders dropped a fraction. If he wasn't a friend then perhaps there was a chance.

'And Salim?'

His honed features seemed to tighten, as if he was annoyed by her effrontery in questioning him. But what could she lose? She already faced the worst if he deported her back to Dhalkur.

After what seemed an eternity he spoke. 'Again, I don't know Salim intimately. I wouldn't call myself a friend. But I respect him.'

There'd been no mention of him respecting Fuad. Because he wasn't a fan, or because he was playing some double bluff, trying to entice her into revealing too much? These last couple of days she hadn't known who she could trust, until the unexpected meeting with Yunis and his offer of help.

Tara's head, still thick from the effects of her journey, began to throb.

'You were about to tell me why you didn't simply apply for a new passport.'

He was determined to get an answer, wasn't he?

'I didn't actually *lose* my passport.' She snatched in a quick breath then kept talking before her courage failed. 'Fuad confiscated it and refused to give it back.'

Saying the words brought it all back, the disbelief and horror. Her voice wobbled on the words and she looked down at her hands, pleating the material of her skirt. She smoothed out the fabric then placed her hands on the arms of her chair, trying to appear calm even though she wasn't.

'Are you going to explain?' Impatience threaded his voice.

'It depends. Are you going to send me back?'

'Clearly you don't want to return. But before I decide what to do with you, I demand an explanation. Especially,' his dark eyes pinioned her, 'if I'm to expect fallout from Dhalkur. I don't want an international incident. Your uncle and I have worked hard to improve relations between our countries, but old grievances still simmer and it will be some time before I'd call our relationship friendly.'

He sounded so reasonable. As if she were being paranoid. But the last week had turned her view of the world as basically safe and normal totally on its head. And she knew nothing of this man.

'Truly, I never meant for any sort of incident. I was hoping to get clear away without being discovered.'

'Without a passport or money?'

His gaze raked her light cotton dress and simple sandals, as if noting her lack of even a handbag.

Tara did have money with her, tucked into her bra with her driver's licence, but she wasn't going to reveal that.

She shrugged. 'I didn't have much choice. I was a prisoner and I had the chance to get away, so I took it.'

When he said nothing, just watched her with that glittering gaze, she knew she had no option but to tell him everything, or at least enough to satisfy him.

She spread her hands. 'My mother died last month and about ten days ago I had a visit from representatives of the Dhalkuri embassy in London. They had a message from my uncle, asking me to return to sort out some of my mother's affairs. A few days later, after I'd arranged some time off work, I travelled with them to Dhalkur. I saw my uncle and Fuad and talked to a lawyer about a…bequest from my mother.'

No need to go into detail about the property her mother had inherited from Tara's grandfather and never mentioned, or that her solicitor in London didn't know about. The property which was now worth a fortune because of the rare earth metals discovered there, ready to be mined.

'I was a guest at the palace and at first I felt welcome.' For about a day, until Fuad's bizarre announcement. 'My uncle is very ill and Fuad has taken charge.'

The palace had an entirely different feel to the last time she'd visited. The servants didn't smile and the large kennel of pure-bred hunting dogs, her uncle's pride and joy, was empty. Fuad had ordered the dogs be got rid of—destroyed if homes couldn't be found for them. He'd always hated them, because they, and most animals for that matter, didn't like him.

'Go on.'

Tara looked up, dragging herself back from old memories. 'On the second day Fuad announced that he intended to marry. He said it would bolster his reputation as a solid leader to have a wife and potentially a family on the way. He said the country didn't want a repeat of the insecurity when my grandfather didn't have a clear male heir for so long.'

'He believes marrying will advance his cause beyond his brother's?'

Tara was on the point of saying *nothing* would make Fuad a better prospect than his brother, then recalled she didn't yet know how far she could trust this man.

'He seems to think so. He also thought, for the reasons you've mentioned, that marrying into my grandfather's bloodline would cement that advantage.'

She swallowed hard, trying to remove the bitter tang from her tongue.

'In other words, he wants to marry *you*.'

Did that unreadable face change? Did she imagine the tiniest flare of something in those midnight eyes?

It would be nice to believe him sympathetic but she couldn't count on it.

'Yes. He does.'

She shivered at the memory of Fuad's expression when she'd turned him down. And later, how anger had melded with a possessive hunger that frightened her to the core.

'I couldn't go to my uncle for help. He's too sick.' Tara looked down at her hands. 'He's dying.'

She'd never been close to him but he'd been kind over the years in his own way. His views on women were old-fashioned, but he'd be horrified to know of Fuad's threats.

'I know. I'm sorry.'

There it was again. Something in the Sheikh's tone drew her eyes up to meet his and she had the impression that stern face fleetingly softened.

Was it an illusion because she desperately needed this man's sympathy?

He looked like someone who'd never be bullied by her cousin. He looked like the sort of man who...

No, she had no time for feminine fantasies. Her situation was too desperate.

Tara hurried on. 'Fuad threatened to keep me prisoner till I agreed to marry him.'

That wasn't all he'd threatened. He'd made pointed reference to her small size and strength compared with his. He'd been determined to claim her, one way or another.

Another shiver skated down her spine and her nostrils flared as she remembered the smell of him when he'd grabbed her arms in a vice-like grip and thrust his face towards hers. Only the appearance of a messenger from his father's doctor had made him break away.

That was when Tara realised she had to make a run for it. Fuad wasn't making empty threats.

She already knew about men who grabbed what they wanted from helpless women.

'Ms Michaels? Tara?'

She looked up to find the Sheikh leaning forward, his brow pleated. In concern?

Their gazes locked and Tara had the strangest feeling of connection. Of understanding.

Then, abruptly, he sat back and the moment shattered.

'He can't touch you here. You have my word on it.'

'Thank you.' Blood rushed through her body, her ears filled with the sound. She swallowed, her throat suddenly scratchy. 'Does that mean you won't send me back?'

Raif looked into clear green eyes that looked huge in that tense face and felt an unwilling pang of sympathy.

Initially it had been her pouting mouth that had drawn him. And, yes, that small but utterly feminine body. Now, so close he saw every emotion flitting across her features, he discovered Tara Michaels' expressive eyes were her most potent weapon.

Ever since she'd appeared at his feet, like a surprise birthday gift unwrapped for his pleasure, he'd had difficulty focusing on anything else. Even while he was questioning Yunis, the head of the master weavers' cooperative who'd delivered her to the palace, part of Raif's mind had been back in this room with this runaway.

'No. You're safe for now.'

'For now?' She leaned towards him, hands clasped together as if in prayer. 'What do you mean? What are you planning to do?'

Raif raised one hand. 'Be calm. I've promised you'll be safe in my home. You must be content with that while I decide what's to be done.'

Already she was shaking her head, her dark hair, which she'd secured in a long plait, sliding over one shoulder. Raif refused to watch the way it teased her breast. 'I know what's best. I need to return home immediately, to England.'

'Why? Is someone waiting there for you? A man who can protect you?'

Where had that come from? Yet he found himself canting forward, waiting for her answer.

'I don't need a man to protect me.' She sat straighter, as if to make up for her diminutive size. 'I can look after myself.'

Raif refused to say the obvious, that she hadn't been able to do so up till now.

But that was unfair. She'd been isolated in the royal palace. The royal servants would have done Fuad's bidding even if they didn't approve of his actions. With his father terminally ill and failing more each day, his was the power behind the throne. Raif's contacts across the border had already reported a number of troubling changes as Fuad sought to establish authority in the country.

Not for the first time Raif wished Fuad's younger

brother, Salim, were home. Raif didn't interfere in politics across the border but it was obvious Dhalkur would be unstable under Fuad's temperamental influence. As for the years of work Raif had put into improving relations between the countries...

He suppressed a sigh.

He'd need to tread carefully. This was a complication he didn't relish.

Yet he knew he'd never hand Tara Michaels to her cousin.

It made sense not to give the man a bride who might win him the sheikhdom. But Raif knew it wasn't the future of the sheikhdom influencing him.

It was her expression, alternating between determination and vulnerability. That proudly firm chin, betrayed by the tiniest wobble of dismay. Those pouting lips, downturned now in disapproval. That body, petite but perfectly formed.

Silently Raif cursed. For he felt his body's quickening. The desire not just to protect the victim of a bully, but also to taste this woman's passion.

Would that mouth be as soft as it looked? Would those rapidly rising breasts fit his hands as exactly as he imagined?

His jaw tightened, muscles flexing hard as he banished the unruly thoughts. Raif never let lust override logic. Attraction and passion could be enjoyed, but always within set limits.

Besides, she needed help. Not another man slavering over her. He had no doubt Fuad's interest in his cousin wasn't solely for political reasons. The woman was a pocket Venus.

Disgusted at his thoughts, Raif concentrated on what must happen next. He had yet to confirm the details of her story. His contacts in Dhalkur had mentioned the arrival of the Sheikh's niece but she hadn't appeared in public. Raif needed to check that this was the same woman.

'Yes or no, Ms Michaels? Have you a protector in England?'

Fire simmered in her bewitching eyes. Her mouth turned mutinous. 'No.'

Raif exhaled slowly, telling himself it wasn't relief he felt that she didn't have a man in her life. It was no business of his, except in so far as she might have a champion.

'But the law will protect me there. I—'

'Tell me,' he broke across her protest, 'these representatives from the embassy who visited your home, they were men?'

'Yes.' She looked puzzled.

'Old or young?'

'Young.'

'Two young men. Fit-looking?'

'I… Yes, I suppose so.'

'And your flight from the UK was with a commercial airline?'

'No.' She was frowning now. 'It was on a private jet from a small airport.'

Raif nodded. 'Did it not occur to you to wonder why your cousin should send two people to invite you to Dhalkur? Surely one would do? Even a phone call from a lawyer.' He paused as he saw his words sink in. 'Instead he sent two young, presumably strong, men to your home.'

'You think if I hadn't agreed to go they'd have abducted me?'

Her face paled and Raif almost regretted stripping away her illusions. But her safety depended on it.

'I think Fuad leaves little to chance. He knows what he wants and he's determined to get it.'

'You don't think I'll be safe in London.'

'I don't.'

He watched her swallow, her hands clenching against the vivid crimson of her dress.

'I…see.' For a moment he caught a quiver on her lips before she flattened them and looked away, staring wide-eyed across the room as if she'd never before seen a potted orchid. Or was it the bookcase beyond that she stared at?

When she turned back her eyes looked glassy but she was calm, except for those restless hands knotting and unknotting in her lap.

'That complicates things. I'm afraid I'm not quite sure what to do now.'

Unwilling admiration stirred. He'd heard of the British stiff upper lip. Given her situation, her desperate escape attempt and her dramatic entrance, he wouldn't have been surprised if she'd succumbed to tears. He was profoundly grateful she hadn't. He abhorred shows of feminine emotion.

Which was still no reason to take a hand in this.

Raif didn't interfere with Dhalkuri politics. It was the first rule of good international relations.

Yet this woman was, however unintentionally, a guest under his roof. She deserved protection.

He *wanted* to protect her.

The thought of returning her to Fuad's less than tender mercies made his mouth curl at the sour taste on his tongue.

As did the idea of handing the man an asset, in the form of a bride, who'd help win the throne. Raif would far prefer it if Fuad's brother, Salim, inherited. A sensible, capable ruler rather than an unstable, egotistical one.

'For now, you don't have to worry about that. Rest here tonight and we'll meet tomorrow to discuss your options.'

CHAPTER THREE

TARA SOAKED HER stiff body in a deep bath. Even her arms finally stopped aching in the warm water. Dark bruises encircled her upper arms from when Fuad had tried to force himself on her.

That was in the past. Thanks to the Sheikh.

He seemed decent, if remote. There was no reason to believe him in league with her cousin. If so, surely he'd have packed her back to Dhalkur straight away.

Yet exposure to Fuad had made her wary. Politics was a devious game. She remembered her cousin's covetous look when he talked of her inheritance. Perhaps Sheikh Raif wanted a share of that? How much did he know about her?

Tara firmed her lips and sank back in the soothing water.

She had no option but to accept his offer of a bed for the night. She'd just have to be on her guard while she worked out her next step.

Except she had no idea what that would be.

Anxiety skated through her.

Technically London was home, so it had made sense to head there. Except Sheikh Raif had shown her how that might play into Fuad's grasping hands.

She gnawed her lip, pondering where she'd be safe.

London felt like a temporary stopgap. She and her mother had moved there after the mining accident in Africa that killed her father. Before that they'd lived in Asia, Australia and South America—wherever his work took him.

Maybe that was why Tara had felt restless in Britain. She was used to moving on. London was invigorating but the clouds and damp got her down. She longed for wide skies and warmth.

She'd been tempted to move from the UK in search of

adventure but then her mother was diagnosed with cancer and Tara had shelved any thought of travel till her mother recovered. But after four years there'd been no recovery.

Her chest squeezed. Memories crowded, her beloved mum fading before her eyes. Yet she'd been indomitable to the end, making Tara promise to make the most of her life when she was gone.

Tara swallowed the familiar knot of hot grief that clogged her throat.

She loved her job as sales clerk for a top-class jeweller, but going back to her old routine didn't feel like making the most of life. Once she'd had plans to study and become a gem expert but that seemed a long time ago.

Tara sighed and let her head sink back. Scented steam curled around her, courtesy of the maid's lavish hand, scattering bath salts and rose petals.

The last few years she'd had little time to rest. At work she'd had to hide her emotions and be the consummate professional. At home and then at the hospice, she'd put on a brave face, talking about future travel plans, or outings with friends, anything to see her mother smile and relax.

After her recent stresses, Tara could handle some decadent luxury. Yet she felt like an imposter here. She was a sheikh's granddaughter but she'd never felt royal, never experienced such luxury, even at the Dhalkuri palace.

When Tara was shown to this suite with its courtyard, sitting room, dressing room and bathroom with a tub the size of a small swimming pool, she'd been ready to protest that there'd been a mistake. But tiredness had won out.

She'd had an ultra-quick shower, then fallen into blessed oblivion, sleeping the afternoon away, till a maid brought tea and honey pastries.

Sheikh Raif's hospitality made her think more kindly of him. Even if he looked down that handsome nose at her. And made her uncomfortably self-aware.

Tara frowned. Strange how different his regard was to Fuad's. Her cousin had stared at her in a hungry way that made her feel like ants swarmed across her skin.

Once or twice she'd seen something in Sheikh Raif's eyes that made her body heat. He'd sized her up with the swift judgement of a connoisseur of women. Yet, despite that, and his ability to infuriate her, he hadn't made her feel that dreadful skin-crawling sensation she experienced with Fuad.

Or on that night when she was seventeen and her date spiked her drink. Someone had seen what happened and rescued her before he could assault her. Yet she retained a horribly vivid memory of his leer as he reached for her while she'd been unable to move or defend herself. That awful sense of ceding control still haunted her dreams. It had been reignited this week under Fuad's threats.

Yet, here in Nahrat, Tara's body came to life in new and disturbing ways under the Sheikh's dark gaze.

It was remarkable. For years she'd been wary of men, especially attractive ones, like the guy who'd doped her. Yet caution wasn't her first instinct around the Sheikh.

She shifted, acutely aware of the warm water caressing her body, the tug and lap of it against bare skin.

Tara thought of hooded black eyes, proud features, so severe they shouldn't be handsome but were. The man was powerful, macho and used to getting his own way.

Her heart raced. What would it be like to be wanted by a man like that?

She couldn't believe she even wondered. Surely he was the sort to impose his will on a woman.

A husky chuckle escaped as she realised her foolishness. She'd never find out how it felt. He saw her as a political hot potato, not a potential lover.

Which was good. If ever she sought a lover it wouldn't

be someone like Raif of Nahrat, so proud he'd probably click his fingers to summon his latest woman.

Yet that wasn't right. Something about his eyes and sensual mouth betrayed the ascetic's face. Tara imagined he'd be a demanding lover but a generous one.

Suddenly she was tingling all over. Beneath the warm water her nipples budded and between her legs there was a tiny ache.

Horrified, she surged to her feet and reached for a towel.

Her clothes had been removed for washing. In their place was a long caftan of silk so fragile it felt like a butterfly's wing. It was of deep amethyst, embroidered in gold around the neckline with its deep central slit, and around the wide wrists. Instead of her sandals there was a pair of delicate slippers, covered in embroidered amethyst silk.

She'd never possessed anything so fine.

After a second's hesitation Tara lifted the dress over her head. The silk on bare flesh felt decadently luxurious, making her once more hyper-aware of her body.

Tara huffed her self-disgust. First she'd been unsettled by Sheikh Raif, and now by new clothes and a temporary lack of underwear. She was in a strange place with strange clothes and people she didn't know. That was all. Tomorrow morning, when she had her own belongings back, she'd feel herself again.

Flipping her hair back over her shoulders, she opened the door and crossed the bedroom. She needed a computer to check flights.

If only she knew where she was going. Once more fear curdled her insides. Fuad had power on his side and she didn't even have a plan.

'Hello, Tara.' The deep voice stopped her on the threshold of the sitting room.

She blinked, taking in the darkening night sky through the windows and the cosy glow of lamps.

A figure rose from where he sat on the far side of the room. He wore a suit. The top button of his shirt was undone, its crisp white fabric accentuating the dark gold of his flesh.

Tara's heart beat high and hard. She told herself it was a natural fight or flight response to finding a stranger in her rooms.

Except she'd known his identity instantly. That voice was unmistakeable. Even when he'd jabbed questions at her and looked disapproving, Sheikh Raif's voice had warmed her insides, making her think of dark, rich coffee and pastries dripping honey syrup.

Of addictive treats and secret cravings.

She pressed a hand against her swift-beating heart, then dropped it as the silk she wore pulled across her unfettered breasts, reminding her she was naked beneath the single layer.

That did nothing for her composure.

'I hope you don't mind if I call you Tara. It seems likely that you'll be here for some time.' He didn't move closer, but remained near the entrance to her suite.

As if waiting for her to invite him in?

It would be nice to think so. To forget that, as absolute ruler of this country, and owner of this vast palace, he could go where he chose.

Another tickle of doubt stirred. *Could* she trust him?

Gathering her scattered wits, Tara crossed the room, noticing things she'd missed in those first moments. Like the small dining table drawn up near a window, with place settings for two.

Like the way the mellow lighting accentuated the strong lines of his face and gleamed on his dark hair.

'Of course.' What choice did she have? At the moment he was her only protection against Fuad. She wouldn't antagonise him by refusing such a simple request, even if it felt safer when he called her Ms Michaels.

'And in private you may call me Raif.'

Tara blinked. She may not be a real princess but she knew enough of her mother's family to understand this was an extraordinary privilege.

He must have read her face. 'You have a problem with that? It's not a difficult name to say.'

The corner of his mouth hooked up, as if her reluctance amused him. Could he read her so easily? Or did she imagine it? Now his expression was infuriatingly inscrutable, as it had been earlier.

'I'm just surprised.' She paused and swiped her tongue around her suddenly dry mouth. 'Thank you... Raif.'

Tara stepped closer.

'Has something happened? You said I might be here for some time.' She'd hoped to be on her way quickly, putting as much distance as she could between herself and Fuad. A single border wasn't enough.

Now she did read the Sheikh's... Raif's expression. The raised eyebrow, then a tiny nod, as if of approval.

'Please, sit and be comfortable while I explain.' He gestured to the dining table. 'I took the liberty of arranging to eat with you since we have more to discuss.'

Tara felt a flurry of nerves.

Because he had news she needed to sit down for? Or at the thought of dining with this man who made her more viscerally aware of herself as a woman than anyone she'd met?

'Of course.' She took the chair he indicated while he made a brief call on his phone.

'Dinner will arrive shortly.'

He settled opposite her and Tara had the uncomfortable realisation that, even up close and wearing the western clothes she was used to, he stood out from other men.

It wasn't just her imagination.

She opened her mouth to ask what had happened, when a knock on the door interrupted her.

The staff must have been waiting for his call. For the next few minutes cold drinks and an array of dips, breads, and other starters were placed before them. Then a man in a chef's uniform wheeled in a heat-proof trolley and revealed an array of succulent skewered meats and vegetables. The aroma of herbs and charcoal roasting made Tara salivate. It was a long time since her afternoon snack.

When the attendants left Raif said, 'I thought it best to serve ourselves in private. We won't be interrupted.'

His words evoked a memory of Fuad, who'd been eager for privacy with her. Wariness stirred.

Tara's gaze shifted from the food to the man. There was nothing lascivious in his regard. Raif—it worried her how easily she adapted to using his name—wasn't talking about seduction but business.

She smiled, her tight shoulders easing as she accepted a plate.

'I'm convinced the safest place for you to be for the fore-seeable future is here, in my palace.'

'Define foreseeable future.' She looked at his stern features, remembered he was the supreme authority in this country and added, 'Please.'

'Until the next Sheikh is proclaimed.'

The serving spoons she was using clattered onto a plate of chargrilled vegetables.

'But that could take...' Tara shook her head. 'I thought maybe a day or two to sort myself out,' and, if he'd help her, to obtain a passport. 'I want to be well away from Dhalkur.'

'Fuad can't reach you here. You're safe under my protection.' Raif helped himself to salad and grilled lamb.

But Tara couldn't be so sanguine. 'I can't stay indefinitely.' Bad enough to feel beholden to this man for a short stay. To linger... The idea made her uncomfortable.

Straight black eyebrows lifted and his features took on an austere expression that made her wonder if he felt insulted.

'I'm so grateful for your help, Your M… Raif. It's wonderful to know my cousin can't reach me. But I need to go home.' Long enough to sort out her affairs, including her job, and find a bolthole outside the city.

'Because someone is waiting for you?'

Tara frowned. That was the second time he'd asked.

'No. No one.' Stupidly her throat constricted on the word and heat prickled her eyes, making her blink. She had friends in London but it was her mother who filled her mind.

'Forgive me.' His voice was surprisingly gentle. 'That was thoughtless. You mentioned your mother died last month. I didn't mean to dredge up painful thoughts.'

Meeting his steady gaze, she saw genuine regret.

It was unexpected. It made him suddenly more real. Not merely an autocratic leader or an astonishingly sexy man, but someone as human as she. Someone who made missteps and regretted them.

'It's fine. I like thinking of her.' Yet her smile wobbled. Because now there were so few people she could talk to about her mum. 'She was a special woman.'

'I'm sure she was, to produce such an indomitable daughter.'

Tara's eyes widened. Her? Indomitable? She'd been scared of Fuad and nervous about the trip here; all she could think of was how weak and vulnerable that made her.

'You don't think so?' Raif gestured with the serving spoons, and when she nodded began filling her plate.

She shrugged. 'I'm pretty ordinary.'

His smile took her by surprise. It began at the corner of his mouth, a tiny crook of amusement that slowly extended, curving his lips and creasing his lean cheeks into an expression that made her heart patter too fast. Even his eyes seemed to glitter more brightly as he surveyed her.

'Believe me, that entrance of yours was anything but ordinary. My poor chamberlain still hasn't recovered from the shock.' He put down the servers and sat back, his gaze catching hers, making a little pool of heat simmer deep inside. 'You didn't let that daunt you. You were as proud as any princess I've met.'

For a second longer Tara let the unfamiliar but invigorating heat spread and dance in her veins. Then she shook her head.

'I told you, I'm no princess.' After hearing her mother speak of the restrictions of royal life she was glad to be a commoner. 'I need to get back to London to ask my employer for more leave. To pack my flat up and rent it out while I find somewhere Fuad can't reach me.' Easier to say that than admit Raif's kingdom felt too close to her cousin.

'Ah.' Raif took a sip of sparkling water then put his glass down.

'What is it?' Tara had a bad feeling. 'You've had some news, haven't you?'

Those straight shoulders shrugged. 'My people have done some checking, which was made easier with your driving licence. Thank you for that.'

Tara nodded. She'd realised it would be easier for Raif to check her story with proof of identity.

'So you know for sure I am who I say I am.'

'Indeed. Sources in Dhalkur confirm something significant happened at the palace. Staff are on alert. Guards are patrolling the streets, searching premises and vehicles. There's a heightened presence at transport hubs and border crossings.'

No trace of a smile on Raif's face now. That lovely warmth she'd felt at being labelled indomitable faded. She found herself rubbing her hands along her silk-clad arms as a chill enveloped her.

'He's looking for me.' Her voice emerged husky.

'He is. But he won't find you. If you stay here.'

Tara heard the certainty in Raif's voice, felt its reassurance. Yet it wasn't enough.

'I need to get well away from Fuad. It's wonderful of you to help me but I can't impose—'

'Because you want to go back to your normal life.'

She nodded. Even if she had to go somewhere else, where Fuad couldn't locate her.

'I'm afraid that's not possible. Not yet.'

'Why not?'

'My staff report that your flat is under surveillance by men from the Dhalkuri embassy.'

Tara's stomach dropped, the morsel of food she'd eaten turning to lead.

'Fuad is already looking for me in London?' Of course he was. Why hadn't she thought of it sooner?

'More than that.' Raif's expression was grim. 'The Dhalkuri government has put out an alert for you. It's requested information if you cross the border into Nahrat and we understand they made the same request of the British authorities. Presumably they didn't stop there. Who knows which other countries have been contacted?'

Tara's fingers clawed at the fine linen tablecloth.

'I haven't done anything wrong! I'm not a criminal.'

'You left the country without a valid passport. But they haven't gone through Interpol, presumably because Fuad doesn't want to trump up fake criminal charges if he plans to marry you.' She fought a shudder at the thought. 'There's no warrant for your arrest. But, given you're part of the royal family, any such request would be considered seriously by other countries.'

Tara shook her head. 'I'm not royal. Fuad never thought

so in the past.' Years ago, he'd taken delight in telling her how unimportant she was, her only link to the old Sheikh being through the female line.

Raif didn't bother to argue that point. 'While the UK government is unlikely to hand you over without a hearing, we both know Fuad will bypass the law if he can. Once he knows where you are...'

Raif let the sentence dangle but she had no trouble finishing it.

Once Fuad knew where she was he'd force her to return. He was devious and determined. Inevitably her mind conjured images of being bundled, gagged and bound, into a car and taken to a private airfield and a private plane. Of being helpless, unable to protect herself.

Pain seared her chest as her lungs tightened.

'Tara.' She blinked as warmth blanketed her clenched fists. She looked down to see Raif's hand, large, tanned and capable, covering hers.

She looked up and his dark eyes captured hers. 'Don't panic.'

She swallowed. 'It's hard not to. This is like something out of a thriller movie.'

'Except this will end quietly and calmly. Your uncle only has a week or so left.' Tara opened her mouth to ask how he knew, then shut it. Raif would be well-informed of major events in the region. He'd already mentioned information gained from sources in Dhalkur. Sources that didn't want Fuad to inherit?

'You need to wait till the new Sheikh is crowned. Once he's in control Fuad won't need to marry you to establish himself.'

Except it wasn't just her royal links her cousin coveted. He also wanted access to the wealth she'd inherited.

But maybe Raif was right. Maybe once Fuad became

Sheikh he'd be too busy running the country to worry about her.

'When that happens, I'll arrange a new passport for you and put you on a plane to London.' His mouth curved in a reassuring smile. 'Meanwhile, for the next couple of weeks, you'll stay here incognito as my personal guest.'

CHAPTER FOUR

SLOWLY, ALMOST RELUCTANTLY, Raif released her hand and sat back.

That reluctance was unexpected and he didn't like it.

Ignoring the tingling on his palm, he reached for her glass and held it out to her.

'Drink,' he ordered. 'You'll feel better.'

He had no idea if she would, but he didn't like seeing her distressed.

A warning sounded in his brain.

This woman was a complication he didn't need.

True, he'd do anything to prevent Fuad inheriting. But interfering in Dhalkuri politics came at a cost. That was why there was animosity between the countries. For centuries both nations had tried to take control of the other, either overtly or behind the scenes.

Two generations ago there'd almost been war between them. Raif's grandfather had broken with centuries of royal tradition and married for love. Totally besotted with his bride, who hankered after life in the international jet set instead of a dutiful one, he'd ignored everything but her. The country had been left wide open for Dhalkuri infiltrators and insurgents. War had only just been averted and the damage to the country had taken years to overcome. It was only when Raif's father took the throne that the nation really recovered.

Relations were, at best, wary, though Raif and the Sheikh of Dhalkur had worked to increase cooperation.

Tara Michaels, with her big eyes and obstinate chin, was trouble. Looking at her put him on alert.

In the seventeen years since he'd ascended the throne at thirteen, Raif had learned to think before he acted. His grandfather's errors had been held up by his mentors as a lesson in the dangers of following his heart instead of his head. But he was still a man who knew an opportunity when he saw it. A man who capitalised on such opportunities.

Besides, sheltering Tara Michaels wasn't simply about thwarting her cousin's plans. It was an act of simple decency. Raif had never warmed to the Sheikh of Dhalkur's eldest son. If the rumours about his temper and violent ways were even half true, Raif wouldn't leave a dog in his care, much less a woman.

Raif's determination to get involved had nothing to do with the clenching awareness he felt whenever he met Tara's clear gaze. Or the fact that each shuddering breath made her pert breasts rise hard beneath her gown.

That conservative garment should be an effective cover-up, but not when she forgot to wear a bra. He could see the points of her nipples and the way her breasts occasionally jiggled against the rich fabric, as if unrestrained.

Despite his good intentions she kept reminding him she was a desirable woman, not merely a diplomatic problem.

Was that why he'd reached across and held her hand?

The result had been a raking shudder of awareness.

Yet even that wasn't all of it. The lost look in those great eyes, her mix of fear and determination, had touched him in a way that was quite separate to her feminine allure.

'It's very kind of you to invite me to stay.' She bit the corner of her lip and Raif wished she wouldn't. It made him want to smooth that lush mouth. Even, perhaps, test it with his own.

Abruptly he pushed his chair back. Being in her suite wasn't a good idea. He'd organised a meal here, thinking of her comfort and keeping her presence secret. Now he realised his mistake.

Raif got to his feet. 'Make yourself at home. If there's anything you need you have only to ask my staff.'

'You're leaving?' She looked stunned and who could blame her? He'd eaten nothing.

But, aware that his growing appetite wasn't for food, he needed to leave. It was unacceptable to think of Tara as anything other than someone needing his help. Raif didn't take advantage of people under his protection.

Even if he was almost sure some of her covert glances were appreciative. Nor had he missed the quick thrum of the pulse at her wrist when he'd held her hand.

Of course her pulse quickened! She's worried about Fuad coming after her.

'I'm not hungry.' *Not for any of the dishes on the table.* 'I simply wanted to update you and assure you that you'll be protected.'

She rose, hands clasped together.

'I can't tell you how much I appreciate your help. It's kind of you to help me. Especially given my unorthodox entry.'

She meant the way she'd sneaked across the border. But Raif's thoughts went to the memory of her, all golden limbs, long hair and lush curves, sprawled at his feet like some offering.

He drew a deep breath, feeling the blood of his ancestors pound through him. They'd been protectors of their people but also men with no compunction in claiming any prize that caught their eye.

Tara Michaels, with her small but emphatically feminine figure, her bright eyes and seductive pout, was enough to catch any man's eye.

Raif inclined his head, telling himself her looks didn't influence his actions. 'I'm happy to assist. My only condition is that you stay within the palace and out of public spaces. The fewer who know you're here the better.'

* * *

Tara prowled through the Courtyard of a Thousand Mosaics. But standing under a colonnaded walkway, as big and as beautiful as the cloisters of any cathedral, she barely took in its beauty.

Three days ago she'd discovered this place and been blown away by it.

Millions of exquisitely hand-painted tiles in shades of blue, green and gold decorated the floor, walls and even the bottom of the shallow pools in the centre of the garden. That colour scheme, the glossy-leaved citrus trees and the tinkling sound of a multitude of fountains, created a cool and peaceful ambience.

She'd been charmed. She'd been enchanted too with the Sheikha's Rose Garden, where arbours heavy with fragrant climbing roses invited you to relax.

Then there was the Sheikh's private library, stocked with thousands of books in several languages. The gymnasium. The lap pool.

So many facilities at her disposal. All tempting, all gorgeous, and none satisfying.

Tara was going stir crazy.

She hadn't even been allowed to wash her own clothes. After her first night in the palace she'd woken in that comfortable-as-a-cloud bed to discover the wardrobe full of clothes and shoes, all in her size. There were western-style dresses, one of them like the crimson wraparound dress she'd worn when she arrived. Except the new one was in a vibrant green, of some clingy, fragile fabric. Then there were the long traditional dresses in jewel colours, each more beautiful than the last.

Yet, despite the luxury, without some occupation she felt like a prisoner.

Tara slumped onto a shaded seat. She had nothing to

complain about and every reason to be thankful. She *was* thankful.

Her pulse galloped as she remembered being isolated in her uncle's palace, Fuad threatening retribution if she didn't give in to him.

But after four days cooped up, Tara longed for people to talk to, a purpose, even a change of scene.

She was too stressed to lose herself in a book. The staff were polite but kept their distance and the only other person she saw, briefly, was Raif. Every day he'd share coffee with her and update her on the latest news from Dhalkur. He'd ask if she needed anything and she'd say no. Then he'd nod and leave.

When he did, Tara felt even more alone.

Four days of luxurious isolation, following a week's imprisonment in Dhalkur, still felt like confinement.

Tara was used to being active. Working. Caring for her mother. Having responsibilities. But after a couple of phone calls, including to her work in London, asking for more leave, here she was, without a purpose.

She shot to her feet, annoyed at her moping. There must be some other place she could explore. Anything to pass the time that lay so heavy.

Tara was heading back through the private section of the palace when she noticed a door she hadn't seen before. Opening it, she discovered the sitting room where Raif had questioned her that first day. She must have been too upset then to take in the view from the long window.

A minute later Tara was out on the balcony, breathing deep and grinning from ear to ear. Her rooms were in the secluded centre of the palace. This wasn't secluded. This felt like freedom!

Before her was a wide strip of parkland and then the multi-coloured buildings of the old city. She was close enough to make out people on the streets below the ramparts of the citadel. Further away, new buildings and a forest of cranes attested to the capital's thriving commercial hub.

She heard traffic, a dog barking, watched a woman hanging out washing on a flat roof that doubled as a garden with pots of what might be herbs. Tara inhaled, catching the scents of the city and something delicious, as if the breeze blew from the old spice markets that she'd read were only a few streets away.

A boy and a dog galloped up the street that separated the palace from the city. A few minutes later another boy appeared with a football. Soon they were kicking the ball about in the open ground. In no time two impromptu teams had formed.

Tara leaned on the railing, her spirits lifting as she watched the game and the bustle of people. To be an unseen observer of the life in the city...

She blinked, her smile freezing, as one of the footballers pointed and several heads turned her way.

Instantly she stepped back from the railing.

What had she been thinking? She'd felt like an unseen observer but she wasn't invisible.

To her horror the balcony door didn't open easily from the outside. Was it stiff or had it automatically locked?

Eventually the latch turned with a click and she hurried inside, her heart racing as if she'd been part of that energetic football game. Her palms were damp as she shut the door. But one final look revealed that no damage had been done. The kids were engrossed in their game again and no one seemed to be looking this way.

It wasn't till the next morning that she discovered her mistake.

'His Majesty requests your presence in the audience chamber.' The chamberlain didn't quite meet her eyes and Tara remembered his shock when she'd tumbled out of the carpet in that very room.

'In the audience chamber?' Tara's nape prickled. Usually she met Raif in a sitting room or his office.

He hadn't returned to her suite since that first night and Tara tried not to mind his withdrawal. The man ruled a nation. She was an unwanted guest. Of course he had no time for her.

Even if she spent far too many hours thinking about him.

The chamberlain frowned and finally met her stare. He didn't look happy.

'Yes, he has a visitor, the Dhalkuri ambassador.'

Tara took an involuntary step backwards, bumping into the sofa from which she'd risen. Her hand went to her breastbone, to where her heart hammered.

'He's come to take me back!' Her voice stretched thin, her mind racing to avenues of escape. She'd even turned instinctively towards the doors leading onto the private courtyard, but there was no escape that way.

Fear flooded her, and frustration. She didn't even know where the exits were in this vast place.

'You have nothing to fear.' The words made her turn back. The few times she'd met the chamberlain he'd looked serious, if not disapproving. Now his expression softened. 'His Majesty will look after you.'

Even so, Tara trembled from head to foot.

She'd put her trust in Raif and now it would be tested. What did she really know of his motives?

'Very well.' She smoothed her hands down her thighs, realising she wore the same wraparound dress as when she'd arrived. Was that an omen that she was about to return? She told herself not to be fanciful. 'Give me a minute to tidy my hair.'

When the doors to the audience chamber were opened and the chamberlain led her in, Tara was glad she'd taken the time to put her hair up into a chignon. She wished she'd also changed her clothes into something more sophisticated.

She felt daunted, not just by the opulence of the vast room decorated in white, royal blue and gold, but also by the men waiting for her. The ambassador stood grim-faced before the royal dais where Raif sat enthroned.

Tara tried to take heart from the fact he hadn't been invited to sit, that this was clearly a very formal interview, but instead that merely highlighted the seriousness of the moment.

She looked up at Raif, hoping for reassurance, but found his attention on the ambassador, not her.

Gone was any trace of the man who'd shared coffee and been kind, if in a slightly formal way. In his place was a monarch, imposing on his gilded throne. As she crossed acres of inlaid marble his face was unreadable.

Was the chamberlain right? Would Raif protect her? She was a stranger. Why should he risk harming his relationship with his closest neighbour for her sake?

'Ms Michaels.' Even his voice sounded different, portentous somehow.

'Your Majesty.' She curtseyed, only lifting her head when he spoke again.

'The Ambassador of Dhalkur has approached me with a representation from your cousin Fuad.'

'With respect, sir,' the ambassador said smoothly, 'from His Majesty the Sheikh.'

'Ah, from the Sheikh himself? Obviously I misunderstood. I believed the Sheikh's illness is so advanced he's no longer issuing instructions or messages and that his son is acting as his proxy. I'm glad to hear his illness is not so grave.'

The ambassador opened his mouth then closed it, looking discomfited. 'This is a private matter, sir. If I might speak alone with Ms Michaels.'

Tara clasped her hands together so she didn't wring them. She darted a glance in Raif's direction, wishing she could borrow some of his composure. Still, he didn't meet her gaze. 'I'd prefer to hear the message here,' she said.

The ambassador's head reared back. He hadn't expected that. Tough. Even here in Raif's palace she had no desire to be alone with Fuad's messenger.

The man cleared his throat. 'Your family asks that you return to the palace. Your uncle needs you and your cousin also charged me with saying he's concerned about you, alone, so far from home.'

'You may tell my cousin there's no need for concern. I'm comfortable and safe.' She paused, giving emphasis to the last word. 'As for my uncle needing me, I'm afraid there's some confusion. My uncle—'

'No confusion, I assure you.' Yet the ambassador wasn't looking at her but at Raif. 'Within these walls I can reveal that our beloved Sheikh is, in fact, very ill. Is it any wonder he wants Ms Michaels by his side?'

'Frankly, yes,' Tara answered, wiping the half-smile from the man's face. She turned to Raif, for some reason needing him to understand. 'My cousin rejected all my attempts to spend time with my uncle, even going so far as to give orders that I wasn't to be admitted to see him.'

That had hurt. She and her uncle weren't close, but the man was dying and she'd wanted to provide what support she could. What had Fuad feared might happen if she spent time alone with him?

'One day I did manage to see my uncle.' Because a kind nurse had let her slip in. 'But after a while he said that he preferred the ministrations of medical professionals. He made me promise not to come back to him.'

Her throat closed. What he'd actually said was that he didn't want his niece hanging around his deathbed. He'd been trying to protect her, as if she hadn't seen her own mother fade away before her eyes. He'd said his goodbyes and told her to leave.

Tara blinked and stood straighter. Her uncle was a decent man and the nearest she had to family now. She'd be sorry when he died.

The ambassador's eyes rounded but he pressed on. 'It's a very difficult time, to be sure. But all the more reason to draw close to your family, to offer your support as your cousins face this looming tragedy.'

For her cousin Salim it would be a tragedy. But for Fuad, his father's death would give him supreme authority, something he craved.

Tara's chin lifted. 'As they supported me when my mother died?' Her voice thickened. 'My cousin Fuad sent his condolences three weeks after her death. Even then, the message was primarily to summon me to discuss my mother's estate.'

Salim had contacted her straight away, offering support and sympathy. The difference between his concern and his brother's lack of it had been starkly obvious.

The ambassador's face grew mottled.

'There is also the question of your affairs. Such a significant inheritance would fit more naturally under the control of your male relatives. Used properly it will benefit the whole country.' He spread his hands and faced the throne. 'Far be it from me to accuse Ms Michaels of lack of womanly sympathy or appropriate respect—'

'Good,' Raif said, his voice cutting. 'Because your role as ambassador doesn't give you the right to criticise Ms Michaels. Or pass judgement on what she should do with the land she's inherited. Or to make assumptions about recent circumstances which, I *hope*,' he leaned forward, 'you were not involved in.'

There was no mistaking the steel behind his smooth tone. Or the horror on the ambassador's face. Raif, his expression stern and gaze piercing, looked every inch the absolute ruler. A man used to wielding ultimate power.

Tara felt her breath shudder out in a sigh of relief. Raif had said nothing all this time and she'd begun to fear he'd side with the ambassador.

'But Your Majesty—'

'Do you have any further information to put before me, or perhaps something new to tell Ms Michaels?'

The ambassador goggled up at him. 'I was instructed to accompany her back personally.'

Raif nodded. 'A sensible arrangement. It's been brought home to me recently that women alone can be prey to all sorts of dangers.'

Tara stared up at him. Sensible? Surely he didn't mean to force her to go with this man?

'Your Majesty—' she began.

'If Ms Michaels chooses to return you'll be informed and can escort her personally. But as, at the moment, she plans to remain in Nahrat,' he turned to her and she nodded her confirmation, 'there's nothing more to be done than to thank you for your message and send our very best wishes to your Sheikh and his sons. I'm thinking of them at this difficult time.' He paused, then added, 'My chamberlain will see you out.'

The ambassador looked ready to protest, but Raif's implacable expression stopped him. The chamberlain ushered him out.

It wasn't till the pair had left that Tara filled her lungs with a deep, sustaining breath. Her hands, locked before her, were clammy and her heartbeat was loud in the silence.

She blinked and bowed her head, telling herself it was over. She was safe. Raif hadn't given her up, though his silence as the ambassador spoke had worried her.

Her legs wobbled terribly and she wished she had something to hang on to. But the only piece of furniture in the room was the gilded throne.

On the thought she looked up and movement caught her eye. Raif, rising from that imposing seat and stepping off the royal dais. He paced towards her and Tara shuffled her feet wider, stiffening her legs.

He didn't stop till he stood immediately before her and she arched her neck so she could meet his eyes. The man didn't need a dais. He was tall enough and imposing enough to impress without it.

'That was totally avoidable,' he said, in a low voice that lashed like a whip. 'Exactly what part of staying in the palace, out of the public eye, don't you understand?'

Raif looked into those clear green eyes, registered her flash of surprise, and felt anger ramp up.

Anger that he knew would be better directed at the bumptious ambassador or, better still, Prince Fuad, pulling strings to secure his runaway cousin. Yet his ire rose like a living, breathing beast within him.

It should never have come to this. Hadn't he *warned* her?

The sight of Tara, alone and seemingly fragile, facing down their visitor, had clutched at something deep inside Raif. At one point her mouth had crumpled, before she'd thrust her shoulders back and confronted her cousin's emissary. As he saw that sign of weakness Raif's belly had clenched and he'd had to force himself not to intervene and put himself between her and the ambassador.

That would have inflamed an already disastrous scenario.

This situation was fraught enough without him appearing as anything but impartial, in public at least. He might be supreme ruler of his own country but he trod a very delicate path, harbouring a foreign runaway. A *royal* foreign runaway.

Didn't she understand that?

The fact that he'd been forced to sit passively and allow that scene to play out had tested his endurance to the limit. Raif had wanted to take charge, deal with the ambassador and let diplomacy be damned.

His instinct to protect this woman was so compelling it went beyond a desire for justice and fair play. This was something different, more potent, and he didn't like it one bit. It felt like a form of weakness, and that fuelled his temper.

He was *not* weak. He'd never allow a woman to undermine his duty to his nation.

'I didn't go out. Truly. I've stayed in the palace the whole time.' Her chin jerked higher but now, instead of applauding her feistiness, Raif didn't like her attitude. She had no cause to look at *him* that way. He'd been the one to stop her being dragged back to Dhalkur.

He took a slow breath and fought the seething fury inside.

'No. Instead you flaunted yourself on the Sheikh's private balcony, the place where rulers appear to their people at major celebrations.'

Her mouth sagged open and Raif had the satisfaction of knowing she hadn't deliberately sabotaged the secrecy surrounding her stay. But that was no comfort, given the inevitable, severe repercussions.

He closed his eyes for a second, drawing on the reserves of strength that had seen him through years of diplomatic negotiations and ruling a country full of proud, opinionated, indomitable people.

It didn't help that when he looked down again Tara appeared put out, as if *he'd* done something wrong, not her.

'I didn't know it was your balcony. No one told me.'

He shook his head. What did she want? Signs at every

door for her convenience, explaining the purpose of each space?

'The fact that it was clearly visible to the public should have stopped you. How do you think the Dhalkuri authorities discovered you were here? You were seen. Photos were taken. The press is humming this morning with the story of the strange woman in the palace.'

'I'm sorry. I didn't realise. I was restless after days being cooped up.'

If she'd looked repentant Raif would have ended it there. He dealt pragmatically with issues, not wasting time apportioning blame. But Tara Michaels stared back at him as if *he* were at fault. As if a few days as his pampered guest was some sort of trial.

What more did the woman want from him?

She'd already got under his skin to an alarming extent. He thought of her when he should be working, or sleeping. He found himself thinking about that sultry mouth of hers and how it would feel on his skin. Which in turn made him feel guilty.

He almost heard his patience snap.

'I gave you an instruction and you disobeyed me. Don't you *want* my help?'

She drew herself up straighter, as if from just below his shoulder she could stare him down. Her hands jammed onto her hips in an attitude designed to provoke.

'I'm not your servant.' Her tone was fire and ice, lashing at his skin and drawing it tight.

Raif felt his hands clench at his sides and his teeth grind. 'No, you're my guest. My uninvited guest.'

For a second he saw something unreadable flare in her eyes but before he could decipher it she spoke again, her lip curling disdainfully.

'If I'm such a burden, I'll leave. If you give me that passport you promised and show me the exit, I'll be on my way.'

Infuriating woman! As if she'd be going anywhere now. He'd had enough of her attitude.

She opened her mouth, no doubt to lambast him again, and it was too much.

In one swift movement he wrapped his arm around her waist and hauled her against him.

There! He almost heard his body's cry of relief. As if he'd waited months to feel her against him instead of days. Her soft curves fitted perfectly in his embrace.

Her eyes were huge, her lips apart, but she didn't speak. Just looked up with something in her expression that sent a buzz of anticipation through him.

Raif waited a split second then surrendered to the force that had driven him since the moment she'd tumbled out of the carpet to lie so provocatively at his feet.

He bent his head and covered her mouth with his.

CHAPTER FIVE

IF SHE'D WANTED to stop him she could have. Raif's grip was firm but not unbreakable.

Instead Tara stood where she was. She might even have leaned towards him, her palms to his chest for balance. The feel of his hot, honed body beneath her hands sent a tremor of excitement through her. But that was nothing to the impact of his kiss.

There was no hesitation. No fumbling to get the right angle. Nor was it punishing, despite his anger.

Raif kissed like he seemed to do everything else: decisively. With impeccable talent.

Perfectly.

Tara swallowed a sigh of pleasure as his mouth possessed hers. It was persuasion and invitation and such pleasure. Inevitably she responded.

How could she not?

For days she'd been acutely aware of Raif, not just as a protector, but also as a man who drew her lonely body into tingling awareness. Even the warning voice of past experience, telling her that men weren't always as they seemed, died under his kiss.

This was better than any of her fervid imaginings.

Tara leaned closer, higher, hands fisting in his clothes and tugging him down to her.

The arm around her back tightened. Heat blossomed where she fitted between his thighs. Her wayward mind imagined them wedged together like this but without so many clothes, and suddenly she had trouble getting enough oxygen.

Raif's hand lifted to her jaw, her cheek. She felt the slight burr of calluses against her skin and shivered, her senses deliciously heightened. Long fingers pushed past her ear, into her hair, gripping, massaging, and delight whirled through her, making her shake and her knees loosen.

She inhaled the scent of male spice and sandalwood, absorbed the rich taste of him, and needed more.

Her hands rose up the back of his head to tunnel through thick hair, clamping his skull and holding tight.

A low sound vibrated from his mouth to hers, a deep, murmuring growl of masculine pleasure. Tara's nipples peaked hard against him, heat drilling down to that needy spot at the apex of her thighs.

Was this why she'd felt so ready to stand up to Raif? Almost taunting him when she could see he was annoyed? As if she *wanted* to spur his anger till he snapped. As if she hoped he felt this electric spark too.

That couldn't be it. Her anger had been justified. He had no right to order her about.

And yet...

And yet her righteous indignation died as he swept her close and made her feel things she couldn't remember ever feeling.

Desirable. Cherished. Powerful. As if she could level mountains with a sweep of her hand. And lose herself utterly in this man's earthy desire.

This wasn't just a kiss. Their bodies strained together like twin halves of a long-separated whole, and it was blissful.

In fact, as she squirmed closer she felt...

Raif stepped back so abruptly she swayed, bereft of his anchoring frame.

He didn't reach out to support her. Instead he put even more distance between them, his brow scrunching into a mighty scowl. His hands clenched in fists at his sides.

Tara's heart skipped a beat then plunged. Hadn't he felt the magic?

Her ragged breathing was loud in her ears. Her heart hammered and a voice in her head told her to close the gap between them and kiss him again, because what they'd shared was too good to stop.

Where that voice came from she didn't know. In twenty-three years she'd never heard it before. Usually she heard a jangling alarm if she got close to intimacy. A warning to beware. Not this time.

Tara blinked up, transfixed by the change in Raif's expression. A shiver racked her and now it wasn't a hot shudder of excitement but cold, so cold.

He'd looked annoyed and impatient before. Then, in the seconds before he'd claimed her, she'd seen something flare in those dark eyes. Something reckless and eager.

Had she imagined it?

Now there was the downward tilt of his eyebrows and lips, deepening grooves bracketing a grim mouth and the flare of aristocratic nostrils as if they scented something unpleasant.

'That shouldn't have happened.' He stood stiffly. His jaw clenched as if with pain. Or disgust.

Disgust that he'd touched her?

A horrified shudder swamped Tara. She'd got it wrong.

Seconds ago she'd thought him aroused. Instead he'd kissed her out of pique. He'd been angry and didn't like her challenging him. So he'd silenced her.

And she'd let him. Worse, she'd loved every moment. Every touch, every breath, had been a revelation.

Because she had such limited sensual experience after years supporting her mother through the grief of losing her father, and then through illness?

'It *definitely* shouldn't have happened,' Raif repeated in case she hadn't got the message.

Because, of course, she wasn't the sort of woman the

exalted Sheikh of Nahrat would kiss. She was an *uninvited guest*.

Had he really kissed her to stop her words? Or had he—the thought stirred a sick feeling in her stomach—simply been curious? After all, she wasn't like the sophisticates he usually mixed with.

Anger shot through Tara's blood and crawled across her skin, drawing it tingling tight.

'You're right.' She almost spat the words. 'It shouldn't. I don't want you touching me again. *Ever*. Is that clear?'

He might be a sheikh. He might have power, wealth and an unassailable aura of machismo. He might have an inflated view of his own worth, but he was *not* her superior. He was a man, as flawed as the next one. Nothing gave him the right to use her that way.

For all Tara knew he was no better than Fuad. The press reports she'd read about Raif were almost fawning, continually singing his praises. But none of them investigated the real man behind his royal authority.

'Don't worry! It's a mistake that won't be repeated.'

But Tara barely heard. Through the fog of anger and hurt, something the ambassador had said suddenly lodged in her brain. Something she should have noticed before.

'You knew,' she said in a strangled voice.

'Sorry?'

'You weren't surprised when the ambassador mentioned my inheritance. You didn't ask what he meant about the nation benefiting from it.'

Tara's eyes narrowed on the man before her. Was that discomfort on those strong features? It was impossible to tell.

'I don't see the problem. It's straightforward. Your mother died and left you property.' He folded his arms, emphasising his broad chest and his annoyance.

Tara stared back, crossing her own arms. 'It's more than

that. You weren't surprised or interested because you already knew about it.' Her voice rose. 'You *knew* what my inheritance is. You mentioned land, not money or a house or something more general.'

Now Tara saw it. The shimmer of confirmation in his dark eyes, despite the fact his mouth remained as still and stern as before.

Dismay hit, hard as a fist to the ribs.

She'd escaped Fuad but now she was stuck in Sheikh Raif's palace, unable to leave until he provided the passport he'd promised.

Awful doubt stirred in her belly then snaked through her, sending out slithery coils of fear.

Had she escaped one man determined to use her for his own ends, only to find herself at the mercy of another? A man who was simply better at hiding his motives? She should have guessed. Shouldn't have let herself be lulled into ignoring those hard-learned lessons about self-protection.

'So?' He looked utterly supercilious.

'How long have you known about my inheritance?'

'What does it matter? It's a minor point.'

Her stomach plunged towards the floor. He didn't want to answer. She had a terrible feeling she knew why. Because he, too, wanted to get his hands on her inheritance.

Why else hide her from her cousin? Why treat her as his personal guest and lavish such luxury on her?

The last couple of weeks she'd learned how far an unscrupulous man would go.

'Tell me,' she demanded. '*When* did you find out about the land I've inherited?'

Land which had recently been found to contain large quantities of rare and valuable substances. Usually found in very small deposits unsuitable for mining, this large deposit could be a huge boost to the economy, or, if Fuad married her, to his personal fortune, because under local law Tara owned both the land and its mining rights. If Fuad married her, he'd control both.

Finally Raif answered. 'I heard rumours of a significant find of rare elements weeks ago. I had confirmation around the time you arrived.'

Tara's chest cramped. She was right. A sour tang filled her mouth.

'You're well informed. Do you have spies in the Dhalkuri court?'

He shook his head. 'No spies. The find is no secret. I have business and diplomatic contacts through the region. It's no surprise I'd hear such significant news.'

Why hadn't Tara thought of that? Why had she assumed all he knew of her was what he'd discovered after she arrived?

'I should have known.' How foolish she'd been, trusting this man.

'Known what?'

She had to hand it to him. Raif did haughty like no one else. When Fuad aimed for hauteur he merely managed arrogant and thuggish. Tara looked up at the man before her and wondered what, if anything, would discomfort him.

Probably nothing. He had too high an opinion of himself.

'That this,' she waved her hand, 'your hospitality, comes at a price.' The thought of how he'd played her like a complete innocent spurred her indignation. It felt all the worse because she'd liked him.

More, she'd been attracted. His magnetic looks combined with his kindness had suckered her into believing he was on her side. Instead it seemed she was still stuck in the nightmare that had begun in Dhalkur.

Tara swallowed, pushing down a horrible feeling of self-pity, and concentrated on anger.

Raif's mouth thinned and his folded arms fell to his sides. 'What exactly are you saying, Tara?'

'It's an unlikely coincidence that you took me in, a complete stranger, and went to such lengths to protect me. Especially when all the time you knew I have a potential fortune. A fortune I'm told would benefit any nation.'

She knew about grasping, predatory men. How had she allowed herself to forget?

For a second, for two, Raif merely stared down at her, eyes glittering and nostrils flaring.

Tara gave him a death stare of her own. She refused to let him intimidate her.

'Is that why you kissed me?' She had to stop and clear her thickening throat. 'Were you hoping I'd be so blown away that I'd fall under your spell? That you'd persuade me to give you access to my inheritance?'

Her mouth trembled so hard she bit her bottom lip to stop it quivering.

Because she *had* fallen under his spell. Even before the kiss she'd been fascinated by him. When he'd taken her in his arms she'd all but gone up in flames. Even now, racked with hurt and indignation, part of her yearned for his touch, his taste, the passion she'd discovered in his embrace.

How naïve she'd been.

Raif took a step towards her, his gaze like obsidian, black and hard.

'You really think,' he paused and shook his head, 'that I have designs on your inheritance?'

'Why not? My cousin does. Apparently this cache of minerals will bring the owner immense wealth.'

'And how, precisely, would my kindness give me access to that? Do you imagine I want to *marry* you for your money?' Disdain dripped from every syllable, puncturing Tara's certainty.

She hadn't thought that through. But surely there

was something fishy here? To go from that kiss to such contempt?

'I don't know. I just know it's unlikely a man in your position would go to such lengths to help someone ordinary like me. But if you thought you could butter me up and do some deal to get access to the land…' She shrugged and spread her hands.

'This buttering up…it falls short of marriage, then. Is my dastardly plan to seduce you into sharing your mineral rights?'

When he put it like that, it sounded preposterous. But he was hiding something, she sensed it.

'You *did* kiss me.'

'Oh, well, in *that* case, I must be up to no good,' he sneered. 'It never occurred to you that you're a beautiful, infuriating woman and that even a man of honour might be goaded into unwise action as a result?'

Tara gaped at him. Beautiful and infuriating?

Raif thought her beautiful?

He shook his head. 'Of course you didn't. You're so fixated on your cousin you make the insult of assuming I'm like him. No!' he continued when she opened her mouth. 'Don't speak. You've already said more than enough. Come with me.'

He swung towards the door but Tara stood firm.

'Where are you going?'

'You think I want your wealth. Well, there's something you need to see.'

Tara had the uncomfortable feeling she had been at least a little ridiculous. And yet—

'Ow.' She flinched as he took her upper arm.

Raif scowled and released his hold. 'Do we need the dramatics? My grip wasn't tight.'

Tara blinked at the pain searing her arm.

'Tara?' Her face must have revealed her discomfort, for his expression altered. 'What is it?'

She shook her head but he was already lifting the soft cotton of her sleeve.

Tara knew what he'd see and for reasons she couldn't explain wished he wouldn't. Having anyone else view the massive bruises made her shrink inside.

Raif's face turned grim. His jaw had a hard line and a pulse throbbed at his temple.

Slowly, as if consciously not making a move that might startle her, he rolled up her other sleeve, while she stood motionless, wishing this was over.

'Fuad did this?'

Tara shivered. Not with cold, but because of a new note in Raif's soft voice.

She'd heard him annoyed. She'd heard him indignant and angry but that was nothing to the lethal note she heard now in that quiet tone.

She darted a look up but he was examining her arms. She turned her head. His fingers hovered above the ugly purple-blue bruises that were beginning to turn a lurid shade of green.

'Yes.' She shivered, swamped by the memory of Fuad grabbing her, shoving her up against the wall, threatening her. The way he'd pawed at her dress, only stopping when interrupted by someone with an urgent message, made her stomach turn.

'He'll pay for this.' Raif spoke so softly Tara almost didn't hear him, as he rolled her sleeves down to cover the discoloured flesh.

It was easier for Raif to concentrate on drawing Tara's sleeves back into place, than to meet her eyes.

Shame filled him, along with anger at the sight of her

injuries. That shame was unfamiliar, a burning sour taste in his gullet.

He'd made his share of mistakes but couldn't recall anything to compare with this. Nothing to rival the potent whirl of guilt.

The sight of Tara's injuries sickened him.

But not as much as the realisation he'd lost control and hurt her. The throbbing pain and confusion in her voice as she'd accused him of using her gouged his conscience.

She was wrong about his motives. He wasn't interested in her money.

But she was right about one thing. His motives weren't pristine.

He'd lusted after her from the moment she'd fallen at his feet. And, while he told himself his actions were pure, he'd kept his distance, seeing her only for a short time each day, because he feared what she did to his self-control.

Self-control! Where was that when he'd kissed her half senseless?

His thoughts flew to the grandfather he'd never known, legendary for his loss of control in respect of one single woman. But this wasn't the same. Raif's was a passing attraction, made more intense by proximity and the dramatic circumstances. He wouldn't let it destroy him.

Yet Tara was right to be suspicious. Right to wonder if he wanted to seduce her. Not because he was after her inheritance but because he wanted *her*.

Even now, he felt that tell-tale quiver of heat in his groin, legacy of their kiss and the feel of her sweet body clamped against him.

Raif inhaled deeply, trying to find his equilibrium, but only succeeded in drawing in her rose and cinnamon scent. It was rich, earthy, yet elegant. Like the woman herself.

He hadn't been thinking when he kissed her. Or at least, thinking only with his body, not his brain. His twin needs, to silence her and to taste her, had eradicated sensible thought.

That was why he'd let her subsequent doubts get under his skin. She'd grazed his pride and he'd been so unsettled by that embrace he'd reacted in anger.

But the sight of those bruises brought reality back with a vengeance. The ugly marks reinforced her vulnerability.

If ever he needed to be the man he prided himself on being—honourable, honest, a champion of the weak—it was now.

'I'm sorry, Tara. That should never have happened. Either my touch on your arm or the kiss.'

He paused, wondering how best to explain without revealing how close to the edge of sanity she drove him. He couldn't share the complete truth, that she tempted him too much.

He met her questioning gaze. 'I was angry that you doubted me but that doesn't excuse what I did.' He set his shoulders back. 'It won't happen again.'

As he said it, the taste of her lingered in his mouth, rich, ripe and intoxicating. Denying himself another taste was tantamount to torture. But so be it.

She watched him gravely. Did her straight shoulders drop a little at his words?

'I'm sorry too. I leapt to conclusions. I shouldn't have accused you the way I did.' She drew a breath that seemed to shudder right through her. 'I know you're not like Fuad.'

Damned by faint praise!

But after what had just happened, Raif would take what he could get.

'Thank you.' He paused then forced the words out. 'I'm not used to being questioned. Or having my intentions doubted.' He shook his head. 'I'm used to speaking and being instantly obeyed. And believed. When you thought I was scheming—'

'You don't have to explain. I provoked you.' She spread her hands wide, 'Like you provoked me.'

Raif nodded. 'Neither of us acted well. Can we agree to draw a line under this and move on?'

'Yes. Of course.' She met his eyes then looked away and it struck him that that she seemed diminished. By regret over her actions or worry about the future?

'Excellent.'

It wasn't excellent. It was a damned shame. Because despite his apology, he wasn't sorry about that kiss. The kiss was something he wanted to repeat.

Raif bit back a sigh. It struck him that if he'd ever needed a lesson in humility, and not becoming too prideful, Tara Michaels was the woman to provide it.

'Will you come with me now?' He gestured for her to precede him.

Was that a flicker of doubt in her expression? Then she nodded and Raif felt a surge of pleasure that she trusted him, this far at least.

CHAPTER SIX

As THEY DESCENDED deep into the living rock beneath the citadel, the woman beside Raif grew tense.

In other circumstances he'd be tempted to touch her hand, reassure her. Except he'd just learned how dangerous it was to touch Tara Michaels. He wasn't foolish enough to do it again.

'What's down here?' She sounded far more tentative than moments ago when she'd fired up at him.

Did she think he was leading her to a private dungeon?

'Storage vaults. My ancestors kept grain supplies as protection against famine. There's also a well and massive water cistern. The palace was built to withstand siege.'

'No dungeons?'

He'd been right. She *was* nervous.

'No dungeons.' He didn't explain that his ancestors had believed in swift justice, rather than locking up prisoners for years. That wouldn't reassure her.

'Here we are.' He stopped before a steel door and Tara's eyes widened. The contrast between old stone walls and high-tech security was stark. After completing the security authentications he stood back as the door swung open. Lights flicked on inside.

'After you.'

Tara shot him a doubtful look, then entered.

She took only a couple of steps then stopped, her breath an audible hiss. She turned to take in the display cases all around the room. 'These can't all be real.'

'They are. Every one.' Raif put the tips of his fingers to her back, gently urging her further inside, feeling again that abrupt zing of energy through his body from that point of contact.

If anything were needed to remind him to keep his distance, that did it.

And the heavy craving deep inside. A craving for one more taste, one touch.

Raif stepped to one side, distancing himself. Yet her tantalising fragrance lingered in his nostrils.

'These are incredible!' Glowing green eyes held his, then she turned to study a nearby display. Its centrepiece was a curved dagger in a gold scabbard, studded with precious gems. The hilt was of gold surrounding one of the biggest faceted emeralds the world had ever seen.

Her eyes rounded. The royal jewels had that effect.

Raif watched her move from the dagger to a solid gold platter, its rim studded with precious cabochon rubies, then to a small casket decorated with diamonds.

Now she bent over another case, her gaze intent. Raif moved closer, curious to see what held her so rapt.

'Look at the workmanship. Isn't it amazing?'

Of all the riches in the cabinet it was the smallest, a bangle studded with small stones the colour of cranberries.

'See the gold work? The intricate beading and the exquisite forms?'

Raif leaned closer, drawn by her excitement and assurance as she described the methods some long-ago goldsmith had used to create the decoration of tiny birds and flowers.

'And the stones?'

'Spinels. Don't they have a fabulous colour?' But once again she was exclaiming over the fine workmanship.

It fascinated him that she was drawn by the craftsmanship, not how expensive the piece, or how bright the gems. Usually visitors stared at the biggest, most glittering pieces. Some didn't make it past the emerald dagger.

Then he remembered a detail from the report he'd received on Tara Michaels. She worked as a sales assistant in an exclusive jewellery store. Raif had thought of her as merely a smiling face at a cash register. Now he realised his mistake.

He'd underestimated her. Again.

The idea discomfited him.

Upstairs he'd taken out his frustrations on her, kissing her, only to discover Tara wasn't a woman to be so easily silenced. She'd stood up to him as few people did. Even if her doubts about him weren't correct, she'd been right to wonder about his intentions.

He should have known not to expect her to be predictable. Tara Michaels was many things, including a problem of increasing proportions, but predictable wasn't one of them.

'You have a real interest in these.'

She looked up, surprised. 'Who wouldn't? They're unique. This is an extraordinary collection.'

Raif nodded. She wasn't the first to say so. He'd been urged to have the treasury inventory updated and permit the public display of some pieces. But it wasn't high on his list of priorities.

Now, though, an idea began to form.

Tara made a sweeping gesture with one hand. 'I feel privileged to see this, but why—?'

'Why bring you here?' It had seemed a good idea. Now Raif felt the gesture was too crudely obvious. Too much like bragging. 'To prove I'm not after your inheritance. My nation is rich and my personal wealth significant. I thought seeing this would convince you.'

Of course he wasn't scheming to get her inheritance.

She'd known it almost as soon as she'd accused him. But she'd been so upset after what happened in the throne room, and by Raif's repudiation after their kiss, she hadn't been thinking straight.

Tara's gaze drifted across the vast room lined with priceless treasures. No wonder he'd been insulted at her accusation. Her cousin Fuad might be hungry for money, but not so the Sheikh of Nahrat.

She felt foolish.

'I apologise. It was a crazy idea, I know.' She focused on his chin, rather than meet those intense eyes that she found so worryingly attractive. 'I shouldn't—'

'Of course you should.' His words jerked her gaze up. This time Tara felt a little judder of delight as their eyes locked. 'You've learned your family is trying to exploit you. If you don't stand up for yourself, who will?'

Raif paused and then, remarkably, his mouth rucked up in a hint of a smile that did devastating things to Tara. Warmth trailed through her, eddying lower and lower to places she didn't want to think about.

'I applaud you for standing up for yourself.'

'You do? That wasn't the impression you gave.'

He inclined his head, a groove dimpling his cheek as his smile grew wry. 'I overreacted. It's rare for anyone to take me to task, or question my judgement. No one else does except my aunt.'

'I'd like to meet your aunt.' The words escaped before Tara had a chance to think better of them.

Instead of annoying him, the comment made his smile grow. And with it that fluttery feeling inside her.

'She'll enjoy meeting you too. She's in the US, visiting friends. It was her carpet you stowed away in.'

'I see.' Tara wasn't sure what to say. The mention of her unorthodox arrival brought heat to her cheeks. Then there was Raif's implication that she'd be here when his aunt returned.

Once more he seemed to read her thoughts. 'I'm afraid that for your safety your stay here will be extended. Now Fuad knows your location he'll set people watching in case you leave.'

Tara nodded, repressing a shudder.

'But there's an upside.'

'There is?' She couldn't see one. She was still a prisoner, even if in a gilded, beautiful palace.

'Of course. You said you feel restless after being cooped up. How would you like to be my guest at a dinner tonight?'

Attending a royal event was nerve-racking. Especially as Tara was busy fretting over Fuad's next move. His ambassador must have reported back by now. But at least, compared with her cousin's bullying behaviour, a royal dinner shouldn't be too daunting.

Tara smoothed her hands down her dress and told herself she had no reason to be nervous. They were just people, even if they were the sort who frequented royal dinners. She'd never attended such an event. Her visits to Dhalkur had always been as a private citizen.

She pivoted before the mirror, pleased that she'd stand up to scrutiny thanks to the stunning clothes Raif had provided.

The sapphire-blue dress draped her curves, cinching in at her waist and flaring in a flirtatious ripple around her legs. Tara loved it. It was what she would have chosen if she had an unlimited budget. She'd never worn haute couture but knew this cobweb-fine silk with hand-sewn detailing around the deep V neckline was expensive.

What would Raif think when he saw her?

That shouldn't matter, and yet...

This morning he'd kissed her till her head spun and her senses sang. The memory made the fine hairs on her arms stand up and her insides quiver. She'd been with him every step of the way. Resisting had never entered her head.

He'd acted out of temper but she'd felt, or thought she'd felt, his body stir against hers. As if it wasn't just annoyance he experienced or the need to impose his will. Afterwards he'd disarmed her with his apology and wry confession that he wasn't used to being crossed.

That had only made him more attractive.

Too attractive.

He confused her. Tara wanted to trust him, and so far it seemed she had every reason to. Yet, despite her profound attraction, she couldn't quite accept he had no ulterior motive. There was something, some secret he kept from her. Or did her situation make her paranoid?

He had ultimate power and she had none. That, above all, made her nervous. The feeling of powerlessness evoked panic.

She was a refugee, dependent on his charity till she found safety elsewhere. Despite her family connections, she wasn't royal. She'd never been inducted into that exclusive clique. She'd grown up with two wonderful parents who loved her and the chance to live in some fascinating places. They'd had enough money to live comfortably but they weren't rich or powerful.

A knock on the door sounded.

'Coming!' Tara slipped on her sapphire-blue shoes. When she straightened the door was open, revealing Raif's tall frame.

Tara's breath seized. She swallowed, her mouth suddenly dry. She told herself not to be silly, but her body had other ideas. Her nipples peaked as if vying for his attention and low in her belly that needy sensation was back.

He looked stunning in made-to-measure formal clothes. She recalled the strength of his arms lashing her to him and the taste of his firm mouth as he bent her to him and she went up in flames. Even the texture of his hair against her fingertips had been incredibly erotic.

'Raif.' Her voice was a betraying wisp of sound. 'I wasn't expecting you.'

He strolled across the room towards her, his movements easy with fluid grace.

Another little shimmy of excitement started up inside. Was there anything about this man that didn't appeal?

Yes. His determination to have his own way.

'I thought you'd like an escort. You don't know the other guests. I'll introduce you to make it a little easier.'

Easier! Walking in to a royal dinner with the Sheikh? She'd hoped to slip in quietly and not draw attention.

'That's very kind. Thank you.'

A faint smile curved his lips as if her words pleased him. 'Shall we?' He gestured to the door then stepped back, as if not wanting to crowd her.

Or not wanting to touch her. Despite her determination to be cautious with him, the thought jarred.

As they turned down a wide corridor decorated with beautiful murals, Raif kept his distance. A message that he had no intention of repeating their kiss?

She already knew that. Yet disappointment took root.

What had she expected? That he'd see her in her finery, sophisticated and even a little sexy, and be smitten?

The rhythm of her high heels clicking on marble faltered as she realised that was exactly it.

She wanted Raif to be smitten.

Wanted him to admire her. Not see her as a problem or an annoyance.

She wanted him to regret rejecting her.

Fool. Fool. Fool.

This was dangerous.

'Tara, are you okay?' Warmth teased her as his fingers gripped her elbow. Her sleeve was no protection against his heat, or the shimmery wave of longing radiating from his touch.

'Fine, thanks.' She pasted on a smile and looked up at

him. Her heart gave a mighty thump that confirmed her misgivings.

She was too old for a crush on the man who'd saved her. This was something different.

Raif was so close she could lean in to rest her head against his chest.

Being short, she'd spent most of her life proving she was perfectly able to look after herself and defying those who equated her lack of height with a need for them to make decisions for her.

Strange that now, looking up into Raif's gleaming gaze, acutely aware of the latent power in his tall frame, all Tara felt was the desire to burrow closer.

As if being pressed against his big body would be the most wonderful thing in the world. The disparity in height didn't make her defensive, ready to reject a casually patronising attitude. Instead, his powerful body beckoned.

Tara swallowed hard, inhaling the faintest drift of sandalwood.

She wanted to surrender to those forces he'd unleashed a few hours ago.

'New shoes,' she murmured, to explain her stumble. Then wished she hadn't when Raif, still holding her, looked down. Tara felt supremely aware of his scrutiny. Did he like the way the high-heeled shoes enhanced the curve of her calves and made her legs look longer?

'Very pretty.'

She could *not* feel his gaze drifting up her legs. Yet her skin tingled as if from a caress.

'Thank you.' Quickly changing the subject, she found herself promising once again to repay him for the clothes.

Gravely he heard her out then said merely, 'If it pleases you to do so, of course. But it's my pleasure, especially as I get to enjoy seeing you look so lovely.'

Tara opened her mouth then shut it. She couldn't object

because he'd left it up to her to decide whether to pay him back. As for the comment about how good she looked, she'd seem churlish to object to that. It wasn't Raif's fault she felt self-conscious.

'Shall we go?' He stepped close again, leading her through the palace. 'There will be some guests tonight that I think you'll find interesting.'

By the time they reached the public rooms Tara was looking forward to meeting the people he'd described. Until a footman opened a door and they stepped into a long chamber that took her breath away.

The vaulted ceiling was midnight-blue, dusted with sparkling stars that she discovered later were white sapphires. The walls were a muted gold, decorated at the base with mosaics of lilies that looked almost real. A long, elaborately set table extended down the room, and at this end stood a crowd of beautifully dressed guests, all watching her.

Every head bowed. The men inclining from the waist and the women curtseying, making Tara shockingly aware that she had her hand tucked through the Sheikh's elbow.

People did not touch a sheikh, especially in public. She moved to withdraw her hand, but Raif forestalled her, his other hand covering hers.

Fortunately the guests were too polite to reveal shock, but as she and Raif circulated there were lots of curious glances. Clearly her presence caused a stir. Because she was from Dhalkur, or because he escorted her?

Raif introduced her as niece to the Sheikh of Dhalkur, here on a personal visit. That was nicely vague and made her sound like the sort of person who might belong at a royal event.

Instead of an intruder.

She shivered as Raif escorted her to her place at the table then excused himself, saying protocol dictated he sit with representatives from another kingdom.

Tara told herself she was relieved not to spend the evening with him. Yet she felt a jangle of disappointment, watching him go to the head of the table, stopping along the way to speak to more guests. A couple of beautiful, sloe-eyed women hung on his every word, their smiles too inviting for Tara's liking.

'He's very impressive, isn't he?' She turned to find an auburn-haired man smiling at her, his accent familiar from time she'd spent in Australia.

'Impressive?' She pretended to ponder.

'Our host. Urbane and sociable, but with a mind like a steel trap when it comes to business.'

'And what is your business, Mr...?'

'Fletcher. Steve Fletcher. I'm a geologist. And you're—?'

'Tara Michaels. Passing through before heading back to London.'

She read a glint of appreciation in his eyes. 'But here long enough to share dinner.' He gestured to the table where their names were inscribed on neighbouring place cards. 'The evening is looking up already.'

Tara laughed. She'd forgotten how upfront Australians could be.

As the evening progressed, her neighbours proved friendly and fascinating. On her other side was a woman with a warm chuckle and an infectious sense of humour who headed a medical research team. Across the table was a curator from the national museum whose specialty was old jewellery, and his wife, a teacher of English, eager to practise her language skills.

How long since she'd simply enjoyed chatting with others?

Through the last stages of her mother's illness and in the dark weeks that followed, she'd been absorbed in grief.

Then had come the trauma of imprisonment in her uncle's palace. No wonder she revelled in her new acquaintances.

As for her brighter than usual smiles, they weren't about proving to herself that she didn't miss Raif. Or hurt reaction to his grim expression whenever she found him watching her.

Had she offended him in some way, breaking some royal protocol?

Tara firmed her jaw. If so, maybe she wouldn't be allowed out in public again. She intended to make the most of it. Ignoring Raif's dark stare, she turned to the man beside her.

CHAPTER SEVEN

THE EVENING TESTED Raif's patience to the limit.

It had begun badly when Fuad had phoned, something he'd never done before. Ostensibly the call had been about the old Sheikh's declining health, but soon he'd moved to increasingly shrill demands that Raif send Tara back.

The man sounded obsessed. Or perhaps simply desperate. Raif had heard the Dhalkuri Royal Council wasn't all in favour of Fuad taking the throne, so he was probably grasping at any way to shore up his position.

Raif had barely hung on to his temper during the call. He'd finally ended it by saying Tara was here as his most *personal* guest, leaving Fuad to splutter indignantly over what that might imply. The conversation had left him seething and even more determined to support her.

Since then Raif had spent the evening watching his most conservative guests struggle to hide their affront that he'd personally escorted a single woman to dinner, something he'd never done before. And not just any woman, but a Dhalkuri!

On top of that he had to watch Tara smile at that too-attentive Australian.

Pain circled Raif's jaw and he forced himself to relax and unclench his teeth.

He'd asked his secretary to ensure she was seated near the museum curator, given their shared interest in old jewellery. The Australian he hadn't met, but, given his senior role in a mining company, Raif had imagined someone older.

Not a young man who leaned too close to Tara. Who made her laugh that low, throaty laugh that Raif felt like the drag of velvet across his skin.

Raif wanted Tara to laugh like that with him, not some upstart Australian.

He wanted her smiles for himself.

Raif's fingers tightened into a fist and he had to focus on relaxing them. On smoothing his frown.

How could he be distracted by one tiny woman? One at the centre of a diplomatic furore that Raif really didn't need.

Yes, she was vivacious.

And unbelievably sexy.

And annoying.

And stronger than she looked.

Touching her today—okay, more than touching—had unleashed forces Raif usually kept well under control.

He was profoundly disturbed to discover his control of his libido had slipped again.

Raif's control had never slipped before Tara Michaels tumbled into his world.

He'd been provoked into kissing her but he'd pulled back. Because she was under his protection. And because Raif didn't do unbridled passion. Ever.

This hot surge of feeling was new and distracting.

The Australian pulled out her chair as everyone rose from the table and Raif wanted to shove him away from her.

For a moment he toyed with the notion that it was jealousy he felt, but dismissed it. He was never jealous.

He'd never needed to be. As the only child of loving, if strict, parents, he'd had a charmed life. Until his early teens when they'd died and he'd inherited the sheikhdom. But he'd had sound advisors to ease him into his new role. Everything he'd ever wanted had been within his grasp.

As for wanting Tara, that was natural. She was attractive and intriguing. He'd wanted women before. The difference was that this time he couldn't have her. *That* was why his response seemed so intense.

Farewelling his guests, Raif managed to keep his gaze off Tara till finally it was time to join her.

'Ms Michaels.' He resorted to formality for the sake of those around them.

'Your Majesty. What a lovely evening.' Her smile hit him square in the chest.

Still the Australian lingered. 'Your Majesty,' he said. 'Thank you for tonight's dinner. It's been an honour and a pleasure.'

Raif inclined his head. 'You're welcome, Mr Fletcher. I hear you're to begin work in the outer provinces.'

'Not straight away.' His gaze flicked to Tara. 'I thought I'd stay in the city and see the sights first.'

'Really?' Raif frowned. 'I understood from your CEO that he expected you on the ground immediately.'

The enterprise was in part funded by the crown. It might be timely to ensure an early start to the geological survey, as originally planned.

As the chamberlain ushered the last guests out Raif was surprised at the satisfaction he felt, watching the ruddy-haired Australian go while Tara remained here, at his side.

Possessive as well as jealous?

He couldn't be.

Raif was simply pleased she was here where he could protect her.

He'd never allow Fuad to get his hands on Tara.

Or the Australian?

'You enjoyed yourself?' he asked, leading Tara away.

Her smile widened and Raif dismissed the Australian from his thoughts.

'It was lovely. Thank you. Just what I needed. It was terrific to meet such interesting people.' She shrugged. 'I'm a bit of a people person and I've spent too much time alone with my thoughts.'

'I'm pleased you had a good time. It must be a relief that you don't have to hide from public view anymore.'

Though, judging by Fuad's reaction tonight, her presence here would fuel more trouble. And the backlash wouldn't just be from across the border.

Already there'd been talk about what Tara was doing, alone and unchaperoned in the palace. About what his relationship was with a woman from the Dhalkuri royal family.

As Dhalkur and Nahrat were traditional enemies, and many believed that shouldn't change, Raif had to tread carefully.

He hadn't been careful when he'd entered the banqueting hall with her hand on his arm.

Raif had acted deliberately, defying anyone to express disapproval. Knowing his action would eventually be reported to Fuad. He was determined to signal that Tara was under his protection. Everyone, Fuad and his representatives, as well as Nahratis who might take issue with her presence, needed to know that.

Raif had crossed a boundary when he gave her sanctuary and had no intention of going back on his word now. No matter the repercussions. Only his support kept her free. It was what any decent man would do. It was *not* a sign of personal weakness.

'Here.' He opened a door and ushered her inside a sitting room.

'I thought you were taking me to my room?' Was that disappointment in her voice?

Did she want him in her private suite? His brain snagged on the notion, till he told himself not to be distracted.

Nevertheless, his gaze caught on her as she moved to take the seat he indicated. She was poised and sexy in those high heels that turned her gait into a sensuous sway. The subtle sheen of blue fabric shimmered across her breasts and hips.

Raif swallowed, his throat sandpaper dry.

He'd given orders that she be provided with a wardrobe suitable for a princess. It would have been easier if his orders hadn't been followed so assiduously.

Easier but much less enjoyable.

Besides, it wasn't her clothes. Alone of all the women tonight, Tara wore no jewellery, and if she wore make-up he couldn't see it. Yet the golden glow of her skin, her fine eyes and glossy dark hair with its hint of mahogany red were embellishment enough.

She'd look good in anything.

Or nothing.

Raif took a seat opposite, corralling his thoughts. 'We have things to discuss.' He wouldn't tell her about Fuad's call, though. That would just worry her.

She sat demurely, hands in her lap. Raif's gaze dipped to her mouth, dark pink and lush, then back to her questioning eyes.

'Now it's public knowledge you're here, you can have more freedom.'

He'd thought her eyes pretty before. Now they turned bright as polished gems. He'd pleased her. Stoically he squashed thoughts of other, more personal ways he might please her.

'That's wonderful!'

'You'll still have to be careful. No dashing into the city unescorted.'

Because her cousin was desperate and underhanded enough to have thugs waiting for a chance to grab her. Nor could Raif completely discount the possibility that one of his own people might assist, believing it inappropriate that their Sheikh associate with a woman whose family was seen by some die-hards as the enemy.

'You think Fuad would snatch me off the street?' Her eyes rounded.

'You know him better than I do. What do you think?'

'I wouldn't put anything past him.' She chewed her lip. 'So what did you have in mind?'

'Two things. You met the jewellery curator from the national museum tonight. It looked like you got on well.'

'We did. He and his wife are charming and his work is so fascinating.'

'I'm glad you think so. He's persuaded me to update the inventory of royal jewels. You can assist him.'

'Me?' Her brow pinched. 'I'm no jeweller. I don't have formal qualifications.'

'You have a good eye and a real appreciation.'

She shook her head. 'An appreciation, yes. I've picked up a bit over the years, but I'm not an expert.'

'I'm not looking for expertise—the curator will provide that. I thought it would appeal to you.' Though it was, now he thought about it, unpaid work. 'If you're not interested—'

'Oh, I'm interested! If you think I can really help, it would be wonderful.'

Raif nodded, pleased his plan was so well-received. 'It will mainly be a matter of taking notes, and, knowing the curator, listening to his thoughts on the history of each piece.'

A smile tugged her lips and it struck him again that Tara was a woman who didn't need adornment to be attractive. That smile alone would entice any man. Awareness shivered low in his belly.

'I'd like nothing better! If you're sure he wants me. He doesn't already have an assistant?'

'His assistant will be busy at the museum.' Raif's old friend was thrilled to be given the go-ahead for the project and if it kept Tara occupied so she didn't feel isolated... 'So, that's sorted. My staff will arrange a meeting.'

'You said there were two things.'

Raif nodded. This next was trickier. Not for her, but for him. Yet he had no intention of bowing to Fuad or any diehards who held a grudge against Dhalkur. It was time for change.

'I'd like you to come on my visits around the capital and later to a provincial centre.'

Her eyes flashed to his and he read her excitement. 'I'd love to get out. What would I have to do?'

Raif told himself that wasn't elation he felt at her excitement. She chafed at staying here, that was all. How different she was to the women he knew who'd enjoy relaxing in luxury, waited on hand and foot.

'You'll see the sights, attend a few receptions, meet some locals. You won't have a formal role, but you'd participate in any welcome festivities.'

'I can do that.' But now her smile suddenly crimped tight. 'Thank you. You're very kind, very...thoughtful. I've put you to a lot of trouble.'

'Tara?' Was it a trick of the light or did her eyes shine over-bright?

She looked down, restlessly smoothing the shimmery fabric of her skirt.

He wanted to take her hands. The woman he'd come to admire was feisty and determined, sometimes too much so. He didn't like this glimpse of what looked like sadness.

'I thought you'd be happy to get out of the palace.'

Tara swallowed, feeling the lump of scalding emotion in her throat. Stupid to be upset now when nothing was wrong.

It was his kindness that undid her. The reminder that, uninvited guest though she was, Raif tried to make her stay pleasant. She still couldn't believe he was allowing her the chance to work with an expert cataloguing those exquisite treasures. But it was the idea of getting outdoors again, away from the confinement of four walls that most affected her.

She blinked, forcing back the prickle of tears.

It had been the same when her cousin Salim had contacted her on her mother's death, asking what she needed, what he could do to help. His thoughtfulness had threatened to undo her then. As Raif's did now.

She'd been through so much her emotions were shot.

'I am happy. I'm thrilled.' She pasted on a smile that she hoped reflected excitement, though her facial muscles felt too tight. 'With all your other responsibilities I'm amazed you have time to think of me. I can't tell you how much I appreciate it.'

Raif's forehead knotted and he waved a dismissive hand. 'It's nothing. Others will make the arrangements.'

Yet it was only because of his intervention that she wasn't at Fuad's mercy. And Raif had gone further. He turned her stay into something other than another incarceration. Tara felt guilty that she'd doubted him, wondering if he was like Fuad, aiming to grab her fortune.

Her ribs tightened around her fast-beating heart.

Raif made her feel so much. He had an uncanny ability to rub her up the wrong way and bring her to bristling, uncharacteristic antagonism. Yet despite his arrogance and her occasional doubts he was kind, considerate and far too appealing. He made her feel scary, unfamiliar yearnings.

Tara shot to her feet, afraid of where her thoughts might lead.

When Raif had invited her to join him after dinner she'd wondered if he was going to kiss her again. She'd been on tenterhooks, wondering if he'd take her to his suite.

Instead he really did want to *talk*.

It wasn't talk she wanted from him.

If she stayed much longer there was a chance she'd reveal that. Her pride couldn't take another rejection.

'Thank you, Raif.' She paused as he rose to tower above her. She only had to take a couple of steps to close the space between them. A couple of steps and she could put her hand on that sturdy chest, feel his heartbeat, smell his heat and sandalwood spice scent. Reach up and cup his jaw. Pull his head down for another kiss. 'I'd better go.'

'Are you all right?' Concern laced his tone, roughening it deliciously as he stepped nearer.

Tara shivered as her body reacted. She arched her neck back to hold his gaze. His eyes gleamed brighter than ever, obsidian-black. Yet to her fevered mind his gaze looked soft, not hard. Beckoning, not distant.

She swallowed again, nostrils flaring as she inhaled his unique male scent.

'I'm fine.' Her fingers flexed and she realised with a jolt that she was imagining dragging her hand across the dark olive skin of his cheek. Down to the sharp line of his jaw. Would his skin feel rough there? Her palm prickled as if tickled by imaginary stubble.

Tara whipped her hands behind her back, like a child caught reaching for forbidden goodies.

'I'm just very tired.'

That was such a lie. She was wired. She wouldn't sleep for hours.

His eyes widened infinitesimally.

Did he guess she lied?

Could he sense the current of awareness passing through her? It hummed in her veins and across her skin, drawing her nipples into tight buds and making her far too aware of that hollow, needy sensation deep inside.

Tara licked suddenly dry lips then forgot to breathe as Raif followed the movement of her tongue.

A heavy whump of sensation punched through her. She canted towards him, drawn by his magnetism.

His eyes glowed and his nostrils arched as if he scented her arousal in the thickening air.

One second more. One move…

With a rush of blood to her head Tara pulled back, stunned that she still had the power to. She swallowed, regret lodging hard against her breastbone as she conjured the words she needed.

'Thanks again, Raif.' Her voice thickened on his name and the taste of it almost undid her resolve. As did the fire in those burning eyes. 'It's time I turned in. Goodnight.'

She swung away, movements clumsy, feet leaden, and walked to the door.

Every step she waited for his voice calling her back, or the touch of his hand on her shoulder, pulling her against him. Confirming that she wasn't alone in this. That he too felt this…yearning.

Instead, with her hand on the door, she heard, 'Goodnight, Tara. Sleep well.'

Her mouth trembled but she kept her head high. No matter what, she'd vanquish her attraction to Raif. She *would*.

CHAPTER EIGHT

THE NEXT FIVE days sped by. Tara met Raif daily but he never hinted at anything like intimacy by word or look.

She found that deflating, even though she'd decided she had to conquer her attraction. Surely something that affected her so suddenly couldn't last?

Yet Tara enjoyed the companionable time with him. It made her feel calm and grounded, which was baffling because she'd never needed anyone else to help her do that.

Each day she went out with the Sheikh's entourage. She had no official role but Raif always took time to tell her about each venue and introduce her. It was so fascinating that she managed not to mind the curiosity she provoked.

Her favourite excursion was to the old covered markets, inspecting building improvements. For Tara it was a chance to enjoy the vast array of goods on sale, from carpets, brass and copper wear, leather goods and silks to huge mounds of vibrantly coloured spices and fruit.

As well, each day she spent hours in the royal treasury. She'd been nervous at first, conscious of her lack of formal qualifications. But to her delight she found herself up to the job. Sometimes she even noticed things her new colleague missed. Like identifying the design work around some emeralds as South American, thanks to her years living there. That led to a new line of investigation on the source of the piece.

It made her think of reviving her idea of getting formal qualifications. She'd put that on hold when her father died and she'd moved with her mother to England, and again when her mother became ill.

Lulled by the rocking motion of the four-wheel drive crossing the desert, Tara was musing on that when they reached the summit of a huge sand dune and stopped. Her breath caught at the scene below her.

All around were shades of ochre and gold, and above, the bright blue of the sky. Before them, between the dune and a rocky cliff, lay a miniature forest of green. Tall, graceful palms towered over other, shrubbier trees and she caught the tantalising glint of water.

'An oasis!' Thrilled, she turned to see Raif in the driver's seat, watching her.

Tara's ease shattered as her pulse quickened. There was something about his gleaming eyes that made her insides flutter.

'You like it?' Raif's voice burred softly, making her pulse thrum an unfamiliar beat.

Tara yanked her head back to the view.

'It's amazing. I've never seen anything like it. The change from barren sand to lush greenery is so sudden.'

Was she babbling? Suddenly Tara felt self-conscious. Surely she imagined the change in his expression. Just because she found him fascinating didn't mean he felt the same. He'd been nothing but a perfect host for days.

How disappointing she'd found that!

The sun glinted off the vehicles that had gone ahead.

'Are those tents I see?'

'They are. This is our campsite.'

Surprised, Tara turned back to him. 'I thought we were visiting towns. That we'd stay there.'

'Afraid you'll miss out on amenities?' His mouth flattened. 'Don't worry, you'll find the camp quite comfortable.'

'I didn't mean that. I'm just surprised. I'd love to camp in the desert. I've never done that.'

He held her gaze, then nodded. 'I'm glad to provide a new experience.' He started up the engine and drove downhill, manoeuvring over the treacherous surface with consummate skill. 'The towns are over there.' He nodded towards a distant blue ridge. 'We'll go there later.'

The oasis was fascinating. It had a peaceful quality, enhanced by the fact their accommodation was set away from vehicles and attendants.

Raif led her into a grove sheltered by tall palms where two big tents sat side by side.

Crazy to read anything into the way they were located together. It was just that, unlike the guards and other attendants, she was Raif's private guest.

Nevertheless, Tara was supremely conscious of the man beside her. As always, she felt their disparity in height. But now the difference between them seemed even more pronounced. She was hyper-aware of his athletic body, from his loose-limbed stride to his upright stance and innate air of assurance. Even the easy swing of his arms reminded her of the power in those big hands when he'd held her close and kissed her. When all she could think of was losing herself in the glorious oblivion of passion.

'I'll leave you to freshen up before lunch.'

Quickly she nodded, not turning to meet his penetrating stare and definitely not trusting her voice to respond evenly.

'Then we'll head out for a site visit.'

In other words, despite the exotic setting, this trip was business. Not a romantic getaway.

Tara swallowed and scraped her voice together. 'I'll look forward to it.'

'See you in half an hour.'

'I'll be ready.'

She felt his stare but pretended to be fascinated by the sprawling tent before her as he strode the few metres to his own, even larger tent, topped by the royal standard that stirred in the breeze.

Taking a deep breath, Tara silently berated herself. Raif's expression when they'd stopped at the top of the sand dune was *not* heavy with desire. Even if it had made her hot all over. As for his regard just now, he probably just wondered why she was so silent.

See? She could be sensible. That was a first step in conquering her awareness of him.

Pushing aside the canvas flap that served as a door, she walked into her desert accommodation.

And stopped short at the sheer Arabian Nights beauty of it.

The tent looked big from the outside but it was larger inside, with a high ceiling that emphasised the sense of space. Rich carpets in jewel hues covered the floor and some of the walls, creating a sense of lush opulence.

Tara was reminded of an ornate jewellery box she'd catalogued the day before. Of solid gold, it was set with precious and semi-precious stones that created a rainbow of colours. Here, a similar kaleidoscope met the eye, but whoever had decorated this space knew what they were doing. Despite the range of colours, they blended together harmoniously.

The long swathes of filmy material around the bed gave it a rich feel, as did the burnished brass tables and silk cushions covered in exquisite embroidery. There was even a bowl of deeply scented roses on an inlaid wooden chest of drawers.

Shaking her head, Tara took off her shoes, curling her toes into the deep pile of the intricately patterned carpet.

Her mother had been something of an expert on carpets, given that the headquarters of the Royal Guild of Carpet Weavers, established by Tara's grandmother, was next door to the Dhalkuri palace. Tara's mother had been in and out of the place throughout her childhood—hence her friendship with Yunis—and she'd taught her daughter well. This carpet was not only beautiful but also old and very, very precious.

A huff of dry laughter escaped Tara's throat.

This was how Raif went camping?

Had she really thought, even for a second, that he was interested in her paltry fortune?

Her stunned gaze took in the gorgeous space. All it needed was an ornate lamp with a genie to make it the stuff of fantasies.

Or a tall, dark handsome man with hard features and an even harder body...

The thought set her insides shivering again.

On bare feet she crossed the room, discovering a wardrobe complete with a range of her new clothes. Not just the ones she'd chosen for this visit, but also some made of that butterfly-sheer silk, beaded at neck and hem.

The sight of those glamorous, sensuous outfits set up a jangling sensation inside, but she mastered the urge to wonder if they'd been packed for Raif's benefit.

That wasn't going to happen. Despite what some eager maid assumed.

Spying another door, Tara discovered a well-appointed bathroom complete with fluffy towels and a range of toiletries. Another vase sat on a bench top, this time filled with scented gardenias.

Tara was stunned by the level of luxury. She knew Raif had grown up in enormous wealth, but he seemed a man who didn't need opulence to be happy. The vehicle he'd driven today had been serviceable rather than luxurious and his clothes, though well-made, weren't ostentatious.

Were there sybaritic touches in his accommodation too? Or was his personal space more restrained? Had he specifically asked his staff to create this amazing bower for her? More likely a helpful staffer had pulled out all the stops for His Majesty's guest.

Or perhaps Raif brought his lovers to this beautiful place. Maybe these furnishings were used whenever he wanted a discreet love nest for his latest amour.

Pain jabbed between Tara's ribs.

Nose wrinkling at the direction of her thoughts, she washed her face and hands, then let down her hair and brushed it before arranging it high in a severe knot. Ignoring the delicious silks in the wardrobe, she located a cool cotton dress and low sandals.

She'd give no one reason to believe she was here as Raif's lover.

For once Raif had trouble concentrating. Usually nothing distracted him from his job.

Right now, that job was listening to the elders of the town where a new solar energy farm had been established. Yet as they discussed changes in the region, job opportunities and the impact of newcomers moving into town, Raif's attention wandered.

To Tara, of course.

He'd organised the oasis stay because it was one of his favourite places, where he went to unwind. He'd thought its natural beauty would soothe Tara in this difficult time and when she'd first seen it, it seemed he'd been right.

Delight jolted adrenaline into his blood when he'd seen her wide stare and stunned smile. But doubts crowded at her reaction when she learned they were to stay the night. Perhaps camping, even with every possible luxury, wasn't her style. Perhaps, after all, she didn't appreciate the peace and majesty of the place as he did.

Strange how that had felt like a personal blow. He'd felt rebuffed, sharing a place that was special to him, only to face her lukewarm enthusiasm.

He'd gone out of his way to make her accommodation special. As if his staff couldn't be trusted to provide what was necessary.

As if he wanted her to fall for the place, to appreciate it as he did.

To appreciate him?

Raif wasn't so needy.

With an effort he dragged his attention back to the current discussion. Two elders with differing opinions debated between themselves. Time to rein them in and turn the discussion in a more constructive direction.

'Sir!'

The head of his close personal protection team approached and Raif frowned. Despite his professionally schooled features, Raif read the man's tension.

'A word, sir. Urgently.'

All heads turned and the debate petered into silence.

Raif rose. 'Excuse me a moment.' He found it hard to believe there was a threat. His people were loyal.

'There's trouble at the community centre, sir.' Once outside, his bodyguard slanted a look across the square to the building where Tara was taking tea with the local women.

Raif's heart stumbled to a halt then accelerated into a rackety beat.

'Tell me.' His fingers closed around the guard's arm. All was quiet. Too quiet?

'A young woman with a baby slipped out from a back room. She reported armed men in the building. Strangers, with a different accent. She thinks from Dhalkur.'

The hairs at the back of Raif's neck stood up.

Were they here for Tara? It should be impossible but it was the only reasonable explanation. They were fifty kilometres from the border. Even Fuad would be wary of an armed incursion into sovereign territory. Which meant it likely the men were a rogue group, easily denied by Fuad if something went wrong. And likely more dangerous than trained soldiers. Raif's heart plummeted.

'You believe her? It's not some story?'

'No, one of my men saw an armed gunman attempting to slip out. He had a woman with him. We believe it was Ms

Michaels. When he saw my man he shouted an order over his shoulder and withdrew. Now the entrance is locked from the inside. We've heard male voices and women crying.'

Raif made to cross the square, but the bodyguard stepped in front of him.

'Please, sir. You need to leave this to us.'

'What do you have in mind? Storming the building? With scores of hostages in there?'

He shook his head, his brain conjuring and rejecting one scenario after another. Armed intervention could end in a bloodbath.

'How many men?'

'We've identified only two voices.'

Vaguely, Raif was aware of his quickened breathing, his hurried pulse. There was a sick feeling in his gut as he thought of vulnerable women, held by gunmen. Of Tara. His heart lurched. He'd promised her protection. Yet he'd brought her into danger.

As Sheikh, he had a responsibility to all his people trapped in there and to their families.

As a man it was the thought of Tara that filled his mind and iced his veins with fear.

Tara stood, hands bound, watching the two armed men. Fear was a harsh, metallic taste on her tongue and her pulse raced ten to the dozen.

A quick glance over her shoulder revealed all the women standing, silent, behind her, their expressions a mixture of fear and defiance. A couple of them had protested when the men had bound Tara's hands and tried to hustle her out of the building. They'd been struck down with vicious blows, but now their quiet sobs had stopped.

Guilt sat heavy in Tara's chest. She'd brought this horror on these friendly women. These men were Dhalkuris and it was her they wanted.

Her senses strained to heightened awareness as terror dragged every muscle tight.

Fuad wanted her alive. But if something went wrong, as it now appeared, would they dispose of any witnesses? The men looked panicked. Panicked men made mistakes, which could work in her favour, or ramp up the danger.

Better they take her, than endanger all these people. If she offered herself as a willing hostage, surely whoever was outside would let them pass. She'd be delivering herself into Fuad's hands but there was no other option.

Tara stepped forward. 'I'll come with you quietly if you let the others go. The guards will let you pass if I'm with you.'

She slammed to a halt as a woven hanging on a far wall lifted. Her eyes widened. It took a moment to realise what she saw wasn't the wall breaking, but someone entering through a door hidden by the traditional weaving.

There was a shout, the gunmen swivelling. Then Tara's heart stood still as Raif stepped into the room.

Relief filled her, till she saw those ugly weapons pointed at him, and her knees went to jelly.

He said nothing, nor did he look at her after one sweeping survey of the large room. Instead he lifted his arms from his sides and slowly turned on the spot. His movements were measured, confident even, and his austere expression revealed no fear. His regal bearing, as much as his snowy robe and head scarf, put him in a different category to the two men before him, dusty and nervous-looking despite their weapons.

'Don't come any closer,' one of the men said, his voice grim.

'I'm unarmed.' Raif's voice rang through the strained silence with the authority of total assurance. 'I come in peace to discover why you're threatening my people.'

One of the intruders whispered something to his companion. The other shook his head, then growled, 'We're here for the woman.' He jerked his head towards Tara. 'We have no interest in the others. Let us pass and no one will be hurt.'

'She doesn't want to go with you.'

'It doesn't matter what she wants. She belongs in Dhalkur. Our orders are—' He broke off when his companion whispered something in a rough voice.

Perspiration beaded Tara's forehead and nape. The men *were* from Fuad. Her hands trembled and it took everything she had to stand there, upright, instead of cowering. The sight of Raif, so strong in the face of danger, gave her strength.

'You're mistaken. Ms Michaels belongs in Nahrat.'

The younger, more agitated of the men shouted back. 'You lie. She's a Dhalkuri like us. We're taking her home.'

'I am Sheikh Raif ibn Ansar of Nahrat and I do not lie.' He paused, letting that sink in. 'I tell you now, if you try to leave without my permission, you'll be cut down by my guards.' The younger man opened his mouth but Raif ignored him. 'And we *will* uncover your identities.' His voice deepened to an impressive resonance as a savage light flared in that dark stare. 'If you harm anyone here, you have my word, it won't just be you who pays the price. I'll invoke the old ways. Your families will pay as well. And if you have no families, your friends and associates. I vow it on my family honour, on the names of all my forefathers.'

Silence engulfed the huge room. It was so thick Tara felt it press down like a huge, invisible weight.

Now the gunmen were in whispered conference. Their plan of an easy kidnap while the Sheikh's guard was busy on the other side of the town was in disarray.

Tara kept her eyes on the younger one, watching the restless jig of his fingers on the gun. Her stomach clutched in fear.

'Your Majesty.' The older man spoke. 'We wish no violence. It's the woman we want. We'll leave in peace if we have her.'

For answer Raif stepped away from the wall, pacing closer to the men and their raised weapons.

'That I can't allow. Ms Michaels is mine.' His voice rang out, clear and forthright. Tara felt the world swoop and dip around her. 'And,' Raif continued, 'as all the world knows, what I have, I hold.'

Oblivious of the muffled gasps from the audience of women, Raif turned his head, his glittering eyes snaring hers, sending a blast of sheet lightning shearing through her insides. 'That's so, isn't it, Tara? You belong to me.'

She knew he said this for the benefit of her would-be abductors. Yet in that strange moment, when the world seemed to telescope around them so there was just her and Raif, Tara felt the truth of it. The powerful whump of sensation, like a blow to her chest, confirmation that, yes, she belonged to him. She was tied to this man by sexual desire and by something more profound that she had no name for. A yearning that had settled deep in her bones.

'Yes,' she croaked, barely above a whisper. She lifted her chin and stepped towards him on wobbly legs. 'Yes,' she spoke louder, 'I belong to you, Raif.'

Maybe it was the use of his name, as if she really *were* his woman, but she saw the intruders' expressions alter.

'That's far enough.' The younger one waved his gun and she stumbled to a stop.

But now Raif was walking towards her, shoulders back and gait steady, as if he strolled in some grand, royal procession.

'I said—'

The older gunman stopped him, whispering urgently in his ear, his hand pushing the barrel of the gun down.

Tara felt light-headed as Raif reached her, his hand comfortingly warm as it enveloped hers. She looked up at him, torn between fear and relief, but he wasn't looking at her. His attention was fixed on the two men.

'You have my word that if you lay down your weapons and leave with me now, you will be treated humanely. You will be taken to the capital and held there while we negotiate with the Dhalkuri authorities. I will allow you to stand trial there, rather than here in my realm.'

It was an enormous concession. Especially since it was clear that these men acted under Fuad's orders. Once in Dhalkur they wouldn't be put on trial. Though facing Fuad in a temper if they failed would make anyone tremble.

Their whispered discussion took for ever. Even with Raif's hand holding hers, she couldn't feel calm. When Raif squeezed her hand then released it, she almost grabbed at him, but he approached the gunmen.

Her heart leapt in her throat, but there was a change in their demeanour. Even the jittery younger man looked less belligerent. Was it possible Raif's words might persuade them? Or would they take their chances, using her or Raif as shields? That must be tempting, yet she'd seen the impact of his promise of vengeance. The Sheikh of Nahrat would make an implacable enemy.

Raif spoke to them again, so low she couldn't hear.

Then suddenly, things changed. Before her widening eyes she saw the men put their weapons down and step to one side, hands in the air. At a command from Raif the covering over the door where he'd entered lifted and several armed guards arrived, surrounding the intruders.

After that everything happened quickly. The weapons and the men disappeared. Women surrounded her, offering reassurance and undoing her bound wrists. From them she gathered that the discreet entrance Raif had used led to a small back room. One of the younger women had retreated there to feed her baby before the attackers arrived. She'd raised the alarm with Raif's men.

It all felt unreal, even the relieved chatter of the women and the offer of sweet tea, until she caught sight of Raif over their heads. He was talking to a security staffer but his eyes were on her. Once more that black stare was unreadable but Tara didn't care. She was grateful they were both unharmed. That moment when he'd walked right up to the gunmen... She'd have nightmares about that for the rest of her life.

The crowd parted and there he was. Raif, his features more drawn than usual, but reassuringly strong and solid. A great shudder racked her and she knew it was true. They really were safe.

He put his hand out and she placed hers in it, curling her fingers around his, drawing on his strength.

Raif led her out and she went with him, willingly.

CHAPTER NINE

RAIF DIDN'T DRAW a full breath till he had Tara back at the oasis. Her attackers were under armed escort, heading for the capital.

Used to taking charge, being the one people looked to in a crisis, he'd projected an aura of calm when dealing with the gunmen and townspeople. Yet inside he was a mess. Seeing those men threatening the defenceless women, threatening Tara...

He never wanted to face anything like it again.

Despite his show of arrogant certainty, he'd been worried his intervention wouldn't end the potentially deadly hostage drama. But he'd had to try. His gut clenched as he imagined the bloodshed if they'd tried to force their way out.

The drive to camp was silent and, though Tara hadn't dissolved into tears, her silence worried him. The sooner he got her back to the palace the better.

'We'll have you back in the city soon,' he said as they reached their tents. 'I've ordered a helicopter. We'll be back at the palace before sunset.' His own chopper had been diverted to bring in a medical emergency from an outlying area to the city and other nearby helicopters were either in use or undergoing repairs. Raif firmed his mouth. Waiting was tough but medical emergencies took priority, even now.

'I don't need to go to the city.'

Raif surveyed her pale features. 'You'll feel better somewhere safe, away from a reminder of what happened today.'

Her eyes grew huge in her face and he cursed himself for scaring her. 'You mean there's still danger?'

'No. Everything's fine.' He resisted the urge to take her hand again. Unaccountably he'd felt better with it firmly clasped in his. 'Forces have been deployed on the border and elsewhere through the province. But initial enquiries make it seem certain those two acted alone. There's no sign of anyone else.'

Raif paused, listening to the chatter of a tiny bird in the trees, feeling a tiny breeze ruffle his clothes. It was peaceful here and he knew specialists were already busy, searching out every detail on the two prisoners and how they had crossed the border.

'I'm sorry, Tara. I never guessed Fuad would make such a drastic attempt. I shouldn't have brought you.' Bile rose as he thought of how close she'd come to being taken.

'Don't apologise. You're the man that saved me, remember? Besides, you couldn't have known Fuad would try anything like this, an attempt under your very nose and in your own territory! It's outrageous. Almost...unhinged.'

Raif read the fear and outrage in Tara's face and the stew of fury in his belly stirred hotter. He'd known Fuad was ruthless, but this showed him to be obsessive, willing to risk an international incident.

'Presumably he thought a couple of men might succeed where a larger force couldn't.'

Her lovely mouth tilted up in a crooked smile that carved a hollow in his belly. 'He reckoned without considering you. I've never seen anything so brave. Thank you, Raif. I can't begin to thank you enough.'

Horrified, he raised his hand to stop her words. His bravery, if that was what it was, had been born of desperation and guilt. He'd put Tara and his people in danger. He couldn't rid himself of the horror of the moment when he'd realised the peril.

'It's over now. That's what matters.' He nodded to the tent. 'There's time for a shower before the chopper arrives.'

Tara shook her head, shafts of filtered sunlight playing on the rich mahogany tint of her hair. 'Please don't send me back. I'd like to stay.'

It was the last thing Raif expected. 'Surely you'd feel better away from what happened—'

'I don't think so. You're staying here, aren't you?'

For a second Raif thought she implied she'd rather stay where he was, then he realised Tara needed reassurance on the journey.

'I'll accompany you to the palace and see you settled.' His staff could do that but Raif remembered how she'd clung to him earlier, only releasing his hand so he could drive her here. It was nothing personal. 'Later I'll return. My business isn't finished and I want to go back tomorrow to see the townspeople are all right after today's scare.'

Tara nodded. 'I do too. They were very kind, very supportive. I'd like to visit them again and thank them.'

Raif frowned, folding his arms across his chest. He knew she was brave. The way she'd stood alone, apparently composed, when facing her would-be abductors, proved that. But he'd felt her hand shake, seen the trembling breaths she took afterwards. Beneath her apparent calm lay distress.

'It's a nice idea. I'll pass on your thanks and good wishes. But I think—'

Once again she interrupted. She was the only person, apart from his aunt, who did that. It was still so unexpected it stopped him mid-sentence.

'Can't I think for myself? I *want* to stay.' Her eyes blazed. '*Please*, Raif. I promise to stay in the background, not make a nuisance of myself. But we left so quickly I feel bad about not staying to thank them.' Her gaze dropped. 'And even though your palace is nice, it sometimes feels like a gilded cage. I'd much rather be out here, where I can breathe.'

Stunned, he stared at this remarkable woman.

Had anyone else ever dismissed the royal palace as *nice*, preferring to stay in the desert?

Actually, now he thought about it, his mother had loved

coming here with his father. She always returned to the palace with a glow in her cheeks and warmth in her eyes.

'Where you can breathe?'

She looked up. Those green eyes seemed darker, maybe because her face was pale. 'I live in London now but I spent years in small settlements, often in remote areas, wherever my father's mining work took us. I like the quiet out here and the beauty of it.' She paused. 'Besides, going back now I'd feel like Fuad was controlling me again, forcing me to cower in hiding, rather than do what I think right. Like visit those women who stood by me today.'

Raif exhaled slowly, trying to recall if anyone had so continually defied his expectations and disrupted the smooth running of his arrangements. Not that he blamed Tara for today's attack. He was the one at fault there.

She looked at him so earnestly, but he didn't miss the signs of fragility. That taut stance, as if it took extra effort to stay upright, the shadows in her eyes.

Whether she admitted it or not, Tara needed time to recover. She shouldn't be standing out here, she should be resting.

'Very well.' At his words her high shoulders dropped and a glimmer of a smile curved her lips.

'Thank you, Raif.'

His forehead crinkled and his hands curled tight as he fought the dart of pleasure he felt, hearing his name in that husky, grateful voice.

'On condition that you rest. And that, if you feel worse, you let me know.' The camp medic had checked her out but Raif was determined to look after Tara better than he had before.

'I'll be good, I promise.' Another ghost of a smile. This time he caught a hint of mischievous laughter in her expression.

An inner voice told him he wasn't interested in Tara being good. He'd much prefer her to be bad. With him.

He strode forward and yanked open the entrance to her accommodation, gesturing for her to go in. The sooner she was out of sight the sooner he might get hold of himself. Tara tempted him to forget honourable intentions.

When she was inside and only a trace of her rose and cinnamon scent lingered to tease him, Raif spoke. 'Rest now. Tomorrow we'll visit the town together. And Tara?'

'Yes?' Her voice sounded eager, despite her obvious weariness.

'For the record, you're not a nuisance.'

Once he might have thought so. Especially as she stood up to him and provoked him as no one else dared.

Now he found her perplexing, challenging, admirable, and distracting.

And dangerously tempting.

The oasis was a calm paradise. Tara heard the gentle burble of spring water as she stood in the doorway of her tent, watching diamond-bright stars pinprick the black velvet night.

The day's warm zephyr had given way to a cooler breeze that brought the indefinable scent of the desert. It teased the filmy silk caftan she'd put on after her shower, reminding Tara that beneath the crimson material she was naked.

It hadn't seemed worth dressing properly after she'd showered and washed her hair. Instead she'd curled up on the wide bed and fallen almost instantly asleep.

She'd slept through the arrival of dinner, an array of delicious dishes left on a tray.

Now, replete after grazing on the delicacies, she felt restless.

Her afternoon sleep had been plagued by disturbing

dreams yet she'd woken feeling better. The light-headed, nauseous feeling of shock was gone.

Tara looked at the towering cliff beyond the oasis and felt no fear. There'd be no more armed men coming after her. Raif would see to that.

It surprised her how implicitly she trusted him, given the doubts she'd once had. Time and again he'd proved himself an ally. Standing up for her with the Dhalkuri ambassador. Taking her under his wing and organising work in the treasury that would challenge and fascinate her.

Facing down two armed gunmen to save her.

She swallowed, her hand clutching the delicate fabric at her chest.

When she'd seen him threatening those men with vengeance, when he'd paced towards her, full of autocratic certainty, her heart had been in her mouth.

If he'd been shot because of her...

It didn't bear thinking about. Yet she couldn't banish it from her mind.

Raif was so vibrantly alive, so charismatic, it physically hurt to imagine him slumped and bloody on the floor. Which could have happened if he hadn't cowed her abductors with the sheer force of his willpower.

He was a remarkable man.

She'd never met anyone like him.

Tara *trusted* him. The knowledge filled her like bright sunlight after a long winter.

That had to be why she reacted so strongly to him. From the first he'd been larger than life. Now it felt like he'd taken over her mind. She couldn't stop thinking about him.

It wasn't just her mind he'd taken over. Her body was affected too. That was the real reason for tonight's restlessness. Today's incident had played a part, sharpening her awareness of her feelings. Of the fragility of life and how easily it could be snuffed away. She'd lost both her parents far too young. Thinking of Raif facing down those men reminded her how easily things could have ended badly.

She shivered and wrapped her arms around herself.

Today had changed things irrevocably.

Tara had been determined to keep a safe distance from Raif. Her past and her current situation making her wary. But now everything seemed stripped back, revealing the truth she'd tried to avoid.

She wanted more from Raif than protection.

She wanted far too much.

Tara was a pragmatist. She knew she couldn't have Raif's friendship permanently, much less a special place in his regard. Once she left he'd move on with his life, as she must. But she was woman enough to understand that he felt *something* for her. Something that had prompted him to kiss her. Sometimes she caught his eyes on her and read hunger there, before he saw her watching.

Desire. *That was* what made her edgy now. Suspecting Raif wanted her, even if he didn't want to want her.

Her yearning, after today's tumultuous events, felt impossible to resist. Was that what this restlessness was? A primitive acceptance that life could be short and opportunities needed to be seized?

It eclipsed her ingrained belief that temporary relationships weren't for her. That if ever she were to be with a man it would be in a loving relationship such as her parents had shared.

Tara drew a slow breath and dropped her hands, smoothing damp palms over her hips and thighs, feeling the caress of gossamer silk against bare flesh.

Instead of regaining control of her racing thoughts, the gesture made her wonder how it would feel if Raif ran his hands over her, dragging the silk against her skin. Would those powerful hands be tender or urgent?

Her nipples budded and her breasts tingled, weighted

with a heaviness directly linked to the aching hollow sensation low in her body.

For so long she'd felt at the mercy of others, of circumstances she couldn't control. That was about to change.

Raif slung his damp towel over his shoulder and tugged on cotton trousers, casually tying the drawstring.

It had been a productive couple of hours.

The Dhalkuris were in prison and, in hopes of an early release, had given their names and details of how they'd crossed the border. Predictably, they hadn't admitted they were under instructions from Prince Fuad. They'd confirmed that only the two of them had entered his kingdom, yet Raif's forces were monitoring the border so closely not even a stray lamb could get through.

His mouth tightened. What the pair didn't realise was that it would be a long time before they'd be released into Dhalkur. He had no intention of letting violent offenders loose. He wouldn't send them to Dhalkur while Fuad held the reins of power.

The pair would remain imprisoned in Nahrat until Raif saw fit to release them for trial.

Preferably when Salim, rather than Fuad, took the throne.

Raif would do everything he could to ensure that happened. It was good to practise non-interference in a neighbouring state. But it was another matter when the leader of that state threatened the peace. If Fuad was made Sheikh it would be like living next door to a rabid wolf.

Raif had already contacted Salim with news from his homeland, and about Fuad's treatment of Tara. As expected, Salim had been shocked. Fuad had withheld news that their father was fading fast, obviously hoping to keep Salim out of the country so he could be crowned Sheikh unopposed.

This afternoon Raif had also informed Salim of the attempted armed kidnap.

Matters were about to come to a head. Salim planned to arrive unannounced in his homeland and was meanwhile in confidential long-distance discussions with the royal council, who feared what would happen if Fuad became Sheikh.

Raif lifted the towel to rub his damp hair and strolled back into his bedroom.

He'd finish his visit tomorrow then return to the capital. He wanted Tara somewhere safe till the ructions over the border were finished and—

'Raif.'

He looked up and slammed to a halt, his heart crashing against his ribs.

'Tara?' He swallowed. For a second he'd thought her an apparition conjured by his unruly imaginings.

She stood in shadow inside the door, wearing not her usual western clothes but a dark full-length dress, her long hair around her shoulders.

His pulse beat hard in his temples. She was covered from neck to ankle yet his obstinate brain processed the sight of her and thought of sex.

'Why are you here?' His voice grated, his throat suddenly raw. He dragged the towel from his hair, holding it at his side in one clamped fist.

'I needed...' she paused, then her chin came up '...to see you.'

She stepped out of the shadows into the lamplight and everything within him stilled.

Everything except the sharp, animal instinct that turned him taut and watchful. The instinct of a hunter surveying succulent prey. Of a male scenting his mate.

His gaze traversed her, slowly, though every detail of her appearance had been branded into his consciousness in that first instant.

Her hair was a ripple of dark silk shot with reddish high-lights. Her features were composed and serious, as if she'd come to parley over some vital treaty. Yet even the slight pucker of her forehead and the challenging angle of her jaw couldn't detract from the lush invitation of her sultry mouth.

A great thump of awareness reverberated through Raif. He felt it in his chest, his groin and right down to the soles of his bare feet.

The dress skimmed her curves, clinging in all the right places. The fabric must be thin because her nipples stood out against it. As she moved closer, past a lamp set on a low table, the light shone through the fabric, outlining her body in loving detail.

Raif stared. Was it wishful thinking or was she naked beneath that red dress?

'Are you unwell?'

Tara stopped and shook her head, her long hair cascading over one shoulder. 'No, I'm fine.'

She looked better than fine.

She looked—

'Are you scared? Believe me, you're completely safe here.' He'd made sure of it. There might be no guards in sight but no one could get into the oasis without being stopped. Even the air space around the encampment was closely monitored.

Another shake of her head. Raif watched her lustrous hair shimmer in the light, slipping across one pert breast. He swallowed hard, fighting the rising tide of urgent desire.

'I'm not scared. Not any more. Not with you.'

Raif breathed out in a rush, nostrils flaring and ego swelling at her words. She felt safe with him. She trusted him.

She trusted him…

'Good. Then I'll see you in the morning.'

Instead of nodding agreement as any of his subjects

would have, Tara angled her chin higher, drawing attention to the line of her slender throat. How did the woman manage to appear both vulnerable and feisty?

'No. Please.' She drew a deep breath then expelled it. 'Can't I stay?'

Raif tried to concentrate on her words but his attention fell inevitably to the sweet jiggle of her unfettered breasts beneath the blood-red dress. Heat jagged through him, soldering the soles of his feet to the floor. Which was as well because he was appallingly close to forgetting his promises to himself and yanking her into his arms.

'No, you can't. We'll talk in the morning.' To reinforce the dismissal, not least to his own wayward body, he crossed his arms over his chest. 'Go to bed, Tara. I don't want you here.'

Tara was surprised at his harsh dismissal. His words cut like a lash, abrading her sensitive flesh. She shivered, suddenly cold despite the heat in her belly, and folded her arms around her body.

Raif's attention dropped from her face to her breasts. She felt the silk pull tight there. Her nipples jutted so needily that at any other time she'd be embarrassed.

But she wasn't. Because, despite his words, she'd seen the way Raif's eyes tracked her body.

The same way she'd tracked his.

She'd stood in the shadows, her mouth turning desert dry as he walked from the bathroom wearing only a pair of lightweight trousers that sat low on his hips. Every time he moved, her heart was in her mouth, wondering if they'd slide down to reveal more of his honed body.

He was a perfect study of male musculature. Tara wished she could draw so she could capture every powerful line of that rangy frame. And that tantalising dusting of hair across his muscled chest, the faint trickle of a dark line down to the waistband of his trousers. The taut abs.

Tara inhaled quickly, yanking her gaze up to his face, to discover Raif's attention straying over her body.

She'd never welcomed such frank masculine appraisal. But this was different. Tonight, it exactly matched her own needs.

'Tara, did you hear me? It's too late for talking.'

She jumped and focused her thoughts. 'I'm not here to talk.'

His eyes widened and she had the rare feeling she'd stunned him. Then they narrowed to gleaming ebony slits.

He shook his head and a muscle flicked in his jaw. 'Go, Tara. *Now.*'

Did she imagine a hint of desperation in that hard voice? Of course she did. Raif didn't do desperate.

Yet she'd come this far and she refused to retreat with her tail between her legs. Especially when she'd *seen* the interest in his glittering eyes. Felt it now in the thick atmosphere that despite the desert chill seemed to radiate heat.

Letting her arms drop, she walked up to him, so close she saw tiny beads of moisture clinging to his hair.

Tara put her hands on his shoulders and stretched up on tiptoe, her silk-clad body colliding with his hot, hard frame.

Still he didn't move, just stared down with unreadable eyes.

Nervous, she licked her lips and, remarkably, felt his powerful frame jerk beneath her touch.

'I want to stay. With you.'

Then, fearing rejection but too desperate to let that stop her, she wrapped one hand around the back of his skull. She splayed her fingers in slick, damp hair and pulled his head down to hers.

CHAPTER TEN

TARA'S LIPS TOUCHED Raif's and electricity fizzed through her, as if she'd tapped into a current. Her mouth moved against his, relearning its shape. Still he didn't move. That hard, half-naked body was unyielding, unbending.

Was he going to reject her, as he'd done after their kiss in the palace?

Had she got it wrong, imagining desire in his eyes?

Disappointment vied with desperation. She'd be utterly humiliated if he pushed her away and said he wasn't interested.

Leaning in, she slid her other hand up to his neck, mapping searing hot flesh with her palm.

Her breasts swayed against his torso, only a layer of silk separating them. It felt like the most wondrous, momentous thing in the world.

A low burr of sound teased her. Something rough and raw that she couldn't identify, till she realised she felt as well as heard it. It was a deep growl from the back of Raif's throat, vibrating into her mouth as his lips opened.

One moment he was as still as a living statue and the next he came alive in a surge of power. One arm lashed her waist, pulling her hard against him. His other hand forked through her hair, pushing it back, cupping her jaw as he tilted his head and took her mouth with ruthless efficiency.

Tara's knees gave way. She clung as he took her weight, lifting her against him. She had a second to thrill at his sheer strength, lifting her with one arm, till her thoughts frayed.

Everything was heat and ardour, the lush softness of lips, the hard thrust and swirl of tongues, the possessive grasp of Raif's hands that made her feel both aroused and secure.

Tara's fingers curled into his hair, clutching as she kissed him back.

She'd never known a kiss like it. Her experience was limited and the one time they'd kissed previously it had been...perfect.

This wasn't perfect.

It was too powerful, too utterly overwhelming for *perfect*.

This was a maelstrom she wasn't sure she'd survive.

She didn't want to survive it.

Tara wanted to lose herself in this rush of desire. A whirling kaleidoscope of sensations and desperate longing.

She inhaled sandalwood and something else rich and spicy and utterly compelling. The aroma of Raif's skin and wet hair. She felt the scorching touch of his skin. Tiny detonations of exquisite awareness peppered her flesh.

He bowed her back and she opened to him, giving everything he demanded, feeling his body press intimately against her. Between her legs bloomed moisture and that needy ache.

Tara dragged a hand down to his jaw and shivered as his skin there, textured rather than smooth, tickled her palm.

The shiver grew into a shudder as Raif broke their kiss, turning his head to plant a kiss on the centre of her palm. A deep, drawing kiss that sent more of those electric currents sparking through her.

She heaved in a gasping breath, then another, her breasts rising against his muscled chest, the glorious friction overloading her senses.

Tara's eyes snapped open and there were Raif's, black as sin and wickedly inviting, snaring hers.

She looked into that midnight gaze and wanted everything it promised. Every decadent pleasure from slow seduction to urgent ecstasy.

His mouth moved against her palm, tickling, and when

he lifted his head he was smiling. Not the coolly superior half-smile he'd turned on her when she annoyed him, or the wide grin she'd seen once or twice when he was genuinely amused. This was intimate, a mere quirk at the corners of his mouth that spoke of satisfaction, or perhaps expectation. His eyes were heavy-lidded, his lips dark from their passion.

'You have three seconds to tell me you've had second thoughts.' His voice ground low, so she felt it deep in her abdomen. Even that warning felt like a caress. Because she wanted this, wanted Raif.

'I don't need three. I'm sure. I want you, Raif.'

Hyper-aware of every moment, every breath, Tara cupped his face, sliding her thumbs over the soft cushion of his bottom lip. She quivered as fire shot to her breasts and from there straight to her sex. At the feel of Raif's mouth against her skin, the realisation that he was about to give her access to his beautiful body.

His smile turned lop-sided in an expression that made her heart jangle.

'In that case, princess, your wish is my command.'

He slipped an arm beneath her legs, lifting her high against his chest. From this angle she had a scrumptious view of his decisive jaw and the chiselled planes of his face as he crossed the room.

Tara leant her head against his collarbone, wondering again how it was that with this man she didn't mind being held in a way that reinforced the disparity between them. His size and power compared with her softening eagerness.

Yet she didn't feel weak in Raif's arms. She felt triumphant, eager, and incredibly aware of her femininity.

He bent, lowering her to stand beside the bed. As he straightened, he grasped the shimmery ruby silk and drew it up her body, higher and higher. Its softness teased her sensitive flesh till he reached her shoulders and Tara oblig-ingly raised her arms, feeling silk skim up and away.

There was an arc of colour as Raif tossed the garment away, leaving her utterly naked before him.

Tara swallowed, torn between nerves and pride. She wanted him. She wasn't ashamed of that. Yet she'd never been naked before a man.

She'd never, to her dying day, forget Raif's expression as he surveyed her.

His skin drew so taut across his features his cheekbones looked razor sharp. His nostrils flared wide and his broad chest rose hugely as he dragged in air. As if for a moment he'd forgotten to breathe and needed extra oxygen. His eyes, gleaming before, burned with a searing heat that kindled fire across her skin.

Slowly he shook his head.

Pain thudded through her chest. Was it rejection after all?

He looked so grim. So tense.

'What is it?' she whispered.

Once more Raif's mouth rucked up at one corner and her heart lurched. 'I don't have the words.' Suddenly she realised it wasn't reluctance she saw in his face but admi-ration. 'You're exquisite, Tara.'

The fire was inside her now, roaring along her veins. She stood straighter, chin up and shoulders back, her breasts thrusting towards him.

His hungry stare settled on her breasts and instantly that prickling, heavy sensation was back. She shifted her weight, conscious now of the plush silk carpet beneath her feet, the whispery touch of cool air on her flesh and the tiny distance between them.

'So are you.' Looking at him made her salivate. She wanted to drag her hands down his chest, feel the ridges of muscle and the soft dusting of body hair. Her fascinated gaze strayed to his pale cotton trousers, tented with his arousal.

Tara's breath hitched and held and she wondered if her lungs had forgotten how to work.

But she waited, taking her lead from him. She'd made the first move but as for the rest...

Instinct was fine but she didn't want to admit her inexperience. She had no idea how Raif would react but she wanted nothing to interrupt this. Besides, her virginity was her business.

He lifted his hand and she anticipated the touch of long fingers on her bare breast. Instead, to her surprise, he snagged her hair, pushing it back over her shoulders, then cupped her cheek.

His expression and the gentle caress of his roughened hand against her face undid her. She swayed forward and suddenly he was there, drawing her to him.

She almost cried out at the sensation of his hot, satiny flesh against hers. The tickle of his chest hair, the delicious friction. It was too much yet not enough.

Thankfully Raif must have felt the same because a moment later they were lying on the bed, and for the first time in her life she felt a man's weight on her. Tara shuffled her legs wider and with a grunt of satisfaction he sank harder against her.

This time his kiss, while just as ardent, was slow, as if they had all the time in the world.

Tara revelled in it. She adored the taste of him. The weight of him pressing her onto the soft coverlet. The feel of him everywhere. There were so many sensations her brain was in danger of overloading.

Yet above it all, or perhaps beneath it, as it seemed to underscore everything, was the feeling Raif cherished her. He demanded but he coaxed too.

As if she needed coaxing. What she needed—

He must have had the same thought, for he lifted himself a little, propping himself up on one arm, pulling half off her to rest on his hip. Tara wanted to object. She missed the delicious sensation of his body against hers. But before she voiced a protest, his index finger tracked down to her chest, tracing around her breast in ever-diminishing circles.

Tara's breath backed up in her lungs as he leaned down. Raif's hair was ebony in contrast to her paler skin as he put his mouth to her nipple and sucked.

She gasped, a raw sound that might have been his name, and gathered him close. She felt the flick of his tongue and that was wonderful too.

Tara squirmed, half turning on her side, trying to bring herself up against him, till he pushed his knee across her, holding her against the bed with one powerful thigh.

Her eyes widened, astonished that his superior strength, as well as his caressing mouth, should be so exactly what she wanted.

She didn't feel threatened, just aware of his power, and shockingly turned on by it.

Raif lifted his head, surveying her, and she was stunned that the sight of his lips, wet from sucking at her breast, shot a surge of wanton hunger through her.

'I want you, Raif.' Strange how the words emerged clear and even. As if she weren't teetering on the brink of something cataclysmic. She felt it in the shuddering waves coursing through her, heading down to centre on her sex.

'And you'll have me, *habibti*. Soon.'

He lowered his head to her other breast and Tara arched off the bed, as high as his restraining thigh allowed. But even that was a caress, a teasing reminder of how it would feel when finally he lay over her again and joined them.

Impatience soared. She didn't want to stop the marvellous feelings he created but she wanted...

Her mind blanked as his palm slid down her abdomen,

straight through the silky hair at the juncture of her thighs, and unerringly through moist folds to that tiny, sensitive bud.

Her breath clotted as she jerked beneath him, eyes snapping wide and focusing on a lamp of filigreed metal that hung from a rafter.

Raif circled her nipple with his tongue while his finger circled her core. Every muscle and tendon in her body tightened.

Tara dragged her gaze down to find him watching her. That black gaze was a caress too, hot and sure. His lips closed on her again as he stroked her hard between her legs and suddenly, like the onset of a sudden summer thunderstorm, there was the electricity. Inside her. A current that jumped and sparked and sent her up in flames.

Her eyes closed as ecstasy took her, flinging her into another dimension where only Raif's anchoring body kept her safe.

She shuddered and cried out and through the exquisite bliss could still see Raif's glowing eyes from behind her closed lids.

Rapture took a long while to fade but eventually Tara felt herself float back to the real world. To the realisation Raif was no longer there.

Panic eased when she saw he'd moved to one side and was rolling on a condom.

The sight was fascinating. And daunting.

She tried to distract herself by pondering the fact he'd had the foresight to bring condoms. Had he expected this? Or did he take them wherever he went?

Somehow that didn't fit with what she knew of him. Raif was incredibly virile and attractive but he struck her as very selective when it came to sex.

Maybe that was her ego talking.

He saw her watching and his mouth hooked up in recognition and promise. When he moved, the weight of his lower body settled between her legs while he propped himself up on his elbows above her.

Despite the climax he'd given her, or because of it, Tara felt overloaded with sensation, absorbing the differences between them as well as the astonishing way they fitted together.

Almost fitted together. Her breath came in agitated puffs as she thought of what was to come. She wanted Raif, more than she'd ever wanted anything, yet this was uncharted territory.

His forehead crinkled. 'Okay, *habibti*?'

'More than okay,' she found herself replying. 'I was taking a moment. You feel...*we* feel...'

'Fantastic together.' His smile widened, making her insides dance and the tension disintegrate. 'But nowhere near as good as we're going to feel.' He breathed deep. Tara registered his shuddery breath and the fast tic of his pulse at his throat. 'I'm afraid it's beyond me to wait any longer.'

Something swelled high in her chest, tenderness and something much stronger. He'd given her pleasure before taking his own. His gallantry vanquished hesitation. She smoothed her palms up his bulging biceps to latch on to his shoulders.

'I don't want to wait.'

Raif took her at her word. He slipped one hand beneath her, tilting her pelvis up, and suddenly there he was, sinking into her, all that heat and power sliding flesh into flesh.

Until it felt as if something caught. Tara's lip snagged between her teeth, her lungs stopping. Raif paused and beneath her hands his muscles turned steel-hard. She blinked and met his questioning gaze.

He was going to withdraw, wasn't he? Withdraw and send her away?

Tara's fingernails dug into his shoulders. She planted the

soles of her feet on the bed and pushed up, increasing the pressure where they joined. A brief burn of pain sheared through her then Raif slipped deeper, so deep it seemed he lodged right up against her heart.

She blinked, trying to find her equilibrium, but her lungs wouldn't fill and her breath came in short gasps.

Raif slid an arm around her waist and rolled so they lay on their sides, still joined, but minus that feeling she was being crushed.

Tara drew air into starved lungs, surprised to discover that feeling of fullness, while still strange, was intriguing rather than nerve-racking.

Warm fingers brushed her cheek, pushing her long hair off her face. 'You're full of surprises, aren't you, Tara?'

Raif's ebony eyes locked on hers, unreadable but for that shimmer of heat.

'It doesn't matter.'

Part of her couldn't quite believe they were talking when their bodies—

'It *does* matter.' His voice was pure gravel. 'But not enough to stop this.' He pulled her knee higher up his thigh, then his hand found her breast as he moved against her. Tara gasped as delight coursed through her.

Raif did it again, with a slow deliberation that seemed to spin out the remarkable sensations till there was room for nothing else in Tara's brain but the wonder of it.

Again and again he pushed and now she moved her hips, anticipating each sure thrust, squirming a little at the teasing skirl of delight when he touched her...there.

'Raif?' She pulled him towards her, needing to feel him against her as little shivers set up inside.

She only had to ask once. A moment later she was on her back, Raif's body covering her like a warm blanket.

He held himself still, though the hammer beat of his heart against her chest revealed how much that cost him.

Tara lifted her head and brushed her lips against his jaw and Raif moved. His lips found hers, his kiss slow and lush as he resumed that wonderful rhythm. Shimmers of heat spread as Raif brought her closer and closer to—

The world shattered. Tara clung on tight and gasped out her pleasure. She had no words to describe the ecstasy Raif brought her, or the rolling wave of rapture that enveloped her. It was impossibly perfect.

Until Raif shuddered hard, his body pumping against her, head thrown back and superb torso strung taut. Then perfect got even better.

Still shuddering with delight, she wrapped her arms around him and hugged hard, overwhelmed by the need to assure him she was here, anchoring him. Protecting him.

It seemed the most natural thing in the world, holding Raif as she sank into the dark velvet folds of oblivion.

Raif crossed his arms and stared into the starlit night, cool air chilling his naked body. He welcomed that, welcomed anything to drag him out of the sensual fog he'd been in since Tara sauntered into his tent.

All this time he'd fought to hold back, to resist the temptation of her. Especially because of the worrying suspicion that he had begun to feel too much for Tara. More than simple desire.

Then she'd rocked up at his bedside, watched him with those sultry green eyes and said she wanted him. He had no resistance against her air of fragility mixed with feistiness.

Of course he hadn't resisted. She was a grown woman, even if his conscience whispered she was vulnerable, on the run from her cousin, traumatised by today's events.

He hitched an uneven breath as heat washed through him. Not the heat of passion but shame.

For all those reasons he should have held back.

If they weren't enough, she'd been a virgin. There'd been

a moment as he entered her slick, fragrant body, when he'd met resistance and thought of pulling back. Only for a second. Because virgin or no, Raif had had to have her.

This need had simmered in his blood so long. Today's drama had only notched the heat to boiling point.

But once was definitely not enough. He wanted Tara in ways that made every other lover blur into nothingness.

He raked a hand through his hair, considering a midnight dip in the oasis's tiny pool. But it would take water frigid from an ice floe to douse his hunger for Tara.

His jaw tightened. He wasn't used to doubting his actions or second-guessing whether he'd done right. Every cell in his body screamed that sex with Tara was the best thing he'd done in years. His thinking brain, what was left of it, knew he'd complicated everything. One way or another there'd be a price to pay.

Yet instinct told him having Tara had been inevitable from the moment she rolled out of a carpet at his feet.

With a sigh, he turned and lifted the flap of his tent. He should be thinking of how to minimise the repercussions. Instead his thoughts centred on the sight of Tara in his bed, her hair a lustrous curtain splayed across pale gold skin.

Raif's heartbeat quickened as his gaze snagged on luscious breasts, then trailed down to the indentation of her navel then further, to the hint of a dark V beneath the fine sheet.

She shifted. Jade-green eyes met his and he swore he almost heard the sizzle as his libido caught fire again.

'You're awake.' His husky voice betrayed him.

He'd thought she was out for the count.

'Yes. I went to the bathroom and had a wash.' Was that a dusting of pink on her cheeks? Did she regret what they'd done?

'Are you sore?' He swallowed, his throat scratchy.

She shook her head and that mahogany-tinted hair slid

around her breasts. That, and her secretive stare from under long, dark lashes, made him harden.

Tara's gaze dropped to his groin and he swelled more.

'No, I'm not sore at all. I feel wonderful.'

Beneath the sheet she moved restlessly. Raif read the quickened rise and fall of her breasts and the way her lips parted. His own blood pumped harder, faster and in one direction.

'Excellent.'

He was at the bedside in moments. His doubts didn't stand a chance in the face of Tara, naked and inviting in his bed. He didn't give a damn about complications, political or otherwise. All he cared about was this.

Raif prowled up the bed to kneel above her. He made himself pause, waiting for assent, finding it in her smile. He leaned down and kissed her. She opened instantly, eager but in no way submissive.

Then he felt soft fingers close around him, making him judder and catch his breath as lightning shot through him.

Raif's hand clasped hers and for a moment he was tempted to teach her how to touch him there. Except he was determined that this time he'd make the pleasure last longer than a couple of minutes. For both of them.

Tugging at her wrist, he anchored it to the bed. With his other hand he stripped the sheet away then captured her other hand. She was panting now, her breasts jiggling, tempting him.

Despite his earlier performance, Raif, generally, had formidable self-control. He didn't let himself get distracted. Still shackling her hands at her sides, he moved down, kneeing her thighs open, inhaling the sweet, spicy musk scent of Tara's arousal. He tasted her, delicately at first, and even that had her writhing beneath him.

He looked up, across an expanse of golden skin, to meet wide eyes that seemed to eat him up. He licked and she jumped, a soft keening sound emerging from that sexy mouth. He licked again, wondering how it would feel if she was to return the favour, using that sultry mouth on him.

He almost came on the thought, urged on by another of her desperate cries.

Raif couldn't recall any lover testing his control as Tara did. It wasn't because of her innocence. If anything, that was a weight on his conscience. Maybe it was her enthusiasm. Yet he'd had adventurous lovers before.

Was it because she was forbidden fruit? Messing with a Dhalkuri princess was fraught with problems.

Raif gave up wondering, concentrating instead on the unique taste of her, the sound of her approaching ecstasy and the feel of her quivering body beneath him.

He'd barely started when she came apart and once more Raif had to concentrate on controlling his body's response. He waited till well after Tara had subsided into satiety before rolling over to find a condom. Condoms he'd packed because, though he'd warned himself not to pursue her, he kept imagining Tara in his bed.

He'd never imagined she'd invite herself there.

His smile was taut, almost painful, as he settled over her.

Instantly she wrapped her arms around him, her sleepy smile pure welcome.

Raif positioned himself, then, watching Tara's face, slowly drove forward, revelling in her tight heat. A ripple of muscle contracted around him. A legacy of the orgasm she'd just had?

Her smile grew and he realised she'd done it deliberately. He retaliated by covering her breast with one hand and gently squeezing. Her smile faltered.

Raif lowered his head to her mouth. Tara offered her lips in a slow, luxurious kiss that made him forget he was the experienced one and she the learner.

They were equals in this. Equals as never before in his experience.

His brow twitched in confusion but already his body was driven by desire, not logic. He drew back then thrust again into welcome warmth, feeling her rise to meet him, circling her hips in a little shimmy that threatened to blow the back off his skull.

Where had she learned that?

The thought died as they moved again and the sensations were, if possible, even more exquisite.

Raif lingered on the brink, pride dictating he prolong this. But he reckoned without the desperate, powerful rush that hit him out of nowhere. A rush of physical sensation but something more too. Something he registered in his mind as much as his body.

A sense of relief, of excitement, of rightness.

A sense so powerful that for a second it almost eclipsed the physical pleasures bombarding him.

Then, kissing Tara with something like desperation, he moved again, taking them both over the edge into a world that felt bright and new as never before.

CHAPTER ELEVEN

TARA STOOD BESIDE Raif as the town elders welcomed them, and wondered how everything could seem the same when everything had changed.

Raif still looked every inch a ruler and she…well, the mirror this morning had shown she looked the same, if you discounted a slight flush in her cheeks, and lips that looked a little fuller.

In one night she'd become addicted to the taste of Raif. And to other things: the hard press of his athletic body, the magic of them moving together, and the husky sound of his voice in her ear as he caressed her and made her boneless first with longing, then with satisfaction.

Nor was the change just about physical awareness. There was something more. Something profound that she had no name for and didn't want to think about. When she thought of Raif, which was all the time, she felt…

No, this wasn't the time to examine her feelings. Especially as she suspected she'd be uncomfortable with what she discovered.

She stiffened her knees, standing taller.

Instantly Raif turned his head to look at her. He'd been like this all morning, as if their night together left him attuned to any shift in her mood. As with his touch, it made her feel precious, but it scared her that he was so hyper-alert to her emotions as she still grappled with them.

Gleaming black eyes snared hers. Tara's breath backed up into her lungs as she read concern and intimacy there. He'd looked at her that way all morning.

Raif had wanted her to stay behind, saying she'd feel better for a rest after her sleepless night.

It was true she felt a little wobbly, but not in a bad way. In a glorious way.

Did she sway? It was hot in the sun and she'd taken off her sunglasses for the official welcome. For a second the shadows seemed to stir then she felt Raif's hand at her elbow, holding her steady.

She sent him a grateful smile then froze. He shouldn't touch her, should he?

But no one seemed to notice. Maybe things were different in Nahrat. In Dhalkur no one touched the Sheikh in public and nor did he touch anyone else. Handshakes were usually limited to other heads of state.

Then she remembered the way he'd led her into the grand dining salon with his hand at her elbow. Clearly the rules were different here.

Raif squeezed her elbow and she relaxed. He thanked the town elders for their welcome and they entered the town, heading towards the square.

It looked completely different.

Yesterday the open space had obviously been swept and tidied for the royal visit. But today it was transformed.

Bright banners fluttered everywhere and all around the square stood potted plants, some heavy with citrus fruit and others with roses. Tara guessed householders had brought in their precious, carefully tended plants. Gardens were hugely prized in this arid region and the townspeople had created an amazing, if temporary, one. There were even pots of herbs scenting the air.

A huge awning extended from the community centre out into the square and deep in its shade sat two cushioned chairs. Around it stood what looked like the whole population. Sunlight gleamed on traditional curved knives tucked into the men's belts. It sparkled off the women's jewellery. Some wore scarves sewn with gold coins and medallions.

Others wore long, handsome heirloom necklaces, and in the hush Tara heard the tinkle of bracelets.

'Raif?' She kept her voice low. 'What's happening?' Yesterday people had been neatly, if soberly clothed. Today they were dressed for a festival.

He didn't turn his head and in profile his proud features looked almost stern. But then, he was facing into the sun.

'A celebration.' He paused. 'They're glad to see us after what happened yesterday.' Tara nodded, understanding the need to rejoice after coming so close to violence the day before. 'Relax and enjoy it.' Raif turned to her, his lips curving up into a disarming smile that made her wish they were back in his bed, naked.

Did he read her thoughts? Hunger flared in those midnight eyes. Her lips parted as she inhaled the spice scent of Raif's warm flesh and sandalwood soap. A shiver raked from her nape to the soles of her feet.

'Hold that thought, *habibti.*' His voice was so low she might have imagined it if she hadn't seen his lips move. 'Later.' His fingers tightened on hers, squeezing. Then he drew her forward towards the crowd.

The next hour passed in a blur. There were so many people to meet. Even strangers from outlying villages had been drawn in. And after making their obeisance to their Sheikh, it seemed they all wanted to see her too. Tara lost track of the number of people she spoke to, babies she admired and smiles she returned.

She was especially glad to see those women who'd been with her yesterday. But when she thanked them for their support, they shook their heads and said they'd done nothing. Even the women with bruised faces, who'd tried to prevent Tara's abduction, made light of their actions.

Yet Tara felt warmed by what they'd done, and the way

they crowded around today, checking on her and apologising that something so terrible should happen in their town.

She had a moment of stark shock when several offered congratulations, wishing her and Raif a happy future together. Her face flamed as she explained Raif's words had been solely to free her.

The women were delighted when Raif joined her, temporarily leaving the men. He put them at ease, insisting a frail, elderly lady take a seat in the shade.

This was a different man to the one she'd seen before. He was still an authority figure, but away from the pomp of the palace, among ordinary people, Raif was relaxed and approachable.

He chatted with everyone from local officials to new mothers, from young men hoping to work in an enterprise he'd organised, to the poorest of the poor.

There was dancing and a display of marksmanship that Raif took part in. Tara wondered why she was surprised. His people liked and respected him and it seemed the feeling was mutual. Today he wore a smile more often than a frown and there was no sign of that blank, imperious stare.

Tara saw not a sovereign but a man. Watching him laugh with rival sharpshooters made her wonder how much Raif's responsibilities weighed on him. When did he get time to relax?

An image filled her head, of Raif lying spent, chest heaving, his flesh hazed with sweat, a satisfied smile curving his mouth. *Then* he'd been relaxed.

Abruptly Raif turned his head. Their eyes met.

There it was again. That whump of connection.

A moment later he was forging through the crowd towards her. 'Ready to go?' he murmured.

'Yes, please.' She looked around. 'But before we leave, I think you should explain to them. Some of the women believed what you said yesterday about me being your woman.'

'I've spoken to the elders. Don't worry. They understand the situation exactly.' Raif's eyes held hers and heat pulsed through her. 'Right now we have other priorities.'

Fire kindled at his look. Heat rose like a tide from her breasts to her cheeks.

His smile widened. Fifteen minutes later, they were on their way.

'This isn't the way to the oasis.'

Beside her at the wheel, he nodded. 'You've got a good sense of direction.'

'It's easy to tell. We're not on a paved road.' She looked ahead where a companion vehicle rounded a curve. 'From the direction of the sun we're heading away from the oasis.'

'Not everyone would realise that.'

'I've lived in remote areas. Learning to orientate yourself is an important survival skill.'

Raif slanted her a glance. 'You seem disappointed.'

She was. The look he'd given her and his talk of other *priorities* made her assume—

A warm hand covered hers, his thumb stroking her wrist. Instantly she felt breathless and shivery.

She bit her lip, suddenly unsure about admitting her desire. Last night and this morning Raif had made intimacy easy. But despite those moments in the town when she'd felt that familiar communion with him, she'd also been reminded of the gulf between them.

'I'm disappointed too, Tara.'

'You are?' She swung around to see his eyes on her before he turned back to the road.

'I want nothing more than to be alone with you, *habibti*.' The endearment feathered through her insides like a caress. 'Today's festivities tested my patience to the limit. I'd rather have been back in our bed.'

Our bed. Crazy how his choice of words buoyed her.

Tara turned her hand and clasped his. 'Then why not go to the oasis?'

'Don't tempt me. You don't know how close I am to doing just that.' He withdrew his hand and put it on the wheel. 'We couldn't stay at the oasis indefinitely. We're returning to the capital. Apart from anything else, that means I can have you completely to myself without interruption.'

Tara shivered at the promise in his deep voice.

'Apart from anything else?'

He shrugged. 'Communications are better at the palace, if there's any more trouble from Fuad. Plus I want to speak with your cousin Salim again.'

'You've spoken with Salim?' That surprised her. 'I thought you weren't friends?'

'Acquaintances more than friends, but he needed to know how ill his father was. Fuad had kept the full gravity of the situation from him.'

Tara nodded. That was typical of Fuad. 'You're calling him now to tell him about the attempted kidnap?'

'He already knows. I sent a message yesterday. He has to know how desperate his brother is.' Raif paused for a beat. 'But it's better if I'm on hand in the capital if he needs assistance or advice.'

In other words, if Fuad tried anything desperate again. Tara shivered, rubbing her hands up her arms, feeling the tenderness where bruises still lingered.

'So you're supporting Salim? I thought you didn't want to play politics?'

Raif steered the vehicle around a tight curve as they crested a ridge. 'I don't. But I'd rather have a reasonable man running Dhalkur than someone as unstable as Fuad. Besides, I'm involved whether I like it or not.'

'I'm sorry.' Tara clasped her hands in her lap, remembering how he'd been forced to face the ambassador when she'd broadcast her presence in the palace. 'I didn't mean to embroil you in all this.'

'I know you didn't. It's okay.'

She shook her head. 'It's not. I've brought nothing but trouble.' A hard weight filled her chest as she remembered Raif facing those armed men, basically challenging them to shoot him. Tara swallowed, trying and failing to eradicate the metallic tang of fear. 'You should never have had to confront those men. What were you thinking, putting yourself in danger?' Her voice rose. 'You should have left it to the professionals.'

And let it end in a siege and bloodbath?

But he heard the tremor in her voice and knew Tara needed comfort, not an argument. He covered her hands again, noting how chilled they were. Strange that yesterday, though obviously shocked, she'd seemed to recover quickly. Was this delayed reaction?

Raif pulled over to the hard edge of the road and switched off the engine. Turning, he saw defiance and vulnerability in her tense features. Was there ever a more challenging woman?

For the last three hours he'd been torn between wanting sex and worrying over the new complication today's celebration had highlighted. Now both those faded from his mind.

'It's over, Tara. You're safe and so am I. There'll be no more incursions across the border, no one coming to snatch you. Precautions have been taken.'

Her mouth crimped in a crooked line. 'You think *that's* what worries me?'

She blinked, her eyes glittering brighter than usual. Despite what she'd been through, he'd never seen her cry. Yet she was moved by strong emotion.

Raif drew a slow breath as it struck him she was upset *about him*. He'd let her earlier words about him leaving the situation to the professionals wash over him as a platitude. It was only now, looking into accusing green eyes, that he realised the depth of her fear.

For him.

Something grabbed at his belly. A feeling he didn't recognise. Warmth suffused him, and tenderness. It seemed remarkable that, in the midst of her own troubles, Tara was concerned about him.

Because she cared.

Raif's breath expelled, only to rush back so quickly that for a second he felt dizzy.

He could count on the fingers of one hand the people who cared for him personally. Oh, there were people who'd miss him as Sheikh if he died. He was generally popular. And there were lots who saw it as their duty to look after him. But there had been no one close since his parents died. Apart from his aunt and a few good friends, no one who'd feel his loss personally.

Raif froze as he digested this strange sensation. Tara's fear for him, and his concern to minimise her distress.

His feelings were more than the usual need to do the appropriate thing. This was personal, on a level he'd never experienced.

Her hands turned beneath his, her fingers gripping so tight he knew she was reliving those moments staring down the barrel of a gun.

'Why would you *take* such a risk? You could have ended up dead in a pool of blood. Talk about reckless—'

'Shh. It's over now. Everyone is safe.' He lifted his hand to her jaw, feeling her throbbing pulse.

'But why were you so foolhardy? I couldn't believe it when you spoke to them that way.'

Raif undid his seatbelt and leaned across, brushing her mouth with his. Tara's breath was a sweet exhalation as if of relief, then her lips moved tentatively against his.

That unfamiliar feeling intensified—that grabbing at his gut, and the heat welling in his chest, the tingling in his blood.

He deepened the kiss and she met him halfway. Gone was her hesitation, replaced by the confident woman she'd been last night, inviting herself into his bed.

Except it hadn't been so simple. Tara had been a virgin and, once the first flush of arousal wore off and he'd been able to think, he'd registered her lack of experience.

How had he not seen it?

Simple. He hadn't wanted to because that would mean stopping, and he was too selfish for that.

Now he leaned in, gathering her close, deepening the kiss, revelling in the rising tide of delight that obliterated every concern as she pressed against him. Her mouth was both sweetly yielding and demanding.

Till her seatbelt obstructed him. Tara gave a muffled sound of frustration and fumbled at the clasp.

But the moment pierced his self-absorption.

Raif was used to indulging in sex without interruption. He *never* stole kisses in the middle of an official convoy where his security team would be scoping out what had made him stop his vehicle, setting up an observation post to ensure no one came near. He *never* kissed a lover in public. He was always discreet, ensuring his lovers' names didn't become fodder for gossip.

And here he was, necking on a public road.

He covered Tara's hand and reluctantly drew back.

'Best not.' He met her unfocused eyes and felt desire vie with duty. 'Not here, where anyone could see us.'

Tara turned to stare at the deserted road, deserted because his staff would have stopped any traffic. She looked dazed. Which was how he felt.

This attraction was rooted far deeper than anything in

his experience. It was about feelings as much as sexual desire. Which made it unique.

Damn it. He didn't have the time for unique or for a relationship. This morning had revealed he had a PR situation of monumental proportions to manage, on top of a desperate lunatic poised to take command of the neighbouring kingdom. And still he wanted to forget common sense and sink back into Tara's lush kiss.

A chill feathered his spine. Was this how his grandfather had felt, driven by feelings for the one woman who could blind him to duty and responsibility? Who'd lured him into the illusion of love to the detriment of all else?

Raif frowned and sat back, annoyed at how tough it was to move away from Tara. In broad daylight. With his entourage waiting and guessing the cause of the delay.

This felt like loss of control. It *was* loss of control. A complete anathema to a man whose life was about leadership and duty.

He thrust aside the thought of his grandfather. Raif could handle this. He could have Tara and maintain control.

'I want you, Tara,' he ground out. 'But let's wait till we're home.'

He'd never kept a lover in his home before. Always he conducted his liaisons away from the palace. It was another difference from his previous relationships and it felt significant.

'Good thinking.' Her voice sounded shaky but he couldn't read her features as she lifted her hands to smooth her hair then, discovering the damage his questing hands had caused, taking out the pins to let it down.

Raif watched transfixed as she began plaiting those long tresses. How could the mere sight of her fixing her hair undo him? Because it reminded him of the feel of that silken hair wrapped around him in the night? How it had felt in his hands as he'd lost himself in her sweet body?

Abruptly he tugged his seatbelt and snapped it closed, then started the engine.

The four-wheel drive topped the next rise and there was the first vehicle in his entourage pulled over, waiting. It moved out onto the road and led the way. A few seconds later Raif saw in his rear-view mirror the next vehicle in the convoy.

Had they seen him kissing Tara?

He wasn't ashamed of Tara, or what they shared, yet Raif didn't like turning her into an object of speculation.

His mouth twisted in a grim smile. Too late. He'd already done that. By claiming her as his yesterday, before scores of witnesses, he'd thrown her straight into the public eye.

'Raif?'

'Yes?'

'I understand the theory of why you walked in unarmed yesterday. I know what your intentions were.'

Raif silently congratulated her. That was more than he'd done at the time. Oh, he'd weighed the options and made a considered choice, but in reality he'd been compelled by a force stronger than logic. He'd simply known he had to save her.

'But I can't imagine how you'd think it would work, or how you could *do* that. Calmly walk in and confront those men, putting your own life on the line.'

It really was worrying Tara. Raif opened his mouth to remind her that it was over and they were safe, then reconsidered. She needed an explanation.

He didn't want to try to explain the urgent need he'd felt to protect her, no matter what the odds. Instead he stuck with the obvious.

'It's what I was trained for. I was raised to step in when necessary and not shirk my responsibilities.'

'But you're not a hostage negotiator!' There it was again, distress colouring her voice.

'Actually, I do have those skills. But my real experience is in diplomatic and trade negotiation. I negotiate all the time, when my people bring problems and expect me to solve them.'

'That doesn't explain why you'd walk, unarmed, into danger. You've got a whole team employed to protect you!'

He shot her a sideways glance. 'Leadership is a two-way street. I'm protected and enjoy the many benefits of being Sheikh, but I have to be ready to protect my people.'

Raif paused, seeking words to explain. 'My father raised me to understand that, behind the pomp and glamour, I have a duty to Nahrat. Even at a cost to myself. I must be ready to make a sacrifice if necessary.'

'I doubt many world leaders would do what you did.'

He lifted his shoulders. Few were put in such situations.

'Maybe I take my responsibilities more seriously since I inherited the throne early. I've striven to be a leader my father would have been proud of.'

Raif stopped, surprised to hear the admission. It wasn't something he'd voiced before, yet, sitting here with Tara, it seemed natural to speak of such things, to make her understand.

'You loved him,' she murmured.

'Yes. Him and my mother both.'

It had been tough losing them. He'd missed them terribly. They'd been a close-knit family and, despite his aunt's care, even she didn't fully understand the burdens of kingship.

Raif had been petrified of doing the wrong thing. He'd listened hard to his advisers and his temporary regent, training to be the best Sheikh he could be, always asking himself what his father would do in difficult situations.

'It must have been terribly hard to lose them at a young age.'

Surprising how her sympathy pierced the emotional armour he'd worn so long. For a second he felt it again, the raw grief and fear, but at the same time Tara's understanding felt like balm.

'It was a long time ago.'

'Does that matter? Losing your parents is a blow, whenever it happens.'

It was a reminder that Tara still grieved for her mother.

Guilt snaked through Raif's belly. It reminded him of the serpentine hiss of his conscience last night as Tara slept beside him. That voice had deplored his selfishness, taking advantage of a virgin newly alone in the world and on the run from a sadistic cousin. It taunted, saying no decent man would have behaved as he had.

Quickly, he changed the subject. 'Maybe because I acquired the habit of authority early that gives me a different perspective.'

He heard a huff of laughter. 'You can say that again. One thing I've noticed about you, Raif, is that you always expect to get your own way.'

The humorous note in Tara's voice relieved some of the tightness in his chest. 'You'd prefer a man who can't make up his mind? Or who doesn't have the strength to stand up for what he believes in? I think not.'

Tara might argue with him but those arguments held an undercurrent of sparking awareness. Tara gave as good as she got. She'd be bored with a man who gave in to her all the time.

From the corner of his eye he saw her shake her head. 'There has to be a happy medium. The way you strolled in yesterday, as if you owned the place—'

'I do. It's my country, remember? My people. I had to act. I couldn't allow Fuad's thugs to take you.'

Tara's indrawn breath hissed. 'I still don't know how to thank you properly. I can't believe what you did for me.'

Her fingers curled around his forearm and he turned to meet her serious face. She looked lost, her eyes huge.

Something shifted inside Raif. He needed to wipe that look away.

Deliberately he pinned on a knowing smile and raised her fingers to his lips. 'As for thanks, I'm sure we can arrange something in the privacy of the palace.'

Her laughter told him he'd distracted her for the moment. Yet his thoughts returned inevitably to the implications of yesterday's actions.

Tara thought him brave or foolish to walk in unarmed. Yet it had been the only way he could think of to save her. Claiming Tara as his had worked. Because her captors, like his subjects, understood what it meant when the Sheikh of Nahrat publicly claimed a woman as his.

In their eyes he wasn't talking about a mistress, but a wife.

That was what had saved her. The kidnappers had known there'd be no escape from retribution, ever, if they took Raif's spouse. That he'd pursue them mercilessly and with all the force of his authority. His forebears had a reputation for being just, but when crossed they were renowned for ferocious ruthlessness.

It was as well Tara didn't yet fully understand the reason for today's festivities. He'd let her think the townsfolk were celebrating a peaceful end to the siege and squashed her qualms that some believed she was his woman.

Because now definitely wasn't the time to tell her. She was distressed by yesterday's events, still shocked. He'd explain later, when she was less agitated and they could talk it through without possible interruption. Besides, he didn't want a scene in public.

He'd find the right time, *later*.

Everything had changed irrevocably. News of what had happened would fly faster than the wind across the desert.

Today's celebration was just the beginning.

As far as his people were concerned, he'd chosen Tara as his bride.

CHAPTER TWELVE

RAIF DIDN'T MANAGE time alone with Tara when they reached the palace. That fantasy he'd had—of taking her straight to bed—was just that, a fantasy. The sort of thing an ordinary man might do. Not the ruler of a nation.

He sighed, rolling his shoulders as he finally headed towards her suite. It had been a long afternoon.

At least he'd seen her settled before turning to the urgent matters waiting for him. It wasn't till she was safely in her rooms at the heart of the palace that Raif admitted his relief.

There'd been no danger to her today. He'd taken every precaution to ensure that. But seeing her in his home, knowing that here no one could harm her, Raif had felt some of the tension hugging his shoulders roll away.

How was it that a woman he'd known such a short time affected him so?

His usual preference was for tall blondes and, though he chose intelligent woman as his lovers, they never tested his patience as Tara did. She seemed to go out of her way to get under his skin.

Perhaps it was the combination of intriguing, attractive woman and challenge. Or the dramatic circumstances of her arrival.

Or perhaps it was something altogether different. Raif enjoyed a challenge as much as the next man but his feelings for Tara were deeper than that. As for the drama that surrounded her—he had no need for more excitement.

This was about Tara herself. She drew him. Her body, definitely. Her personality, surprisingly yes. He'd never known a taste for stubborn, feisty women, but in Tara her verve was something he relished. Her care of him...that was something new, but instead of being disturbed by it, Raif welcomed it.

He'd never known feelings like these, so he had no compass to follow. Previous experience indicated that his fascination must wear off, as he'd never had a lover he wanted permanently. On the other hand, he'd need to choose a wife some time and circumstances had forced him to choose Tara.

Circumstances?

Honesty forced him to admit he could have left the rescue to his expert team. The odds were they'd have ended the siege without injuring the hostages.

Except those odds hadn't been enough. Raif couldn't contemplate any risk to Tara.

He'd claimed her in the heat of the moment, but he'd been fully aware of what he was doing. He'd walked into the situation with his eyes wide open and didn't regret it.

Raif hadn't known her long, but he'd been with her through crises. Times of stress provided a unique opportunity to see the core of a person.

In Tara he saw a woman who was honest, who had courage and tried to be indomitable. He admired her loyalty, the way she'd been almost more concerned for the man who'd brought her over the border than herself, fretting over whether he'd been set free. Nor was she interested in Raif's wealth. Tara might be an expert on jewellery but she'd never hinted that he might give her an expensive gift. The woman was even determined to pay him back for the clothes his staff had procured!

She was vivacious yet kind, as he'd seen in her interactions with his staff and citizens. Plus, she could hold her own at a royal event. She was a quick learner with an innate sense of self-worth that would help if he made her his Queen.

As would her royal lineage, for it was still expected that the Sheikh would marry someone from a significant family.

Raif paused a few paces from her door.

Was he really going to do it? Take Tara Michaels as his bride?

It was an unorthodox match. Some would baulk at his marrying a woman from Dhalkur. This afternoon he'd fielded concerns from a number of respected advisers. Yet for everyone who bemoaned such a royal bride there was another who applauded what they saw as an attempt to bury the enmity between the two nations.

Ultimately the decision was Raif's.

Did he want to be shackled with an obstinate, independent, foreign wife?

His preference was to have Tara as his lover. Raif hadn't planned to marry yet. But he *did* want Tara.

His chest tightened as he wondered if his feelings bore some resemblance to his grandfather's weakness. But Raif wasn't allowing personal emotion to undermine logic. He was weighing the pros and cons.

He looked at the door to her suite, thought of her waiting for him, wearing that eager, almost flirtatious expression she'd turned on him this morning.

Raif's brain slowed as other parts of his body responded.

His options were limited. He accepted the situation or removed Tara from the palace straight away, in the process losing face with his people. As far as they were concerned, he'd promised himself to this woman.

He thought of those green eyes that gave a window into her thoughts and desires, her lush mouth, and the rush of attraction between them.

Raif's mouth curled in a slow smile.

He strode towards her suite.

Tara answered the door within moments.

Had she been waiting for him?

Her dress, the colour of dark grapes, clung to her sensational curves. Her lustrous hair spilled around her shoulders almost to her waist, making his palms tingle as he imagined sifting it through his fingers. Her eyes were veiled by long lashes but her ripe lips wore that sultry pout that turned him inside out.

'Tara.' There was a world of want in the word and he barely cared.

Her chin rose, her lashes lifting, and he read both hesitation and need in her expression.

He understood the feeling. Their situation should make him hesitate too. How much more complicated for her, who'd been a virgin last night, and was still dependent on his charity for her safety?

'I missed you.' It was remarkably easy to admit. Instantly he was rewarded by a smile that made his chest pound and his mouth dry. Such a little thing to pack so much power.

'I missed you too.' Her voice was husky.

Raif lifted his hand to that shining hair, winding it around his fist. He tugged, gently, and she came.

This close the rapid rise and fall of her breasts was a teasing caress, making his lungs stall on a sharp inhale. The scent of roses and cinnamon, and warm, willing woman, sneaked into his nostrils, shutting down his capacity for higher thought.

'You were gone so long.' Her pout was back, igniting a sizzle that ran straight to his groin.

'I had urgent things to sort out. But I came as soon as I could. No one will interrupt us now. We have all night.'

The thought should have been an incentive for him to take his time but instead his hunger was urgent.

'I want you, Tara.' Desperately, but he managed at least to keep that word between his lips.

'Good.' Her brow puckered in a hint of a frown that

he found ridiculously adorable. 'I've been waiting and waiting.' Her mouth crimped. 'I thought you might have changed your mind.' Raif had to bend his head to hear her final words.

He shook his head as he looped his free arm around her waist and held her against him. He saw the moment she felt the press of his erection and was intrigued to see colour warm her cheeks.

Tara was such a fascinating mix, of eagerness and innocence, of feistiness and compliance. If he took her as his, life wouldn't always be easy. She'd argue and expect things he mightn't want to give. She'd make up her own mind, which meant he'd have to negotiate and persuade.

But what was life without challenges?

'There was urgent business I had to see to, but believe me, *habibti*, through it all I thought of you.'

Wrapping both arms around her, he lifted her off her feet. Her eyes popped wide then she looped her arms around his neck and pressed a kiss to his jaw.

Longing shivered through him. An urgency to have this woman *now*, to claim her as his own.

He didn't make it to the bedroom. Barely made it to the first long sofa. They collapsed onto it, Raif taking her weight then rolling on the deep cushions to pin her beneath him.

The body-to-body contact shredded his control, undermining his intention to make this last. Instead he pulled back, skimming his hands down to her thighs and tugging her dress up.

His breath came out in a whoosh as the hem rose to her waist and he saw she was naked beneath it.

'You're not wearing underwear,' he croaked out.

'I was expecting you to come, so it didn't seem worth bothering.' Her mischievous tone drew his gaze to her eyes.

Gone was the diffident innocent, in her place a delightful siren.

Oh, he was definitely going to come. 'Excellent. I hope this turns into a habit.'

With a shudder of terrible need, he reefed the dress up and off her body, leaving her naked and alluring. One delicate hand moved across her breasts as if she contemplated covering herself.

'Don't. Let me admire you.' Raif caught her hand and put it on his belt buckle while his eyes ate her up.

His breath disintegrated as she started unbuckling his belt then strove to undo his trousers that now stretched tight across him. Her hands brushed him and Raif discovered it was the most arousing foreplay he'd ever experienced.

With one quick movement he hauled his shirt over his head, tossing it aside. By the time he had a condom out of his pocket she'd pulled his zip down.

Rolling to one side, he sheathed himself then drew a deep breath that trembled on the brink of surrender. This would be quick, but not so quick he sacrificed Tara's pleasure for his.

He stroked between her legs, delighting in the slick dampness he discovered and the inviting way her thighs fell open. Now all he had to do was hold off long enough to—

'Don't!' Tara clutched his wrist as if to stop him, though her hips lifted off the bed towards his caress.

'What's wrong?' The words almost choked him. His blood was thickening, his brain clogging.

She tugged his hand and he let her pull it away. 'I'm so ready I can't last if you do that. I want you inside me.'

Never had Raif been so eager to oblige. He fell between her soft thighs and had to grit his teeth against the urge to spill himself there and then. Tara's knees lifted around his hips then he felt her ankles on his back as he surged forward and joined them in a single stroke that was so easy, so right, it felt profound.

'More,' she whispered against his collarbone and he gave it, withdrawing and returning, deep and slow and so satisfying that already he felt the flutter of her climax begin.

Raif told himself it was satisfaction he felt and anticipation as his body responded to the slick, tight embrace of hers. But there was much more. Tenderness and…

His thoughts frayed as she bucked up against him, precipitating an avalanche of sensation.

Instinctively he curled an arm around her, holding her to him as he took her mouth in a desperate kiss that mirrored the wild plunge of their bodies.

There was a blast of white-hot light, a mighty tremor as if the earth shook deep beneath the citadel, but Raif was barely aware of either. His only consciousness was bliss and the scents, feel, taste and sound of Tara joining him in ecstasy.

The next morning, Tara decided that if she let herself think about it, she'd worry she was addicted to this man. Even the approving way he watched her from under lazy lids as she brushed her hair made her feel different. Powerful, like some Scheherazade who so easily entranced her lover, yet at the same time incredibly self-aware, conscious that she was out of her depth with Raif.

He was a king and she a sales assistant. He was used to ordering and being obeyed and she was used to thinking for herself. He was a sensual, generous, experienced lover and she had nothing to guide her during intimacy but instinct and observation of how Raif responded to her touch.

Yet those thoughts crowded to the back of her mind when they made love, or chatted desultorily. When he spooned her body against his and fell asleep holding her.

Or when he faced down armed intruders to save her.

Something shuddered through her, the same emotion she'd been trying to ignore for days, but it wouldn't fade.

Tara yanked her mind back to the present, telling herself there was no time to dwell on that. Not with Raif here, watching her dress.

She'd never before realised that having a man watch you dress could be as arousing as having him strip your clothes away, something at which Raif was expert.

'You're beautiful, Tara.' His smile lingered, then he flicked a glance at his watch before straightening the cuff of his richly embroidered bronze silk coat, making her wonder if he was nervous.

The idea was impossible. Raif stood tall and proud in his magnificent clothes, his features relaxed, his eyes gleaming as they took her in.

She was the one who felt nervous.

'Are you going to explain what's happening?' It was mid-morning and she'd barely surfaced after an incredible night of lovemaking. Her legs felt a little wobbly and she had that floaty feeling that she'd discovered came from intimacy with Raif. He'd spent the whole night with her, sharing breakfast in her suite, then leaving her to catch up on sleep while he went off for meetings.

An hour ago, he'd returned. Twenty minutes later, in the shower, holding her against him after she sobbed out her ecstasy, he'd announced they had an appointment in another part of the palace. He'd asked her to wear something stunning, since there would be photographers.

Deciding it was tied up with proving to Fuad that she wasn't returning to Dhalkur, Tara complied. There was something about Raif now, a tightly leashed energy, that told her this was important to him. Infuriatingly he refused to explain yet, saying he would when the moment was right. She owed him so much, it seemed paltry to cavil.

Tara found a dress of teal green that fell in soft folds to just below her knees. Tiny beads in teal, jade and a shade of rich blue adorned the bodice, catching the light when she moved.

Now, as Raif looked again at his watch, she twisted her hair high into an upswept style that she hoped looked classically elegant.

She had no jewellery but the dress was so feminine and sumptuous she didn't think it mattered.

She opened her mouth to ask if the outfit would do when he beat her to it.

'You look perfect, *habibti*. I'm honoured to accompany you.' Raif lifted her hand and bent over it, touching it with his lips and forehead in a courtly gesture that made her heart somersault.

Caution warned that she was in too deep. That she should at least set some ground rules for this affair. But she had no idea what they'd be. She loved being with Raif. Loved everything about the way he made her feel. Loved…

Tara drew in a sharp breath, stunned at the dangerous direction of her thoughts.

However wonderful this interlude, their paths lay in different directions. Raif's in Nahrat and hers… Well, she had yet to find out where she'd go. She was almost sure London wasn't for her. But she'd work it out later.

Pinning on a smile to hide the sudden dip of distress inside, as if she'd taken a step into nothingness, she turned to Raif. 'I'm ready.'

How had she ever thought his eyes cold? His expression was so warm she felt an answering flush suffuse her. It wasn't even sexual, it was…affectionate? Tara blinked, wondering if she read too much into his satisfaction.

But there was no time to probe, for he linked her arm through his and led her out of the room.

Tara was hyper-aware of Raif's tall frame next to hers,

the way he shortened his stride for her. That warmth within intensified into something else. Something strong and true.

For a second Tara acknowledged the emotion, even named it. She swallowed hard as the truth of it resonated through her.

Then, with a shiver that traced from her nape to her soles in her new shoes, she blocked those thoughts.

That particular emotion, for this man, could only spell disappointment and unhappiness. She couldn't dwell on it now. It was impossible.

Later, when she had leisure to think, distress would hit, and desperation.

For now all she could do was put on a brave face and hope he wasn't perceptive enough to realise she felt far more than lust for him.

As they approached the public rooms first one then another courtier appeared in the doorways, bowing as they passed. Raif inclined his head and kept walking.

Tara looked around, puzzled. 'What's going on?' she whispered.

'They're paying their respects,' he murmured, leading her into a familiar sitting room. 'Don't worry, I'll explain soon.' A door on the other side was open and Tara recognised the balcony where last week she'd leaned out, enjoying the view of the city, only to create a furore of speculation.

A figure moved towards them. It was the chamberlain, bowing deep to Raif, then, to Tara's astonishment, to her.

'Everything is ready, Your Majesty.' He turned to her and smiled. It was the first time he'd done so. 'Madame.' Then, before she could question him, he bowed out of the room.

'Raif? What's happening? I don't understand.' Unease feathered her spine.

Beside her Raif drew a deep breath. Beneath her arm

his was rock hard. With tension? 'Is everything okay? Is there some problem? Has Fuad caused trouble for you?'

A wry smile carved deep grooves in his cheeks but there was no humour in his eyes. They looked serious. 'I find it refreshing that your concern is for me, *habibti*, after all you've been through.'

His expression grew tender and Tara basked in it. Once more it felt as if her heart rolled over in her chest. How had she come to care about him so much?

She had no idea, only knew she did.

She cared. Too much.

Tara had a terrible feeling her heart might crack when it was time for her to leave.

He drew a slow breath and covered her arm with his hand. 'My people want to see you. They've travelled from outside the city to do so. I thought we'd have more time to prepare before this happened but they're even more eager than I anticipated.'

Tara became aware of a dull murmur from beyond the open windows. It was a low roar of sound that reminded her of the swell of the sea. Except they were inland. Her skin prickled.

'Why would they want to see me?'

For a second it seemed he wouldn't answer. A muscle flicked in his jaw and his nostrils flared as he took a deep breath. Then his dark gaze captured hers. 'Because I claimed you as my woman. By Nahrati custom that makes you my bride.'

CHAPTER THIRTEEN

'BRIDE?' TARA FELT her eyes grow round.

She wanted to make some quip because obviously Raif couldn't mean what it sounded like.

Except Raif's expression was serious to the point of being stern. He looked magnificent and regal, so different to the man who'd made love to her in the shower an hour ago.

Tara remembered his hard body behind hers, her palms flat to the wall and his hands on her breasts as warm water sluiced down and they shattered together in waves of rapture. She'd needed Raif's support not to crumple to the floor.

So often in the last week she'd turned to Raif, depending on him. Yet now it was Raif undermining her world.

'You mean as in *wife*?'

'Wife-to-be.' He paused as if choosing his words. 'Under Nahrati law and custom you're my betrothed.'

'That's...unbelievable!'

He raised his shoulders. 'Yet it's true.'

Tara frowned, trying to fathom what was happening. 'Are you seriously trying to tell me you accept this custom? That you're meekly going to pretend we're an item because of some words you spoke in the heat of the moment?'

One of his sleek black eyebrows rose. 'We *are* an item. Or do you dispute that?' He didn't wait for her answer. 'It's not a matter of accepting, but facing facts. From the moment I called you mine everyone understood what that meant.'

'Everyone except me!' Tara wrapped her arms around her middle, holding in the waves of emotion that battered her.

'The important thing was that your kidnappers understood. That's why they gave themselves up, because they knew I'd be merciless in seeking vengeance if they abducted my woman.'

Raif's woman.

The words reverberated through her as they had two days ago. Did she feel horrified or outraged?

Or even secretly excited? Because despite her efforts not to face it, Tara was pretty sure she'd fallen in love with Raif.

She'd pretended not to notice that particular revelation, because noticing meant facing that hers was a hopeless case.

Love hadn't figured in her plans, at least for the near future, and as for marriage, surely that was a long way off. She'd told herself not to expect too much from this affair. It was just sex, for him at least, not the basis of anything long term.

Now here he was talking about her as his bride. Which would make him her husband. It was ludicrous. She wanted to laugh at the absurdity of it. Except her emotions were so jumbled she might end up in tears instead.

Still Raif refused to smile and break the tension clogging the air between them.

Tara hefted a breath, trying to find something to ground herself.

'Were you really going to take me out there without explaining?'

That was better; outrage and brewing anger were better than shock and that feeling of helplessness. She didn't allow herself to think of her sliver of delight at the news.

As if marrying Raif were really an option!

'No, of course not.'

Tara looked at the open door to the balcony. 'You left it rather late to tell me.'

She chilled to the marrow. He'd known but he hadn't told her. She felt manipulated. Duped.

Powerless in this impossible situation.

Raif reached out and tugged her arms free, took her hands in his, smoothing his thumbs over them in a soothing motion he'd used before. Then, she'd welcomed the connection between them. Now it felt like he was using his knowledge of her weaknesses against her.

Did he guess how she felt about him?

The idea stole her breath, leaving her horrified.

It was one thing to discover she'd fallen in love for the first time. In love with a man who had so little in common with her that their lives barely intersected. It was another to think he had also realised.

'I know it's a shock. I should have told you earlier,' he finally admitted ruefully. 'But I thought it would save an unnecessary argument if you saw for yourself how things stand.'

'You waited this long to avoid an argument? That's outrageous. I had a right to know.' Her voice rose.

'I agree. But if I'd told you what was happening you'd have refused to leave your suite and come here, wouldn't you?'

'Yes. No!' She shook her head, not sure what she'd have done, but suspecting he was right. 'Maybe.'

'See? I'd hoped for time to break the situation to you gradually but it's been thrust on us sooner than even I had imagined. Whether we like it or not, this is unavoidable. There was no point wasting time arguing with you over it when you can see the reality for yourself.'

He gestured to the open window through which that ponderous hum seemed louder than ever. 'That—thousands of people gathered to wish us well—is the reality.'

'That's what that sound is?' Tara swallowed, her throat scratchy.

'It is. Look.'

Raif moved to one side of the full-length windows and

pulled her close. Automatically Tara inhaled that delicious scent of sandalwood, freshly laundered clothes and essence of Raif, warm and spicy. She felt that dizzying spiral of longing and the desire to lean into his big frame. Instead she peeped out at a sea of people. The streets and park, the rooftops and windows were obscured by crowds. Not only crowds but also Nahrati flags and banners featuring a golden scimitar on a scarlet background, the symbol of the royal house.

It was like something out of a movie. Unreal.

She shook her head. 'It's impossible.'

'Of course it's possible. All you have to do is step out onto the balcony. You've done it before.'

Sharply she looked up and caught the glimmer of a smile in that dark gaze.

'You think this is *funny*?' Her breathing fractured as she struggled to drag in enough oxygen.

'Of course not. But nor is it some terrible tragedy. They want to cheer you, not hurt you.'

'You can't seriously ask me to go out and pretend to be your fiancée.'

His gleam of humour vanished. 'I'm not asking you to pretend. You *are* my fiancée. Why not give the people what they want? Just the sight of you.'

Tara shook her head, grappling to understand how he could seem so sanguine. 'But it would be a lie. We're not—'

'I don't lie, Tara.' He paused, his gaze searching. 'Is it so much to ask? I've protected you. Saved you from abduction twice now. My people have stood by you even when they were threatened by armed intruders. All they want is to wish us well. Would you deny them that?'

He made it sound like all that had happened was her fault, but she was an innocent victim.

Yet it was true the townspeople had been endangered

because of her. Raif had gone out of his way to keep her safe, not once but twice.

She owed him.

He didn't say it but the knowledge hung between them, weighing on her conscience.

A hundred arguments formed in Tara's head. All the reasons it was a terrible idea to go out and let those eager citizens believe in a marriage that wasn't going to happen. But Raif's words caught at her. He'd done so much for her, more than she could reasonably have expected. His people had supported her, a stranger from another land, even when they were threatened with violence.

How could she not do this when so many people were waiting for her? How long would they stay there, waiting, if she didn't show?

Tara breathed a shuddery sigh and nodded, resolving to worry about what happened next when this was done.

'Okay. But then we talk.'

Raif wasn't surprised at the roar as he led Tara onto the balcony. The story had spread of how she'd stood proudly before her attackers, offering to go with them. Of how she'd fretted for his safety as he persuaded the men to surrender and of her concern for the other women. All tipped the scales in her favour, despite the fact her family came from Dhalkur.

His people were fighters, proud of their heritage and distrustful of strangers, yet they prized gallantry and had a strong romantic streak. Tara's strength in the face of danger, and Raif's action to save her, had caught their imagination.

It seemed even the naysayers were changing their minds about her, in the face of the tide of public opinion.

In her shimmering green gown she looked radiant. A truly beautiful bride-to-be.

Raif suppressed a tight smile. He was the only one who knew her radiance owed as much to temper as excitement.

His Tara was nothing if not feisty and he expected a battle royal when they were alone together. He almost looked forward to it.

Maybe he was tired of people who wanted to agree with him. Particularly women.

Maybe he anticipated using more than compelling arguments to convince her to marry.

Whatever the reason, he smiled easily, proud as he stood beside her.

How many other women would carry this off as Tara did? He'd been right to wait till the last moment to tell her. If he'd explained earlier there'd have been arguments and attitude. This way the force of her anger was channelled somewhere useful, presenting a proud and happy face for the people of Nahrat.

Nor did she have time to wonder about how Fuad had reacted to the news. Raif remembered Fuad's voice, almost incoherent with rage over the phone, and vowed to avoid mentioning her cousin for as long as he could.

'You do this very well,' he murmured as she lifted her hand and the noise swelled.

'I haven't *done* anything,' she said through her smile. 'They'd applaud anyone who stood here with you.'

There was some truth in that, except Raif knew Tara's attitude in the desert town had won hearts. As had her charm at the couple of events she'd attended in the city. That, combined with his people's belief that he'd never choose a woman who was anything less than perfect for him and his nation, did the rest.

That was the remarkable thing. Tara was in many ways his perfect match. More suited than the contenders his aunt and royal advisers insisted on bringing to court.

'My people know I would never bring just *anyone* here.'

He caught her hand and brought it to his lips, smiling as he saw her eyes catch fire. He knew that look, as he knew that tremor in her hand. 'I would only bring my future wife.'

The words resonated through him. Instead of feeling caged or caught out by this turn of events, Raif felt satisfaction.

He kissed the back of her hand then her palm, and the crowd went wild.

Raif barely noticed. He was busy watching Tara fight and fail to hide her response. The sultry, veiled look, the parted lips, the swift rise of her breasts beneath the beaded dress, and the scent of her, rich and sweet with a slight undertone of musk that betrayed arousal.

He lowered her hand and turned to face his people. 'One last wave.' Then, with cheers filling the air, he led Tara inside and closed the doors behind them. Releasing her, he strode to the door on the other side of the room and locked it.

'What are you doing?' Tara's voice was breathless and carnal excitement scudded through him. Raif knew that tone of voice, but first things first.

'Ensuring my chamberlain doesn't bustle in. You wanted to talk.'

Raif suppressed a smile as he saw her disappointment. Soon, he promised himself. He gestured to a sofa and waited for her to sit before crossing the room to sit beside her.

Tara shot him a look that confirmed she'd expected him to sit opposite her. But they weren't strangers or enemies. She was his woman and he preferred to be beside her. Besides, he had no compunction about using their phenomenal attraction to win his case.

'Tell me what's bothering you.' He took her hand and laced her fingers with his.

'Bothering me!' She swung round to fix him with a stare. 'This whole farcical set-up!'

'Unusual, I admit, but not farcical. Believe me, this is not a situation I take lightly.'

She swallowed and nodded and he knew she fought for composure. 'Good. That's…good. Then how do you plan to get us out of this?'

Raif stroked her fingers, enjoying the way they fitted into his. 'Our betrothal will end in the usual way, with marriage.'

Tara's hand jerked and he firmed his grip. 'You've got to be kidding.'

'I'd never joke about such a thing.'

'You can't want to marry me. And I don't want to marry you.'

Raif's fingers tightened reflexively till he realised and relaxed his hold. 'Have you enjoyed being with me, Tara?'

'Of course. But that's not—'

'Relevant? It's very relevant. We have a connection that's very rare.' He paused and stroked her hand. 'With your lack of experience you may not understand how rare.'

Her brow wrinkled. 'Is that why you're going along with this? Is it tied up with some antiquated idea about having taken my virginity?'

It was true that weighed on his conscience. It was also a source of fierce pride and excitement, knowing he was her first lover. But he was more concerned with being her last and only lover.

'I've never been with a virgin before, *habibti*, but, despite the honour of knowing you gave me your innocence, that wouldn't make me offer for your hand.'

She shook her head emphatically. 'You haven't offered. This isn't a marriage proposal. It's a stunt, a PR exercise.'

'That's what's bothering you?' Raif leaned closer, capturing her other hand where it pressed her collarbone. He kissed one then the other, inhaling her rose and cinnamon scent. 'Tara Michaels, would you do me the inestimable honour of marrying me?'

Instead of melting at his words, she stiffened. Tara shot to her feet, pulling free and stumbling towards the window before swinging to face him, eyes wounded. 'That's not funny.'

'I wasn't aiming for humour.' Raif stood, pride stiffening his spine.

'You're seriously talking about marriage?'

Did she think he made a habit of proposing? Never had Raif offered marriage. Never had he thought about spending the rest of his life with any woman, though he'd known it was his duty to marry one day to secure the throne.

'Deadly serious.'

Once more she shook her head. He reminded himself the circumstances were extraordinary.

'Why should I marry you? I barely know you.'

Raif's patience splintered. He'd been prepared for arguments and doubts but not that tone of disdain, as if she didn't care for him at all. As if his offer wasn't worthy of consideration.

His hands clenched at his sides as he drew himself up. He thought of all those beautiful, talented, amenable women who'd come to his court, vying for his attention and a chance to become Sheikha of Nahrat. He'd been attracted to some, but not enough to contemplate marriage. Now, when circumstance forced his hand, his honourable offer was spurned.

'You think I'd planned to marry a woman brought to me by a rug seller? A woman whose entry to court was in a rolled-up carpet?'

There. That proved it. The scorn in his voice showed how little he wanted this match.

Tara should be grateful the truth had won out. Instead

she felt a hot ball of misery form in the pit of her stomach. Her mouth crumpled and she had to work to face that derisive stare.

'One of the reasons I've been so diplomatically successful in the region is that I'm single,' Raif said after a lengthy silence. His flash of anger had disappeared. 'Several nations hold hopes of closer ties with Nahrat through a royal marriage.'

Had he a *tendre* for some other woman? The idea tore at her. She knew so little about Raif.

Except that, despite the hurt and dismay, part of her wanted to say *yes* to his proposal, as if marrying a man she'd known less than two weeks was a sane move. As if he hadn't cornered her into this.

'So this engagement...' the word was bitter on Tara's tongue '...would scupper that.'

Raif inclined his head. 'It would. But there are other benefits.'

Tara blinked. How could he look at her with familiar warmth in his eyes when a moment ago he'd scorned her?

'Name one. Apart from the fact that your people expect it, and that we're sexually compatible.'

His eyebrows rose as his voice dropped to a decadently low rumble. 'More than compatible, Tara. What we have is unique.'

'Marriage is about more than sex.'

'I agree. It's about constancy, support, respect, patience. Being a partner. I believe we can be all those things to each other.'

That surprised her. He spoke as if he really understood what made a successful marriage. His words evoked memories of her parents, who'd been so happy together.

'You look surprised. But I have the example of my parents. They were very happily married.'

'It was a love match?'

Dark eyes held hers, his look compelling. Tara had the uncomfortable feeling Raif read the thoughts behind her question and silently cursed herself for asking.

'It was an arranged match, in line with family tradition, but there was respect and affection.' He paused. 'Is that why you're hesitant? Because you want a declaration of love?'

'No!' Her voice was strident, almost blotting out his words. Her skin crawled at the idea Raif read her feelings. 'But marriage between two strangers is doomed to fail.'

Even if another Tara, one deep inside, thought marrying Raif was the best idea she'd ever heard.

'You will have my respect and support, Tara. I will help you every step of the way.' His brows drew together in a hint of a frown. 'It's true I'm used to getting my own way, but I promise to work on sharing, on negotiating. You won't find me unreasonable.'

From a man who'd spent years as the ultimate power in Nahrat that was an amazing concession. Did he realise her frozen horror at the idea of having no control in her own life? Her heart beat faster.

'I promise to be faithful too. There will be no other women.' The way he spoke, his gaze holding hers, his voice low and deep, made her shiver with something like excitement. 'And I expect faithfulness from you.'

That was no problem. Tara suspected that after being with Raif, no other man could compete.

Then she realised where her thoughts were heading and pulled back. 'You still haven't told me what you'd get out of this. Apart from good sex and avoiding a scandal. Surely marrying a woman brought to the palace *by a carpet seller* is beneath your dignity.' Her heart pounded as she recalled Raif's contempt.

'Forgive me, Tara. That comment was uncalled for.' Raif spread his hands, his apology taking her by surprise. 'You bruised my pride, saying you didn't want to marry me.'

That wasn't what she'd said. The idea of marrying him was far too tempting.

'We're well suited, you know. Both determined and proud. Both questioning. Both...attracted.' He paused. 'I'd acquire a wife with warmth and people skills that will be beneficial in a royal bride. You're royal too, though you don't admit it. And, despite negativity from those who object to me taking a Dhalkuri wife, tying our nations is good for peace.' His lips twitched in a smile that tugged at her heart. 'Plus, I'd be marrying an heiress.'

Tara thought of his reaction when she'd accused him of wanting her inheritance. He clearly had no need for her money. She ignored his joke. 'There are people who object to the betrothal?'

He shrugged. 'Some still see Dhalkur as the old enemy. I hope to change that. Our marriage would bring us closer to long-term peace.'

Tara stared at Raif. His expression was reasonable, his stance open. Yet she couldn't believe his fatalistic acceptance of the situation, as if he had no choice.

This was a man who made his own fate. The way he'd faced down her abductors, strolling in despite their weapons, proved that. Something else was going on here. She just didn't know what.

Tara thought back to how he'd held her arm, not just in the desert town, but here in the palace, when he led her to dinner. Had he been staking a claim then? If so, why?

'You don't need to say yes straight away, Tara.' Suddenly he was right before her, so close she had to lift her chin to meet his eyes. 'I know this is a shock and you need time to get used to the idea.'

A warm arm wrapped around her waist, tugging her close. He was all muscle and hard bone, and everything inside her melted. Tara fought to keep her mind focused on their conversation, but her body remembered the ecstasy they'd shared.

'Let me help you get used to the idea,' he murmured as he kissed her neck, sending shivers of delight through her. 'I...'

Raif's mouth brushed the corner of hers as he lifted her high against his solid chest. Tara tried to gather her thoughts and her resistance. She needed to think this through, but as he lowered her to a wide sofa and joined her there, it was impossible. Nothing mattered but the magic Raif wrought on her eager body. She'd have to think later.

CHAPTER FOURTEEN

TWO DAYS LATER, the news came that Tara's uncle was dead. Raif broke it to her and she was glad of his presence. The way he held her close in his arms, not talking, just offering the comfort of his embrace, was pure solace.

The death had been expected—and she hadn't been close to her uncle—but it felt as if the final family link to her mother died with him. Her uncle had known her mother well and had been able to reminisce with Tara about her. That had been precious.

'You'll be okay,' Raif murmured, not asking, but reminding her.

'I know.' Yet she didn't break his hold.

Theirs was a crazy relationship. Though they lived together and slept together, Tara had refused to accompany Raif to any public events since they'd appeared before his people.

She sensed his impatience, but to her it felt like a lie, letting everyone believe they were to marry.

Even though Raif seemed convinced they would.

No matter what argument she made, he'd reiterate that actions had consequences, that they needed to face their situation and make the most of it. He talked of respect and admiration, companionship and caring, and Tara slid further under his spell, despite her attempts to be clear-headed.

When Raif was near it was hard to imagine life without him. His personality was bigger than life-size. He had such presence that around him she felt energised in a way that made her old life seem humdrum and stale.

And because she loved him.

Now, alone in her suite a day later, she faced that truth. Did she really want to return to grey London and work selling gems for other people to wear? Did she want to turn her back on this man who, infuriating and challenging as he could be, made her feel stronger and more alive? With Raif she even felt cherished. She told herself it was an illusion, that he was making the best of their situation, yet it felt real, and her vulnerable heart responded wholeheartedly.

If she wasn't careful one day soon she'd give in and agree to marry him.

The thought sent her to her feet. She'd been stuck inside too long. She needed to get out and think.

Raif had flown out early to pay his respects at her uncle's funeral, which traditionally was a male-only affair, and attend the new Sheikh's coronation.

The thought of Fuad made her more restless than ever.

She left her apartment and made for the palace's main entrance. With the funeral and coronation today she'd be safe to venture out. Fuad would have no interest in her once he was crowned and Tara was desperate to get away from the palace.

Maybe she'd visit the spice markets and lose herself in the sights, sounds and smells. Or visit a park or explore the streets of the old city.

She'd reached the grand vestibule when a man stopped before her. He bowed. 'Ms Michaels. I'm afraid I can't let you pass.'

'Sorry?' She stared, recognising him as one of Raif's security staff. 'I'm just going for a walk.'

She spread her hands in an open gesture. She didn't even have a purse. A reminder that everything she had here she owed to Raif's largesse.

'Even so.' His voice was apologetic but his solid form barred her way. 'His Majesty asked that you remain in the palace.'

Asked? He hadn't asked. He'd ordered.

Just like Fuad.

Shock was an iron clamp across her shoulders and neck. It weighted her lungs, making it hard to breathe.

Tara blinked and turned away, making for the other side of the vestibule, only to have another guard step from the shadows.

She slammed to a stop, the hairs at her nape rising. This was ridiculous! She was safe from Fuad now. There was no reason for Raif to keep her here.

She looked out to the warm sunlight, the bustling city she'd never really explored.

Her heart beat faster. She could make a run for it. But the guards would catch her before she got far. She stood, fuming, the feeling of isolation growing. She hadn't minded when Raif was here but now it struck her like a blow.

'Good morning, Ms Michaels.' It was the chamberlain, smiling as he crossed the vestibule. 'Please, come inside and let me see to whatever you require.'

'I want to go out.'

His smile slipped. 'I'm afraid that's not possible until His Majesty returns later today. Please.' He put his arm out, ushering her back inside.

For a moment she wavered, wondering if they'd use force if she stalked outside. Then common sense stopped her. She'd embarrass them and herself.

Her argument was with Raif. What was he thinking, to lock her up when there was no need? Didn't he understand she'd spent too long locked away? This was too much like being Fuad's prisoner. Though Raif tried to protect her it felt like control, and that chafed. More so now when she felt trapped by his marriage plans.

Reluctantly she accompanied the chamberlain.

'Thank you, Ms Michaels. Now, if there's something I can get you?'

'Nothing, thank you.' She was tired of being alone but she didn't have the patience for polite conversation with

Raif's man. She wanted to make her own decisions, not feel her every move was being managed. She didn't even have her work in the treasury to distract her as her colleague was out of the city visiting family.

Tara drew a slow breath. Who would she visit if she had the chance? Not the remnants of her family. There were friends in London but no one particularly close. The realisation intensified that sharp pang of loneliness. It wasn't long since she'd lost her mother.

'You'll have company tomorrow,' the chamberlain said. 'His Majesty's aunt is returning. She's eager to meet you.'

Tara didn't doubt it. His aunt was probably hurrying home to check out how unsuitable Raif's bride-to-be was. Had he told her how Tara had arrived in the palace, and how he'd been forced into naming her as his to save her life?

She shivered. Was she supposed to wait here meekly, to be inspected like some broodmare prior to purchase?

That was unfair, she knew it was. But this, today, was the last straw.

For weeks she'd felt trapped, unable to make the slightest decisions for herself. Even falling in love, at times glorious and exciting, was tainted with the knowledge Raif didn't return her feelings. He wanted to marry because it was expected. Even so, she suspected there was something he wasn't telling her. Another reason behind his insistence.

Maybe he did want access to the mineral wealth she'd inherited after all. Or maybe relations with Dhalkur were worse than she'd imagined and marriage would stop a complete rift between the countries.

Whatever his thinking, he didn't love her. The chances were he never would. If she stayed she'd be trapped, not just by people's expectations but by her yearning heart.

A trembling started in her knees, a sick feeling in her stomach. She remembered being truly helpless as a teenager when choice had been stripped from her by a guy who intended to take rather than ask.

Raif wasn't like him. Raif protected her.

Yet he kept making decisions for her.

Could she live here, loving Raif, but never having the freedom to express it, or the freedom to make her own choices?

'Ms Michaels?'

The chamberlain was frowning at her.

'Sorry. My mind was elsewhere. Please excuse me.'

It was late when Raif returned. His steps quickened as he thought of Tara waiting for him, and the news he had for her. He imagined her bright smile, her relief, the way she'd sink into his arms—

'Tara?' What was she doing here, on a chair outside his study? 'Are you okay? I was coming to your suite.'

She stood and he saw she wore the raspberry-red dress she'd had on the day he first saw her. His lips twitched in appreciation. She looked alluring whatever she wore but he had a particular fondness for that simple dress, especially given how easily it opened.

'We need to talk.' Instead of turning to walk with him, she opened his study door and stepped in.

Raif halted, puzzled. Where was her welcome smile? Why talk in his study instead of in her suite, where there was a comfortable bed?

He followed, closing the door.

'How did today go?' She stood on the far side of his desk and for the first time in ages didn't meet his eyes.

Something wasn't right. He felt it in his bones.

'Your uncle was farewelled with appropriate honours.' He paused. 'And the coronation took place, but not as most people expected.'

'What happened?' *Now* she met his gaze.

'The royal council voted in favour of Salim rather than Fuad. The only person surprised was Fuad.'

'You mean Salim is Sheikh? That's wonderful!' Tara shook her head. 'What part did you play in all this?'

'Me? It was the Council who chose the Sheikh.' All Raif had done was ensure Salim got into the country despite his brother's attempts to keep him out. And speak privately with some of the country's powerbrokers about what a future would look like under Fuad's rule.

'Whatever it was you did, thank you. That's a marvellous outcome.'

Raif heard the warmth in her tone and crossed to her, only to see her stiffen and step back. He froze, reading her tense body language.

'What's happened?' He'd been sure she'd be safe from Fuad's machinations here, but desperate men did desperate things. 'Did someone try something?' His heart stilled on the thought.

'No one had a chance, since I wasn't allowed out.' The mutinous twist of her lips betrayed her thoughts.

That was the reason for her distance?

'It was a precaution. I couldn't trust Fuad not to try to grab you at the last moment.'

'He thought he was going to be made Sheikh. He wasn't thinking about me today. Besides, if you thought that way you should have discussed it with me.' The clipped way she enunciated each word made it clear she wasn't pleased.

'Would you have been happier if you'd gone out and his men abducted you?'

She folded her arms under her breasts and he fought to keep his attention on her face, not her cleavage. 'I'd have been happier if you'd talked to me instead of making decisions for me.'

Raif spread his hands. 'It was for the best.' He paused then admitted, 'I don't want anything happening to you.'

For a second it looked like she understood. He read warmth and longing in her glittering eyes and an answering heat filled his chest.

'You made me a prisoner.'

'Sorry?'

'You locked me up so I wasn't *allowed* to go out.'

'I explained—'

'I spent a week as Fuad's prisoner and then, from the moment I arrived here, you dictated what I could do and where I could go.'

Raif shook his head. 'I don't recall that stopping you. Who was it who announced her presence to the world by slipping out onto the royal balcony?'

'That was one mistake.'

'You haven't been a prisoner. You've been an honoured guest.'

She'd been received with all hospitality. Had she no concept of what he'd done for her? The rules he'd broken, the backlash he'd faced to keep her safe? Hadn't he lavished care and affection on her? Hadn't he shared himself in ways he never had with any other woman? He'd offered her marriage!

'I haven't once ventured out of here except with you. Not once!'

Her contrariness annoyed him. 'Now you blame me for protecting you from Fuad?'

'You're deliberately misunderstanding.' Her chin hiked high and this time Raif found it infuriating rather than attractive.

'What, exactly, is your problem, princess?' He realised his mistake as he drawled the last word and glimpsed hurt behind her anger. He stepped nearer. 'Tara, I—'

'My problem is that from the day I arrived you've told me what to do. You've made every decision. You've given me no choice. I'm not even allowed to go for a walk in the city without your approval. I have no *freedom*. You're trying to railroad me into believing we have to marry because you called me your woman when you saved me.'

At least she acknowledged he'd saved her!

Raif stood taller, feeling her words like a smack to his pride. He'd done everything he could for her. More than anyone could reasonably expect.

'This is the thanks I get?'

'See? I question you and you stare down that superior nose of yours as if I shouldn't even dare to speak.'

'You're twisting this out of proportion.'

Tara jammed her hands onto her hips. 'No, I'm telling you what it's like from where I stand.'

Again Raif saw pain in her eyes and the crumpled corners of her lovely mouth. He was torn between wanting to haul her into his arms and wanting to put her in her place.

Except her place was a moot point. He'd told himself at first she was simply someone who needed his help. Then she'd become his lover and life got much more complicated. Claiming her as his betrothed should have simplified things yet it all felt tangled. His reasoning, his feelings, and certainly her responses.

Raif was used to making considered decisions and implementing them. He was used to knowing he did the best for his people. Most times he was right.

Tara robbed him of that certainty. She made him feel...

That was the problem. She made him *feel*.

'From where I'm standing there's something fishy about this. There's something you're not telling me. I can't believe you'd marry a complete stranger just because you called her your woman. All it would take is a few words from you to correct the situation.'

Raif's belly clamped and he felt an unfamiliar surge of panic skitter through him. 'Are you calling me a liar?'

'I'm saying things aren't as black and white as you make

out.' She breathed deep then said in a rush, 'I want to leave. If you'll lend me the money I'll go to London tomorrow, or tonight if there's a flight.'

He couldn't be hearing this. It felt like everything had turned to slow motion. 'Lend you money?'

'I'm good for it. I've got money in the bank and I'm an heiress, remember?' She shot him a haughty look that chilled his blood. Where was his warm, welcoming Tara? 'Or are you going to say that passport you promised isn't ready? Which reminds me, you didn't return my driving licence. Are you withholding them to keep me imprisoned here?'

Never in his life had Raif felt such incandescent rage.

On top of everything else she doubted his word. He'd done everything for her. He'd planned to give her even more. His thoughts skidded to a halt, shying away from that. He stalked to his desk and yanked open a drawer.

'Here.' He slapped the temporary diplomatic passport onto his desk with her licence. 'I was going to give it to you tomorrow.' After he persuaded her into an early wedding.

Raif had the satisfaction of seeing her mouth drop open, but her surprise only inflamed his temper. No one ever had insulted him so. Tara had turned what should have been triumph into bitter dispute and sour disappointment.

Disappointment? It felt like more than that, but Raif had no intention of examining his feelings in front of her.

It infuriated him that she had the power to undo him. To fog his brain and destroy his peace and make him feel…appalling. Bruised pride urged him to let her leave, but something stronger made him try one more time.

'What will you do with your precious *freedom*, Tara? Go back to work in a jewellery store? Is that the summit of your ambition? Do you know your mentor from the museum approached me? He's so impressed he wants you to undertake formal studies then work for him long-term.'

Was that a flare of interest in her narrowed eyes? But just as he thought he'd got through to her, Tara's expression turned blank. Where was the enthusiastic, fascinating woman he knew? Why was she hiding? Raif didn't believe this was about her being kept inside today.

'Not interested?' He waited for her counter-attack and got none. His heart sank. 'Why, Tara? Because you're too scared to think bigger? You'd rather live a boring life that doesn't fulfil you than take a risk? Is that why you deny your royal position, because you don't think you can live up to it?' The words spilled from Raif in a furious rush. 'Is that why you reject *me*?'

'I don't want to argue, Raif. I want to leave.'

Everything about her, from her stiff shoulders to her flat stare, told him she'd shut him out. He wanted to rage and force her to argue. He wanted to hold her close and persuade her to yield. But he had his pride.

'If you're so eager to escape this *prison*,' his lips curled on the word, 'I'll arrange a flight tonight.'

Raif waited, daring her to agree. She wouldn't, he knew. Despite her accusations, she cared for him. He felt it in her tenderness, her eager smiles. When she thought about it, she'd—

'Perfect.' Her eyes flashed as she stepped up and swiped the pieces of identification off his desk.

She didn't mean it. She was bluffing. In a second she'd see her error and apologise.

'I don't have anything to pack, so I'm ready to leave as soon as a flight's ready. I'll wait in my room till then.'

To Raif's amazement she swung towards the door.

'Wait!'

She turned back. Was that hope in her eyes? No, it was a trick of the light. She was as ungrateful and obstinate as before.

He reached into the drawer and pulled out a velvet box.

He'd intended to give it to her as an engagement gift, until she'd thrown his generosity in his teeth and made a mockery of everything he'd done for her.

'A going-away present.' Raif didn't push it across the table but tossed it. She caught it but didn't even look at it.

'Thank you for your hospitality, Raif.'

Then she was gone in a flounce of crimson cotton.

CHAPTER FIFTEEN

TARA SHOVED HER hands in her pockets and scuffed the fallen leaves with her boot. The London park was damp from autumn drizzle, perfectly matching her mood.

She'd made the biggest mistake of her life.

Leaving Raif should have been the most sensible decision.

She couldn't marry a man who didn't love her. Or who made every important decision. It would be disastrous. She'd felt herself falling more in love while Raif remained self-contained.

Tara didn't want self-contained. She wanted love as well as passion, partnership not bossiness.

She wanted to be an equal, not a subject to be ordered about.

Yet there was no doubt, she shouldn't have stormed off in a temper. She should have stayed and got to the bottom of Raif's behaviour. Talked with him, negotiated, listened, pried, whatever it took to get beyond his demands and obstinate pride and discover why he insisted on marriage.

She'd achieved nothing by leaving except to sever their connection and make herself utterly miserable.

Tara had spent the last week packing up and arranging for the sale of her mother's home. She'd returned to work only to give notice. Raif had been right. Much as she'd loved that job she'd feel stultified returning there.

She kicked more leaves, watching the flurry of brown and gold, and saw two women across the park staring. Were they going to tell her to get back on the path?

Footsteps crunched on gravel behind her and she realised they weren't looking at her. They were gaping at—

'Tara.'

She swung round so fast she almost toppled.

Her throat seized up even as her heart accelerated.

'Raif!' He looked different. Magnificent but unfamiliar. It wasn't merely the cashmere coat over his open-necked shirt. Unfamiliar lines bracketed his mouth and his eyes looked tired. 'What are you doing in London?'

'I had business to conclude.'

Tara's heart dived towards her toes. For a moment she'd thought he'd come for her. After what she'd said to him it was a wonder he even spoke to her.

'I'm sorry for what I said.' She met his stare. 'I was ungrateful. I know you weren't keeping me prisoner. I—'

'You were under considerable stress. You'd lost your mother then your uncle. You'd been physically threatened and you'd just begun your first sexual relationship. Naturally you were emotional. You felt powerless.'

Her mouth turned down. Her first sexual relationship? It had been much more to her. She didn't want a relationship with any man but Raif. Her throat was so tight it hurt to swallow.

'You're very understanding.'

His shoulders lifted. 'When I'm not in a temper.' Was that a curl of humour teasing his mouth? No, she imagined it.

'Why are you here?' Her sweeping hand encompassed the bare trees and dog walkers.

'I followed you from the house.'

Tara's breath hissed in. 'Sorry?'

'I saw you walking towards the park when I drove up.'

Why would Raif want to see her after all she'd said?

'I'm not pregnant.' Her period had begun the day after she arrived in England. No doubt hormones had played a part in her distress that last day in Nahrat.

His eyes widened. 'I see.'

Tara stood waiting, but he said nothing more. Maybe he

hadn't come to check on possible consequences from their affair? Something tingled inside her.

'Have you heard from Salim?'

She frowned. He wanted to talk about her cousin? 'No. Is he all right?'

'He's fine. But Fuad is dead.' Tara gasped and he continued. 'Straight after the coronation he got in his sports car and headed out of the capital. Witnesses say he was in a furious temper, and the experts say he was doing double the speed limit when he failed to take a curve and crashed.'

Tara hadn't had the energy to follow news reports since leaving Nahrat. But she could imagine Fuad in a fit of pique, flinging out of the palace and taking out his temper in reckless driving. He'd been so obsessed with winning the throne.

'So he won't bother you again.'

That was why he'd come. She met Raif's steely gaze and that little tremor of excitement that he'd come because he'd missed her died.

'I see. Thank you for coming to tell me.'

'That's not all.'

She tilted her head in enquiry. She didn't really want to hear what else Fuad had done. It was too hard standing here, so close to Raif, seeing him look so distant. She thought of the hope she'd harboured, the action she'd planned, and knew they were futile.

'You were right when you said there was something suspicious about my actions. That I wouldn't let myself be forced into marriage.'

Tara blinked and stumbled back a step, shocked by the change of subject.

'What are you saying, Raif?'

He closed the gap between them, filling her vision. She inhaled sharply, dragging in the smell of warm flesh, brisk autumn air and a hint of sandalwood. Her pulse thrummed faster and she dug her fists deeper in her pockets so as not to reach for him.

'I used that as an excuse because I didn't want to let you go.' He paused as if watching for a response. She was too stunned to give one.

'I told myself it was fate but I was simply using whatever reason I could find to keep you close. Looking back, I know I was only too ready to flout the rules where you were concerned, touching you in public at that palace dinner and on other visits. As if I wanted the world to know you were mine, though I didn't fully acknowledge the implications.'

Tara fought for calm as excitement vied with disbelief. She breathed deeply, trying to think logically.

'You mean you didn't think about how others would interpret it?'

He shook his head slowly, his lips curving up in a slow smile that stole the air from her lungs.

'I mean I didn't face what it meant about *my* feelings. I wanted you, Tara. But it wasn't all about sex. I've never felt like this with any other lover. I want you in every way a man can want a woman. *That's* why I want you to marry me. You make me feel complete in ways I'd never imagined. It's a new and scary experience, discovering I'm not the loner I believed myself to be. Finding out a small, feisty stranger has the power to undo me.'

His smile faded and to her amazement Tara heard his breathing turn ragged. She replayed his words, unable to believe what she thought she'd heard.

She felt dazed, as if he'd tipped the world upside down and nothing made sense.

'You still want to marry me?' Her voice shook.

'That's why I'm here. Nothing's right since you left. My staff avoid me because I'm in a perennial bad mood and my aunt thinks I'm pining.'

Suddenly it felt like the sun broke free of the louring clouds, warming her chilled flesh. She told herself it couldn't be true, yet she couldn't prevent hope unfurling.

'Because of me?'

He nodded. 'I care for you, Tara. I care deeply. I know you'll say it's too soon, that we haven't known each other long enough, but—'

'I wouldn't.'

Hadn't her parents fallen for each other at first sight?

Tara swallowed hard and gathered her nerve, taking heart from the emotions she saw in Raif's tense features.

'I feel the same. You were right about my old life not fitting any more. I want so much more. I'm booked on a flight to Nahrat today.'

His hand shot out, closing around her elbow, and she was grateful for his touch as her knees wobbled.

'To see me?'

She nodded, stunned to read in Raif's proud features the same desperate hope she felt.

Suddenly what had seemed impossibly risky became urgent. Shattered hopes reassembled, banishing the shadows of hurt and fear.

'Yes.' Tara had to draw another breath to steady herself. 'Because I love you.'

How easy it was to say the words, after all that soul-searching. But Raif had confounded her fears and doubts.

Powerful arms wrapped round her, pulling her against his chest. Soft cashmere enfolded her and beneath her ear she felt the chaotic pound of his heart. She'd never heard anything so wonderful.

Raif's lips pressed to her hair and then her upturned face.

'That's my line.' He sounded breathless, like a man who'd run for his life. 'I love you, Tara. I don't have the words to tell you how much.'

But his expression told her. And his thudding heart and shaking hands.

'I believed that love would make me weak, which is why I fought it, fought *you*. But this doesn't feel like weakness, *habibti*. It feels right.' Raif drew in a deep breath. 'I have a lot to learn about sharing and not being so autocratic, but I'm determined to make you happy. I'll do whatever it takes, if you'll give me the chance.'

Her heart swelled till she thought she might burst with tenderness and excitement. She lifted her hand to cup his jaw, revelling in the feel of his skin against hers. It had been too long.

'You're wearing the bangle.' He caught her arm and held it out, where the weak sunlight caught the intricate gold work and rich red spinels.

Tara nodded. 'I didn't open the box till I was on the plane here. And when I saw what you gave me, I wondered.' Strangely she felt suddenly shy.

'You wondered why I chose that piece?'

'It's not as eye-catching as some other things in the treasury. It wasn't the obvious choice if you wanted to declare publicly that I was your bride. Since you had it handy when I insisted on leaving, I assumed that's why you had it ready to give me.'

Tara had been torn between hoping that was true and telling herself she was spinning tales out of nothing because she wanted so desperately to believe he cared.

Raif's expression made her heart roll over. 'I chose it because it moved you. You see its intrinsic beauty, the work and dedication, not just bright colour and a dollar value. I wanted you to have something that proved I see *you*, as a woman apart. A woman with her own ideas and preferences. It's not a traditional betrothal gift but it seemed perfect for the woman I want to spend the rest of my days with.'

Tara's throat worked, emotion threatening to undo her. 'Just the days?'

He swept her closer, lifted her off her feet till her face

was level with his. 'And all the nights too, *habibti*. If you'll have me.'

Her eyes misted with emotion. She had the strongest feeling she didn't deserve such happiness after the way she'd deserted him, but she wasn't foolish enough to hesitate. Raif was everything to her. Her present and her future, the man who had her heart.

'How can I resist, my darling?' Tara lifted her mouth to his and let Raif sweep her up into their own private paradise.

EPILOGUE

'YOU LOOK WONDERFUL, my dear. A truly radiant bride.' Raif's aunt straightened Tara's train then gave her a hug.

Tara hugged her back. In the last seven months she'd grown fond of this woman whose incisive wit hid a kind heart. She was a wonderful mentor, helping Raif fill any gaps in Tara's knowledge about Nahrat and the royal court.

'Thank you. The colour helps.' Tara gestured to the cranberry satin, richly embroidered with gold, that matched her antique bracelet, chandelier earrings and the delicate tiara Raif had had made especially for her.

'Nonsense. It's the glow of a woman in love. My nephew is an incredibly lucky man. Fortunately, he has the good sense to realise it.' She smiled. 'If anyone had told me he'd wait a whole seven months to marry when every time he looks at you he eats you up with his eyes...' Her smile turned mischievous. 'You're good for him, my dear.'

Tara shook her head. 'He was the one who wanted a long engagement.'

Raif had put her needs first. He was adamant she needed time to adjust to life in Nahrat, find her feet and make decisions about the wedding.

He didn't want her to feel pushed into marriage too fast. Her accusations about being a prisoner had stung his conscience and though she assured him that was in the past, he'd insisted they wait. He'd made her feel totally treasured. She'd even found time to begin her new studies, intending to fit part-time work in with her royal duties.

Salim entered the room, wearing a grin on his handsome face. 'Are you ready, cousin? Your groom is getting impatient. If I didn't know better I'd think him nervous.'

Raif's aunt laughed. 'Nonsense. It does a man good to

wait for his bride.' After kissing Tara on the cheek and twitching Salim's jacket straight, she bustled out.

Salim looked Tara over. 'I'd ask if you're sure you want to marry a Nahrati but your face tells me you are. Besides, Raif's a good man.'

'I know.' Tara smiled as he hooked her arm through his. During their engagement Raif had proved his love again and again. In thoughtfulness and tenderness, but also in his willingness to listen and be swayed by her. There were still times when they disagreed but always they managed to come to some compromise. And negotiating could be such fun!

'You look like the cat who got the cream,' Salim said as he led her to the door. 'I almost feel sorry for Raif.' Tara lightly punched his arm. 'But only a little. I feel he's getting his just deserts.'

The music began, a royal fanfare that once would have made her nervous about being in the limelight. Now, as Salim led her down the red-carpeted aisle, past hundreds of guests, she felt only elation.

For there, ahead, was Raif, resplendent in gold and white, tall and compelling. His eyes were fixed on her with a look that sealed the air in her lungs.

If ever she'd wondered what love looked like, it was this. Those ebony eyes locked on hers with such intensity she barely registered the crowd, or her cousin as he kissed her cheek and moved aside.

There was just her and Raif, the man she loved. Emotion swamped her, suddenly overwhelming. Then Raif took her hand, his strength flowing into her.

'Ready, my love?'

'Absolutely.'

Then before international royalty and a television audience of millions, Raif swept her into his arms and kissed her deeply, thoroughly and with total disregard for royal protocol.

Tara kissed him right back, her hands clamping his shoulders as she held him close. This last week, when she'd stayed at her cousin's palace, she'd missed Raif terribly. It felt an eternity since they were together.

When Raif finally lifted his head the emotion in his midnight gaze told her all she needed to know.

'I love you, Tara. I always will.'

'And I love you, Raif, for ever.' Her voice wobbled from sheer happiness.

Later they discovered that kiss had made headlines. People around the world sighed over their fairy-tale romance. It was a romance the public would follow through the years as the Sheikh and his Sheikha grew closer and their family expanded.

They created a family tradition of love at first sight and happy-ever-afters.

* * * * *

THE
BILLIONAIRE'S
CINDERELLA
HOUSEKEEPER

MIRANDA LEE

Dedicated to all my loyal readers over the years.
Thank you from the bottom of my heart.
Love from Miranda Lee

CHAPTER ONE

'So, you're looking for a live-in housekeeping position, are you, Ruby?' the lady asked.

Ruby heard the scepticism behind the woman's words. She'd heard it before from the other employment agencies she'd been to. They'd all taken one look at her, along with her less than impressive résumé, and told her they didn't have anything suitable on their books right now.

'Yes, that's right,' she replied, already knowing she'd drawn a blank again.

Ruby suppressed a sigh. If she couldn't get a live-in position, then she'd have to take Oliver up on his offer for her to stay on at his place. Liam had offered to have her too, but really, she didn't want to live with either of her brothers. Neither of their apartments were what you would call spacious. Besides, Oliver's long-time girlfriend, Rachel, lived with him, and Liam's new girlfriend, Lara, had just moved in with him. They needed their own space, as did she.

'You do realise,' the woman said kindly, 'that Housewives For Hire doesn't often have such a position available. We specialise more in part-time casual housekeeping. Rarely live-in. Most of my girls are married women who want to earn money whilst their children are at school.'

'I see,' Ruby said in a flat voice. Obviously, it had been a mistake to come back to Sydney and try to embrace real life again.

But before Ruby could say goodbye and go, a phone

buzzed on the desk and Barbara, the owner of Housewives for Hire, swept it up, mouthing an apology to Ruby as she did so.

Ruby didn't really listen as the conversation was rather one-sided. Barbara just said *yes* and *hmm* a lot whilst tapping on her computer, so Ruby tuned out, putting her mind to the problem of what she would do now, because blind Freddie could see she wasn't going to get a housekeeping job in Sydney. She'd been a fool to think it would be straightforward to get such a position.

Going back to her nomadic lifestyle, however, no longer appealed. It had served its purpose for the past five years, giving her the time out she'd desperately needed. But when she'd turned thirty on her last birthday, a yearning had started growing inside her, a yearning to settle down and do something worthwhile with her life.

Not marriage. Lord no. Ruby shuddered at the thought. After the fiasco with Jason a few years back, she'd decided that marriage would never be her lot in life. Because marriage meant loving and trusting a man with her happiness, and Ruby simply couldn't see that happening.

And let's face it, Ruby thought, *Jason wasn't the only member of the opposite sex to have a strike against him. Your father sowed the seeds for your distrust when you were only nineteen, with your first serious boyfriend, Bailey, compounding your negative feelings shortly after.*

It was inevitable that she would eventually come to the decision to rely on herself, and herself alone. Jason had just been the catalyst that had propelled her into adopting a totally celibate lifestyle, which Ruby found she actually quite liked. She enjoyed the freedom from the emotional complications associated with boyfriends and sex.

To her surprise, she found she didn't miss either. Not one little bit.

The idea had finally taken hold that she could become

a social worker. Over the past few years of travelling and working all over Queensland and northern NSW, she'd come across a lot of unfortunates who could have had different lives if someone had given them a helping hand.

The only problem with this was that social workers these days had degrees.

Gradually, Ruby had come up with a plan. It had seemed so simple on paper. She would return to Sydney and get herself a live-in housekeeping position, not because she really wanted to be a housekeeper but because that way she wouldn't have to pay rent. Rents in Sydney, she knew, were exorbitant, and she didn't have enough savings to pay a bond, plus the first month's rent in advance. On top of that, she could spend her spare time doing an online course to get herself into a university so that she could study for a social science degree.

In her head, by thirty-five she would be a qualified social worker. Ruby knew she was intelligent and if she put her mind to it, she could do just about anything.

Unfortunately, her plan seemed to have one fatal flaw. No one would hire her as a housekeeper, not even here in Sydney where there were loads of such positions advertised. Ruby suspected her lack of experience in such a position was the main reason for her always being turned down, although one of the agencies had hinted that she looked too...sexy.

Now that had really floored her, though, now she thought about it, she had come across this opinion once or twice before over recent years. Lord knew why. Okay, so she had what was considered a good figure nowadays but she wasn't even pretty.

Ruby shook her head ruefully when she thought back to her teenage years. No one would have called her sexy back then. Lord no! The opposite sex hadn't given her a second glance when she was at school. And why would they? She'd been all puppy fat and braces, along with the lack of confidence that went with puberty. It had taken every bit of courage she possessed to apply for a job at a local fast-food place. But from then on her confidence had grown, confidence that had nothing to do with looks. It annoyed her that people couldn't see past the obvious to who she was inside.

Oh, well. Ruby accepted she would *have* to live with one of her brothers for a while till she could get a job as a waitress or bar staff—jobs she was well qualified for and where looking sexy would be an asset. Once she had enough money she would look for shared accommodation, hopefully with a room of her own so she could study in peace.

It wouldn't be as good as her original plan of being a live-in housekeeper but it would have to do, Ruby decided as she waited for Barbara to finish her call. A potential client, it sounded like.

'I see,' Barbara said slowly. 'So this won't be a permanent position, Mr Marshall. Your usual housekeeper will be coming back to work for you eventually.'

Ruby couldn't hear what Mr Marshall said to this.

'Actually,' Barbara went on with a glance Ruby's way, 'I do have a girl who might suit you very well. Yes, she has excellent references.'

Ruby nodded enthusiastically at this. She did have excellent references. Ruby was a good worker, and as honest as the day was long. Employers were always sorry to see her go.

'She's actually here now. Would you like to talk to her? Good. Her name's Ruby. Here she is.'

The ball's in your court, Barbara's eyes seemed to say as she handed Ruby the phone.

'Hello?' Ruby said after a swift swallow. She was not a nervous person, but she did so want this job. Even if it was only temporary. Because then she would have *experience* as a housekeeper on her résumé, which would lead more easily to getting another housekeeping position.

'Hi, Ruby,' Mr Marshall said in a deep and very masculine voice, the kind of voice you mostly associated with radio announcers and soul singers. 'First things first. Have you done housekeeping jobs before?'

Ruby was about to say no when she had a light-bulb moment. Really, why hadn't she thought to mention this before?

'Not professionally,' she said briskly. 'But I ran the family household for seven years from the age of eighteen till I was twenty-five. My mother was ill at the time,' she raced on before he could ask why. She didn't add that her mother had actually died of ovarian cancer a year after she'd finished school, her precious father leaving it up to Ruby to help her shattered younger brothers through school and then university. The rotten mongrel deserted them two months after the funeral to live with his rich mistress in her fancy city penthouse. Yes, he'd given them the family house to live in and, yes, he'd paid the bills, but that had been the extent of his support.

'I did all the cooking and cleaning,' she added, in case Mr Marshall thought they'd been rich enough to pay someone to do that.

'Your mother must have been very proud of you,' he remarked. 'And is she well now?'

Ruby blanked from her mind the grief that still consumed her whenever she thought of her lovely, brave mother. 'No,' she bit out, gritting her teeth at the same time. 'She passed away. Cancer.'

'Bloody cancer,' Mr Marshall muttered, then was silent for a few seconds. 'Sorry,' he said at last. 'My wife died of cancer. Still, no use going on about it, is there?' he continued gruffly before she could make any sympathetic noises.

'Only makes things worse. What's done is done. So, how old are you now, Ruby?'

'Thirty.'

'I see. And what have you been doing with yourself since your mother's death?'

Clearly, he thought her mother had died fairly recently and not a decade earlier. Ruby decided not to enlighten him as it would only mean answering awkward questions that weren't really relevant to this interview. She hated talking about that time in her life. *Hated* it!

'Well, I've always worked part-time in the hospitality industry,' she explained, 'even when I was at school. So once I had the opportunity I took off by myself, travelling all over northern NSW and Queensland, working in various resorts and clubs. I've done lots of things, from serving behind the bar to waitressing to the occasional bit of work as a receptionist. But I'm a little tired of that life, so I've come back to Sydney to find suitable work whilst I study for a degree in social science.'

'That sounds very commendable. And you sound like a very nice girl. Not that Housewives For Hire ever recommends any other kind. I have it on good authority that they're very reputable, so I'm sure you'll be fine for the job. Unfortunately, I'm in London on business at the moment and I won't be back in Sydney for over a week. I hate leaving my house empty so this is what I'll do. My sister lives in Sydney in a nearby suburb—I live in Mosman—and she has keys to my house. I'll contact her and have her meet with you there tomorrow morning. She can show you the house and answer any questions you might have about me. But if you want it, then the job's yours, Ruby.'

If she wanted it? Of course she wanted it. Wanted it like crazy! He sounded like such a nice man. 'Oh, Mr Marshall, that's wonderful. I'll do a good job. I promise.'

'I'm sure you will. Now hand the phone back to Barbara for me so I can give her my sister's details. Yes, yes,' he said impatiently to someone in the background. 'I won't be long. You go down to breakfast and I'll join you there.'

Ruby handed the phone back and just sat there, dazed and elated, whilst Barbara spoke to Mr Marshall and tapped some more on her computer. Finally, the woman hung up and turned her swivel chair to face her.

'You're a lucky girl, Ruby,' she said with a smile on her face. 'Mr Marshall is none other than Sebastian Marshall, head of Harvest Productions, which you may or may not have heard of.'

She hadn't, and shook her head in the negative.

'They produce several highly successful television shows,' Barbara went on. 'I'm sure you'd have heard of them. *Australia at Noon… What Word Am I*? The soapie *Elizabeth Street*. But the jewel in their crown is *Battle at the Bar*.'

'That's a very popular show,' Ruby agreed, despite only having watched it the once. But she'd heard a lot about it and was always meaning to watch the series some more. The hero, or anti-hero really, was a lawyer named Caesar Battle who defended the sometimes indefensible and often won. A loner, he was an enigmatic character who worked hard and played hard but still had an integrity about him that was very likeable. Women lusted after him. Men wanted to be him. The show had won countless awards, especially for its handsome main actor whose name eluded her.

'I'm sorry it's only a temporary position,' Barbara continued, 'but it's better than nothing.'

'*Much* better,' Ruby agreed with a smile.

'The job won't be too hard, either. Mr Marshall is a widower, with no children.'

'So how old is Mr Marshall?' It had been impossible to tell from his voice. A widower, however, suggested someone elderly.

'Forty, according to the internet,' came the crisp reply.

'Goodness. That young.' Ruby suddenly thought of her father, who'd been forty when he began having an affair. A dangerous age, forty. Or so she'd been told.

Thinking of her father always made Ruby angry. Angry and cynical and just a little wary, when it came to her dealings with men. The last thing she wanted was to stuff up this job by presenting herself with the wrong look.

'Does your company have a dress code?' she asked. 'A uniform perhaps?'

'No. My girls wear whatever they like. Though under your circumstances,' Barbara added with a knowing glint in her eye, 'I would suggest dressing conservatively. Professional.'

Ruby glanced down at her outfit, which she considered reasonably conservative. Yes, the skirt ended above her knee and the top did show a hint of cleavage but by modern standards it was hardly provocative. Still…

'That's very good advice,' she said. 'Thank you.'

'Sensible girl,' Barbara praised. 'Now, I'll just contact Mr Marshall's sister and we'll make arrangements for tomorrow.'

CHAPTER TWO

RUBY WAS EARLY. Partly because she didn't want to risk being late, but mostly because she wanted to have a good look at the house—and the area—all by herself.

She'd expected her new boss's house to be posh. Wealthy people who lived in Mosman didn't live in ordinary houses. And she wasn't disappointed. It *was* posh. So posh and so elegant, in fact, that it took her breath away.

'Oh, my…' She sighed as she climbed out of her car and just stared.

The house was white, cement-rendered and two-storeyed, with an architectural style that reminded Ruby of those old Georgian mansions that were popular with the English aristocracy.

Not that this house was on that scale, but it had a size and symmetry that were very pleasing to the eye, with a central ivy-clad portico flanked by two French doors downstairs and the same number of windows upstairs. The front yard was like a miniature Versailles garden, with manicured hedges and gravel areas rather than lawn, highlighted with exquisite pots and water features. The front fence had a solid white concrete base topped with dark wooden slats, and a wooden security gate that opened onto a wide path made of white marble tiles. Not that Ruby could open the gate, but there were gaps you could see through.

For a few moments Ruby wondered if she'd bitten off more than she could chew. But then common sense kicked in. Of course she could do this. She was a very resourceful person. And what was the worst that could happen? She stuffed it up and got fired. Not the end of the world.

Ruby refused to succumb to what her mother used to call the heebie-jeebies.

Ruby smiled at the memory. Her mother had been such a character, a great reader who loved cute sayings such as heebie-jeebies. Being a nervous Nellie was another of her favourites, perhaps because her mother had been an anxious person growing up. She'd confided once that she'd been determined to raise Ruby to be confident and independent in her thinking.

Ruby believed she had eventually achieved this, though only after many life lessons.

A car coming slowly up the street brought Ruby's mind back to the present. When she saw a woman behind the wheel of the Lexus she just knew it was Mr Marshall's sister.

The Lexus pulled in behind her silver Kia Rio, which, whilst not a flash car, was still fairly new and sparkling clean, Ruby having left it at a car wash whilst she shopped last night. She knew how important first impressions were and was glad Barbara had advised her how not to dress. Because Ruby was no fool. She knew that if Mr Marshall's sister didn't like the look of her, she might not be getting this job.

Ruby was pleased with the way the woman was smiling at her. Clearly, the outfit she'd bought last night was spot on. The A-line black skirt reached her knees, and the simple white shirt she'd teamed with it shouted professionalism, especially when combined with black pumps and pulled-back hair.

'Ruby, I presume?' the woman said as she approached. She was slim and blonde and rather glamorous-looking. In her forties, Ruby guessed, but could have been older.

Money did keep women looking young, what with Botox and face peels.

'Yes,' Ruby replied. 'And you must be Mrs Chalmers.'

'Indeed, but do call me Gloria,' she insisted, her blue eyes twinkling with genuine warmth.

Ruby could not help liking her. But then, Ruby liked most people, as long as they were nice to her.

'That's a lovely name,' she said.

'A little old-fashioned. I much prefer Ruby. So, Ruby, what do you think of my brother's house?'

'It's very impressive.'

'It is. I have the keys here. Shall we go inside?'

'Yes, please.'

The inside was as elegant as the facade, with lots of grey marble floors and white walls, and a mixture of pale silk curtains and plantation shutters at the windows. Some of the furniture looked antique, in dark wood, but the overall impression was very contemporary. The kitchen was a dream in mostly white, with every mod con imaginable, including a coffee machine, which Ruby would have no trouble using. There were several reception rooms, and one carpeted bedroom downstairs, which she imagined a housekeeper might use, with a bathroom just across the hallway. Upstairs there were three guest double bedrooms—again carpeted—serviced by a family bathroom, along with a huge master suite, which had its own sitting area, bathroom and walk-in wardrobe.

Though not quite a mansion, it was still going to take some looking after. Maybe she wouldn't have much time to study after all.

'You look a little worried,' Gloria said as she led Ruby through some French doors out onto the huge back terrace, which was set up for alfresco dining. Beyond the terrace was a large lawned backyard along with a rectangular swimming pool to one side.

'Will I have any help?' she asked.

'Goodness yes. There's a cleaner who comes in Monday and Friday to do the floors and the bathrooms. Her name is Janice. Though she wouldn't have come today with Sebastian being away. Then there's a handyman called Tom who does the garden and the pool. Not sure which days he's here, but Georgia will tell you everything.'

'Georgia?'

'Sebastian's usual housekeeper. She's left you the house phone with all the necessary contacts in it, including her own phone number. It's in the drawer in the kitchen just below the cutlery drawer. She wants you to ring her today so she can fill you in on everything Sebastian likes and doesn't like.'

'Right. So what happened that she had to be called away so suddenly?'

'Didn't Sebastian tell you?'

'No.'

'Typical,' Gloria said, rolling her eyes. 'Her sister had a car accident and will be in hospital for several weeks.'

'Oh, the poor love. So where did this happen? Obviously not here in Sydney.'

'No, down in Melbourne. Georgia said she will most likely stay for a good while, even after her sister gets out of hospital. There are three children to look after and her brother-in-law is pretty useless, she said. Anyway, she won't be back for at least three months.'

'Barbara said it might be as long as that.'

'Barbara?' Gloria frowned.

'The woman who runs Housewives for Hire.'

'Oh, right. Look, I'm sorry to love you and leave you but I have some ladies coming over for lunch today and I've still got a lot to do. Here are the keys. Make yourself at home, and please do ring me if you have any questions, though I imagine Georgia would be better qualified to answer them than me. Oh, and one last thing, there's a side driveway which leads down to a huge garage underneath the house. There's plenty of room for your car. Do use it. The remote is on the key ring. Also, Sebastian said to tell you he'll be in contact. Probably by text. Or email. Now, I have to run. Lovely meeting you, Ruby. Give my regards to Georgia when you ring her. Bye.'

She was gone before Ruby could do more than say bye in return, leaving Ruby standing there on the back terrace, still slightly overawed by the place. She'd worked in some fancy resorts but she'd never been in a private home this flash before. Her own family home—which her father had sold once they'd all flown the nest—had been a standard brick veneer house in the Western suburbs with three bedrooms, one and a half bathrooms and no pool. Even so, it had sold for over a million dollars. Lord knew what this place was worth. Or what Sebastian Marshall was worth, for that matter.

Her curiosity piqued, Ruby decided to do an internet search on him after she'd parked her car and settled in. Hopefully, there would be a photo or two so she could see what he looked like. She'd expected there to be a few photos of him around the house but there weren't. Not a one. Clearly, he wasn't into photos. She wondered why. People usually had a few photos dotted around their home, photos of family and loved ones. At the very least, she'd expected a few photos of him with his wife. But there wasn't a single one. All she could think was that he didn't want to be reminded of his marriage, or his dead wife, which was a shame. She loved looking at all the photos of her mother she had on her phone. She'd even had a tribute to her mother tattooed on her wrist with the dates of her birth and death inside a love heart. When you loved someone, you wanted to remember them.

It was a puzzle all right.

Hopefully Georgia could fill in a few of the blanks when Ruby rang her, plus give her a feel for what sort of man her new boss was. A personal connection was much better than the internet. But first she would make herself some coffee with that lovely coffee machine.

There was nothing better than good coffee, Ruby thought as she walked back inside and headed for the kitchen. Coffee always relaxed her, and she needed relaxing after what had been a somewhat stressful morning. But really, it had worked out surprisingly well. Gloria had seemed to like her and the feelings were mutual. And truly, the house was divine. It would be a pleasure living in it and looking after it. On the surface, it was a dream job.

Of course, her satisfaction with the position ultimately rested on the character of her boss. She hoped he would be as nice as he'd sounded on the phone, and not one of those rich, arrogant men she'd met during her working life. Having a lot of money, she'd found, didn't always bring out the best in the male sex.

Such thoughts reminded her to be careful with her appearance during her time here. *Conservative*, Barbara had advised.

I can do conservative, Ruby reassured herself as she switched on the coffee machine.

Okay, so it wasn't her usual style of dressing but no way was she going to do anything to risk this wonderful job. Which meant hair kept up or at least tied back, minimal make-up and jewellery and a very bland wardrobe.

The clothes she wore today were a good start but she would need more. She could hardly wear this outfit every single day, especially once summer got started. It was already very hot and it was only the first week in December. When she rang Georgia she would ask what *she* usually wore during the summer months. And yes, she would subtly question her about what kind of man Sebastian Marshall was.

Ruby wasn't really worried about him, but forewarned was forearmed.

She wasn't to know that fate would conspire against her, making her first meeting with her new boss very awkward indeed.

CHAPTER THREE

WHEN SEBASTIAN EXITED the terminal the heat came as a shock. After spending a fortnight in Europe's winter his body wasn't used to either heat or humidity. Both enveloped him within seconds, making the wait for a taxi very uncomfortable and irritating.

The trip overseas had spoiled him, he realised, the executives of the various companies who wanted to buy his shows sparing nothing in their efforts to woo his agreement to their terms. He'd been chauffeured around everywhere he went, and wined and dined within an inch of his life—not that it had done them much good. Sebastian knew what his shows were worth—especially *Battle at the Bar*—and he'd driven a hard bargain. He would shortly be many million dollars richer, with more money to come. The royalties would roll in for years.

Not that being super rich interested him all that much. After a certain point, what did it gain you really? There was only so much you could spend before it became obscene. He had a lovely home, an excellent wardrobe and a great car. He didn't need a private jet, a yacht, or a holiday home in the Caribbean.

Of course, it was nice to be able to afford five-star restaurants and first-class airfares, along with the best hotels and resorts in the world. Sebastian couldn't deny that he enjoyed the finer things in life. But then, he'd worked hard to be able to afford them. Damned hard.

Still, he would give every cent he had if only Jennifer…

No, no, don't go there, Sebastian warned himself with gritted teeth.

But he was already there, the emotions he'd felt at the time of her cancer diagnosis coming back to haunt him with a vengeance. Not just grief, but bitterness and anger, and that other awful feeling of helplessness. He'd hated that more than anything: that he hadn't been able to *do* anything to save the woman he loved.

Keep looking forward, he lectured himself sternly. *And working hard.* Work was the only thing that kept the memory demons at bay.

He actually loved running Harvest Productions. It had been his saviour, which was a perverse thing to say when his father had had to die for him to inherit the company. But it was strangely true. Sebastian knew that without the challenge he'd faced when confronted with control of a near-insolvent business a few months after Jennifer's death, he would have fallen by the wayside completely. The realisation that he was *needed*, and that he could actually do something to help all those people faced with the prospect of unemployment, had given him the strength to carry on.

'Where you going, mate?' the taxi driver asked as he scooped up Sebastian's luggage.

Sebastian gave himself a mental shake then stepped forward to open the passenger door of the taxi. 'Mosman,' he said as he climbed in.

'Where in Mosman?' the driver asked after he slid in behind the wheel.

Sebastian gave his address, only then remembering that he'd better text Ruby and let her know he was on his way home. He'd taken a flight one day earlier than intended, spending the night in Singapore, being feted by another billionaire who wanted a piece of Harvest Productions. It was amazing how success brought investors flocking. He'd been polite with the man but he hadn't liked him at all, turning down his offers and flying out first thing this morning, landing at Mascot at just after three this afternoon. By the time he got home it would be close to four. Even so, Ruby wasn't expecting him till tomorrow morning.

Not that he thought this would be a problem. They'd exchanged a couple of texts during the past week and she seemed an easy-going kind of girl who had everything in hand and wouldn't be upset by his early arrival.

He quickly sent off a text, explaining the situation, confident of getting a reply before long. Girls these days lived on their phones, didn't they?

The taxi driver chatted away as they headed for town. Sebastian didn't mind and asked the chap what he liked to watch on television. He often did that, gathering honest feedback about what the everyday person liked and didn't like. He was pleased to hear the man's disgruntlement with the current wave of reality shows, which matched Sebastian's feelings exactly. Audiences were getting sick of them and craved more escapist entertainment.

'What do you think of *Battle at the Bar*?' he asked.

'That's one of my favourites,' the man answered as he sped through the harbour tunnel. 'My wife's too. Wouldn't miss an episode for the world. I hope they make another season.'

'I'm sure they will,' Sebastian said a little smugly. They'd already aired four seasons here in Australia and the shooting of the last episode of season five was wrapping up this week. 'Man, it's hot today.' He glanced at the outside temperature on the dashboard. It said thirty-seven.

'They say it's going to be hotter tomorrow.'

'Thank heavens for air conditioning, then.'

'You can say that again.'

Sebastian still hadn't heard back from Ruby, a quick check of his phone showing no messages. His text had gone through but there was no answer. That was odd. He frowned. Maybe he should have contacted her sooner.

The taxi dropped him off with his case, Sebastian giving the man a good tip.

'Thanks, mate,' the driver said, and headed off with a wide smile on his face.

Sebastian unlocked the front gate and wheeled his case along the marble path up to the front door. Once inside, he called out Ruby's name but was greeted by silence. No TV on. No sound at all, except for the air conditioning. It was on downstairs but not upstairs, he soon found out. Sebastian turned it on, throwing his case onto the bed to unpack later when the room was cooler.

It was then that he heard a faint splashing noise coming from outside.

Sebastian moved over to the window, which overlooked the pool, his brain already understanding why Ruby hadn't answered his text. She was in the pool.

And why not? It was blisteringly hot.

Sebastian might have joined her if the woman in the pool hadn't suddenly hauled herself out of the water. For a few seconds, she sat there on the side of the pool, dripping water, before slowly, gracefully, standing up.

Sebastian couldn't help it. He actually groaned, squeezing his eyes shut for a split second before opening them again and just staring.

If ever there was a female body designed to make a man drool, it was Ruby's, especially in that zebra-print bikini she was wearing. Heavens!

It was bad enough when she stood still, but even worse when she began to move, reaching for a nearby towel then lifting a hand to release the clip in her hair. It tumbled down, long black wavy hair, which was in as much abundance as her curves. Watching her walk along the side of the pool, patting herself down with the towel, was an exercise in masochism. Sebastian's male body reacted as most male bodies would, his arousal bringing a surge of dismay.

Sebastian couldn't think of anything worse than having a housekeeper who looked like Ruby. His home was more than his castle. It was his refuge, the only place he could totally relax. How could he relax with *that* sashaying around his house?

Quite attractive was how Gloria had described Ruby over the phone. Talk about an understatement.

Not that he could blame his sister for this situation. *He'd* been the one to hire the girl, sight unseen. He'd mistakenly assumed Ruby was a plain Jane, a homely thirty-year-old spinster who'd spent years looking after her dying mother and now wanted to become a social worker.

It wasn't Gloria's fault. Or Ruby's, for that matter. It was his own stupid fault for jumping to conclusions.

Thank goodness it was only a temporary situation. One day in the not too distant future, Georgia would be back and his life could get back to normal.

Meanwhile…

Sebastian heaved a deeply frustrated sigh before clenching his teeth hard in his jaw and heading downstairs.

CHAPTER FOUR

'RUBY, I PRESUME?'

Ruby's head shot up with a gasp, her eyes widening as she recognised the man standing on the back patio. It was Sebastian Marshall himself, whose images she'd looked up on the Internet just last night.

There was quite a difference, however, between them and the real thing.

First of all, she hadn't realised he was so tall. The photos had all been of him sitting down at a table on television awards night. She saw now that he was well over six feet. He was also even better-looking than she'd originally thought. Talk about tall, dark and handsome!

His photos hadn't done him justice, that was for sure. Then again, they'd all been taken at a distance and in profile. Up close and face on, he was gorgeous, with the kind of strong, manly features that aged well. No one would guess he was forty. His nose was straight and strong, his jawline very square and masculine with a small dimple in his chin. His dark brown hair was cut very short, showing ears that were set close to his head. There were a few lines around his mouth but they didn't detract from his well-shaped lips.

Ruby couldn't stop staring up into his very attractive face, and his even more attractive blue eyes.

So it was impossible for her to miss the narrowing of those eyes. Or the way he began frowning at her.

Automatically, Ruby clasped the towel she was holding

to cover herself more modestly. Her bikini would not be considered risqué when worn on Gold Coast beaches, but it was possibly not the thing to be wearing on first meeting her new boss. She felt half naked, even more so since he was dressed in a business suit, complete with white shirt and tie.

'Goodness me, Mr Marshall!' she exclaimed as she stepped up onto the back patio. 'You frightened the life out of me. You said you wouldn't be home till tomorrow morning.'

'I caught an earlier flight,' he retorted in clipped tones. 'I sent you a text.'

'Really? I'm sorry but I'm sure I didn't get one. When did you send it?' she asked, determined to stay cool, and not become flustered.

'On my way home in the taxi. Clearly, you were in the pool at the time.'

For heaven's sake, she thought a little irritably. *That was a bit late to let me know you were coming home a day early.*

'Yes, I was,' she admitted. 'I've been in there for a while. It's been so hot. Look, I'll just dash inside, have a quick shower and get dressed. Then I'll make you some coffee, okay?'

She already knew from Georgia how much he liked his coffee. And she knew how he liked it. Georgia had also told her that whilst their boss was long on looks he was short on charm.

Ruby could see what she meant.

'I won't be long,' she said as she hurried past him, shivering as her damp skin encountered the cool air inside the house.

Sebastian could not resist turning and watching her walk away from him, her peach-like derriere drawing his eyes, and holding them. Lord, but her body was delicious. Delicious and lush and so sexy it was criminal.

Sebastian suspected his sister had underplayed Ruby's looks because she didn't want to say anything to stop him hiring the girl. She was an incorrigible matchmaker, his sister, always plotting to find him a new wife. He recalled an argument they'd had not that long ago when he'd refused to come to any more of her infernal dinner parties where, naturally, there was always a single female seated next to him, just panting to give him whatever he wanted.

'I know you think I've been living the life of a monk since Jennifer died,' he'd thrown at his sister during that phone call. 'But you're wrong. Yes, I was celibate for a couple of years. Grief will do that to you. But I can assure you that when I want company, I get it.'

'But you never date anyone,' Gloria had argued back. 'You never *bring* a woman to my dinner parties. Or home to your place. Georgia told me. You're always alone.'

'It is possible to have sex without commitment these days, especially when you're travelling overseas and interstate a lot and staying in five-star resorts and hotels. I don't have any trouble.'

'Well, bully for you. But is that all you want, Sebastian?'

'Yes, that's all I want,' he'd stated gruffly. 'I'm not interested in falling in love again or having some woman fall in love with me. I like my life the way it is.'

Which he did. He'd worked out a lifestyle that didn't give him any grief, and he hated the thought of having it messed with. He liked having a sensible middle-aged *plain* woman as his housekeeper. He liked the feeling of peace that greeted him when he came home each evening. He liked living alone, free of potential pain and emotional conflict.

He did *not* like the way he felt at this present moment. Not one little bit.

Sebastian swore, then stalked inside, feeling disgruntled, and, yes, very hot indeed. But he didn't go upstairs and take his suit off. He just took his jacket and tie off, undid the top buttons of his shirt and headed for the kitchen, deciding not to wait for Ruby to make his coffee. He would make his own. He was in the process of doing so when she hurried into the kitchen, dressed in black Bermuda shorts and a black and white striped top, which had a boat neckline and capped sleeves.

Admittedly, with her hair tied back and dressed in ordinary clothes, she wasn't as distractingly desirable as before. But nothing could stop the memory of how she'd looked in that bikini, with her long dark hair spilling over her shoulders. He was unlikely to ever forget it, or what it did to him.

'You should have let me do that,' she said on seeing the coffee was well under way.

'It's all right, Ruby,' he replied, trying to make up in some small way for his earlier abruptness. 'I can make my own coffee.'

'But it's my job, Mr Marshall,' she protested. 'Here. You go and relax somewhere and I'll bring the coffee to you. I know how you like it,' she added with a smile that was as sweet and as perversely sexy as she still was. 'Georgia told me.'

When she came right up to where he was standing by the coffee machine, he caught a whiff of something tantalising. The scent wafting from her person was a mixture of coconut and vanilla. Not perfume as such. Possibly shampoo. Without thinking, he leant closer and inhaled, his nose not far from her hair.

Delicious, he thought once again. Everything about her was delicious. Delicious and dangerous and disturbingly tempting!

Gritting his teeth, he whirled around and strode away before he did or said anything seriously stupid. Ruby was, after all, his housekeeper. Which meant she was strictly off-limits.

So why was it that this thought didn't help dampen what was going on inside him? If anything, her being forbidden fruit made everything harder. Made *him* harder.

'I'll be in my study,' he called over his shoulder. Lord knew what he was going to do in there.

Get a grip! That's what you're going to do, Sebastian. Anyone would think you were a horny teenager, not a forty-year-old man whose libido doesn't run his life.

Still, maybe I should have slept with that woman in London when I had the chance, he thought as he strode into his study and plonked himself down at his desk. Despite what he'd told Gloria, he didn't often indulge in casual sex, only when things got to a critical phase with his male hormones.

Clearly, things were getting to a critical phase, if he were to judge by his body's reactions to Ruby. Okay, she had a great figure and very sexy hair, but Sebastian was used to dealing with seriously beautiful women on a daily basis and, quite frankly, he never had a problem controlling himself around them. Yet the moment he'd laid eyes on Ruby in that bikini he'd got an erection the size of Centrepoint Tower.

Was it just a matter of intense frustration? Of going too long without sex?

He hoped so. Sebastian didn't like the thought that this attraction could be anything but a case of primal lust. To even contemplate anything else was emotionally disturbing, something which always brought with it a deep sense of alarm.

Emotional disturbances and Sebastian were serious enemies.

Thank goodness this was only a temporary annoyance, he reminded himself sternly for the umpteenth time.

CHAPTER FIVE

RUBY DIDN'T KNOW what to make of her new boss, despite Georgia having filled in a few of the pieces of the puzzle that was Sebastian Marshall.

'He's a workaholic,' she'd told Ruby over the phone. 'He lives and breathes Harvest Productions, with little time left over for socialising, unless it's to do with the business.'

When Ruby had asked about the lack of photographs in the house, Georgia had explained that Sebastian—Georgia called him Sebastian—had bought the house fully furnished five years ago and had not changed or introduced a single thing. She'd come with the house, the previous owners having moved overseas to work and sold off everything, including their housekeeper. Georgia said she hadn't minded as she liked working for Sebastian, who was often away and never brought women home.

'Never?' Ruby had asked, surprised.

'Never. His sister told me he never got over his wife's death. Apparently, she was the love of his life and died of cancer. About ten years ago, I think.'

'And there's been no woman since?'

Ruby found that hard to believe. A handsome man like that. And in the prime of his life.

'Not that I know of.'

Ruby wondered about that whilst she finished making the coffee. From what she knew about men—especially successful, good-looking ones—he wouldn't be doing without sex entirely. And if he'd been so devoted to his dead wife, why not put some photos of her around the house? It was as though he were trying to wipe out all memory of her.

The thought persisted that maybe her boss's marriage hadn't been as perfect as his sister imagined. People had believed her own parents' marriage had been great until the ugly truth came out. Her father had been cheating on her mother the whole time she'd been dying of cancer.

Ruby still found that reality hard to stomach.

Shaking her head, she picked up the coffee mug and headed for the study-cum-library, which was at the front of the house.

The door was shut. Ruby knocked.

'Come in,' came the snappy reply.

Ruby sighed, then entered. Sebastian Marshall was sitting behind his desk, a laptop open in front of him. He was staring at the screen, his upward glance both brief and almost dismissive. 'Thanks,' he said, his attention already back on the screen.

Ruby put the mug down by his right elbow then just stood there, waiting for his attention. His eyes eventually lifted to hers, and they were as cool as the air conditioning.

'Yes?' he bit out.

Ruby decided then and there to address his attitude, which she found unacceptable. Unacceptable and unnecessary. Georgia might put up with him being rude but she wasn't going to.

'Mr Marshall,' she began, then hesitated. When he looked at her like that—with hard narrowed eyes—her resolve weakened somewhat.

'Yes?' he persisted.

Ruby gathered herself and went on before she lost her nerve. 'I couldn't help but notice you were displeased to come home and find me in the pool. I was told I could use the pool when you weren't home and I had no idea you were coming home early. I'm sorry I didn't see your text but I never take my phone with me when I swim these days. Last time I did that I dropped it in the water and I had to buy a new phone.' Ruby knew her tongue was running away with her but, Lord, this man was seriously intimidating. Her heart was thudding in her chest and it was hard to hold his penetrating gaze. 'If you don't want me to use the pool at all,' she said, anxiety making her tone sharp, 'then please just say so.'

His sigh was heavy as he leant back in his chair and picked up his coffee, taking a sip before he answered.

'Of course you can use the pool, Ruby,' he said, then took another longer sip of coffee before putting the mug down. 'It wasn't you being in the pool that displeased me. Or you not reading my rather last-minute text.'

'Then what?' she asked, perplexed.

'May I be blunt?'

Was he ever anything else? 'Please.'

'You weren't what I expected...looks-wise.'

Ruby's heart sank. She'd come across a few employers in the past who'd not liked her looks, though they'd been mostly women. The men had never complained.

'I can't help my looks,' she bit out.

'Of course not,' he agreed. 'But you came as a surprise. Gloria said you were quite attractive but you're more than that, Ruby. Especially in a bikini.'

Ruby winced. She supposed that bikini was rather revealing. And whilst she didn't think her face was her fortune, she accepted that her figure was somewhat provocative when half naked.

'I promise I won't wear it again, Mr Marshall.'

'For pity's sake, Ruby, call me Sebastian. Georgia does. And of course you can wear your bikini. Just not when I'm home. And maybe not when I have visitors, which you'll find is reasonably often. Can I assume you know what I do for a living?'

'Yes. Barbara told me.'

He frowned. 'Barbara?'

'The woman who runs Housewives For Hire.'

'Oh, yes. Barbara. Then you know I'm in TV production.'

'Yes...'

'One of my shows is *Battle at the Bar*. I presume you've seen it?' he asked, and picked up his coffee again.

'Just the once,' she said.

'Really? Why just the once?' he demanded to know, banging the mug back down. Clearly, he was quite put out.

She shrugged, all the while trying to think up a reason why she hadn't watched one of the most successful shows on TV more often. 'I don't really like series,' she invented, 'especially crime ones with complicated storylines. If you miss an episode, you get a bit lost.'

'You can always catch up later online.'

'I suppose so,' she admitted, wishing she'd just told him the truth.

'*Battle at the Bar* has won a lot of awards,' he pointed out. 'You should watch it some more. Give it a chance to grow on you. Anyway, that's not why I brought it up. I just wanted to warn you that the star of the show—Zack Stone—often drops by. He's a good friend of mine but he's very fond of pretty girls. He'd probably try to make a pass at you given the chance. But you don't need to worry about him. I'll make sure he behaves himself.'

Ruby laughed. She couldn't help it.

His dark brows beetled into a frown. 'Why the laugh? I'm told he's irresistible to the female sex.'

'Not to me,' she said. 'I don't like men who think they're God's gift to women.' Or men at all much, if truth be told. She'd been through a wild phase when she'd first left home during which she'd gone to too many parties, drunk too much alcohol, and indulged in too much casual sex. She'd finally woken up to herself, however, and stopped before things got out of hand.

After that she'd sworn off men for ages.

But then she'd met Jason…

She'd been working as a receptionist in a hotel on the Gold Coast at the time, filling in for a girl who was away on maternity leave. He'd been a sales representative who stayed at this hotel very regularly. Jason had been movie-star good-looking with blond hair, blue bedroom eyes and buckets of charm to go with it. And he'd made a beeline straight for her.

Ruby had been flattered by his never-ending compliments, despite initially resisting his many requests to take her out. In the end she'd gone for coffee with him and then agreed to go to dinner with him when he was next in town. By then she was very attracted to him and possibly would have gone to bed with him. But thankfully, before he came back, she found out he was married.

To say she was crushed was an understatement, confirming what she already suspected about most men. They simply could not be trusted. But finding out the truth about Jason had the positive effect of turning off her libido entirely. She hadn't had sex for four years and didn't miss it one little bit.

'Just thought I'd warn you,' Sebastian said.

'Thank you, but you needn't worry. Zack Stone won't even get to first base with me.'

'Do you have a boyfriend already?'

'No. No boyfriend.'

'Girlfriend?'

She blinked her surprise at the question, one which no man had ever asked her before.

'No,' she replied.

'I probably shouldn't have asked,' he said, his smile wry.

When their eyes met and held for a long moment, suddenly, something like an electric current zapped across the space from his eyes to hers, revving up her dormant libido, tightening her stomach with the most amazing sexual awareness.

Dismay overwhelmed Ruby as she reached the stunning realisation that she just might want sex again after all. With this man. Her boss!

Ruby smothered a groan as she struggled to gather herself. But gather herself she did.

After all, wanting sex with Sebastian Marshall was only wanting, thank heavens. Ruby believed she could ignore it. Of course she could!

It was as well, though, that he didn't want her back. That much was quite obvious. His concern about her looks had not been personal. It had been professional. He'd been looking out for her, worried that his womanising star might make a pass at her.

'Is that all, Mr Marshall?' she asked, perversely irritated by his own lack of interest.

You should be grateful. Not annoyed.

'Sebastian, remember?'

'Right,' she said, and smiled a stiff smile. 'Is that all, Sebastian?' Lord, but he really was very handsome. And he had a very good body. Without his suit jacket on she could see the breadth of his shoulders. The top two buttons of his shirt were undone, giving her a glimpse of dark hair. She didn't mind a bit of hair on a man's chest. She actually found it sexy. Or she had, once upon a time.

Stop looking at him, she lectured herself. But where else could she look?

'Could you make dinner for eight tonight?' he said.

Ruby took a deep breath. She had to cook him dinner. Which was only logical. She was his housekeeper. But she didn't want to cook him dinner tonight. She needed some time away from him, time to come to terms with the effect he was having on her.

'What would you like?' she asked, surprised at how cool she sounded. Yet she didn't feel cool inside. She felt all jumbled and jumpy.

'Surprise me,' he said and actually smiled up at her. Not a sexy smile. Just a polite one.

Ruby swallowed the huge lump in her throat, thinking that *she* was the one who was surprised. Though the word surprised didn't quite cut it. More like shocked. Stunned. *Shattered.*

Her dream job was turning into a nightmare.

Oh, dear…

CHAPTER SIX

'SOMETHING SMELLS NICE.'

Ruby spun round from the stove top, startled by her boss's sudden appearance in the kitchen. Startled, too, by his compliment. She tried not to stare, but he looked altogether different in casual clothes. Clearly, he'd showered and changed at some stage since she left him in the study a couple of hours ago. His dark hair was still damp, his tall, well-built body now housed in stone-washed jeans and a pale grey T-shirt.

Strangely, she preferred him in his business clothes, perhaps because it made him more out of her league. At the moment he looked like a guy she was allowed to fancy.

And fancy him she did. Big time.

'What are you cooking?' he asked before she could think of something to say.

'Beef stroganoff,' she told him matter-of-factly. 'Surely you've had beef stroganoff before?'

'Possibly. I'm not a foodie.'

'My version is hardly cordon bleu,' she said, wishing he would go back to his former rude self so she didn't have to secretly drool. 'I made it from a packet.'

'Well, it smells great.'

Ruby turned back to stirring, rattled by his unexpected pleasantness, not to mention her increasing awareness of him. Better she not look at the man any more than was strictly necessary. Talking was okay, as long as it wasn't accompanied by ogling.

'It was one of my brothers' favourite meals,' she threw over her shoulder. 'Along with spaghetti bolognese and a lamb roast.'

'I like the sound of all of those,' he said, that gorgeous voice of his making even the simplest compliment sound sexy. 'How many brothers do you have?' he asked, clearly intent on having a chat.

Oh, Lord, she thought, annoyed again by this totally unexpected attraction. Ruby wished he would just take his hunky body back to his study and wait there till she called him for dinner.

But no, that wasn't going to happen, was it? Out of the corner of her eye she saw him pull out one of the kitchen stools and slide onto it. If she was going to stay working for this man, she had no option but to turn round and answer him.

Clicking off the gas ring, she whirled around and dredged up a face that she hoped betrayed nothing but civility.

'Two,' she replied coolly. 'They're twins. Three years younger than me.'

The microwave pinged, letting her know the rice was ready. Good. Now she could serve him dinner and escape to her room.

'Identical?' he asked as she turned away to take the dish out of the microwave.

'No.' She placed the hot dish on a cutting board then looked up at him. 'But very similar. Do you want me to serve your dinner in the dining room or outside on the terrace?'

'I usually have dinner on a tray in my study when I'm alone here in the evenings. That way I can work or watch TV as I eat.'

Ruby should have guessed. Georgia had said he was a workaholic.

'That's fine. You're the boss. I'll just have to find a tray.' And she started rummaging around in the cupboards, banging a few doors as she did so.

Ruby hated the way she was acting. This wasn't like her. She was usually relaxed with people. But not with this man. He made her want to be stroppy. She hated that she fancied him. Hated that he made her heartbeat quicken by just being there.

She noticed him frowning, which in turn made her feel guilty.

'I think I need to apologise,' he said after she'd found a suitable tray.

'For what?' she replied, unsure what he was on about.

'For my attitude when I first came home. I had no right to imply that your looks could pose a problem. Or assume you couldn't handle yourself where Zack is concerned. I can see you're a very capable person who wouldn't accept unwanted attention from any man.'

Ruby was torn between being flattered and still annoyed. Not with him. With herself.

It was an effort to put aside her exasperation and find a small smile from somewhere. 'I have been known to put the odd man or two in his place,' she said, her voice still on the crisp side. 'You really don't have to worry, Sebastian. You're right. I can handle myself. But thank you for the apology. I admit I did feel upset that I hadn't made a good first impression on you.'

Sebastian did his best not to let his face reveal his reaction to her words. He'd come down to the kitchen to smooth things over, knowing full well that he'd been less than welcoming so far. Having a long, cold shower had helped with his frustrated male body, but there was no help for the memory of what had happened when he'd first come home.

No, she *hadn't* made a good first impression. She'd made a very bad, very lasting impression, one that he suspected would torment him for the entire length of her time as his housekeeper. Not her fault, of course, but unfortunate just the same.

It had taken every ounce of his willpower to come in here and act the part of a boss for whom she might actually like to work, instead of the jerk she possibly thought he was. There was no doubt he hadn't made a good first impression on *her*, either. Sebastian was a reasonable judge of body language and he could see Ruby wasn't too happy with him. Which in one way was a good thing. But possibly awkward in the long run. If they were to coexist for the next few months, they had to establish a bearable working relationship. Sebastian had already decided to make himself scarce till Georgia came back but he couldn't be absent all the time. When he was home, however, he was determined to be polite, and pleasant.

'I'm sorry I made you feel that way,' he said. 'Let's start again, shall we?'

Her face showed that she was not going to be won over that easily. Her dark eyes flashed in a way that hinted at something close to annoyance, and her smile looked a little forced.

'But of course,' she agreed stiffly.

'Good. Now I'll just pop downstairs and get myself a bottle of red. I like wine with my meal at night.'

Sebastian was glad to escape down into his wine cellar where the air was almost as frosty as Ruby. His smile was wry as he pulled a bottle of his favourite Merlot from the shelves. If only she knew the R-rated thoughts that kept going through his head about her. No doubt she would quit on the spot.

Which might not be a bad idea. But he could hardly confess to the feelings that had rampaged through his body when he'd first sighted her in that damned bikini, and which he was only now getting under control. Because quitting would not be the only fallout to such a confession.

Sebastian had no intention of saying a single word on the matter, but the irony of the situation appealed to his sometimes dark sense of humour. He was still smiling when he reappeared in the kitchen.

Ruby, however, was not.

She had already set a tray with cutlery, a serviette and a wine glass. The correct wine glass for red, he noted. The only thing missing was the meal.

'Would you like a bread roll with your stroganoff?' she asked crisply.

'No. No dessert either.' Sebastian was suddenly tired of being accommodating. Or perhaps he was just tired. It had been a long and difficult day.

'How long will dinner be?' he asked.

'Not long at all.'

'See you soon, then.'

Swooping up the wine glass, he stalked off to his study. By the time Ruby arrived with the dinner tray he was already on his second glass. The alcohol hit his empty stomach hard, making him tetchy rather than mellow.

'Just put it down here on my desk,' he grumped.

'Right.' She put it down as ordered, her eyes speaking volumes. Clearly, he'd blotted his copybook again.

'What time would you like breakfast in the morning?' she asked in what could only be described as a cool voice. 'Georgia told me you like a cooked breakfast on Saturdays as opposed to weekdays when you just have coffee. She said you make the coffee yourself because you leave for work before most people are awake.'

'True,' he said, thinking Georgia made him sound like

the worst kind of workaholic. 'I like to beat the traffic. But I actually won't need breakfast in the morning, Ruby. I intend to sleep in, then go out for brunch with some work colleagues. We have a lot of catching up to do after my trip. But I'll need dinner tomorrow night. At seven-thirty rather than eight. That spaghetti bolognese you mentioned will do fine.'

'Very well.'

'Did Georgia also mention you have Sundays off?' he asked, already looking forward to a day when she wouldn't be around.

'Yes.'

'Good. That's all for now.' As he dropped his eyes and picked up his fork, Sebastian was sure he heard her sigh. Not a big sigh. A small exasperated sigh. But he didn't look up. He just started eating, refusing to feel in any way guilty for his autocratic manner. He was, after all, not Ruby's friend. He was her boss. And Sebastian aimed to keep acting like a boss for the duration of her stay. That way, he might just stay sane.

CHAPTER SEVEN

RUBY BREATHED A sigh of relief when Monday morning came. Sebastian was up and gone with the dawn, leaving her with no one to please but herself for the day. Janice arrived at nine to clean, followed shortly after by the guy who picked up the laundry each Monday morning. Ruby had intended to help Janice upstairs after he left but was stuck downstairs answering phone call after phone call.

First there were her brothers, each making polite enquiries about the job, as well as asking her if she wanted to join them for Christmas lunch at the restaurant they went to every year and which required early booking. Ruby hadn't returned to Sydney for Christmas during the last five years and had been rather looking forward to a traditional Christmas at one of their places. She hated the thought of being the fifth wheel in their happy foursome and had declined their kind invitation, making some excuse about having to be on deck at the Marshall household.

Before she could surrender to guilt over this little white lie, Barbara rang from Housewives For Hire, wanting to know how she was getting along. No sooner had she finished with Barbara than Georgia rang with similar questions.

She told all of them the same thing: that she was fine, the job was fine, her boss was fine, and that she didn't foresee any problems. And brother, was that a *big* white lie!

Saturday had been sheer torture, especially after Sebastian

came home around five and went swimming in the pool for over an hour. Which hadn't been too bad until he'd called out to her, asking her to bring him a towel, which he'd obviously forgotten. She had done as ordered, of course, which would have been okay if he'd stayed in the pool, but he'd chosen that moment to climb out.

Keeping her eyes off his hunky male body in those revealing trunks had been impossible. Lord, but he was one well-built man!

Hopefully, she'd hidden her feelings from him, feelings that she hadn't experienced in years. Not since Jason, who admittedly had stirred her female hormones somewhat. She'd been very attracted to Jason, but this thing with Sebastian was on another level entirely. This was nothing but sheer lust, as opposed to just attraction.

Ruby accepted ruefully that lust wasn't one of the seven deadly sins for nothing. Talk about tempting!

The only plus to the weekend was having Sunday off. She would have spent it visiting her brothers but they had both been having a weekend away at some hotel in the Blue Mountains, information she'd gleaned from Facebook, so she'd driven out to Parramatta where she'd spent the day in the mall, attempting to do some Christmas shopping. But not very successfully. She'd had trouble making up her mind so in the end had bought nothing. After that she'd gone to a movie, not arriving back at Mosman till late. Fortunately, Sebastian had been in bed by then.

Monday morning had come as a relief with Sebastian gone to work. Out of sight was out of mind! Though all that lying over the phone had put her boss firmly back into Ruby's thoughts again. After finishing with the phone calls, she had just put some coffee on when her phone rang again, her heart jumping when she saw it was Sebastian.

'Good morning, Sebastian,' she said, determined to act normal and not like the uptight creature she was in danger of becoming around him. After all, he couldn't hear her heart thumping away inside her chest, or see the X-rated images running around in her head, the ones that had plagued her after that incident by the pool.

'Hi,' he said. 'Everything okay with you?' he asked sharply, perhaps picking up some kind of vibe.

'Yes, of course. Everything's fine.' That word again. 'What's up?'

'Zack Stone will be coming over for a while this evening,' he announced. 'We'll need dinner.'

'Of course. What would you like?'

'Seafood. Half a dozen oysters each followed by barramundi and salad.'

Whilst Ruby admired a man who knew what he wanted, she was irritated by her boss's ongoing brusqueness. For a while there at the weekend he'd been nice and apologetic, but that hadn't lasted for long. 'What about dessert?' she asked.

'Something chilled. The weather's still damned hot and we'll be eating outside. Zack likes fresh air. Oh, and get a bottle of white wine from the cellar to complement. Actually, make that two bottles of white wine. I know I can trust you to pick well. I saw from your résumé that you've worked in plenty of restaurants and bars.'

'Indeed I have,' she said, thinking she'd met lots of men like him too. Talk about arrogant! But that was what came with men who were too rich, too good-looking and too successful. They simply couldn't help themselves. She supposed Zack Stone would be just as obnoxious.

'Anything else?' she asked archly.

'No. Oh, yes. I'm off to Surfers Paradise next weekend. I leave on Friday and won't be back till Monday so that leaves you free to do as you please over the weekend.'

Thank goodness, she thought. *Now I won't have to se-*

*cretly ogle you all weekend. Or want to slap your face
every five minutes.*

Unrequited lust, she'd come to accept, could make the
sufferer extremely tetchy.

'Actually, that'll be great,' she said brightly. 'I have some
studying to do. What are you doing in Surfers Paradise?'
she couldn't resist asking. 'Business or pleasure?'

His hesitation to answer told her what she needed to
know. People rarely went to Surfers Paradise for business.

'Just relaxing,' he said at last. 'Zack has an apartment
up there which I use occasionally. It's not far from the ca-
sino. I enjoy playing Blackjack.'

Possibly he was telling the truth but Ruby doubted he'd
be alone for long. Casinos were notorious pick-up places.

Ruby knew she had no right to be jealous, but she was
all the same. She'd known instinctively that a man like Sebastian wouldn't do without sex. It wasn't natural.

A fantasy zoomed into her head in which he asked her
to go with him...to spend the whole weekend with him. In
bed, of course.

Just the thought excited her.

Not that he would ever ask her. Lord no! It was just
a fantasy. Or possibly wishful thinking. It was obvious
Sebastian was not the sort of man who did that kind of
thing. Which was just as well. She'd come to Sydney to
make an independent life for herself, not to fall into bed
with her boss.

Get a grip, girl!

'Is Mr Stone going with you?' she asked, pleased to have
herself under control again.

'That chick magnet?' he scoffed. 'Thankfully no. I'm
just there for the gambling.'

'Of course,' she said, her comment having a decidedly
dry edge to it.

He didn't say a word for several seconds. But when he

spoke his voice sounded amused. 'I fear my new house-keeper is a cynic.'

'I fear you could be right,' Ruby retorted before she could think better of it.

'Good. Then you won't fall for Zack's charms.'

'Like I said before, Sebastian, I'm not a fan of that show, or its anti-hero.' Her voice was extra cool, a habit of Ruby's when a man assumed she was a pushover.

'Unfortunately, it's required viewing for all my staff,' he insisted. 'I get the best market research that way.'

'Really.' Thank goodness he didn't produce erotica, then, otherwise she might volunteer for more in-depth market research.

Ruby flushed at the way her mind kept going. Yet was it a flush of shame, or excitement? There was no doubt she was enjoying their repartee.

'What about your other shows?' she asked him.

'I'll give you a list tonight. They are *all* required viewing for employees of Harvest Productions.'

'That's a bit draconian, don't you think?'

'It's just for feedback,' he said.

'Oh, all right, then. Give me the list tonight and I'll look them up.'

'I'll do that. And I will appreciate your opinions, Ruby. You're obviously a very smart woman. Bye for now.'

Ruby hugged the compliment to herself as she hung up. Compliments about her intelligence had been in short supply in Ruby's life so far. Yet she *was* intelligent. She knew she was. Okay, so she hadn't covered herself with glory at school after her mother was diagnosed with cancer, and all her jobs so far had been on the menial side. But that didn't mean she didn't have a good brain.

It pleased her that Sebastian recognised she was smart. And it pleased her, in a perverse way, that he wasn't bowled over by her so-called sexy looks. No woman wanted to be valued for her face or figure alone...though it wasn't a pleasant experience to be dead plain either, as she'd been as a teenager. Ruby hadn't blossomed until after her mother had died. She'd lost some weight and grown her hair, after which she'd finally snared her first boyfriend. Bailey, the rat.

She still wasn't conventionally pretty. But that didn't seem to matter. Men took one look at her and wanted her.

At least, a lot of men did. Clearly, Sebastian wasn't one of them. Which, she supposed, was good news. Yes, he recognised her attractions but obviously didn't feel compelled to act on them. Then again, there was clearly something wrong with him if Georgia had said he never brought a woman home. Never!

The man was a cold-blooded robot, Ruby decided. An emotionless machine. Either that or he was so damaged by grief over his wife's death, that he'd turned off his libido for good.

No, no, that wasn't right. If that was the case then he wouldn't be going away next weekend.

Ruby rolled her eyes, irritated with herself for thinking about the man so much. She had more important things to do. Like going shopping and buying fresh ingredients for tonight's dinner, along with something suitable to wear in front of a TV star.

CHAPTER EIGHT

'DO ME A FAVOUR, Zack,' Sebastian said as he approached his home. 'Try not to hit on my housekeeper tonight, okay?'

Zack threw him a puzzled look. 'And why would I do that? I never have before. Georgia is safe and sound.'

'I'm sure she is. But Georgia's in Melbourne, looking after her sister, who was in a car accident. I have a temporary housekeeper at the moment. Her name is Ruby. And she's a different kettle of fish from Georgia.'

'Really?'

'Yes, really. Younger. Attractive. And unfortunately single.'

'I see.'

'You don't actually,' Sebastian said ruefully. 'But you will.'

'So why am I getting warned off? You want her for yourself, is that it?'

Sebastian laughed. He couldn't help it.

'No,' he lied. 'You know very well I never get involved with my employees.'

'Or anyone else, for that matter,' Zack shot back.

'That's not true. I just like to keep my sex life away from home.'

'Far away from home, from what I've gathered. But we're getting off the point. Why aren't I allowed to chat this Ruby up? You said she was single.'

'She's also a *nice* girl.'

Now Zack laughed. 'Too nice for me, is that what you mean?'

'Yes,' Sebastian said, though he delivered the barb with a smile.

'Lovely,' Zack growled. 'My best friend thinks I'm a bastard.'

'I didn't say that,' Sebastian said, 'but you are a bit of a bad boy with women.'

Zack nodded. 'True,' he said. 'But it works for me, Seb. Bad boys often get the girl.'

'Yes, so I've noticed. Just not this time, please. Keep your bad-boy act buttoned up tonight and try to act like a good guy.'

'Fine. How boring.' His sigh was the melodramatic affectation of an actor. 'Very well. I guess I can channel my inner altar boy for one night.'

'Good,' Sebastian said as he angled into his driveway and headed down to the garages. Because he knew he couldn't stand it if Ruby fell for Zack's charm. And he could be charming. *Very* charming.

Sebastian's stomach tightened with tension as he made his way up the internal staircase, Zack hot on his heels.

'Is she a good cook?' Zack asked.

'Very,' Sebastian threw over his shoulder.

'That's good. I can at least enjoy the food, if not the company.'

Sebastian ground to a halt, then spun round to face his friend. 'What do you mean by that?' he demanded to know, his deep voice echoing in the cement-rendered staircase.

Zack's ruggedly handsome face creased into a wry smile. 'Can you hear yourself? You've been like a bear with a sore head all day.'

Sebastian sighed. 'Sorry. Business worries.'

'Like what? Your trip overseas went well. What have you got to worry about?'

'I guess I'm just a natural worrier.'

'That you are. You should be more like me. Nothing worries me.'

'So I've noticed. But we can't all be like you, Zack. Some of us actually have consciences.'

'Ah, so that's the problem. You do fancy this Ruby but you're her boss.'

Sebastian pursed his lips. To lie or not to lie? In truth he was sick of lying. And pretending. Last weekend had been hell. He shouldn't have come home early and even more stupidly gone swimming. Though it had seemed a good idea at the time. Then, to cap off his stupidity, he'd forgotten to take a towel with him. The way Ruby had looked at him when she'd brought him a towel—as if he was a complete idiot—was etched in his mind.

'Well, do you fancy her or not?' Zack prompted impatiently.

'I suppose I do,' he admitted at last.

'Then why didn't you just say so, for Pete's sake?'

'Because I don't *want* to fancy her,' Sebastian snapped. He didn't want to fancy *any* woman. That was the truth of the matter. After Jennifer's death he'd vowed never to become emotionally involved with another woman. Not as long as he lived.

Not that he was emotionally involved with Ruby. Lord, no. He felt sure he knew exactly what was eating away at him. It was nothing more than lust. Though given she was living in his house, that could develop into a dangerous situation as the weeks went on.

'Thankfully, she's only my temporary housekeeper,' he ground out. 'In a few months, she'll be gone. In the meantime…'

'In the meantime?' Zack asked with raised eyebrows.

'I would prefer not to think of her in your bed.'

Zack smiled. 'I can appreciate that. Nothing worse than the object of your affections being seduced by another man.'

'She is *not* the object of my affections. Just my hormones.'

'Then perhaps you should do something about those hormones. Oh, yes, you already are, aren't you? That's why you're off to Surfers next weekend. Plenty of hot babes up there.'

'You'd know,' Sebastian said.

Actually, getting laid wasn't his chief reason for going away. He just wanted to put some distance between himself and Ruby. He certainly didn't want a repeat of last weekend. Of course, if some hot babe made a line for him, it might be wise to succumb. Though, damn it all, sleeping with anyone other than Ruby did not appeal.

He was damned if he did and damned if he didn't.

Sebastian's sigh held frustration. 'I suggest we get ourselves inside before Ruby wonders where we are.'

CHAPTER NINE

RUBY HAD BEEN wondering where they were for some time. She'd heard Sebastian's car go down the drive, followed by the whirr of the garage doors, and she'd expected them to make an appearance shortly afterwards. But a few minutes had gone by and still no show. The door from the stairwell remained steadfastly closed.

The delay did nothing for her sudden attack of nerves.

Racing down to her bedroom, she checked her appearance, one glance in the wall mirror bringing a satisfied sigh to her lips. She wasn't wearing any make-up tonight but her olive skin and her dark, heavily lashed eyes did not suffer from a lack of enhancement. And the black shirtdress she'd bought, thinking it was perfect housekeeper fare, somehow didn't look as dowdy and plain as she'd hoped. It did, in fact, look very smart.

She sprayed her hair, which was trying to escape the tight bun she'd imprisoned it in. Feeling more confident, she thought, *If that actor bloke tries to chat me up, I'll put him in his place, quick-smart. I'm good at that!*

No sooner had she finished with her hair than she heard Sebastian calling out to her from the kitchen.

'Ruby, where are you?'

'Right here,' she said as she hurried from her room, smoothing down her skirt with clammy hands on the way.

Sebastian's guest looked her up and down, his icy blue eyes showing curiosity rather than lechery. He really was an attractive man, but not a patch on Sebastian, who was seriously handsome. In her eyes, anyway. She adored the way her boss looked tonight in his grey business suit, especially with that white shirt and red tie. Zack, on the other hand, was wearing jeans and a black singlet top, which showed off his heavily tattooed arms. His dark brown hair was too long, in Ruby's opinion, and rather messy, whereas Sebastian's dark brown hair was always superbly groomed in that short-back-and-sides cut, which she liked. Sebastian looked like a gentleman whereas Zack looked every inch a bad boy.

'Nice to meet you, Ruby,' Zack said when Sebastian introduced her, 'Sebastian has been speaking highly of you. Says you're a great cook.'

Goodness, she thought. No smarmy comments, or long meaningful gazes. Just normal eye contact and polite compliments.

'That's nice of him,' she said, relieved. 'I'm okay but no cordon bleu chef. I hope you like seafood.'

'Of course he does,' Sebastian said, not looking at her at all as he removed his jacket and tie. 'I wouldn't have asked for it, otherwise. Come on, Zack, we'll have a pre-dinner drink in my study. Ruby,' he added with a quick look her way, 'let us know when you're ready to serve.'

And just like that they were gone, leaving Ruby wanting to strangle Sebastian for she knew not what. For not fancying her, she supposed. Still, she figured she should be grateful that Zack Stone wasn't going to be a pest this evening.

But she didn't feel grateful for anything at that moment. She just felt peeved, even more peeved when she called the men to dinner half an hour later and neither of them said anything about the table, which she'd gone to great pains to set beautifully.

By the time Sebastian complimented her on her choice of wine she was in no mood to be gracious. Her smile felt forced, her movements as she set the oysters down in front of them decidedly brisk.

'Glad you like it,' she said, then retreated to the kitchen before she showed her displeasure.

They disposed of the oysters quite quickly but seemed happy to sit and drink the wine till the main course was ready. The evening had turned balmy after the suffocating heat of the day. The sky was clear above and the stars had come out. Not that Ruby took much time to look at them. She was too busy cooking the barramundi, which was not an easy fish to get just right. Nothing worse than overcooked fish.

Luckily, it all turned out well. Sebastian's guest was especially complimentary. The walnut salad and fresh bread rolls she served with the barramundi were also a hit, even with Sebastian, which went some way to improving Ruby's mood. A more genuine smile lit her face as she removed their empty plates.

'How long before you want dessert?' she asked when she saw Sebastian open the second bottle of wine, which had been chilling in the ice bucket next to the table.

'Leave it for half an hour,' he told her, and was in the process of pouring them both a glass of wine when his phone rang.

'Damn it,' he growled. 'Should have turned it off.'

'You can always let it go to voicemail,' Zack said.

'Better not. It's my sister. She wouldn't actually ring me unless it was important.'

Ruby had a sudden premonition that somehow this phone call would affect her, and not in a good way. She wasn't sure how till Sebastian rose to his feet.

'I'll take it inside,' he said, and left her alone with Zack.

Uh-oh, Ruby thought as she cast their visitor a wary glance.

'Sit down, Ruby,' the man himself said and gestured to

the chair adjacent to him. 'Would you like a glass of wine? You've done nothing but work all night. And possibly all day, by the look of this table.'

'No, I don't want any wine,' she told him, and made no move to sit down.

Zack smiled. 'No need to stress,' he said. 'Your boss has already given me strict orders not to try anything. He thinks you're far too nice for a bastard like me.'

'Oh!' she exclaimed. 'How rude of him to say such a thing!'

'Maybe, but he's quite right. You *are* far too nice for a bastard like me. Now, go and get yourself a glass.'

Ruby decided then and there that she liked Zack Stone. She didn't lust after him, however, which was just as well since he had a charm that she could see would be dangerous to the wrong woman.

When she returned with a glass and sat down, Zack didn't fill the glass straight away. Instead he reached out and took hold of her wrist—not in a lecherous way—and turned it over.

'Who's Ava?' he asked as he stared at the small heart-shaped tattoo.

'My mother,' she replied thickly.

He frowned at the dates before letting her wrist go and looking up at her.

'You must have been young when she died.'

'Nineteen,' she admitted, then waited for him to ask more questions.

But he didn't.

'My mother died when I was young too,' he said at last. 'But not as young as you.'

'Please don't tell Sebastian,' she said quickly, glancing over her shoulder lest her boss suddenly reappear.

'Why not?'

Ruby sighed. 'It's complicated.'

'Fair enough. We all have our secrets. And yours is harmless enough. Let's have some wine.'

Ruby was glad for the conversation to move on. Glad too of the soothing effect of the alcohol. It still amazed her how upset she could get when she thought of her mother's death. Though maybe it was her father's behaviour at the time and afterwards that kept her distress alive. Men could be such bastards.

She stared at Zack over the rim of her wine glass and wondered what his secrets were. Something deep and dark, she suspected. But any musings about her guest were cut dead by Sebastian stomping back to the table, his face grim.

'Well, my weekend at Surfers is off,' he growled as he slumped into his seat and swept up his wine glass.

'Why?' Zack asked before Ruby could. 'What's happened?'

'My mother's birthday is what happened. It's next Saturday. Gloria was going to take Mum out for the day but her doctor husband has to go to some medical conference in Adelaide and he wants her to go with him. Which means yours truly has to do the honours.'

Ruby rolled her eyes at him. 'Is that all?' she said as she rose to her feet. 'You should be thankful you have a mother.'

He did look a little shamefaced at this comment. 'Yes, yes, I know that. But she's just so difficult to please. Never likes anything on restaurant menus. She used to drive my father mad when he was alive. He liked interesting food. But not Mum. She prefers the plainest fair.'

'Then why not bring her here and I'll cook her something she likes?' Ruby suggested before it sank in that it would be better if he took his mother out for the day. The whole day!

'What a good idea,' Zack said. 'This is a great girl you have here, Sebastian.'

Ruby could have sworn that Sebastian threw his friend

a decidedly caustic glance. Ruby realised he was probably thinking Zack was trying to butter her up.

Sebastian sighed. 'Thank you for the offer, Ruby. That's very kind of you.'

His warm compliment brought a sudden flush of heat to her whole body.

'Time for dessert?' she asked, her voice going a little high, as it did when she was agitated.

'Absolutely,' Sebastian said. 'What is it?'

'New York-style cheesecake. What do you want with it, ice cream or cream?'

'I'll have ice cream,' Zack said before Sebastian answered. 'And plenty of it. This damned heat is getting to me.'

'It's supposed to storm tomorrow,' Ruby told him.

'Good.'

'Not good,' Sebastian snapped. 'We're shooting outdoors tomorrow.'

'I'm sure we'll cope. It might add some atmosphere to the episode if it rains. The way it is, that scene is a bit bland.'

Sebastian frowned. 'You think so? I thought it was intense.'

'It didn't read that way to me.'

'Why didn't you say so earlier?'

'I would have, but we were discussing other things, remember?'

Ruby decided it was time to go. 'Sorry to interrupt, but what do you want with *your* cheesecake, Sebastian?'

He stared at her for a long moment before a wryly amused smile quirked the corner of his mouth. 'I'll have what Zack's having,' he said, bringing a laugh from Zack.

'Very funny, Seb.'

Ruby didn't think it was funny, the quote from the well-known romantic movie causing her mind—and her body—

to zing with the type of sexual tension that was difficult to ignore.

Ruby knew there would be nothing fake about her orgasms if she ever went to bed with her boss. Not that she ever would. But it was still a struggle to focus on the present moment and not some ridiculous fantasy.

'That reminds me,' she said, looking straight at Sebastian with a cool, businesslike expression. 'You didn't give me the list of your shows like you said you would.'

'Sorry. I forgot. I'll get my PA to email you the list and the screening times tomorrow.'

'Right,' she said, and went to get the desserts, feeling ridiculously hurt that he'd forgotten. It was silly really. Very silly. But then this whole business of being attracted to Sebastian was silly. He wasn't interested back. Yet, in that perverse way of human nature, this only seemed to make him even more attractive to her.

Ruby had spent the last few years fending off the attentions of the male sex. It was ironic that the one man she wanted to want her, *didn't* want her.

She supposed she should be grateful for that. Sebastian wanting her would have caused trouble in the end because she would have been faced with the dilemma of working women everywhere. Should she or shouldn't she?

Sleeping with the boss was never a good idea. *Never!*

Nevertheless, it was a wickedly exciting idea when Sebastian was the boss in question. Ruby should have been shocked at herself for even thinking about it. But she did think about it. Endlessly. And she wasn't shocked. She was aroused.

Oh, dear, she thought as she spooned the ice cream onto the plates of cheesecake, stuffing a big spoonful into her overheated mouth at the same time.

Do try to cool it, Ruby. You're on a good wicket here. Don't do anything to spoil it!

'This looks delicious,' Zack said when she put his dessert in front of him. 'Did you cook it yourself?'

'No. I bought it from this wonderful bakery not far from here. It's where I got the bread rolls from too.'

'A good bakery is worth its weight in gold,' Zack said. 'So is a good housekeeper,' he added. 'You're a lucky man, Sebastian.'

Sebastian's lips pressed grimly together as he cast his friend an exasperated glance.

'I do know that, Zack,' he bit out. 'Ruby is a find, that's for sure. That's all for now, thank you, Ruby. We won't have coffee. We'll just finish off this wine.'

'Okay,' she said, and traipsed back to the kitchen, not sure whether or not she was pleased with all those compliments. There was something…odd…about them, as though Zack and Sebastian had some secret agenda going on involving her. She couldn't think what. Maybe it was all in her imagination. There was a lot going on in her imagination, all of it about Sebastian.

Ruby stacked the dishwasher slowly, her head going round and round with frustrating thoughts. When she heard the men come in from outside and walk towards the front of the house, she returned to clean off the rest of the table. She heard the front door bang shortly afterwards and was in the process of making herself some coffee—which didn't keep her awake like most people—when Sebastian made an appearance. Alone. Clearly, Zack had taken a taxi home.

'Did Zack make a nuisance of himself when I was taking that call?' were his first words.

Ruby turned from the coffee machine to eye her grim-looking boss. Lord, but those blue eyes of his could go quite dark when he was angry.

'Not at all,' she replied. 'He was very nice. Quite the gentleman, really.'

Those eyes narrowed further, his high forehead bunching into a frown. 'You *like* him,' he said, almost accusingly.

'Yes, I do.'

'I did warn you about him.'

'Sebastian, stop,' she said firmly. 'I like Zack, but not in that way.'

'I find that hard to believe. Most women drool over him.'

'Then I'm not most women. I assure you, he's not my type. On top of that, I'm just not interested in men at the moment.' Just one man in particular. 'I've come back to Sydney to study for a degree. I want a career, not a boyfriend. Men cause complications.'

'You don't want to get married?'

'No. Marriage is not for me.'

His head tipped to one side as he studied her. 'Why is that, Ruby?'

'That's a very personal question,' she told him with more than a touch of anger.

It brought him up short. 'You're right. It's none of my business. I apologise.'

'Accepted. Do you want coffee?'

'God, no. I've already got enough to keep me awake tonight. By the way, thanks for offering to cook dinner for my mother next Saturday night. That was very kind of you.'

Their eyes met and Ruby's heart melted with that squishy feeling she always got when anyone talked about kindness, and mothers.

'My pleasure,' she said thickly. 'Do you know what foods your mum likes most?'

'Not really. Give Gloria a ring tomorrow and ask her.'

'I'll do that.'

A rather long look passed between them, a look that had Ruby's heart pounding behind her ribs.

'Is there anything else?' she asked at last, just to break the awkward silence.

'No,' he said brusquely. 'I'm off to bed to try to get some sleep. I have an extra early call tomorrow. Goodnight.'

And he was gone, leaving Ruby to stare after him with a mixture of longing and curiosity. What a strange man he was. One minute caring about her welfare, the next dismissing her abruptly. She decided then and there that when she spoke to his sister tomorrow, she would try to find out a little bit more about him, and about his late wife.

CHAPTER TEN

'RUBY!' GLORIA EXCLAIMED. 'How nice to hear from you. I hope there's nothing wrong.'

'No, no,' Ruby replied. 'Unless you count the rain. Isn't it strange? We were all dying of the heat and praying for rain, then when it comes, it's annoying.'

'I know exactly what you mean. Janice was complaining about it this morning. Said she hates having to use the dryer all the time instead of hanging the washing out on the line.'

For a split second, Ruby wondered why Gloria was talking about Janice's washing, till she remembered Janice was Gloria's cleaner as well as Sebastian's.

'I don't have a clothes line here,' Ruby said. 'I send all the washing out, as per Georgia's instructions.'

'Lucky you.'

'They do a brilliant job, I have to admit. And it saves me a lot of ironing. Anyway, Gloria, the reason I'm calling is because I've offered to cook your mother a special birthday dinner here on Saturday night and I wanted to find out what sort of food she liked.'

'Goodness! That's brave of you. Mum's hard to please where food is concerned. I usually take her to a buffet where she can pick what she likes. She's very fussy.'

'Perhaps I should give her a call and ask her personally what her favourite meal is.'

'Actually, I think that's an excellent idea. Her number's in your house phone, under Frieda Marshall.'

'Right. So is there anything else I should know about her?'

Gloria chuckled. 'So much I don't know where to start. Just make sure the table setting is pretty and use the dining table inside. She hates insects almost as much as she hates the heat.'

Ruby frowned. 'You make her sound like a grumpy old woman.'

'She's not. Not really. Just hasn't got enough to think about. But she'll love this personal attention. Trust me on that. Thank you so much, Ruby. You're very thoughtful.'

'Just trying to help my boss out really. He seemed in a bit of a panic about it all.'

'Really? That doesn't sound like Sebastian.'

'Perhaps panicky is an exaggeration. More like put out that he couldn't go to the Gold Coast for the weekend.'

'He was going up to the Gold Coast for the weekend?'

'He *was*.'

'He never said. What was he going there for?'

Ruby realised this was the opening to find out some more information about Sebastian but the words got stuck in her throat. Which was just as well, for it would sound as if she was prying, and Gloria was no fool. She would put two and two together and conclude that Ruby fancied Sebastian. Which, unfortunately, she still did.

'I have no idea,' Ruby said with feigned indifference. 'I'd better go and ring your mum. I'm off to the supermarket later and I'll want to know what to get.'

After they said their goodbyes, Ruby rang the number for Frieda Marshall straight away.

'Hello?' came the slightly quavering answer.

Gosh. She sounded as if she was ancient. Yet she couldn't be all that old. Seventy perhaps?

'Is that Mrs Marshall? Mrs Frieda Marshall?'

'Yes,' she replied in the same wobbly voice. 'Who's this? You're not Georgia.'

Ruby realised that Georgia's name must have come up on the caller ID. She was, after all, using the house phone.

'No. I'm Ruby. Sebastian's new housekeeper. Georgia was called away to a family emergency and I'm standing in until she gets back.'

Frieda gasped. 'A family emergency? What kind of family emergency?'

Ruby explained the situation, all the while amazed that Sebastian hadn't thought to tell his mother what had happened.

'Poor Georgia,' the woman murmured. 'And poor Sebastian. He'll be lost without her. Who's going to organise his firm's Christmas party? It's not long till Christmas.'

'That's all under control,' Ruby informed her, thankful that it was. 'Georgia booked the caterers in advance and all I have to do is make sure the house is clean.'

It took Ruby a good five minutes to worm out of Frieda what she would like for her birthday dinner. What she wanted—she said rather sheepishly—was rissoles.

'Rissoles?' Ruby echoed, thoroughly taken aback.

'Yes. Beef rissoles,' Frieda said eagerly. 'And mashed potatoes. Lovely creamy mashed potatoes. The cook here is all right but her mashed potatoes are always lumpy.'

'I make good creamy mashed potatoes,' Ruby told her with a catch in her throat. It had been one of the foods her mother had been able to manage when she was on chemo. Ruby closed her eyes for a long moment before blinking them open again.

'And what about dessert?' she went on. 'Any favourites there?'

'I really shouldn't eat dessert. I've put on a few pounds lately.'

'But you must have dessert. It's your birthday. Come on, Mrs Marshall, it's your special day. You deserve a treat.'

'Oh,' the old lady said with a happy sigh. 'What a lovely

thing to say. All right, then,' she went on, sounding less trembly now. 'I adore lemon meringue pie and I haven't had one in years. Do you think you could buy one somewhere?'

'Buy one? I suppose I could try, but I'd prefer to make one fresh.' Ruby was confident she could find a recipe on the Internet.

'Are you sure? I know they're a bit fiddly to make. My mother used to make them when I was a girl and she always complained.'

'I'm a good cook, Mrs Marshall. I'll cope.'

'You are kind. And do call me Frieda.'

'Thank you. Much better than Mrs Marshall. Now, what time do you like to eat, Frieda?'

'Not too late. I get tired.'

'Would you rather have lunch?'

'No. I like the idea of dinner.'

'Okay. What say I get Sebastian to pick you up at five-thirty? You can have a pre-dinner drink with your son, then dinner will be ready at six-thirty. How's that?'

'Sounds perfect. But you might have to buy some sherry for my pre-dinner drink. Sebastian won't have any. He never has any.'

'I'll get some in. What kind of sherry? Dry, sweet or cream?'

'Cream.'

'And what would you like to drink with your dinner?'

Frieda hesitated before answering. 'Er…could you buy a bottle of spumante? Sebastian won't have any of that in the house, either.'

No, he wouldn't. Ruby could see by his cellar that he was a bit of a wine snob, like most wealthy men. They looked down their noses at drinks like spumante.

'Any particular brand?' she asked.

'No. Any bottle will do. They all taste the same, don't they?'

Ruby knew this wasn't true and decided to buy the most expensive.

'Can you think of anything else you might like, Frieda?'

'No, not really. I've already given you a lot of work. But thank you so much.'

'My pleasure. I'll see you Saturday, then.'

'Saturday. Yes. Oh, how exiting. I'll have to go and tell the girls. Bye, love. And thank you again.'

Ruby stood still for a long moment after she clicked off. Love. She'd called her *love*, which had been her mother's favourite endearment.

Oh, dear…

Ruby forcibly straightened her shoulders then went to pick up her tablet to look up recipes for lemon meringue pie. The rissoles she could manage with her eyes closed—her brothers adored rissoles—but the pie might have to have a dry run on Friday because she wanted everything to be perfect for Frieda, and not just because she was Sebastian's mother, but because it was her birthday. And everyone deserved to be spoiled on their birthday.

CHAPTER ELEVEN

RUBY WAS IN the fresh vegetable aisle of the supermarket when her phone rang. Her heart jumped when she saw the caller identity. Jumped, then raced.

'Sebastian,' she answered with creditable cool. 'Hi.'

'Hi to you too. I've just had a call from my mother. She said you rang and asked her what she'd like to eat on Saturday night.'

'Yes, I did. Is there a problem with that?'

'No, of course not. She was very complimentary about you. Said she prefers you to Georgia.'

'Really?'

'Yes. Really.'

'What about you?' Ruby asked cheekily before she could think better of it. 'Do you prefer me to Georgia?'

His hesitation gave her the answer to her stupid question. Or it did until he sighed.

'You both have different qualities, Ruby. Georgia certainly never cooked my mother a birthday dinner. As I said last night, you're a very kind person.'

Ruby was glad he couldn't see her blush this time. Or the way his compliment affected her.

'She's sweet, your mum. By the way, how old is she?'

'Seventy-three. Why do you ask?'

'She sounded fragile,' she said. Or she had, at first.

'That's a bit of an act,' Sebastian said. 'She's as healthy as a horse.'

'I see. Still, I did wonder why she wasn't living with you. It's not as though you don't have the room.'

Sebastian's laugh was dry. 'My mother would never live with me. She says I'm a misery guts. Not to mention a workaholic. She told me she'd be talking to the walls after a while, since I'm never at home.'

'Oh. What about Gloria?'

'God, no. Gloria has two teenage boys. Mum couldn't stand the noise.'

'Have either of you actually offered?'

'We both did and she refused. Look, she likes living in the retirement village. She has lots of friends there. Now stop playing the social worker, would you?'

'But I wasn't!'

'Yes, you were, Ruby. I suspect you're an incorrigible fixer. Trust me when I say my mother is happy where she is.'

Ruby pulled a face at this, knowing full well that his mother wasn't *that* happy. If she was she wouldn't have been so grateful for Ruby offering to cook her a special birthday dinner.

'Now on to my real reason for this call,' Sebastian swept on before Ruby could think of a suitable comeback. 'I realised this morning that I'd forgotten to talk to you about the Christmas party I throw for my staff every year. It's booked for Friday next week. I'm worried it might be too late to hire the party people we usually use.'

'You don't have to worry,' Ruby said. 'Georgia already had that organised. She booked the caterers well in advance. She told me they bring everything, do everything, and even clean up afterwards.'

'Good old Georgia.'

'She's certainly very organised. So how many people are coming to this party?'

'A lot.'

'Twenty? Thirty? More?'

'At least fifty.'

'Wow. That is a lot. So who will be there?'

'Are you fishing to find out if Zack is coming?' he asked sharply.

Ruby suppressed a sigh. 'Not at all. Is he coming?'

'I would imagine so. Speaking of work matters, I also just remembered that I forgot to get that email sent to you about the times of my shows. Sorry. I'll get my PA to do it, asap.'

'Please don't. I really don't have time to watch much television at the moment, Sebastian. I have a lot of studying to do.'

'Already? I wouldn't have thought any course would start until well after Christmas.'

'That's not the case with online courses. They start when you want them to start. I will find time to watch *Battle at the Bar*, but not the others.'

'Okay. The latest episode airs this Friday. You can tell me what you think on Saturday at breakfast.'

'I'll be glad to. So, what do you want for dinner tonight?'

'Didn't I tell you? I won't be home for dinner any night this week.'

'No, you didn't tell me,' she said, feeling quite put out. Yet she should have been grateful. Out of sight was out of mind, right?

On the other hand, absence also made the heart grow fonder...

Don't be silly, Ruby, she lectured herself. It's not your heart involved here. It's something much more basic.

'More time for me to study, then,' she quipped. 'Anything else you've forgotten to tell me?'

The sudden silence down the line unnerved her until she heard him clearing his throat.

'You sound like you're catching a cold,' she said.

'Could be. I hate the rain. Have to go now, Ruby. If I don't see you before I'll see you on Saturday morning at breakfast. I'm looking forward to hearing what you thought of Zack's show.'

'I'll take notes,' she said brightly. No point in giving away the fact that she would miss his company, even if his presence frustrated her like mad.

His sigh sounded weary.

'Are you all right, Sebastian?' she asked.

'Yes. Like I said, we're having a few problems with this last episode. But nothing that can't be fixed, I hope. Bye.'

'Bye,' she returned, but he was already gone, leaving Ruby with a strangely heavy feeling in her chest.

CHAPTER TWELVE

BY FRIDAY, THE rain that had dogged Sydney all week had finally begun to clear. Sebastian's sexual frustration had begun to clear as well, intense work and several days away from Ruby's provocative presence doing the trick. But that hiatus was now over and he had to face the weekend ahead, with all its accompanying difficulties.

The thought of bringing his mother over for a home-cooked dinner tomorrow was not something Sebastian was looking forward to. His mother would take one look at Ruby and think what Gloria had probably thought when she first met her. That she was wife material.

He wished his mother and sister would abandon the hope that he would marry again one day. Because he wouldn't. They simply didn't understand his resolve after Jennifer's death never to risk a serious relationship with a woman again. The truth was he simply could not bear to go through what he'd gone through ten years ago. It had scarred him for life, time not having dimmed the feelings that welled up within him every time he thought of Jennifer dying like that. He shuddered whenever he thought of falling in love again, of leaving himself vulnerable to such pain. Lust he could cope with, but not love. It bothered him how much he already liked Ruby. He would have to be careful around her. Very careful.

Sebastian took some time to fall asleep that Friday night, despite the late hour he'd come home, late enough for Ruby to be safely in bed. He woke on Saturday morning with a start, his head turning to stare at the pillow next to him, a tortured groan punching from his throat.

Ruby wasn't there, of course. It had all been a dream, a wildly erotic dream where Ruby had been lying naked in his bed with her gorgeous hair spread out across the pillow, her eyes glazed from hours of lovemaking.

The trouble was he could remember the lovemaking so very well—though one could hardly call it lovemaking. It had been nothing but sex of the raunchiest kind. Primal even. He'd been a beast. A crazed beast. Not like him at all. But it had thrilled him to the core, and left him to wake up still cruelly aroused.

Groaning, he opened his eyes and swung his legs over the side of the bed.

Such acute physical frustration bothered him enormously. He wasn't used to it. After Jennifer died he hadn't wanted sex for a couple of years. Then, when his male hormones had finally demanded he listen to them, it hadn't been with this kind of intensity. He'd been able to satisfy his sexual needs by having the occasional fling when he was away from home.

He could have been away from home now, he thought irritably, having his sexual needs met.

But he wasn't. He was here. And his needs were staring him in the face. No doubt his arousal was mainly because of that damned dream, but also partly because he'd be seeing the object of his desires this morning. There was no avoiding Ruby. No escape. Today was going to be hell, starting with breakfast.

Oh, well. No use putting off the inevitable. He had to face his nemesis sooner or later. But first he determined to do something about the dreadful state he was in.

Gritting his teeth, Sebastian hauled himself onto his feet and headed for the bathroom.

* * *

It was five past nine before Sebastian made an appearance in the kitchen, Ruby's spirits lifting at the sight of him.

'There you are,' she said. 'I was beginning to think you weren't ever going to come home.'

He said nothing to this, instead picking up the newspaper, which was delivered every Saturday and which she'd placed on the breakfast bar.

A silence descended as he attempted to remove the plastic cover, giving Ruby the opportunity to observe him stealthily. He looked tired but still handsome, casually dressed in fawn chinos and a white T-shirt. His dark hair was still wet from the shower and his face unshaven, which was unusual for Sebastian. His grooming was usually perfect. Yet the stubble suited his masculine face. And added to his sex appeal.

Unfortunately.

'What do you want for breakfast?' she asked after he succeeded in freeing the paper of its stubborn confines.

'A tall glass of orange juice to begin with,' he answered, finally looking up at her. 'Then a couple of poached eggs on toast followed by lots of coffee. I'll eat outside,' he finished up.

'Right,' she said through gritted teeth. For whilst Ruby was getting used to his on-off brusqueness, it still offended her. Why couldn't he just be nice?

Lord knew why he put her libido in such a twist. She didn't really *like* him all that much, but it seemed lust was not necessarily connected with liking.

He didn't go outside straight away. Instead, he just stood there on the other side of the breakfast bar, frowning at her old jeans and the very large apron that covered her from neck to knee.

'Yes, I know,' she said with a defensive shrug of her shoulders. 'I look a fright in this apron. But I've been cooking pastry, which can be messy. Don't worry, I'll look decent by the time your mother comes.'

'I'm sure you'll be perfect,' he bit out, spinning on his heel and stomping outside.

It was at moments like this that Ruby didn't just dislike him. She *hated* him. But then he spoiled everything by smiling at her when she brought the juice outside.

'Sorry for being grumpy,' he said. 'It's been a tough week.'

'That's all right,' she said, and smiled back at him before she could stop herself.

Their eyes met over the rim of the glass and her heart turned over. Dear God. As much as she wanted to keep hating him, she just couldn't. He wasn't a hateful man. Not even remotely.

'So did you watch *Battle at the Bar* last night?' he asked after he took a huge swallow of juice.

'I did.'

'What did you think of it?'

'It's an exceptional show,' she said truthfully, glad to have something to distract her from her escalating feelings for this man. 'I doubt there's anything else like it on TV at the moment. It hooks you in within five minutes and keeps you on the edge of your seat for the whole hour and a half. The story last night was riveting and Zack was just brilliant. If ever I get into trouble with the law, I'd want someone like him in my corner.'

'He is good, isn't he?'

'Better than good.'

'Why do you think that is? I sometimes try to work out what appeals to people about him so much. Is it just his looks, or his acting? Or both?'

Ruby considered her answer for a few moments, aware that Sebastian was watching her. Watching and waiting. 'I think it's the passion of the character he plays,' she said at last. 'Caesar *cares* about his clients and he shows it. Of course,' Ruby added, 'it does help to have a strong plot, not to mention all that sex.'

'True. Sex sells,' Sebastian said, then drained the rest of his juice. 'Thank you for that very intelligent critique, Ruby. Could I have the eggs now?' he asked as he picked up the newspaper and started reading.

She had been dismissed.

Ruby wanted to scream. Or hit him. Or both.

Instead, she turned and started to walk back inside, holding her temper with great difficulty.

'What about the coffee?' he called after her.

Ruby stopped, then turned back round to find him folding the paper up and putting it down. 'You said you wanted it *after* your eggs,' she pointed out tartly.

'Did I? Well, I've changed my mind. I'd like it now.'

'Coming right up,' she said through gritted teeth.

It was a good ten minutes after that she brought him the coffee before she returned with his eggs, her mood still dark.

'Ah,' he said, looking down at the eggs. 'This looks so good. Thank you, Ruby.'

Ruby stifled a sigh. He'd done it again. How did he disarm her when she was mad at him?

'So, did Gloria drop by yesterday with the presents for Mum?' he asked before he started eating.

'Yes. I put them on the dining table, ready for her.'

'Good. I have to go out after breakfast so I won't need any lunch. I have a meeting with the writers of Zack's show, then I'm taking them out to lunch as a thank you for all the extra hours they put in this week.'

'They fixed the problems, then?'

'Yes. They got it right in the end, which is just as well. Nothing worse than a season ending on a bad note. You have to end on a high.'

'I would imagine so,' she said thoughtfully. 'You…er… you won't be late home, Sebastian, will you? Your mother will be upset if you're late picking her up.' She didn't add that *she'd* be upset if tonight didn't go well, after all the work she'd done.

'No, Miss Worrywart,' he said as he picked up his knife and fork. 'I'll be back in plenty of time to get ready for tonight's ordeal.'

'It doesn't have to be an ordeal,' she chided him.

The corner of his mouth lifted in a wry smile. 'That's a matter of opinion.'

When he dropped his gaze and began to tuck into his eggs, Ruby realised she'd been dismissed again.

One day, she thought frustratedly as she made her way back to the kitchen, *I'll tear strips off that man.*

What Ruby didn't realise was that that day had already arrived.

CHAPTER THIRTEEN

SEBASTIAN RETURNED TO the house shortly after four-thirty, disappearing straight upstairs without even bothering to say hi. Ruby faintly heard the sound of his shower running. And running. And running.

Truly, she thought as she shook her head from side to side. Just as well he was rich. His water and electricity bill must be enormous!

She herself had already showered and dressed some time ago, choosing to wear her black shirtdress. *Again.* Still, it did look good on her. Her make-up was subtle and her hair imprisoned in a knot at the nape of her neck. The house was spotless, the dining-room table set with pretty new place mats, and all the food prepared, including that infernal lemon meringue pie, which had turned out to be a real pain in the neck. She'd tried three recipes during the week, only the third one meeting with her approval. Even then, she'd had Tom and Janice do a taste test yesterday on a trial pie. Thankfully, it had met with their approval, so she'd given the rest of that pie to them to take home and made a fresh one this morning; Ruby had read that meringue was better consumed on the day it was made.

She was a little nervous about the evening ahead, but excited as well, glad that she could make the day memorable for Sebastian's mother.

He hurried downstairs shortly after five, cleanly shaven and dressed in stylish navy-blue trousers, teamed with a blue striped shirt, open at the neck. He looked refreshed and utterly gorgeous, but with a grim set to his mouth, which suggested he wasn't looking forward to the evening ahead.

'I hope your mother doesn't live too far away,' she said, glancing at the clock on the wall.

'Don't fret. She's less than ten minutes away at Clifton Gardens. In a very *exclusive* retirement village, I might add. It costs me heaps. I should be back by five-thirty, as long as she's ready and doesn't keep me waiting. See you.'

And he was gone again, leaving behind the faint whiff of a very expensive cologne. Or possibly it was aftershave. Either way, it smelled wonderful.

Ruby took another deep breath through her nose, wallowing in the fragrance. There was nothing she liked better than a man who smelled good.

Some extra butterflies started gathering in her stomach when five-thirty came and went, with no sign of Sebastian. She hoped nothing had gone wrong. Ruby was just beginning to panic when she heard his car enter the driveway. She was busying herself with plates in the kitchen when the door from the stairwell opened and Sebastian ushered his mother inside.

Frieda looked nothing like her son. She was short and plump with a kind face, topped by a cap of wavy silver-grey hair. Her dress was very flowery and didn't flatter her plump figure, but her white shoes and handbag looked expensive, especially her handbag. Ruby had a thing for handbags and could always recognise quality.

'Happy birthday,' Ruby said by way of a greeting, coming forward to give the woman a hug, then a kiss on her cheek.

Frieda flushed with pleasure before throwing her son an exasperated glance. 'You didn't tell me Ruby was so pretty. And so *young*!'

Sebastian rolled his eyes. 'She's not as young as she looks,' he said.

'Well, she's a darned sight younger than Georgia.'

'True. Come on, Mum, come and open your presents.'

The dining room was just off the kitchen, a large conservatory-style room with a lovely view of the pool, the backyard and the skyline beyond. The table wasn't overly huge though it did extend, if needed. Ruby had set only one end of the table with two place settings, the presents piled up on the other end and a vase of fresh flowers in the middle.

'Goodness!' Frieda exclaimed. 'That's a lot of gifts.'

'They're from Gloria as well,' Sebastian told her. 'And your grandsons.'

Frieda opened the cards first, then the presents. She was quite overcome at one stage.

The range of gifts was extensive, including an expensive tablet, jewellery, a lovely scarf, books and chocolates. The tablet was from Sebastian, though Ruby suspected he hadn't done the buying. Clearly, he'd delegated that job to his sister.

Still, his mother didn't know that. Or maybe she did, because she said she would have to ring Gloria straight away and thank her.

Whilst she was on the phone, Ruby asked Sebastian what he would like to drink before dinner.

'I think I'll have a whisky. But don't you worry. I'll get it myself.' And he took off down the hall towards his study where Ruby knew he kept a wide range of spirits on top of a walnut sideboard.

'Ready for a sherry now?' she asked a teary-eyed Frieda once she got off the phone.

'Oh, yes, I could do with one. Where's Sebastian?'

'Getting himself a whisky.'

'Let's hope it improves his mood,' Frieda said with a sigh.

'Yes, let's,' Ruby returned, and both women exchanged a small smile.

'I shouldn't criticise him,' his mother said, taking her glass of sherry. 'He's really a good son. Do you know about his wife dying of cancer?' she whispered, all the while watching for Sebastian's return.

'I do,' Ruby said, nodding.

'It broke his heart.'

'Yes, I can see that.' And she could.

'I hoped he would meet someone else and get married again. But he doesn't want to.'

Ruby could see that too. It shouldn't have bothered her, but it did. Which was crazy. It wasn't as though *she* wanted to marry him. Heavens no. She just wanted to…

Her X-rated thoughts weren't entirely banished when Sebastian strode back into the room, a glass of whisky in his hand. When he lifted it to his lips, her eyes followed, her heart quickening. What she wouldn't give to be that glass of whisky…

'Excuse me, I need to go and cook now,' she said quickly. 'Why don't you two go outside with your drinks? It's lovely out there at the moment. The rain has chased away the heat and the insects. I put some nibbles on the table earlier. I'll call you when dinner's ready.'

They did as instructed but when Ruby finally called them inside, Frieda took one look at the two place settings and insisted Ruby eat with them.

'Maybe she doesn't want to, Mum,' Sebastian said when Ruby hesitated.

'Don't you have enough food for three, dear?'

'Yes, I do. But I… I'm not family.'

'Nonsense. You *feel* like family already, doesn't she, Sebastian?'

Ruby experienced some sympathy for her boss at that moment. His mother had really backed him into a corner.

He looked totally frustrated with her, his eyes carrying exasperation before he finally surrendered, a small rueful smile playing on his lips.

'Yes,' he said. 'She does. Please, do join us, Ruby.'

Surprisingly, the evening went quite well, especially after she brought out the bottle of spumante, which Frieda consumed with gusto. The rissoles and mashed potato went down a treat but the *coup de grâce* was the lemon meringue pie, served with whipped cream. The gushing compliments from Frieda made all the trouble she'd taken worthwhile. Ruby hummed as she made the coffee, warmed by the feelings she always got when she made people happy, confirming her decision to become a social worker.

Frieda lingered longer than Ruby expected. She wanted to chat with Ruby a lot, asking about her life and her travels. Not that Ruby told her the whole story—more an edited version of it. After all, Sebastian was listening. Listening intently, she noted, and watching her with the sort of narrowed eyes that might have indicated interest on another man. But not Sebastian. He was just curious about her, she decided. Not attracted.

It was just after ten when his mother announced it was time she went home, with Sebastian obviously eager to take her. Ruby sensed he'd had enough.

'This is the best birthday I've ever had,' Frieda praised as they gathered up all her gifts and carried them down to the car. 'What a shame Ruby won't be here next year,' she added. 'Are you sure you can't fire Georgia and keep her, Sebastian?'

A look of horror flickered across his face before he could hide it. 'Afraid not, Mum,' he replied. 'But she'll be with us a while yet.'

'Yes. Yes, I suppose so.' Frieda looked disgruntled for a moment, then her face brightened. 'You'll have to bring

Ruby to Gloria's for Christmas Day. Gloria always does a turkey with all the trimmings.'

Now *that* was the sort of Christmas celebration she liked.

'Ruby might have other plans, Mum,' Sebastian said before she could jump at the invitation. 'She has family here in Sydney.'

'Actually, I don't have other plans,' Ruby said truthfully. 'I'd love to come. If that's all right with you, Sebastian. And Gloria, of course.'

Their eyes met, his betraying nothing. Nothing at all. It annoyed the hell out of her that he didn't find her even a little bit attractive. But then, perhaps he didn't find any woman attractive these days. Maybe that was why he never brought a woman home. Because his libido was dead and buried, alongside his wife. Clearly, she'd been the love of his life and he had no room in his heart for anyone else. Maybe he *had* only been going to the Gold Coast to relax.

But even as Ruby worked through these thoughts, she wasn't entirely convinced. For she had been aware of *something* simmering between them tonight. Women did have good antennas about these things. And hers had been twanging all night.

But maybe she was wrong. Maybe it was her own stirred hormones twanging away. In truth, she hadn't been able to stop looking at him surreptitiously as she'd chatted away with Frieda. Looking at him, and wanting him. This lust business—especially when it was one-sided—was a right pain in the—

'I'm sure Gloria would love to have you,' Sebastian said briskly, putting an end to her musings. 'Now, come along, Mum. You said you were tired.'

'Thank you again, dear,' Frieda said, coming forward to give Ruby a goodbye hug.

Ruby was glad when they left. She, too, was quite tired. It didn't take her long to finish clearing away the table and put on the dishwasher. Ruby decided not to wait for Sebastian to come home before having her shower and going to bed. He wouldn't expect her to.

She was just about to dive in between the sheets when there was a knock on her bedroom door. Her stomach tightened with instant alarm.

'Yes?' she called out warily.

'Are you decent?'

Ruby glanced down at the elongated T-shirt that she wore to bed. It was white with a colourful beach-side logo on the front, which hid her underlying nakedness to a degree. But not entirely. Nipples like bullets were hard to hide. She reached for her blue cotton housecoat, pulling it on and wrapping it around herself as she walked to the door.

'Yes?' she repeated once the door was open.

To give him credit, he did look at her for once like a normal man, his eyes going from her released hair down to her bare feet. But once his eyes returned to hers, there was nothing there but cool politeness. 'I just wanted to thank you personally for all the trouble you went to today. You went above and beyond the call of duty.'

'My pleasure,' she said, dismayed and, yes, disappointed. Which was silly. What had she been imagining? That he'd come to her bedroom to seduce her at long last?

She wished.

'Mum thinks you're lovely,' he said.

Ruby's smile was stiff. 'That's nice.'

'I think you're lovely too...'

It was all so unexpected. Ruby was shocked, both by the sudden thickness in his voice and the unmistakable hunger that zoomed into his eyes. When his desire-filled gaze dropped to her mouth, she sucked a breath in sharply. For surely he was going to kiss her. Any second now, he was going to step forward, pull her into his arms and crush his lips down on hers.

A wave of longing—no, *craving*—swept through her. For it was what she wanted more than anything else in the world. Ruby knew it wouldn't stop at kissing. She couldn't *bear* it to stop at just kissing. She wouldn't *let* it stop at just kissing.

'Sebastian,' she said, the uttering of his name filled with her own hunger. She had never in her life felt anything as intense as the desire gripping her body right now, not to mention her mind. There was no room in her head for any other consideration. No thought of common sense, or consequence. No care for the future, just the here and now, and this utterly overwhelming need.

He stared at her hard for several seconds, his eyes glittering with the same need. Then, suddenly, he shuddered and turned his back on her.

'Goodnight, Ruby,' he threw over his shoulder, and started to walk away.

CHAPTER FOURTEEN

RUBY WAS STUNNED. For a split second she just stood there, staring after him, until a fury rose within her. It wasn't the fury of a woman scorned. It was the fury of a woman crushed by the disappointment of him rejecting what was clearly a mutual desire. There she'd been all this time, thinking he didn't want her. But he had. He *had*!

Yet despite this, he was walking away…

It was too much.

'Don't you dare walk away from me!' she exploded.

He stopped and turned back to face her, his expression disbelieving.

'I beg your pardon?' he bit out.

'You heard me,' she retorted.

'I thought I must have been mistaken,' he said coldly. 'So what's your problem?'

'*My* problem,' she threw at him. 'I don't have the problem here. *You're* the one with the problem. I can't work out if you're some kind of masochist, a sadist, or a coward.'

His nostrils drew together as he sucked in sharply. 'I would think carefully before you say any more, Ruby.'

She tried to rein in her temper but she simply couldn't.

'Good grief, what's wrong with you? Are you going to deny the way you looked at me a minute ago? Trust me when I say I know that look. You wanted to make love to me. And I wanted you to, more fool me. I was ready to jump into bed with you just like that,' she said, clicking her fingers at him. 'I was yours for the taking. But what did you do? You bolted.'

His eyes darkened to a stormy blue, his hands curling into fists by his sides. 'I was trying to be a gentleman,' he ground out. 'More fool *me*. But you're wrong about me wanting to make love to you,' he went on grimly. 'I didn't want to do *anything* to you that smacked of love. I wanted to have sex with you, Ruby. I wanted to ravish you sense-less. That's why I walked away. Because I knew a nice girl like you wouldn't want that.'

Now it was her turn to suck in sharply.

His admission was not only surprising, it brought with it a measure of guilt, plus a huge wave of temptation. Ruby knew she should step back and think about the conse-quences of what she was about to say, but she was beyond that. She wanted Sebastian on any terms.

'You're wrong about me,' she said, desperate with desire for him. 'I'm not as nice as you think. I've had sex without love in the past. Please don't walk away, Sebastian. Not tonight. I need you, just as much as I think you need me.'

'I doubt that,' he muttered. But he didn't walk away. Instead, he covered the distance between them with a few swift strides, sweeping her up into his arms just as she'd imagined earlier, his mouth swooping down to crush hers.

His kiss was savage, his lips demanding. But, oh, how she loved it, opening her mouth to the thrust of his tongue, her body already aching to feel the thrust of hard maleness pressing up against her stomach.

The kissing continued as he wrenched the housecoat off her shoulders, his hands dropping to her thighs, taking the hem of her T-shirt with them as they travelled up to her bare buttocks. There he cupped her bottom, kneading the soft flesh till she was moaning into his mouth. He didn't stop kissing her, even when he lifted her up; didn't stop as he carried her upstairs to his bedroom. Once there, he tipped her back onto the bed, spreading her legs and leaving her exposed to his gaze as he stripped off his clothes.

Ruby just lay there like that, stunned by her level of arousal. She wasn't used to this kind of need. This degree of wanting. This kind of sex.

She could hardly wait.

And neither could he, by the look of him. Once he was naked, her arms reached out to him and he fell into them, groaning as he did so. He entered her swiftly, his thrusting urgent but, oh, so satisfying. Ruby came with a rush, stunned by the intensity of her orgasm, calling out his name as the first spasm struck. He stopped for only a second to stare down at her before returning to his frantic rhythm. His climax was just as strong, his body shuddering at length. Finally, he collapsed upon her, his head buried in her hair.

His ragged breathing took ages to calm, by which time Ruby's whole body had surrendered to a deeply drugging peace. The craving was gone, at least for the moment. Before she could think, or experience any regret, she fell fast sleep, oblivious to the not so nice feelings that would face her when she awoke.

CHAPTER FIFTEEN

SEBASTIAN WOKE FIRST, shocked to find himself still on top of a sleeping Ruby.

Oh, dear God, he agonised. *What have I done?*

He groaned as he carefully withdrew, then, without looking back, he headed for the shower. There he stood under the jets of hot water for ages, his head pressed against the tiles, his thoughts whirling.

He should never have gone to her door last night, should never had said those stupid words.

I think you're lovely too…

Of course, he hadn't expected her to react the way she had when he'd walked away. My goodness, she'd been furious with him. And the things she'd said, the things she'd accused him of being…

What were they? A sadist, a masochist and a coward.

Sebastian knew he wasn't a sadist. But he had to admit that he'd suffered from a degree of masochism ever since Ruby had come to live with him. He'd been permanently aroused whenever he was around her. Last night, the dinner with his mother had been sheer torture, having to sit there and watch Ruby all evening, watch her and want her.

He hadn't imagined for a moment that she was as attracted to him as he was to her. She'd certainly hidden it well. But the moment she'd revealed her own hunger for him he'd been lost. Totally lost. He could still feel her lips, her tongue, her hot, wet body.

Sebastian hadn't experienced that kind of passion since…since *never*, he suddenly realised. Sex with Jennifer had never been wildly spontaneous like that. It had been good. Of course it had. But there had always been an element of control. On her part. Not his. She'd liked to put aside special times for lovemaking. She'd never indulged in a quickie. Never been so overcome with desire that she couldn't wait.

Thinking back, Sebastian accepted that whilst Jennifer had loved him, she'd never really *needed* him. Not in life, or in death. But that hadn't made losing her any easier.

That brought him to Ruby's last accusation. That he was a coward.

Sebastian sighed. Maybe there was an element of truth in that accusation. After his experience of losing Jennifer, Sebastian had withdrawn into a shell from which he hadn't emerged for a long time. Even then he hadn't been able to consider a relationship with another woman, settling for one-night stands and the occasional holiday fling. He'd always kept these encounters well away from home, so that nothing could come back to haunt him.

Sleeping with Ruby broke all the rules he'd been living by.

Common sense demanded that he ask her to leave. But how could he possibly do that? Maybe, just maybe, he wouldn't have to. He suspected Ruby might do the deed for him and just quit.

And maybe she wouldn't. Sebastian obviously found it hard to read her because she'd shocked the life out of him last night. Thinking about her explosive passion still amazed him.

Sebastian snapped the taps off and reached for a towel, dismayed when he noticed he was already aroused again.

'Hell on earth,' he muttered under his breath as he

wrapped the towel firmly around his waist then reached for the bathroom door.

He found Ruby sitting on the edge of the bed, her shoulders slumped, her head bowed. Her head jerked up when she heard the door open, distress in her eyes.

'I suppose I'll have to quit now,' she said.

Such a prospect did not sit well with Sebastian, which was perverse, given he'd already decided it would be easier if she quit.

'I'm so sorry,' she blurted out before he could say a word. 'It's all my fault. I know it is. You tried to walk away but I wouldn't let you. I provoked you. I don't know why. No, that's a lie. I do know why. I wanted you to make love to me. No, that's a lie as well. I didn't want you to *make love* to me. I wanted you to have sex with me the way you said. You know? Nothing to do with love at all. And you did. And I loved it. I really did,' she choked out, then burst into tears, her head dropping into her hands.

Sebastian couldn't bear it, seeing her cry like that, and accepting all the blame. He rushed over and sat down next to her, wrapping an arm around her shaking shoulders and drawing her close to him.

'You just needed sex the same way I did. I dare say you haven't had any for a while, have you?'

She shook her head from side to side. Was that a yes, or a no? Did he care either way? Probably not.

'Same here,' he said. 'Now stop crying and let's talk about this situation like sensible adults.'

Hopefully, he could manage that, though he suspected that what was under his towel might influence what he had to say. Thank goodness she was still wearing that T-shirt. If she'd been sitting there naked, he wouldn't have stood a chance of a rational conversation.

Ruby looked up at him with wet eyes. 'I need to go to the bathroom first and freshen up.'

'Freshen up,' he repeated before the penny dropped. He hadn't used a condom—another one of his rules broken. Oh, God…

'Now I'm the one saying sorry,' he said, sighing. 'I should have used a condom. Let me assure you that's a first for me so you don't have to worry about STDs. What about birth control? Are you on the pill?'

'Yes,' she said. 'Though I'm not sure why. It's been years since I had sex. Now I really *have* to go to the bathroom.'

He stared after her, stunned by her announcement that it had been years since she'd had sex. No wonder she'd liked it so much. Still, he couldn't help wondering what had happened in her past to make her choose a celibate lifestyle. Especially looking the way she did. She certainly wouldn't be short of admirers.

But he had no intention of asking her. Sebastian didn't want to know all about Ruby's life story. The intimacy he craved was of the strictly sexual kind. Lord, but he had to have her again. And soon.

An idea leapt into his head that seemed feasible, though very un-Sebastian-like. He was, at heart, a conventional man. And a careful one. Not that you would think so by the way he'd just acted. The idea was outrageous, he knew, but once it infiltrated his thoughts, he could not put it aside.

Would she go for it? He sure as hell hoped so.

Sebastian climbed into bed whilst she was gone, his body urging him on, despite some lingering misgivings over what he was going to propose. He would have to make it clear to her up front that his proposition was to be a strictly sexual arrangement. No emotional involvement. Just sex. And it would all end when Georgia came back.

Ruby emerged after a few minutes, looking worried. And hesitant. When she saw his towel on the floor beside the bed, her eyes widened.

'Are you expecting me to join you in there?' she asked him.

'Only if you want to.'

She pulled a face. 'That's not fair, Sebastian. You know I want to.'

'Then what are you waiting for?'

She walked round and climbed into the bed on the other side but kept a bit of distance between them.

'Okay. I'm here. You said you wanted to talk about the situation like sensible adults, though I can only assume by your invitation to join you in bed that you don't want me to quit.'

Sebastian had to smile. No flies on Ruby. 'You're absolutely right. I want you to stay on as my housekeeper. But we crossed a line tonight, Ruby, and I'm afraid it's impossible for me to step back over that line. Do you know what I'm saying?'

'Yes. You want to have more sex with me.'

'Yes. I do. And I promise I'll use protection from now on. What do you say?'

Her smile was small and wry. 'I think I could suffer it.'

'Good,' Sebastian said, trying to keep a straight face. She really could be a saucy minx. This was some comfort, as was her admission to having had sex before without love. 'There will, however, be conditions to this affair.'

'*Conditions?*' she asked, her frown indicating she wasn't all that happy with that word.

'Maybe conditions is the wrong word.'

'You could be right there,' she said sharply.

'I shouldn't have called it an affair, either, because it won't be that. It will be an arrangement.'

'An arrangement,' she repeated, as though mulling that word over as well. Sebastian began to feel as if he was tackling this all wrong.

'Look, I'm sorry,' he said. 'I'm expressing myself badly. But the truth is I don't want a girlfriend, Ruby, just you as my lover. I also don't want anyone else to know, or guess, that we're sleeping together.' When his conscience pricked at him, Sebastian steadfastly ignored it. 'What do you think of that idea?'

'Wow,' she said, though she was still half frowning. 'So you want me to be your secret lover?'

'I couldn't have put it better myself,' he said with a relieved sigh.

'Wow again. That's a very daring proposition for a gentleman like you, Sebastian. I mean, you're not a bad boy like Zack. What's got into you?'

'I don't think you have to look far to know the answer to that,' he said, and closed the distance between them. 'You've totally undermined my common sense, along with my conscience,' he added, lifting the T-shirt up over her head and tossing it away. 'So is it a yes, Ruby?'

CHAPTER SIXTEEN

HE KISSED HER before she could answer, one hand covering her left breast at the same time. When she finally came up for air, her head was whirling.

'Er...could you give me some time to think about it?' she asked, wondering all of a sudden whether she was capable of conducting a strictly sexual affair without that soft heart of hers finally getting involved. She didn't want to fall in love with Sebastian. She really didn't. To do so would be futile. And ultimately bring her a lot of grief. Common sense demanded she leave things at a one-night stand and just walk away.

But common sense was no match for the exquisite feelings pulsating through her body at that moment. Already his hand had moved from her breast down between her legs to that area that was pulsating and throbbing.

'How much time do you think you'll need?' he asked, and stopped what he was doing.

'I'm not sure,' she squeaked, desperate by now.

'I need an answer, Ruby.'

'Yes. All right. Yes.'

'Do you want me to continue?' he murmured knowingly.

'Please,' she moaned.

Her orgasm shattered any lingering qualms Ruby had about saying yes. For how could she give up such pleasure? And if it worried her that she would get emotionally involved with Sebastian, or that he would say goodbye to her without a backward glance when Georgia returned, she pushed such thoughts aside. Because already he was inside her, taking her with him to a level of satisfaction she'd never experienced before. She came and she came, her body shattering into a million pieces of pure pleasure. By the time she fell asleep with his arms tightly around her, Ruby's mind had moved beyond something as mundane as worry. She was totally obsessed. With this man, with his body, and the way he could make her feel. She would do anything he asked of her if it meant she could be with him.

The sun was well and truly up when Ruby woke the next morning. Sebastian was still out like a light, which didn't surprise her. He'd outdone himself last night, leaving her feeling exquisitely sated.

What did surprise Ruby, however, was that she was having second thoughts about this...arrangement she'd agreed to. Really, what had possessed her to say yes just like that?

Of course, she *knew* why she had at the time. But that didn't make it acceptable in the cold light of day. Pride demanded she talk to Sebastian about it again, make some *rules* of her own. She wasn't about to be at his sexual beck and call whenever he felt like it, even if being at his sexual beck and call did hold a decidedly wicked appeal.

Ruby cast a glance over at his sleeping form, images popping into her head of the various activities they'd indulged in during the night. She had to admit he was very good at oral sex. She also hadn't shrunk from going down on him, either, even though it had never been one of her favourite forms of foreplay. With Sebastian, however, it seemed she was up for anything.

And she meant *anything*!

Her stomach twisted with renewed desire, bringing with it the temptation to just stay here in this bed till Sebastian woke up.

But if she did that, Ruby feared she would be lost. She had to have some self-respect. She had to make a stand.

You've never been the meek and mild type, she lectured herself, *and you're not about to start now. Now get out of this bed and put some distance between yourself and this infernal man.*

Ruby crawled out very quietly lest she wake Sebastian. Because if he touched her she just knew her resolve would crumble. Once out of the room, she hurried downstairs, collected some fresh clothes and bolted for the nearby bathroom.

She lingered in the shower, shampooing her hair whilst letting the hot water soothe her body, though there was not much soothing for her mind. It was once again a total shambles.

Some loud knocking on the bathroom door brought an end to her tortured thoughts.

'Ruby, how long are you going to stay in there?' Sebastian demanded to know. 'You've been in that shower for ages.'

Now, there was nothing more guaranteed to make Ruby defiant than a demanding man. Who in hell did he think he was?

Ruby snapped off the taps so he could hear her answer, loud and clear.

'Might I remind you, Sebastian, that it's Sunday, which is my day off. I have plans. So if you want coffee, then I suggest you get it yourself. Now, if you don't mind, I'd like to be left in peace to finish my ablutions.' And she turned the taps back on again.

Ruby thought she heard a four-letter word through the hiss of the water. It brought a wry smile to her lips. Yes, this was the way to play it. She couldn't be at his command all the time. A girl had to have some pride.

It was fifteen minutes later before she emerged, dressed

in her favourite black Bermuda shorts and a simple red T-shirt. Her still-wet hair was bundled up on top of her head in a rough knot. She had no make-up on and no shoes on her feet. This she swiftly remedied, slipping on black thongs before padding her way down to the kitchen where Sebastian was sitting on one of the breakfast stools, a mug of steaming coffee in front of him.

'I see you did as I suggested,' she said, trying not to stare at him. It was obvious he was naked underneath the short black silk robe he was wearing.

'I've never minded making my own coffee,' he returned, his eyes glittering with a desire that she found both perturbing and tempting.

'How generous of you,' she said.

He looked at her long and hard. 'You don't like men much, do you?'

'Depends on the man,' came her truthful reply.

'What about me? Do you like me?'

A small smile tugged at her mouth before she could stop it. 'You're growing on me.'

'You're an enigma, do you know that?'

'What do you mean?'

'I can't work you out.'

'Do you have to? I'm your temporary housekeeper. And your secret lover whilst I'm here. End of story.'

'Is that what you expect? That once your time here is over, then we're over?'

Her smile turned wry. 'Of course.'

'And you're okay with that?'

She shrugged, doing her best to ignore the sharp tug at her heartstrings. 'Yes. Of course.'

His face showed a perverse mixture of relief and exasperation.

'When I woke this morning and found you gone, I thought you might have changed your mind.'

This was her chance to say, *Yes, I've changed my mind. I quit and I'm out of here before I do something stupid like fall in love with you. Because there is no future in that. Even if you are actually a nice man. But you don't want love and marriage. You don't want anything from me but sex. Which I thought was all I wanted from you but now I'm not so sure...*

'I couldn't bear it if you changed your mind,' he said, half to himself.

Ruby's heart turned over as she accepted that it was already happening to her. The caring. The emotional involvement. She'd always been a sucker for being needed. And Sebastian needed her. At least for a while.

The time for walking away was gone, Ruby accepted bravely. She'd made her bed, so to speak. Now she would have to lie in it.

She laughed at the irony of that thought.

'What's so funny?' he asked, frowning.

'Nothing important. One thing, though, don't think I'm going to jump into bed with you every time you get the urge. I don't belong to you.'

Obvious relief smoothed the frown lines from his forehead. 'Well, of course you don't, Ruby. I don't always act like a beast, like I did last night.'

Ruby thought she'd better not tell him she'd rather liked that beast.

'Do you mind if I ask you a couple of questions?' she said.

An immediate wariness zoomed into his face. 'That depends on the questions.'

'Were you happy in your marriage?'

'Very. Why?'

'You don't have any photographs of your wife around the house.'

'No,' he said grimly. 'I don't like to remember.'

'Your happiness together, or her dying of cancer?'

'I would imagine you already know the answer. You've been there, Ruby. You know what it's like.'

'Yes. It's very difficult,' she said, her heart going out to the bleakness in his eyes. 'But I don't think it's wise to try to blank it all out. See this?' she said, and showed him the tattoo on her wrist. 'Ava was my mother. I had this done so I would never forget her, or the love I felt for her.'

Sebastian studied the tattoo, then looked up at her, frowning. 'But the date of her death... You said she died five years ago.'

'No. I said I left home five years ago. You just assumed that was when she died.'

'Why did you let me think that, then?'

'It's a long story. Are you sure you want to hear it?'

CHAPTER SEVENTEEN

SEBASTIAN SUSPECTED HE SHOULDN'T, but he couldn't resist. His curiosity was well and truly awakened.

'Yes, I want to know,' he said.

'Right,' she said, 'though I'm going to need some coffee myself first.'

He watched her make it, spending the time drinking his own coffee and trying not to think of how she looked naked; trying not to remember the sounds she made when she came.

It was a relief when she finally started talking, though he was still glad they had a breakfast bar between them.

'My mother was first diagnosed with ovarian cancer when I was seventeen, in my last year at high school. She was already stage four and the prognosis wasn't good. She still fought it, of course. Endured heaps of chemo. Her hair fell out and her weight dropped from sixty kilos to forty.'

'Good God. Poor woman.'

'Yes,' Ruby said bleakly.

'Your father must have been devastated.'

'He pretended to be. But the whole time she was dying, he was having an affair.'

'You're kidding me.'

'I kid you not. Mum wasn't cold in her grave before he took off to live with his other woman. She was rich, you see. A rich divorcee. Dad always wanted to be rich.'

Sebastian could hardly believe what he was hearing.

'Did your mother know?' he asked.

'I think she must have because she asked me to look after my brothers before she died. She didn't ask Dad.'

'So you stayed and looked after them.'

'Yes. I stayed,' she said in the kind of flat voice that hid a lot of emotion. 'Dad let us live in the house. He also paid the bills but I refused to take more of his rotten money than I had to. I worked part-time at the local fast-food place so I could buy my clothes and have some money in my purse.'

Sebastian's heart went out to the poor brave girl whose father had to have been the biggest bastard he'd ever heard of. 'What did your father do for a living?' he asked.

'He was a car salesman. Classic cars, actually. I think that's how he met the rich woman he took off with.'

'Didn't he come back home at all to see how you were faring?'

'Yes. Twice. But on the second occasion I told him what I thought of him and said I didn't want to see him again as long as I live. I meant it and he believed me.'

Sebastian didn't doubt it. Ruby was the type of girl who meant what she said. 'And your brothers? What did they say about not seeing their father any more?'

'They were actually at school at the time of Dad's visit but when they came home, I told them what I'd said and they agreed with me entirely.'

'Both your brothers felt the same way?'

'Yes. They'd totally lost respect for Dad. We all had.'

'And have any of you seen your father since?'

'Not to talk to. I did email him once to tell him Liam and Oliver had graduated from university, and his response was to put the house on the market. He didn't bother to come to their graduation ceremony or buy them anything, not even a card.'

'Good grief. The man just gets worse and worse.'

'Indeed. Thankfully, Liam and Oliver had secured good jobs by the time the house was sold and could afford to rent. The real estate agent said they could take whatever furniture they wanted from the house once it was sold, which I presume Dad sanctioned.'

'How kind of him,' Sebastian said caustically.

'My thoughts exactly. Anyway, once the boys were settled, I took off. I'd had enough.'

'I can understand that. All those years raising your brothers was a lot of responsibility for a young girl.'

'It was tough,' she agreed. 'Dad's betrayal made me so angry. My boyfriend dumping me a year after Mum died didn't help, either. Bailey said I didn't have enough time to be a proper girlfriend. He complained I was always doing things for my brothers. Which was true, I suppose,' she added, sighing. 'Whilst they were loving boys, they could be selfish. And I guess I overcompensated a bit because of Mum dying and Dad deserting us. Still, if Bailey had truly loved me like he said he did, he would have helped me, not dumped me.'

'He certainly should have. When Jennifer was diagnosed, I tried to help. I offered to leave work and nurse her at home but she didn't want me to. She put herself into palliative care in hospital and stayed there until she died.'

'But what about her parents? Surely they would have offered to help care for her.'

'Her parents were both dead. They were killed in a car accident when she was a teenager. Jennifer was raised by her grandparents. By the time she got cancer, they had passed away.'

'I see. It sounds like there were no brothers or sisters either.'

'No. She was an only child. The circumstances of her

upbringing made her very self-sufficient. She didn't like to need anyone. She was so damned tough at times. She told me once that she hadn't wanted to fall in love with me. She confessed she was afraid of losing me. Yet in the end it was me who lost her.' Sebastian's heart squeezed tight as he shook his head from side to side.

'What kind of cancer did she have?'

Sebastian's normal practice would be to stop talking about Jennifer as soon as possible but he couldn't seem to. 'Inoperable brain cancer. It came from a melanoma. She died within weeks of her diagnosis.'

'That's so sad.'

'People said it was a mercy she died so quickly but I couldn't handle it. It was all too sudden.'

'I can understand that. You didn't have time to get used to the idea of her dying.'

Was that why he'd fallen apart afterwards? he wondered.

Only partly, he accepted.

'Mum and I had two years to get used to her dying,' Ruby said. 'I valued that time I had with her. We became very close.'

'I envy you. Jennifer didn't want me to see her suffer, so she pushed me away. Every time I visited her in hospital she would tell me not to come again. I felt so helpless. Helpless and hopeless.'

'That was wrong of her,' Ruby said gently and Sebastian struggled not to cry.

'But that's no excuse for you not having her photos around,' she went on, less gently.

'That's a matter of opinion,' he said gruffly. 'People handle things differently, Ruby. I suggest we change the subject. It's going to be hot again today. How about coming for a swim with me later?'

'Am I allowed to wear my bikini?' she said cheekily.

'Absolutely not. That bikini is the work of the devil. That's what started me off on the road to ruin and damnation, seeing you in that bikini. So no, Ruby, I don't want you to wear that bikini. I don't want you to wear anything at all,' he finished up, smiling the sexiest smile.

CHAPTER EIGHTEEN

RUBY DID HER best to stay cool in the face of the wickedest of temptations, knowing instinctively that if she kept on giving in to this man, she would lose control of her life, and her emotions. She really didn't want to fall in love with Sebastian any more than he wanted her to fall in love with him. He didn't seem to appreciate the danger, however. But *she* did. It was bad enough that they'd started sharing confidences about their lives. Already she felt sorry for him. Already she wanted to somehow fix him.

Compassion and passion were a dangerous mix. Or they were where her soft heart was concerned.

'Sorry, Sebastian,' she said without a hint of the rampant desire raging within her. 'I have plans for today. First I have to do some Christmas shopping this morning. Then I have some studying to do this afternoon. I have an assignment coming up.'

'Can't you at least spare me a couple of hours? Surely you'll need a break from studying at some stage.'

'No. When I study I need total concentration. Going skinny dipping with you would certainly break that concentration, as you very well know.'

'Fair enough. But I can't stand the thought of today without spending some time with you. So how about I go shopping with you?'

'You want to go shopping with me?' she asked, stunned. 'What if someone sees us together?'

'Like who? Gloria's in Adelaide and my mother never goes shopping on a Sunday. No one else matters.'

'I don't know about this, Sebastian,' she said worriedly. It was a strangely intimate thing, to go shopping together. Almost as bad as sharing confidences about your past life.

'I'll buy you lunch out,' he tempted, coming around to pull her into his arms.

She gasped at the feel of his near nakedness pressed against her, her heart racing as desire threatened to overwhelm her. His mouth sought hers and it was so exciting, his kiss, his nearness.

The sound of the house phone ringing startled both of them. Ruby reefed out of Sebastian's arms and snatched it up, glad of the distraction. If the kissing had gone on much longer, she'd have been back in bed with him. And she really didn't want to be that weak.

'It's your mother,' she told Sebastian as she put the phone to her ear.

'Good morning, Frieda,' she said breezily. 'How are you this morning?'

'Very well thank you, Ruby,' she returned, her voice not at all fragile. 'I just wanted to call and thank you for last night. It was a wonderful dinner. You are a wonderful girl. I hope Sebastian appreciates you.'

'I'm sure he does, Frieda,' she said, a naughty smile itching to break out.

'You'd make some man a wonderful wife.'

'You think so?'

'I do indeed.'

'That's very nice of you to say so. I'm afraid I have to go, Frieda. I'm in the middle of making your son's breakfast,' she lied.

'He's a fool, my son,' she muttered and Ruby pretended not to hear.

'What was that, Frieda?'

'Nothing. You go, my dear. Thank you again.' And she clicked off.

'Your mother thinks I would make some man a wonderful wife,' she murmured when Sebastian drew her back into his embrace.

That stopped him in his tracks. 'I'm sure she does,' he bit out. 'Why do you think I want to keep us a secret?'

'She just wants you to be happy, Sebastian. Mothers are like that.'

'Marriage is not necessarily the recipe for happiness. You should have told her you don't want to get married either.'

'Perhaps I should have. Now, I have to get us some breakfast,' she said, pulling out of his arms. 'Time is a-wasting. I'd like to get to the shops before they close.'

An hour passed before they were both properly fed and dressed, Sebastian continually delaying proceedings by kissing Ruby. He couldn't seem to keep his hands off her. Finally, they made it into his car and out to a nearby mall. The place was already packed, yet it was well off lunchtime.

'I'm not familiar with this mall,' Ruby said. 'Is there a department store or just smaller shops and supermarkets?'

'There's definitely a department store. Come on. I know the way.'

When he took her hand in his, Ruby ground to a halt.

'No hand-holding in public,' she said firmly.

'Fair enough,' he replied. 'But I reserve the right to buy you lunch.'

'Okay,' she agreed. 'Shopping first, though.'

'Do you have anything specific in mind you want to buy?'

'Yes. I thought since both my brothers are in live-in relationships, I'd get them some seriously nice sheets and towels. At this time of the year, there are often sales in Manchester.'

'Sounds like a good idea,' Sebastian said.

Ruby couldn't believe how much she enjoyed the next hour. Sebastian was a great help, stopping her from buying navy blue sheets—despite them being a bargain—and insisting she stick to white, both with the sheets and the towels.

'Can't go wrong with white,' he advised.

As they made their way to the car park to deposit all their parcels before having lunch, it occurred to Ruby just how lonely she'd been for a long time. Yes, she'd made friends over the last few years, but they hadn't been close friends, and she'd moved too often to develop deep connections. Sebastian was the first person she'd gone shopping with in ages. And it had been so nice to have someone with her whose opinion she could ask.

Ruby suddenly thought of her mother and how they had always gone shopping together. For food. For clothes. Make-up. Anything and everything. Her father used to complain they were joined at the hip.

Thinking of her father annoyed her, so she shifted her mind to her brothers, who had always brought her joy. But they had their own lives now. She couldn't rely on them to ease her loneliness.

She couldn't rely on Sebastian either, she accepted ruefully. Once Georgia returned, she would be gone, from his life and his bed. She sighed before she could stop herself.

'What on earth are you thinking about?' Sebastian asked.

'Nothing important,' she replied, and dredged up a quick smile.

He frowned at her, then shrugged. 'Okay. I won't pry. You have a right to your thoughts. Are you hungry?' he asked as he zapped open the car. 'I am.'

'Not overly. But coffee would be nice.'

After they finished their coffee, they were making their way past some shops when Sebastian ground to a halt.

'That would be perfect for you,' he said, and pointed to a mannequin in a nearby window wearing a red dress.

It was, indeed, a stunning dress. Halter-necked, with a wide band inset around the waist above a gathered skirt—very short gathered skirt.

'That has Christmas party written all over it,' Sebastian said.

'No way could I wear a dress like that to your Christmas party,' Ruby protested.

'Nonsense. Let's go and try it on,' he said and this time firmly took her hand in his, pulling her into the expensive boutique.

When an attractive young salesgirl immediately approached them, a speechless Ruby let Sebastian do the talking.

'That red dress in the window,' he said. 'Ruby wants to try it on.'

'Certainly, sir,' the girl said happily and hurried away to find one in Ruby's size.

'It looks expensive,' Ruby whispered to Sebastian. 'This whole shop looks expensive.'

'Good. You only get what you pay for, Ruby. Now, no more objections. I'll be doing the paying. Call it a thank you for what you did for my mother's birthday.'

The dress was soon brought to them and Ruby was bundled off to try it on. It fitted perfectly, and looked very sexy on her. Sebastian obviously thought so too when she came out of the fitting room to show him. Desire flooded her as his eyes roved hotly over her. Suddenly, she couldn't wait to go home.

'Perfect,' he said. 'We'll take it.'

Ruby refrained from telling Sebastian that it cost almost a thousand dollars because he was right. He could afford it. And she loved the dress. It was gorgeous.

The salesgirl returned to the fitting room with her.

'You're a lucky girl, having a generous husband like that.'

Something twisted in Ruby's heart. 'He's not my husband,' she said.

'Oh, sorry. Boyfriend, then?'

'Something like that,' Ruby agreed, and smiled at the girl. For how could she say that he wasn't her boyfriend either, that he was her boss and her secret lover?

The girl left with the dress whilst Ruby got changed in her other clothes. She took her time, combing her hair whilst her mind whirled with bothersome thoughts. By the time she emerged from the fitting room, Sebastian had paid for the dress and had the parcel in his hand.

As they left the shop, Ruby decided to say what was on her mind. 'Thank you for the lovely dress, Sebastian, but I can't possibly wear it to your Christmas party. I'm your housekeeper, not a hostess.'

His sigh was full of exasperation as he stopped walking and turned to face her. 'At my annual Christmas party, you are neither, Ruby. This is a staff party and you are a member of my staff. Georgia used to get dressed up. Why shouldn't you?'

'Oh, I didn't realise.'

'No more objections, then?'

'I guess not.'

'Good, because I would like to get you home. Seeing you in that dress has done wicked things to me. I trust you won't come up with any other excuses not to spend some private time with me.'

He didn't wait for her answer, just headed for the car.

CHAPTER NINETEEN

THE DRIVE HOME was agony for Sebastian. He wanted Ruby so badly it was painful. As soon as he'd driven into the garage and switched off the engine, he turned and kissed her. It was possibly a mistake but he couldn't resist. He did stop, however, when disaster loomed. Lord, but she made him act like a randy teenager.

'I think I'd better get you inside, pronto,' he said wryly.

'Yes, please,' she said in a voice thickened with desire.

They only just made it up to his bedroom before they ripped each other's clothes off and fell onto the bed. Once again, their first mating was quick and savage, testimony to their need for each other. Afterwards, he carried her into the shower where they kissed under the water for ages till they were both panting with renewed need.

'I want you to put on that red dress for me,' he said as he dried her. 'Without any underwear, of course.'

He could see the idea excited her as much as it excited him.

She gave him one of those glazed looks, her chest rising and falling as her heartbeat quickened.

'I can't wear a bra with it anyway,' she said breathlessly.

'Yes. I noticed.' He still hadn't forgotten how she'd looked back in the shop. So hot and sexy that he'd immediately become erect.

'Will you take me with the dress on?' she choked out.

'Do you want me to?'

'Yes...'

So he did, getting her to kneel at the foot of the bed with her head on the quilt whilst he lifted the skirt and took her from behind. She moaned when she came, a noise of sheer pleasure. His own orgasm was just as intense.

'You are definitely trying to corrupt me,' she said when he pulled her shakily to her feet.

'I think the corruption is mutual. Now, take the dress off.'

Her inward breath could have been shock, but it felt more like excitement. She was one sexy woman.

Her hands trembled as she undid the side zip before slowly lifting the dress over her head, leaving her standing there once again with nothing on. Her breathing, he noted, had quickened further. His own was decidedly ragged.

'Take your hair down,' he ordered thickly.

Sebastian's gut tightened as she did so. God, but she was beautiful!

'You would tempt a saint,' he muttered.

She laughed. She actually laughed. 'But you're not a saint, Sebastian.'

'No,' he agreed. 'Far from it. Now stay where you are. There's something I have to do.'

He turned from the provocative sight of her nakedness, hurrying into the bathroom where he disposed of the used condom before rolling on another. The fact he was still so erect was as stunning as it was thrilling. He simply could not get enough of this woman. Thankfully, she seemed just as needy for him. He strode back into the bedroom where he climbed onto the bed, dragging in a few gathering breaths whilst he tried not to ogle Ruby too much. But he was wasting his breath. He couldn't stop looking at her. And wanting her.

'What do you want me to do?' she asked shakily.

'Nothing,' he growled. 'Just get that gorgeous body of yours over here.'

She came over to the bed rather hesitantly, which surprised him. Surely she wasn't going all shy on him. But no, she wasn't shy, he soon realised. She was trembling with desire.

'Wow,' she said, reaching out to brush her fingers over his erection. 'That's impressive, considering.'

Now it was his turn to laugh. 'It's been like this ever since I clapped eyes on you in that bikini, Ruby.'

Her eyes clouded and Sebastian worried momentarily that he'd said something to offend her. But then she smiled, and without any hesitation boldly climbed on top of him. Sebastian blinked his surprise. She hadn't taken the initiative before. He'd been the boss in the sex department so far, but he liked her taking charge.

'I could say the same when I saw you by the pool in those indecently tight togs you own,' she said, lifting her hips before taking a firm hold of his erection. Her eyes grew heavy as she eased him inside her, Sebastian unable to stop himself from groaning. Lord, but she was hot. Hot and wet.

'I didn't like you much to begin with, Sebastian,' she said as she began to ride him. 'But I always liked your body. You are one hunky man.'

Sebastian grimaced at her words, not happy that she'd reduced him to just a body. But he was too far gone to protest. He was close to coming, and so was she. He could recognise the signs. Her muscles tightened around him and her head tipped back, her lips parting as she dragged in more air.

He came first, shuddering into her as if he hadn't had an orgasm for years. She followed him with a fierce orgasm of her own, her hands clawing at his shoulders as she kept riding him through it, her eyes closed tight, till finally she stopped. For a long time she just sat on him, her eyes still shut. When she finally opened them, he was staggered to see they were wet with tears.

'What is it?' he asked straight away. 'What's wrong?'

She just shook her head and rolled off him onto the bed, her hands coming up to cover her face as she continued to shake her head from side to side.

Her tears upset him, for tears spelt emotion and emotion was something he'd vowed to avoid. Then again, he'd vowed to avoid sleeping with women like Ruby as well. But, hell on earth, he was only human and she was so incredibly sexy. Unfortunately, she was also an incredibly nice girl. He hoped she wasn't falling for him. If she was, then this affair was over. Pronto.

'You have to talk to me,' he insisted. 'Tell me what the matter is.'

She didn't reply, just sighed the deepest sigh.

Finally, she took her hands away, and Sebastian was relieved to see she wasn't still crying. Though her eyes were a little moist. She blinked as she turned to face him.

'It's nothing drastic, really. I was just overcome by the moment, that's all. I mean, I've never enjoyed sex like I enjoy it with you. It's incredible.'

Sebastian's relief was enormous. She wasn't falling in love with him. Thank God.

'You're the one who's incredible,' he said, and reached to cuddle to her close. 'Incredible all round. And the very best lover a man could have. You are insatiable, woman, and it's fantastic!'

'I guess I can't get used to having gone so sex mad. I mean, till I met you I was quite happy to be celibate.'

'Well, obviously that's not the case any longer. Face the facts, Ruby. You're a grown woman in her sexual prime. By your own admission it's been some time since you've had sex. It was inevitable that one day you'd meet a man who would turn you on. I myself have been on sexual rations for years so it's not surprising I had to break, eventually. Yes, we've both gone a bit sex mad but we're not hurting anyone. There's nothing wrong in what we've been doing. Yes, the arrangement I proposed is unconventional, but if it fulfils our needs at the moment, then why should we care, or worry?'

He tipped her face up and kissed her softly on her lips. 'Now, what say I order us a meal? I'm famished.'

'I am too,' she agreed.

'Okay, we'd better get dressed before the food arrives.'

'All right.'

'Then after we've eaten we'll come back upstairs to bed for the night.'

'Really?'

'Yes, really.'

'I would have thought you'd be too tired.'

'The food will revive me. But if we get tired, we'll go to sleep.'

'Am I to stay the whole night with you? Is that part of our arrangement?'

'I'd like you to.'

'We'll see,' she said. But she was smiling.

CHAPTER TWENTY

'HOW DID SATURDAY night go?' was Janice's first question when she arrived on Monday morning.

'What are you talking about?' Ruby answered, alarmed that Janice somehow knew something.

'The dinner with the boss's mother,' Janice went on, giving Ruby a puzzled look. 'You can't have forgotten.'

She had, of course. The dinner for Sebastian's mother seemed like eons ago. All Ruby could think of this morning was what had happened on Saturday night. And last night. And then again this morning, after Sebastian awoke. The man was insatiable. But then, so was she. Already she could not wait for him to come home tonight and he'd only been gone a couple of hours.

'Oh, the dinner,' she said, hoping she didn't look as distracted as she was feeling. 'It went well.'

'I'll bet she liked the pie. My kids certainly did.'

'Yes, she liked everything,' Ruby said, only then noticing that Janice looked tired, which was understandable. The woman had three school-age children and a husband who Tom said was often out of work. To earn money she worked hard as a cleaner, doing Sebastian's house, and Gloria's, as well as her own place.

'Come and have some coffee before you start,' she offered.

Janice glanced around her agitatedly. 'I should get on with things. The end-of-year presentation at the school is this afternoon and I promised the kids I'd be there. It starts at one-thirty.'

'You should be well and truly finished in time,' Ruby said. 'I'll help you.'

'Would you?'

'Of course.'

'You're a life-saver, Ruby. I… I want to go home and freshen up before I go. Do my hair. Put on a dress. The kids love it when I make an effort to look nice.'

'I'll make sure you're out of here in plenty of time.'

After their coffee, Ruby suggested Janice do the downstairs whilst she did the upstairs, leaving Ruby alone with her thoughts as she cleaned away. She started in the master suite, doing her best not to look at the bed and think about what had transpired there.

In truth, Ruby still hadn't come to terms with her bold behaviour, despite Sebastian's logical argument that they weren't doing anything wrong; that they were just indulging themselves sexually after denying themselves for too long.

It all sounded rational, but something inside Ruby kept ringing alarm bells. It was probably still just lust with both of them, but she wanted to keep it that way. Ruby didn't want to fall in love with her boss. She really didn't.

But such emotions didn't always respond to reason.

Eleven o'clock saw her come downstairs to tell Janice that she was finished upstairs, and if she wanted to go home early, she could.

'But I haven't done the bathroom down here,' Janice protested. 'Or got the laundry ready.'

'I'll do them. You go and make yourself beautiful for your children.'

Janice laughed. 'I'll do my best but I'd need a fairy godmother to look beautiful. I'll settle for nice.'

'Nonsense. You're a good-looking woman. Your husband is a lucky man.'

Janice's flush of pleasure gave Ruby pleasure. She liked making people feel good about themselves.

'He doesn't always think so,' Janice grumbled.

'Then he's a fool! Now off you go. I'll see you on Friday and you can tell me all about the presentation.'

'I'll do that,' Janice said cheerfully as she pulled off her cleaning gloves. 'Thank you so much, Ruby. You're a doll.'

Being called a doll brought a smile to Ruby's face. But once Janice had gone, it occurred to her that she was exactly that to Sebastian. A doll, to be played with for a while but easily discarded.

It was a depressing thought. But not, Ruby accepted ruefully, depressing enough to dampen her desire for Sebastian. She still wanted him to hurry home, still wanted tonight to come sooner than it would. She wanted him to take all her clothes off and, yes, to play with her at length before having all sorts of sex with her. There wasn't a position they'd tried that she hadn't enjoyed. She had no preferences as long as it was Sebastian she was having sex with.

Ruby sucked in sharply at this last revealing thought. Oh, dear. Maybe it was already too late. Maybe she was already emotionally involved with him. Not that it would change things. She was in way too deep to walk away. Just thinking about Sebastian made her fizz with longing. It didn't matter whether it was lust or love driving her actions. Until Georgia came back, she was his for the taking.

Strangely enough, the notion that she might be falling in love with Sebastian didn't upset Ruby as much as she'd thought it might. At least it showed she *could* fall in love. Ever since her father's betrayal, Bailey's cruel dumping, and Jason turning out to be married, she hadn't thought she would ever fall in love with a man. Or trust one, for that matter. Not that she needed to trust Sebastian. Such thinking was only an issue if he loved her back. Which he didn't.

They didn't have a relationship. They had an *arrangement*, and it would come to an end in a few months.

Ruby was wondering how she would survive that when her phone rang, her chest tightening when she saw it was Sebastian.

'Yes, Sebastian?' she answered, trying to sound like a housekeeper and not a woman obsessed.

'I have a problem,' he announced baldly. 'Those bastards I sold my shows to in the UK are trying to pull a swiftie with the contract and I have to go and sort it out. I've already booked a seat on a flight to London tonight but I need you to pack a bag for me and taxi it over to my office. I can't afford the time to come home and do it myself. I have things I have to do here before I go.'

'Can't this problem be fixed up over the Internet?' she said, dying inside at the thought she would not see him tonight after all.

'No. It needs my personal attention.'

'You haven't got a lawyer over there who could sort it out for you?'

'Afraid not. I'm the one and only lawyer I employ.'

'You're a *lawyer*?'

'That's what I was before I went into the television business. Jennifer was a lawyer too. That's how we met.'

'Oh. I didn't know.'

'Why would you?'

Yes, why would you, Ruby? It's not as though you two have ever really talked. You just have lots of sex.

But not tonight. Tonight, Sebastian would be winging his way to London, not to come back for possibly days.

'Don't forget your Christmas party is on Friday night,' she reminded him.

'I'll be back by then. I've booked a return flight that gets in Friday morning.'

'I see.'

'I'm sorry, Ruby,' he said quietly, and her heart turned over. 'I'll only be there a couple of days.'

'You'll be tired for your party.'

'I shouldn't be. I fly first class. I'll sleep on the plane.'

Ruby made no comment to this, having forgotten how super rich he was.

'I could bring your luggage to the airport,' she suggested hopefully. 'See you off.'

'Best not, Ruby. Just send the case to the office.'

'I don't know where that is,' she said, highlighting again how little she knew about this man.

He told her the address and she wrote it down.

'Before you go, Sebastian,' she said before he could hang up on her, 'would you mind if I had Tom put up some lights for the party? I mean, it's not a Christmas party without some Christmas decorations.' There were heaps in the storage room downstairs, obviously left behind by the previous owners.

His sigh down the phone was exasperated. 'You must know by now, Ruby, that I'm not into that kind of thing.'

'Yes, but—'

'Some lights, then,' he agreed abruptly before she could argue with him. 'But not out the front of the house. And no tree.'

'No tree?' she echoed.

'No tree,' he confirmed. 'Okay?'

'Okay.' But, boy, was she going to go to town on those lights.

'I'm sorry, I have to get back to work and you have to get on with packing me a bag.'

'Promise to text me tomorrow to let me know you've arrived safely.'

'For pity's sake, Ruby, this is just what I don't want.'

'All I'm asking for is a simple text,' she said firmly.

Another sigh. 'All right. I'll text you.'

'Thanks,' she said, but he was already gone.

Ruby trudged upstairs, trying to take some comfort from the fact that she knew so little about Sebastian. Because surely she couldn't be in love with a man she didn't know. It was just lust, she decided. Lust and infatuation. He was, after all, handsome and rich and, yes, damned good in bed.

Ruby brightened at this last thought, promising herself that when Sebastian arrived home Friday she would give him a welcome he wouldn't forget in a hurry.

CHAPTER TWENTY-ONE

SEBASTIAN'S PLANE TOUCHED down at Mascot shortly after seven on the Friday morning. Despite having flown first class, he was not rested, sleep having eluded him in London *and* during the long flight.

Sebastian's body sagged like a dead weight as he hauled himself out of his seat. His eyes felt gritty, his head full of cotton wool. Getting through Customs was slow and Sebastian had lots of time to regret having driven his car to the airport Monday. He should have left it at work and taken a taxi. He hadn't anticipated being this exhausted. Unfortunately, now he'd have to drive home instead of just sitting in the back seat of a taxi with his eyes blessedly shut.

Sebastian wasn't looking forward to the drive, or the arrival at home. He suspected by the time he got to the house he wouldn't be fit for much, certainly not the serious discussion with Ruby he'd decided upon during the long hours he'd been awake on the plane. Sebastian was not a procrastinator, but common sense demanded he put this off until he'd had some sleep. Such a situation needed tact and sensitivity. Not Sebastian's strong points. Especially not when he was exhausted.

The traffic home was appalling, peak hour on a Friday enough to try anyone's patience, let alone a man who hadn't slept properly in days. By the time he turned into his street at Mosman, he was practically comatose. Leaving his luggage in the car, he staggered up the stairwell. Ruby was in the kitchen, clearly eager for him to arrive if the smile on her face was anything to go by. That smile precisely underlined why he'd come to the decision he had.

'You're home!' she exclaimed happily. 'Can I get you some coffee? Some food perhaps?'

'Sorry,' he said far too sharply. 'But I don't want coffee right now. Or food, or anything else. I have to go to bed if I'm to function at the Christmas party tonight. No noise for a few hours, Ruby. We'll have coffee together later, when I feel human.'

It killed Sebastian to see the welcoming smile wiped off her face but it had to be done. He was being cruel to be kind, wasn't he? She'd see that he was right in the end.

Turning, he strode off down the hallway, hating himself more than he had in a long time.

Ruby stared after Sebastian until he disappeared. She heard him trudge upstairs and bang his bedroom door shut. Then she heard nothing.

She tried not to feel too hurt, tried to understand. Clearly, he hadn't slept on the plane. Clearly, the contract business he'd been going to fix in London had not gone well. But that was no reason to be so abrupt with her. It wasn't *her* fault.

Still, with Sebastian demanding no noise it was just as well that Tom had done the lawns and pool yesterday. Just as well too that she'd given Janice the day off, saying *she* would do whatever needed to be done. Janice had been super grateful, as the school holidays had begun and she wanted to spend more time with her children. Of course, Ruby's motivation for doing this wasn't all pure kindness. She'd been imagining being alone in the house with Sebastian; she'd thought that after a few days away he'd be as hungry for her as she was for him.

Clearly not.

The erotically charged reunion Ruby had been fantasising about all week was not going to happen, was it?

Ruby tried to be philosophical about it. But it was still disappointing. She'd been so looking forward to being in Sebastian's arms again, to losing herself there and feeling what he alone could make her feel.

She sighed deeply at the realisation that her feelings had gone beyond lust now. Way beyond.

Oh, Lord. What to do?

Nothing, she accepted. She could do nothing. She couldn't make Sebastian fall in love with her. He didn't want that.

She could walk away, she supposed, before her heart was totally broken. Maybe she should. She would have to think about it. Ruby suspected, however, that she simply didn't have the courage. Falling in love made you weak. If she couldn't have Sebastian's heart, she could at least have his body. For a while anyway. Until Georgia got back.

Meanwhile…

Ruby wished she had some housework to do to distract herself but there wasn't any. The house was spotless, not a speck of dirt or dust anywhere. She supposed she could lie down and read a book, but, truly, what an anticlimax.

All the elation and anticipation Ruby had been feeling earlier had totally drained out of her. She'd been so looking forward to today. Not the party so much. Just Sebastian being back.

Okay, so he was tired, and obviously troubled. But that wasn't anything to do with her. He could at least have smiled at her, given her a little kiss maybe.

Perhaps she would just lie down and check out Facebook. See what those brothers of hers were up to. Yes, that was what she would do. That was how she'd kept in contact with them these past few years, though it was their female partners who posted most of the pictures.

Strangely enough, after she'd been doing that for a while her eyes grew heavy and before she knew it she fell asleep. She was awoken by the sound of the house phone ringing and Ruby was startled by the identity of her caller. It was Zack.

'Hi, Zack,' she said, trying not to sound too surprised. Or too worried. Surely he wasn't going to ask her out. She didn't want to have to tell him to get lost.

'Hi, Ruby. Look, I've been trying to get in contact with Sebastian but his damned phone's turned off. Is he there?'

'Yes, but he's asleep. He said he needed a few hours' rest before the party. I don't think he slept on the plane, and I have a feeling that contract business in London didn't go very well. He seemed worried.'

'Did he? Well, it's not about the business. That was all sorted out. Sebastian sent me a text. Look, he's probably just tired. Seb's not at his best when he's tired.'

'What did you want to contact him about? Maybe I can help. I wouldn't dare disturb him.'

'Okay. When he wakes up, tell him I might be a bit late for the party tonight. I will be there though. I promise.'

For such a laid-back kind of guy, Zack sounded somewhat stressed. Ruby couldn't let it go. 'Is there anything wrong, Zack?' she asked.

'Not really,' he said, still sounding odd. 'Just girl trouble. I wanted to ask Seb's advice about something. But no sweat, I'll sort it out myself. See you tonight.'

He hung up almost as abruptly as Sebastian did, leaving Ruby wondering what it was about men that they were compelled to be that way. Talkers, only occasionally. Confiders, rarely. Which was a shame because nothing good came of bottling up problems. If men shared more there would be less conflict between the sexes. Less mental illness as well.

Ruby glanced at the time on her phone. It was only one. There were still four hours to go before the caterers arrived, and at least three hours before she started getting herself ready for the party. She'd already decided not to go to town on her hair and face. Wearing that red dress was glamorous enough, so an hour would do. Rolling over, she picked up the novel she'd been trying to read all week, and started again at the beginning.

CHAPTER TWENTY-TWO

SEBASTIAN WAS ROUSED from his drugged sleep by a rather loud knocking on his bedroom door.

'What?' he said grumpily, his head still heavy from the sleeping pill.

'Sorry to disturb you,' Ruby said through the door. 'But it's gone seven o'clock and people will start arriving soon for the party. I thought you might want to be up and about to greet them.'

'Damn,' he muttered. 'Seven, did you say?'

'Actually, it's ten past.'

'Give me a few minutes and I'll be there,' he said, throwing off the quilt and lurching into the shower.

He started off with warm water, then turned it to cold, swearing under its icy spray until he was well and truly awake. He didn't bother to shave, just cleaned his teeth and combed his hair before heading to his walk-in wardrobe where he pulled on a pair of pale grey trousers, which were lightweight and cool. He teamed them with a favourite navy-blue shirt before slipping his feet into comfy black loafers and hurrying downstairs.

There were other people in the kitchen besides Ruby—a young man and a blonde girl—who were busily setting up glasses on the breakfast bar. But he only had eyes for Ruby, who was wearing that sexy red dress. Despite her hair being up with little make-up adorning her face, she still looked criminally desirable.

Damn, damn, and double damn!

'Hello, Mr Marshall,' the blonde girl said with a bright smile. 'I'm Marcie. We met last year, remember? And this is Josh, my partner in crime and catering.'

She and Josh both smiled at their in joke. Sebastian didn't smile back, troubled that the decision he'd come to on the plane was about to be swayed by the hunger Ruby instantly engendered in him. He told himself it wasn't Ruby herself he'd been missing, but the sex. He wasn't falling in love with her. There was no need to panic. No need to tell her their affair was over after all.

But down deep he knew he was kidding himself. He *was* in danger of falling in love with her. And he simply couldn't go down that road again. Not after what had happened with Jennifer.

'So how are you feeling now?' Marcie went on brightly, clearly undeterred by Sebastian's lack of humour. 'Ruby tells us you've just flown in from London and had to catch up on sleep.'

'I'm fine,' he said, thinking how typical it was of Ruby to chat away to these people as if they'd known each other for ever. Yet she would have only met this couple for the first time today. She was a very gregarious person. Gregarious and utterly gorgeous. Sebastian tried to keep his face impassive as he looked at her. Tried not to imagine reaching up and taking her hair down, then taking her to bed.

'I'll have coffee outside, Ruby,' he said, and spun away.

'Do you want anything to eat?' she called after him. 'You must be hungry.'

'We'll have lots of finger food ready shortly,' Marcie added.

'Just coffee for now,' Sebastian threw over his shoulder.

Ruby carried a mug of coffee out to where Sebastian was sitting at the outdoor table, glancing up at the lights. They were already turned on but wouldn't show to advantage until it got darker. She'd turned them on for a while last night and they'd looked fantastic.

Of course, old grumpy probably didn't like them. Truly, he'd try the patience of a saint at times. It pained her that she still found him so damned attractive, even when he was being a grouch. How she'd fallen in love with him she had no idea, though she suspected it had started the day he went shopping with her.

'The lights look good, don't they?' she said as she put the coffee down in front of him.

'Yes,' he surprised her by agreeing. 'They do, actually. But not as good as you.'

Ruby might have taken pleasure in his compliment if it hadn't been delivered so ruefully.

'Thank you,' she bit out.

'Would you sit down, Ruby? I need to talk to you about something before people get here.'

Ruby swallowed, knowing instinctively that she wasn't going to like what he had to say. The hardness in his eyes rather gave the game away.

'Talk to me about what?' she asked tensely.

'Just sit down,' he bit out.

She sat down.

He sighed and shook his head at her.

'Well?' she prompted when he remained silent. 'What is it? People will be here soon. Or some of them will. And before I forget, Zack rang and said he'd be late. He tried to ring you but your phone was turned off.'

'Fine. Did he say why?'

'Some kind of girl trouble.'

'Of course.' His tone was dry, the implication being that Zack was always having girl trouble. It wasn't anything new.

'What did you want to talk to me about?' she went on when he didn't speak. He just sat there, drinking the coffee.

He finally put the mug down, pursing his lips before spearing her with a narrow-eyed gaze.

'I've had time to think whilst I was away,' he began firmly.

'About what?' she asked. But she had already suspected what was coming, her stomach flipping over before contracting tightly.

'Our arrangement,' he said. 'It's not going to work.'

'Why's that?' Ruby said, her chest tightening as well. 'I thought it was what you wanted.'

His laugh was cold. 'I thought so too.'

Ruby tried not to panic. Tried to keep calm. 'What *do* you want, Sebastian? Do you even know?'

'I know what I *don't* want,' he bit out. 'I don't want to fall in love again. The trouble is, you're the sort of girl a man falls in love with, especially once he starts sleeping with her.'

Ruby felt both flattered and frustrated. 'Is it so bad, falling in love again?' Quite the ironic statement, considering she'd once decided not to go there herself. But it was too late; she was already there.

'Yes,' he said firmly. 'I vowed not to fall in love again after Jennifer died and I mean to keep that vow. I'm sorry, Ruby, but I can't keep on—'

The front doorbell broke their conversation off at that critical point, leaving Ruby hanging. What had he been going to say? she agonised as he abruptly stood up and strode away. Clearly, she soon came to realise, she wouldn't be finding out until this party was over. People started pouring in, surprising Ruby that they'd turned up so early. She thought people were always late for parties these days.

Not this party, obviously. They all knew each other, which was logical. They all worked for Harvest Productions. She met so many new people during the next hour that she couldn't keep their names straight in her head. Still, she was glad she was wearing her lovely red dress because all the women were done up to the nines, some of them very beautiful and glamorous. They were all nice though, which came as a surprise. She'd thought they might all be up themselves but they weren't.

The DJ arrived and set up in the dining room from where the music could flow through the house and outside as well. The music he chose was a mixture of old and new, with some Christmas favourites thrown in occasionally. He was a big hit with the partygoers, if their dancing and singing along was any guide.

The lights were a big hit as well, several guests commenting on the festive spirit.

Ruby didn't feel very festive, despite having downed a few glasses of champagne as she chatted away to the guests. The alcohol didn't help her agitation at all. Or her depression. When Zack finally arrived, Ruby struggled to put a smile on her face. But she managed. Somehow.

'Hi,' she said after she opened the front door.

'Hi to you too,' Zack returned, giving her the once-over but without ogling. 'Wow, don't you look stunning? Red suits you.'

'And black suits you,' she said with her first real smile of the night.

'True.' He grinned. 'Sounds like the party's in full flow.'

He walked into the house—and the party—with his usual easy-going confidence, looking like a typical bad boy dressed all in black. Black jeans. Black T-shirt. Black belt and shoes. Even his tats were black. If she hadn't known he was a famous actor, Ruby would have thought he was a biker.

'Zack!' Sebastian exclaimed when he saw his friend. 'You made it.'

'Yeah,' he replied. 'Just. Did Ruby tell you I called earlier?'

'She did,' Sebastian replied with a swift glance her way. 'So what's up?'

'Nothing. Everything's sorted. What I need is a drink. A *real* drink,' he added when a waiter approached with a tray full of champagne and wine.

'Come with me to the study,' Sebastian said, steering Zack away, leaving Ruby standing there staring after them. Annoyed, she swept another glass of champagne from the waiter's tray and lifted it to her lips, telling herself she really should eat something as well. It wouldn't be a good look for Sebastian's housekeeper to get drunk.

Such thinking had her heading for the kitchen, and the finger food. It was all delicious and very addictive. Ruby tasted just about every selection before heading back to the party, her heart lifting when she saw Zack and Sebastian had left the study, with Zack nursing a large whisky. Sebastian, however, surprised Ruby by choosing an orange juice from a passing waiter. He spotted her raised eyebrows and briefly raised his own, their eyes meeting across the room. It was a strangely intimate moment, one which could only happen between people who knew each other well.

Maybe she knew him better than she thought she did.

Wishful thinking, Ruby.

'Wow. Lights!' Zack exclaimed when he reached the al fresco area. 'That has to be Ruby's doing.'

'Of course,' Sebastian said with a rueful look her way. 'You don't think it was my idea, do you?'

Zack laughed. 'Never in a million years, mate. But they look great.' He turned to smile over at Ruby and she smiled back. Sebastian scowled at both of them.

The DJ packed up and went home at midnight, the party slowly breaking up after that. Most people had come in taxis and left the same way. Even Zack went home in a taxi, which was a good idea since he was plastered. No one asked to bunk down there for the night, highlighting their knowledge of their boss's passion for privacy.

The caterers were brilliantly efficient at putting everything away in the boxes in which they had brought everything, taking all the dirty plates and glasses with them when they left shortly after one. Ruby was very impressed and told them so as she helped them out to their van. There was nothing for her to do after they'd gone except turn the lights off and give the floors a quick going-over with the vacuum cleaner. Out of the corner of her eye she saw two grey trouser legs appear.

'Ruby, stop with the vacuuming and come and sit down,' Sebastian commanded. 'We have to finish our conversation.'

Ruby sighed as she switched off the vacuum cleaner. 'I suppose we do,' she said, resigned to the inevitable.

'I'll be down in my study. See you shortly.'

Ruby put the vacuum cleaner away then trudged down to the study. Sebastian was sitting in the oversized leather chair in the far corner, the one with the standing lamp next to it. He was nursing a rather large whisky, which he lifted to his lips, his eyes spearing hers over the rim of the glass. He didn't look happy.

Ruby sat down in his office chair, her agitation spilling over when he remained silent.

'Well, out with it,' she demanded. 'What were you going to say earlier? Not that I don't already know.'

'What do you already know?'

'You don't want to sleep with me any more.'

'Actually, that's not true. I *do* want to sleep with you. That's the crux of the problem. What I was going to say earlier was that, under the circumstances, I can't keep you on as my housekeeper.'

Ruby's mouth dropped open as his words sank in.

'You're *firing* me?' she blurted out after a few mind-blowing seconds.

'I wouldn't put it that bluntly,' he ground out.

'And how would you put it?' she threw at him.

'I was going to suggest that you hand in your resignation, for which I would compensate you handsomely.'

Ruby couldn't help the disbelieving laugh that punched from her throat. 'You have to be joking. You're going to *pay* me to leave?'

'It seems only fair.'

Fair. Ruby closed her eyes against the crippling hurt in her heart.

'I'm sorry, Ruby,' he said with a weary sigh. 'But I can't see any other way. I never meant to hurt you. Or to interfere with your plans. But if you stay, things will get complicated.'

Complicated. That was putting it mildly.

'Very well,' she said at last. 'I'll go.' Best she did, really. 'But I don't want your damned money.'

'Don't be stupid,' he snapped as he stood up and walked towards her. 'You deserve compensation. It was wrong of me to do what I did, and to suggest such an arrangement in the first place.'

'I went into it with my eyes open,' she admitted ruefully.

'I suppose you did, but that doesn't make me feel any better. Please, Ruby, let me make things comfortable for you, make that dream of becoming a social worker come true. I'm a rich man. I can afford to buy you an apartment. Or just give you cash, if you prefer.'

Ruby realised it probably would be stupid of her to refuse his offer. He was right. He was a rich man. A very rich man. Nevertheless, refuse it she would.

She stood up, her shoulders squaring as she faced him.

'I don't want you to buy me an apartment or give me a great wad of cash. As I said, I went into our affair with my eyes open. I wanted to sleep with you and I ignored the warnings in my head that nothing good ever comes of sleeping with the boss. I'll be gone in the morning. And don't worry, I won't be telling anyone the truth. I'll just say things didn't work out. I'll claim a personality clash. That's always a good reason to quit. But I will expect an excellent reference, plus *some* severance pay. A month's wages seems fair. Okay?' she said as she walked out from behind the desk.

Sebastian caught her before she could escape. 'I can't tell my mother or my sister that we had a personality clash. They won't believe me.'

'Well, that's too bad, Sebastian. You'll have to figure something out. Of course, you could try telling them the truth. That you asked me to leave because we've been sleeping together and you're suddenly scared stiff of becoming emotionally involved. That's the crux of the matter, isn't it?' she threw at him. 'Any kind of relationship is too risky for you, even a sexual one. You might actually start caring for me and vice versa. Shock horror!'

He looked quite crushed by her sarcasm, his hands dropping from her shoulders as his whole body sagged. 'Yes. That pretty much hits the nail on the head. I'm sorry, Ruby, but yes, you're spot on.'

Ruby should have walked out then and there but she couldn't. His expression grew so bleak. And so lonely. Before she could think better of it she reached up and gently touched the cheek of the man she loved.

'There's no reason why we can't enjoy each other one last time, is there?' she said, her fingers running a sensual trail down his face. 'Sort of a going-away present. For me.'

His eyes showed how tortured he felt. And how tempted. His hand came up to cover hers. 'Oh, God, Ruby,' he said with a groan. 'Don't.'

But it was too late. She was already lifting herself up on tiptoe and pressing her mouth to his.

CHAPTER TWENTY-THREE

NO, NO, NO! Sebastian's head screamed at him when he started to kiss her back.

But it was too late, because his lower body was screaming *yes, yes, yes* much louder.

All common sense fled. Her lips enticed him, as did the hot blood roaring through his veins, flooding him with the need to give her what she wanted, what *he* wanted.

Oh, yes, he wanted it, desperately, his hands winding around her back and pulling her hard against him.

But it startled him when she wrenched backwards.

'No. Not here,' she said firmly. 'Come with me.'

She took his hand and led him from the study down the hallway and into her bedroom. There, she drew him over to the side of the bed where she started to undress him.

'Don't say a word,' she said, her voice cool but her dark eyes glittering wildly.

He complied, his tongue thick in his throat as she removed his shirt then his belt and then his trousers.

'Kick off your shoes,' she ordered, which he did, leaving him standing there in just his boxers.

When she hooked her fingers into their elastic waistband he noticed that her hands were trembling. Good, he thought.

Good? What was good about it? He didn't want her nervous. He wanted her wanton and wicked and without one shred of decency. He wanted to hate her for doing this to him.

When she pulled his boxers down he hoped she would go down on her knees before him. That way, it would be just sex with her. But she didn't. Instead, she stepped back and just stared at him, drinking in the sight of him. Not just his erection but his whole body. His face. His chest. His legs. She looked him up and down and sighed, giving him the weirdest feeling that she was trying to memorise him, which was crazy.

Her smile, when it came, was a relief. Because it was all those things he wanted her to be. Wanton and wicked, and, yes, sexy as hell.

She quickly disposed of her lovely red dress and the underwear she had on.

His own smile was just as wicked as hers as his eyes gobbled up every inch of her very beautiful body.

He pounced, making her squeal as he swept her up into his arms and threw her onto the bed.

His hands found all those places that his eyes had admired before moving on to places that couldn't be seen. She moaned beneath the onslaught of his passion. Or was it fury? Maybe a bit of both. Sebastian was beyond thought. Beyond reason. He no longer cared about the emotional risk attached to sleeping with Ruby. He no longer cared about anything but sinking inside her and satisfying the needs that had been tormenting him ever since he met her. She was the devil incarnate, he decided. Teasing him. Tempting him. But he would turn the tables on her tonight. He would not stop until she was begging him to. Once would not be enough. Ten times would not be enough. If she wanted a goodbye present, he would give her a night she would never forget.

Sebastian woke with a start, blinking as he tried to work out what had woken him. Then the sound came again. Muffled but familiar. His phone.

After a wry glance at Ruby, who was still dead to the world next to him, he leant over the side of the bed and retrieved the phone from his trouser pocket.

The identity of the caller eluded him. It was a private number not connected to his contacts menu. If it was a scam call, he wasn't going to be a happy man. Actually, he wasn't a happy man already, his resolve to reduce Ruby to begging not having worked out that way. They had both fallen asleep after that first torrid time, sleeping through until now. A glance at his phone showed it was five-twenty-four a.m. God. Almost dawn. Sebastian tried to blame exhaustion from his trip, followed by the party, but he suspected his age was catching up with him.

'Yes?' he said sharply into the phone, never giving his name to an unknown caller.

'Is that Mr Marshall? Mr Sebastian Marshall?'

It was a woman's voice. Australian. Brisk. Efficient.

'Yes,' he said.

'I'm calling from ER at St Vincent's hospital. We had a patient brought in in the early hours of this morning. Mr Zachary Stone. He's given us your name and number as his first line of contact. I did ring before but there was no answer.'

Sebastian ignored Ruby's hand on his arm, as well as her whispered *what is it*?

'What's happened to him?' he asked anxiously.

'He was stabbed in the stomach. By a crazy lady, according to the patient.'

'My God! Is he all right?'

'He's not on the critical list. And he was conscious when he came in. That's how I have your name and number. Anyway, he's just been taken up to surgery. I can't tell you any more right now, Mr Marshall, I'm sorry. I would suggest you come in, if you can. It's always good for a patient to see a familiar face when they wake up. Though you might have a bit of a wait.'

'That's all right. I'll be there as soon as I can. Thank you,' he added, but she'd already hung up.

'What is it?' Ruby demanded to know straight away. 'What's happened?'

'Zack's been stabbed. By some crazy lady, apparently. He's in hospital, being operated on right now. Look, I have to go.' He jumped out of bed and reached for his clothes.

'I'm coming with you,' she said, doing exactly the same.

'Don't be ridiculous. What will Zack think if you show up there with me at this hour?'

'I don't care what he thinks, Sebastian. I refuse to stay here, worrying myself sick.'

Sebastian hated the jealousy that flared at her words. 'And why would you worry yourself sick over Zack? Is there something going on between you that I don't know about?'

'Oh, don't be so pathetic. He's a friend, that's all. I care about my friends, especially ones who need caring about. Can we stop with this useless bickering and get going?'

Twenty minutes later they zoomed into a space in the hospital car park, neither of them having spoken during the entire trip. Sebastian had been too worried about Zack to talk.

'What if he dies?' Ruby said as they climbed out of the car.

'He won't die,' Sebastian stated with more surety than he was feeling. 'Zack's as tough as an old boot.'

'Is he? I think he has a very soft underbelly.'

Sebastian stopped to stare at her. 'You have a highly intuitive nature, don't you?'

She frowned. 'What do you mean?'

'Most people look at Zack and think nothing can hurt him. But they'd be wrong.'

'Would you like to explain that?'

'No. I wouldn't.'

'Should we take flowers?'

Sebastian laughed. 'Hell, no. He'd be mortified.'

'Okay,' Ruby said, and smiled at him.

Her smile did things to Sebastian that worried him almost as much as Zack's condition. He suspected it was already too late to stop becoming emotionally involved with her. Maybe it wasn't love yet, but it was certainly more than just sex. He shouldn't have let her seduce him last night. It had been one time too many. Where would it all end?

Still, he had more to worry about at the moment than his own stupid self.

'Let's go,' he said, and headed for the lifts.

CHAPTER TWENTY-FOUR

RUBY SAT WITH Sebastian in the waiting room, having been informed that Zack was fine but still in recovery. They would be told when they could see him. Whilst they waited, Ruby got them both some coffee from the machine in the corner of the room, but it was pretty awful.

The wait seemed interminable, broken only by two policemen coming along to interview Sebastian. He told them he knew nothing about the attack, or the woman who'd attacked Zack. They would just have to wait to interview the man himself. The police did say that Zack had made no attempt to protect himself from the knife-wielding assailant, a witness stating that he had just stood there with his hands up and let the woman stab him in the stomach. Twice. Ruby found this news astonishing whereas Sebastian, she noted, didn't seem overly surprised.

Finally, after the policemen had interviewed Zack, they were let into the private room he'd been taken to. By this time it was the middle of Saturday morning.

'Not too long, mind,' an officious nurse named Susan informed them. 'Mr Stone needs his rest.'

Zack did look pale, lying back on a mountain of pillows with lots of tubes and machines connected to him. When they walked in, Zack glanced from Sebastian to Ruby then back to Sebastian, his eyebrows lifting a little.

'How are you feeling?' Sebastian asked, coming forward to place a gentle hand on Zack's forearm.

The gesture moved Ruby. So Sebastian could actually care for someone, could he? It gave her some kind of hope. Though not too much. She suspected he would still want her gone today, despite last night.

'The doctor said the surgery went well,' Zack told Sebastian. 'Isn't that right, Susan?' he directed to the nurse, who was hovering.

'As well as can be expected, Mr Stone.'

'Do call me Zack, please. They said I'd be in here for at least a week. Time for us to become best buddies.'

She blushed. She actually blushed. But her eyes flashed daggers at him.

'None of that, thank you, Mr Stone. Now, I'll be back when you need your catheter bag changing in a quarter of an hour. Until then, try to behave yourself and just rest.'

'Wow,' Sebastian said after she hurried away. 'You won't be winding that one around your little finger.'

Zack pulled a face. 'You could be right there.'

'Tell us about the woman who stabbed you.'

'Nothing to tell. I don't know her from Adam. She's an obsessed fan who's been stalking me for a while. She's been hanging around my building for weeks. Takes photos of me all the time.'

'Did you tell the police that?'

'I reported her to the local cops before I came to your party. That was what set her off—them going to speak to her. She pretended to go away but she didn't. She lay in wait for me till I came home from the party and ran at me, screaming, with a knife.'

'Which you made no attempt to stop.'

'No,' he said in a voice that puzzled Ruby. It was oddly resigned.

'You know why not,' he added sharply, looking straight at Sebastian. 'I couldn't risk it.'

Sebastian nodded. 'I understand.'

Maybe he did but Ruby sure as hell didn't.

'But, Zack—' she began, only to be cut dead by Sebastian's savage glare.

'Ruby wanted to bring you flowers,' he said, filling in the awkward moment.

'What kind of flowers?' Zack asked her.

'Not sure. Sebastian said you wouldn't like them.'

'Then he'd be wrong. I'd love flowers. Why don't you go and get me some? There's sure to be a florist here somewhere.'

Ruby was no fool. She knew Zack was getting rid of her so he could talk to Sebastian alone. Whilst somewhat annoyed, she still went in search of a florist, at the same time determined to find out answers to her questions as soon as possible. If Ruby had one flaw it was an insatiable curiosity about people. She wasn't a gossip but she just liked to *know*!

The florist was down a couple of floors. By the time Ruby returned with a basket full of multi-coloured blooms the nurse called Susan was back, glowering at Sebastian. She rolled her eyes at Ruby, taking the basket from her and placing it on a nearby windowsill.

'I'm sorry, but you'll have to go now,' she said firmly. 'Mr Stone is not long out of surgery and he needs his rest.'

'There's no arguing with that one,' Sebastian muttered as they left.

'She's just doing her job,' Ruby said. 'You can visit Zack again tomorrow. Take him some fruit and some chocolates.'

'Zack doesn't eat fruit. Or chocolates.'

Ruby was quite taken aback. What kind of person didn't eat fruit or chocolates?

'That's most unusual,' she said.

'Just habit. There was a time in his life when fruit and chocolates weren't large on his menu.'

'What time was that?'

'I'm not sure I should tell you. It's Zack's private business. I shouldn't have said anything.'

'Would you at least tell me why Zack didn't defend himself against some knife-wielding stalker? He's a fit, strong man. It doesn't make sense.'

Sebastian gave her a long look, which Ruby couldn't fathom. Something was going on in his head. Something serious and thought provoking. But what?

Clearly, he wasn't about to confide in her, since her question remained unanswered. And why *should* he confide in her? She was about to exit his life. It was a depressing thought, one that she'd managed to keep at bay whilst they'd been visiting Zack. But it had still been there, hovering.

'I'll tell you later,' he whispered unexpectedly as they reached the lifts that would take them up to the level where the car was. 'When we're alone,' he added, nodding towards the group standing next to them.

Ruby was taken aback by this offer, but pleased too. As soon as they reached the privacy of Sebastian's car, she turned to him.

'Please don't start driving before you tell me why Zack did what he did.'

'Very well,' he agreed. 'But you must promise never to tell anyone.'

'I give you my solemn word.'

Sebastian nodded. 'Right. The thing is, Zack spent five years in jail. From the age of eighteen to twenty-three.'

Ruby could not have been more shocked. Zack might look a bad boy but she instinctively knew that he wasn't, not deep down. 'How on earth did that happen? I mean, what did he do?'

'He killed a man.'

'What?'

'It was an accident,' he insisted.

'Look, I believe you. What happened exactly?'

'Zack went up to the Cross to celebrate his eighteenth birthday. There was this guy who was drunk and abusing his girlfriend outside a club. He was calling her names, slapping her around. When Zack stepped in and asked him to stop, the guy started swinging punches. Zack fought back. The guy fell and hit his head. He died a week later.'

'But it was self-defence, and an accident,' Ruby argued, appalled. 'There had to have been witnesses. What about the girlfriend?'

'She turned on him, said it was all his fault. It also didn't help that he couldn't afford a good lawyer. Still, what does it matter now? It's too late to change anything. Zack was convicted of manslaughter. He got ten years, paroled in five.'

Ruby's heart went out to eighteen-year-old Zack. 'The poor boy.'

'You're absolutely right. He was just a boy at the time. He changed his name after he got out. Changed his appearance, too, by growing his hair. He'd had a buzz cut in jail. His mother helped him, shortly before she died.'

'He told me his mother died when he was young,' Ruby said, thinking back to the night they'd chatted together outside. He'd hinted at having a secret, but she would never have guessed this. 'How did she die?'

'She was hit by a cement truck as she crossed the road. It happened not long after he was released from jail.'

'How awful.'

'Yes, his mother was all he had. She'd been a single mum; his dad took off years before.'

'That's so sad.'

'Yes, it is. She's the one who also suggested Zack try out for modelling after he got out of jail and no one would give him a job. He took her advice, but not until after she died. Anyway, that led to him auditioning for acting jobs, and the rest, as they say, is history.'

'It's due to his mother, then, that he became a success.'

'Absolutely. She would have been so proud of him.'

'Maybe she still is,' Ruby said. 'Maybe she's looking down on him from heaven. Maybe she kept him safe last night.'

'That's a nice thought.'

Ruby didn't like to add that she often thought of her mother looking down on her from heaven. It was a comfort when she felt lonely. Though not so much when she was doing things she shouldn't be doing, like sleeping with her boss. And stupidly falling in love with him.

Her sigh was weary.

Sebastian sighed as well. 'At least now you can understand why Zack didn't defend himself last night.'

'He was afraid of somehow going back to jail again. That's so sad.'

'Yes, it is. But it's not a good way to live your life, being afraid,' he said thoughtfully. 'It's stultifying.'

His remark startled her. Then made her think. Was he still talking about Zack being afraid? Or himself?

'We all try to protect ourselves from hurt,' she said, well aware she'd spurned the opposite sex for years for that very reason. 'It's only natural.'

'Yes, but fear can get out of control. And when it does, it's self-destructive. Zack could have died tonight.'

'But he didn't.'

'No, because he was damned lucky.'

'I suppose so,' she said, not sure where this conversation was heading.

But it didn't head anywhere because Sebastian abruptly started the car and reversed out of the space. 'We'll talk some more when we get home,' he said brusquely. 'After I've had something to eat. I'm famished. I can't think when I'm starving.'

And that was that. Silence descended and Ruby was left up in the air.

CHAPTER TWENTY-FIVE

SEBASTIAN HAD LIED. He *could* think all right. In fact, that was all he did the whole way home. Think.

Zack's near brush with death had been a shock, but it had also woken Sebastian up to the way he was living his own life. In fear. Since Jennifer's death, he'd been afraid of falling in love again, afraid of giving away his heart and having it broken, either by death or divorce or some kind of disaster. He'd managed to survive so far by becoming a workaholic but, really, it was a nothing life. And a lonely life.

Ruby was right to call him pathetic, because he was. Any normal man would have been thrilled to have such a woman as Ruby come into his life. But what had he done? Run a mile to begin with, until he couldn't resist her any longer. And then what? He'd tried to control things by coming up with that ridiculous proposition.

She would surely pack up and leave today if he didn't stop her. So yes, he had to stop her.

Maybe not tell her he loved her. That would be a step too far at this stage. But he had to show her that he cared. And he had to offer her something better than a strictly sexual arrangement.

'I hope you're not expecting me to cook you breakfast before I leave?' she said tartly when he stopped the car outside the garage and waited for the door to rise.

'No,' he replied carefully.

'Good. Okay. When do you want me out by?'

He turned to her, his eyes determined. 'I don't want you to leave at all.'

Her own eyes widened. 'You don't?'

'No, I want you to stay.'

'But last night, you said…you said…'

'That was last night. Things have changed since then. Could we talk, Ruby? Really talk?'

He had rarely seen her so flummoxed. 'I… I guess so.'

'Good.'

In the end, she did cook him some breakfast. Nothing complicated—just French toast and coffee. They ate it outside on the terrace, Sebastian doing his best not to look as nervous as he was. He wasn't confident she would say yes to what he intended to propose. Ruby was strong-minded, not likely to be flattered or manipulated into what he wanted. She could very well tell him to get stuffed and still leave. It wasn't as though she were in love with him. She'd made it quite clear that she wasn't. Finally, when the toast was gone, he bit the bullet and spoke up.

'The thing is, Ruby. I care about you. It's not just the sex. I want you to stay. I want you to be my girlfriend.'

Ruby's heart stopped beating. 'Girlfriend?' she repeated, stunned by this totally unexpected announcement. When he'd been so dour during the drive home, she'd been sure it was all over; that she was to be out of the door that same day.

'Yes. Girlfriend,' he repeated, standing up and coming around the table to sit in the chair next to her. 'But only if you want to, of course.'

'Only if I want to…'

'Yes.'

Her joy was instant. But so was the temptation to tease him. 'Well, let me see now…'

When a sheepish smile spread across her face, he shook

his head at her. But his blue eyes sparkled. 'You are a minx,' he said, reaching out to cup her face before leaning over and kissing her.

It was a gentle kiss. A loving kiss, nothing but lips. It surprised Ruby. Sebastian was usually a passionate kisser. But she liked the tenderness of his mouth, and his hands. Liked it a lot.

When his head lifted, he opened his mouth to say something, but then he closed it again and just shook his head at her.

'Don't take this the wrong way, Ruby,' he said at last, 'but I still want to keep our relationship a secret for a short while.'

'Our relationship?' she said, startled by his use of the word.

'Yes. Relationship,' he confirmed. 'A proper one. The trouble is, if we tell my family and friends that we're an item, they'll start interfering. I want to keep you to myself for a while at least, whilst we figure this out.'

Ruby didn't know what to say. She was thrilled that he wanted her as his girlfriend, but wary over him wanting to keep it a secret, even for a short while.

His smile was reassuringly warm, however. Warm and quite sweet. 'You've made me break all my life rules,' he said. 'You know that, don't you?'

'You've made me break a few of mine as well,' she returned, his words slowly sinking in. Did she dare hope he might feel for her what she felt for him? Or was that too good to be true? He hadn't said he loved her, just that he cared for her. It wasn't the same.

'Sebastian,' she said when her wariness raised its ugly head again.

'Yes?'

'I understand why you would want to keep us a secret for a while, especially from your mother. But I don't want to spend Christmas Day with her, pretending to be just your housekeeper. I mean, for me, having a real relationship shouldn't be about pretending.'

'You're right,' he said. 'It shouldn't. We'll tell them all on Christmas Day that we're dating, okay?'

'Yes, all right,' she said, suddenly worried that they might think she'd taken advantage of her position to seduce Sebastian; that she was some kind of gold-digger.

'If it really bothers you, Ruby, I'll ring them up and tell them today.'

'No, no,' she said hurriedly. 'Please don't. Christmas Day will do fine.'

'Why are you frowning, then?'

'I don't know. I guess I… I'm worried your family might think badly of me.'

'Why on earth would they do that? My mother already loves you.'

Ruby sighed. 'I suppose you're right.'

'I am right,' he said, and gave her another kiss. 'So what are we going to do today, girlfriend?'

'Nothing much. I'm awfully tired.'

'In that case I think we should go back to bed. I might even let you go to sleep.'

'Thank you very much,' she said, giving him a peck on the lips. 'If you do, you might get a reward when I wake up.'

CHAPTER TWENTY-SIX

SEBASTIAN WAS REWARDED HANDSOMELY, pleased to finally make love to Ruby with true affection in his heart. The sex they'd been having had been physically exciting, but it was even better when it was an expression of love. Oh, yes, he'd finally come to terms with his feelings for Ruby. It was love that he felt for Ruby. True love. Deeper than he'd ever felt before.

He'd loved Jennifer, but it had been a young man's love. Passionate, yes. But selfish. Lacking in maturity and understanding.

He understood Ruby. Understood that she'd been hurt in the past, that she'd had her faith in men shattered. That father of hers had been appalling. Then, when she'd needed him the most, her boyfriend had dumped her. Sebastian suspected there'd been other creeps in her life as well.

It would take a while to win her trust and her heart. Yes, Ruby lusted after him. Maybe she even cared about him a little. But he doubted she loved him. And why would she? He'd hardly been all that loveable. But he aimed to pull out all the stops from this day forward. He wanted her to love him, wanted it more than he'd wanted anything in his life.

Sunday dawned fine and sunny, Ruby waking in Sebastian's bed, feeling wonderfully rested and sated. Sebastian's lovemaking had taken a tender turn the night before, but she didn't mind. She liked him taking his time, liked looking into his eyes and thinking how much she loved him. They'd snuggled up and talked for ages before falling asleep, Ruby happy to find out more about Sebastian—the man, not just Sebastian her boss and secret lover. He liked movies, which was a given, considering his profession. He liked reading. Liked swimming. She'd confessed to her own love of all three, which seemed to please Sebastian a lot.

Unfortunately, as she lay there the next morning, thinking about how much she loved the man lying next to her, Ruby's happiness slowly began to fade. She began worrying about what would happen when Georgia came back, when she was no longer conveniently living in his house. Did Sebastian plan to set her up in an apartment nearby and visit her on occasion?

He didn't know her very well if he thought she would go for such an arrangement.

When Sebastian started to stir, Ruby told herself to stop with the infernal thinking and worrying. *Enjoy what you have right now, you foolish girl. Because that's all you can be sure of in life, isn't it?*

'Did I tell you that Harvest Productions has closed down for the summer break?' Sebastian told her over breakfast.

'No,' she replied, reminding her that there was still a lot she didn't know about Sebastian.

'Yes. We do the same thing every year. It's better to have everyone off at the same time.'

'When do you go back to work?'

'The second week in January. Until then, the television channels run repeats. Or put something else on.'

'What about *Battle at the Bar*? When do you start shooting the next season?'

'Not till late January but it will depend on Zack. Hopefully, he'll be better by then. We'll know more when we visit him today.'

Ruby frowned. 'I was thinking about that. What if we run into other people from Harvest Productions at the hospital? They'll think it's odd if I'm with you. They might put two and two together.'

'I doubt we'll run into anyone. The story's not out about Zack being stabbed yet. I checked the news on my phone earlier and there was nothing.'

'But it won't take long to get out,' Ruby said. 'Someone will talk.'

'Not Zack. He's not into social media. Or media at all, for that matter.'

'What about the police? Or one of the nurses?'

'It's possible. Look, don't worry about running into other people at the hospital. It's none of their business if you're there with me.'

'I suppose so…'

'Come on. Let's get dressed and get in there. The earlier we visit, the less likely it will be that anyone else will be there.'

Sebastian was right. There was no one else in Zack's room, other than the nurse named Susan who was checking his blood pressure. She glanced up as they entered, giving Ruby a look that wasn't entirely welcoming.

'You look a bit better than yesterday,' Sebastian remarked whilst Ruby sat down on a chair in the corner. 'But not much.'

'Don't worry, Seb. Susan says I'll be okay in a week or so. Isn't that right, Susan?'

'If you're sensible and do as you're told.'

'I can't really do anything else, can I? They won't even let me out of bed yet.'

'We'll be getting you out of bed later today,' Susan informed him briskly.

'Thank God for that.'

Ruby was glad when the nurse left the room so they could talk naturally.

'So how are you really feeling, Zack?' Ruby asked.

'Awful. But at least I'm alive. And that nutcase has been arrested.'

'Poor woman,' Ruby said. 'She's obviously mentally ill.'

'Probably. But she needs professional help.'

'Has anyone else been in to visit you yet?' Sebastian asked.

'No. You're it.'

'Do you want me to tell the others at work? I could send out a blanket email.'

'Not yet. Maybe in a day or two.'

'By then it'll probably hit the news and they'll know anyway.'

'Hopefully not. I asked the police to keep it quiet. And the hospital.'

Sebastian nodded. 'Good thinking.'

'From the sounds of things,' Ruby said, 'you definitely won't be out before Christmas. That's only four days away.'

'You're right there. The doctor says I'll be here for longer than that.'

'That's a shame,' Ruby said. 'But we'll come and visit you on Christmas Day. Bring you lots of presents.'

'Nah. None of that. We never exchange presents at Christmas, do we, Seb? But I tell you what.' He directed this at Sebastian. 'Bring me a couple of books from your rather extensive library. Thrillers, preferably. And soon. There's nothing on the TV at this time of year except cricket,' he said, pointing up to the TV mounted on the wall.

'Will do,' Sebastian said. 'I'll bring you a couple tomorrow.'

'Thanks.'

'I can't come tomorrow,' Ruby said. 'I have Janice and Tom coming, and lots of housekeeping things to do.'

'I'll still come,' Sebastian said just as nurse Susan hurried in.

Truly, did she have any other way of moving?

'I have to do Mr Stone's observations,' she informed them. 'I suggest you step outside for a minute.'

Ruby stood up and went with Sebastian into the corridor, having noted his face had gone a bit ashen.

'You all right?' she asked him.

'Yeah. I'm fine. Hospital procedures still get to me a bit. It's crazy, really.'

'No, not at all,' she said gently, and placed a soothing hand on his arm. 'Bad memories.'

He covered her hand with his and smiled at her. 'When we're finished here, Ruby, would you come shopping with me, help me buy my mother a few Christmas presents? Gloria and I don't exchange presents any more. And I always just give the boys money. But Mum likes her presents and I never know what to buy.'

Ruby smiled back at him. 'So what lucky lady usually does the honours for you?'

'My PA. Or Gloria. But I just know you'd be better at choosing. You get people, Ruby. You really do.'

Ruby felt her heart flutter with his compliment. 'I do my best.'

They had a lovely few hours during which Ruby found all sorts of interesting gifts for Frieda, the CBD having a wide range of shops. After they returned their parcels to the car, Sebastian suggested lunch. They found a place that wasn't too busy, both of them sitting down with slightly weary sighs.

When the waitress brought their order, conversation was suspended for a couple of minutes. Unfortunately, silence had a way of bringing Ruby's worries to the forefront of her mind. She wasn't a girl who liked to dwell endlessly on worries if she could talk about them, so once Sebastian had finished his meal she spoke up.

'Would you mind if I ask what you see happening once Georgia returns?'

Sebastian frowned, then picked up his coffee for a swallow before answering.

'I'm sure we'll have sorted something out by then,' he said.

Ruby frowned as well. 'That sounds rather vague. I like to know where I stand, Sebastian.'

'Yes, I can see that. But could we have this conversation again after Christmas?'

Ruby hated procrastinating but she could see that perhaps Sebastian wasn't sure what he wanted at the moment.

'I suppose so,' she said. 'But trust me when I say, Sebastian, that we *will* be having this conversation again. I need to know where my life is going.' *And when my heart is going to be broken,* came the suddenly depressing thought.

'And where do you want it to go, Ruby?' he asked, sitting back and watching her closely.

Ruby sat back also, the suspicion forming that he was trying to see if she wanted more from him than he was prepared to give. If she pressed him, he might end things here and now. If she wanted their relationship, such as it was, to continue, then she had to lighten things up.

She hoped her shrug looked nonchalant. 'Well, as I told you, I want to become a social worker. And to do that, I need a secure roof over my head and time to study. I suppose after Georgia gets back I'll try to get another job as a housekeeper here in Sydney. I don't really want to live with one of my brothers.'

'You still don't want to get married?'

'Lord no!' she exclaimed straight away. To say she wanted to marry him would be the kiss of death.

His sigh could have been relief. Or something else. Ruby wasn't sure and was afraid to hope.

'I'm sorry, Sebastian,' she said, and he threw her a questioning glance.

'Sorry about what?'

'It's Christmas, for heaven's sake. Time to be merry and have fun, not get all serious about the future. We'll worry about next year next year, okay?'

'Okay,' he said slowly, leaving Ruby with the impression that something was still bothering him.

'We should get going soon,' she suggested. 'The traffic is only going to get worse as the day wears on.'

The day ended well after that, their moods having lightened. They chatted away during the drive home, enjoyed dinner together that night, then went to bed together. Ruby wallowing in the pretence that they were, if not really married, then acting as if they were. And if there was a tiny little niggle still at the back of her mind, she steadfastly ignored it.

CHAPTER TWENTY-SEVEN

'HERE ARE THE books you asked for,' Sebastian said as he placed them on the tray table next to Zack's bed.

'Thanks,' Zack said, picking them up and reading the blurbs before looking up. 'I'll enjoy these. So tell me, Seb, how long have you been sleeping with Ruby?'

Sebastian wasn't surprised that Zack had twigged. After all, he already knew how much he fancied her.

'Since a week before the Christmas party,' Sebastian confessed.

Zack looked surprised. 'That long.'

'We decided to keep it a secret.'

'*We* decided to keep it a secret. Or *you* decided to keep it a secret.'

'I guess it was my idea. But Ruby didn't object.'

Zack made a tsking sound. 'I expected better of you than that. Ruby's a nice girl, as you went to great pains to tell me. She won't be happy with being your secret bit on the side for long. You must know that.'

'She doesn't want to get married,' Sebastian said with a sigh.

'What are you talking about? *You* don't want to get married, either. But marriage isn't the only card in the pack, Seb. You could ask her to be your girlfriend. What's wrong with that?'

'Nothing. I've actually already done that. And we won't be keeping our relationship a secret for much longer. We're letting the cat out of the bag on Christmas Day. But the strange thing is, Zack, I've realised I *do* want to get married. I thought I only wanted her to love me but I want more. I want her to be my wife.'

Zack's eyebrows almost hit the ceiling. 'Wow. Now you've really surprised me. You, Mr I-don't-ever-want-to-fall-in-love-and-get-married-again Marshall. Not that I'm surprised it's Ruby who's stolen your heart. She's a great girl. If you hadn't warned me off I might have fallen for her myself.'

'Didn't you hear what I said? She doesn't want to get married.'

'Did she say that to you?'

'Loud and clear.'

'Did you tell her you love her?'

'Well…no…'

'It might be an idea to tell her,' came his dry advice.

'She won't believe me.'

'Then it's up to you to convince her, isn't it? Pull out all stops. Go all romantic. I know you're not used to romantic gestures, buddy, but they work.'

Sebastian had to smile. 'You'd know. But you're undoubtedly right.'

'Of course I'm right. Faint heart never won fair lady.'

'No wonder you get the women, Zack. Poetry, no less. Now I have to get going. I have lots to do.' Already Sebastian's mind was buzzing with ideas. But they would take time. And effort. And money.

At least he had no shortage in that department.

'Good luck,' Zack called after him.

Luck, Sebastian decided as he hurried away, had little to do with success in life.

His first job after leaving the hospital was to go shopping. For a ring. Sebastian refused to countenance failure, so a ring was what he would need. Eventually. After what proved to be a long shopping expedition, he dropped in at the extremely popular Cafe Sydney and spent a small fortune, getting what he also wanted.

It was well after lunchtime as he drove away from the city, hunger pangs telling him he needed to eat. But he needed to get home more. He wanted to see his Ruby. Just *see* her. He didn't need to do anything else.

She wasn't at home, however, when he got there. He texted her immediately and found out she was at the supermarket, stocking up on food, plus a few last-minute gifts. She would be home soon.

Not soon enough for his stomach, Sebastian thought, so he made himself a sandwich and coffee.

'Didn't you eat in town?' she asked when she saw him.

'No,' he said between mouthfuls, his gaze drinking her in at the same time.

'Then what took you so long?'

He could hardly tell her the truth. *I was looking for the right ring for you, my darling.*

But he decided on a partial truth.

'After I visited Zack, I went shopping for something for you. For Christmas.'

'Really? That's sweet.'

'Unfortunately, I couldn't seem to decide what to buy. In the end I settled for taking you out somewhere special instead. I have a booking for lunch at Cafe Sydney on Christmas Eve.'

Her eyes lit up. 'But isn't that a pretty exclusive place?'

'Yes.'

'Then how did you manage to get a table this late? You said all the restaurants would be booked out.'

'I'm a regular customer there,' he said. 'They always keep a table or two free for regular patrons,' he lied. The truth was that he'd made them an offer they couldn't refuse. It would be the most expensive lunch he'd ever had.

But it would be worth it. It already was, by the excited look on her face.

A happy Sebastian tucked into the rest of his sandwich whilst Ruby unpacked her shopping bags.

'Are you going to come with me to visit Zack tomorrow?' he asked her as he ate.

'No. Haven't you heard? The news about his attack is out. It was on the midday news.'

Sebastian swore, then sighed. 'I suppose it was too much to expect to keep it quiet for long.'

'Every man and his dog will be trying to interview him,' Ruby said.

Sebastian laughed. 'I don't like their chances. He won't even do media for the show. Its success comes mainly from word of mouth.'

'They'll still try. And all his work colleagues will be visiting. So no, I won't be going in with you. Sorry.'

'I'll have to go. Keep the vultures at bay.'

'I have things to do, anyway. Present wrapping mostly. I've organised to go over to see Liam and Oliver tomorrow night so we can catch up and exchange presents. Oh, golly,' she exclaimed. 'I just realised I forgot to buy wrapping paper, and gift tags. Truly, my head's not screwed on properly today. Janice said I was off with the pixies and she's right.'

Sebastian could only hope that might have something to do with him.

'Could you buy some wrapping paper for the presents I bought for Mum at the same time?' he asked.

'Yes, of course. I'll wrap them up as well.'

'You're a life-saver. What would I do without you?'

'You'd have Georgia,' she said dryly. 'Or Gloria. Or Janice.'

'Not the same as you,' he said warmly.

'Flatterer,' she said, but with a smile on her face. 'I think you've been spending too much time with Zack. His charm is beginning to wear off onto you.'

Sebastian tried not to feel offended. 'I'll have you know I can be charming when I want to be.'

She laughed. 'Perhaps I just wasn't there at the time.'

'Charm can be shallow,' he pointed out, quite seriously. 'Far better that a man be decent, and sincere.'

She stopped what she was doing and smiled at him. 'It's all right, Sebastian. You don't have to change for me. I like you just the way you are.'

CHAPTER TWENTY-EIGHT

CHRISTMAS EVE FINALLY CAME, the last few days having given Ruby some hope that her relationship with Sebastian might develop into something permanent. She didn't go so far as to imagine love and marriage yet, but who knew? Sebastian was certainly a different man nowadays compared to the rather rude individual she'd first met and who'd been determined not to have a woman in his life ever again after the death of his wife.

The man who took her to bed every night was not that man. Not even remotely.

She dressed carefully for her lunch with Sebastian. She didn't wear the red dress—that was reserved for Christmas Day—but another pretty dress she'd picked out recently, teamed with wedged sandals in a neutral colour. She left her hair down, her only jewellery a gold pendant her mother had given her for her sixteenth birthday. Her make-up was subtle, her perfume equally so.

Sebastian had gone to visit Zack as usual, catching the ferry in so he could have a drink at lunchtime and not be over the driving limit. She was catching a ferry too; the service from Mosman was very good. Ruby had never been to Cafe Sydney before but she knew it was on the top floor of the Customs building, just across from the quay, only a short walk from the ferry terminal.

Ruby did her best not to overreact to Sebastian's invitation but it was impossible not to feel both excited and, yes, positive. That he was taking her out in public was a big step. It was a proper date, not like the other day when they'd stopped off at some small coffee house in the city. Ruby had looked up Cafe Sydney on the Internet and it was one of *the* places to be seen in Sydney. The dining was superb, and so was the view of the bridge and the harbour.

Given its popularity with the rich and famous, they could easily run into people he knew. What would he say to them? she wondered. Would he introduce her as his housekeeper, or as his date?

Only time would tell, she supposed, her stomach aflutter with anticipation.

The weather was wonderful, neither too hot nor too windy. And not a sign of rain or the storms that often plagued Sydney at this time of year. Ruby stepped off the ferry right on twelve-thirty, which meant she would be a few minutes late, even later when the lights turned red, stopping her from crossing the road. As she waited, she sent Sebastian a text saying she was nearly there. He answered That's okay straight away, which brought a sigh of relief. The lights eventually turned green but Ruby still hurried across to the Customs building and there was another minute or two delay because the lifts were busy.

It was a slightly flustered Ruby who was shown to their table at a quarter to one.

Sebastian was already there, looking handsome and sinfully sexy in designer jeans and a blue top, the same colour as his eyes. He stood up when she arrived, like the gentleman he was, and gave her a sweet kiss on the cheek before telling the hovering waiter to give them a few minutes before ordering.

'Sorry, I'm late,' she said on sitting down. 'If I'd caught the previous ferry I would have been too early.'

'It's perfectly all right, Ruby. And may I say you were worth waiting for? You look utterly gorgeous.'

'Oh,' she said, even more flustered now. The way he was looking at her, if she didn't know better she might think he was in love with her. Only then did she glance away from his eyes at her surroundings, her heart beating like mad. 'Oh, my goodness, what a wonderful view,' she said. It looked even better in reality than in the photographs online, especially from their table, which was out on a balcony. 'And what a wonderful place. This is one of the best Christmas presents I've ever had. Thank you so much, Sebastian.'

'My pleasure,' he said, and poured her a glass of champagne from the bottle that he'd obviously already ordered.

'The trouble is, I feel extra guilty now about not buying you anything for Christmas.'

She had tried, but what did you buy a seriously rich man who already had everything he wanted? She didn't dare buy him clothes. Sebastian only wore designer brands, which were out of her reach, financially. Buying presents for her brothers had been easy compared to Sebastian. He was just impossible!

'You don't have to buy me anything, you know,' he said.

'But I wanted to. And I tried. But I couldn't think of anything. Help me out here, Sebastian. Tell me something you want that I can afford.'

'You don't need to buy me anything, Ruby. You've already given me something incredibly valuable.'

'What's that?' she asked, perplexed.

'Happiness,' he said. 'You've made me truly happy again. Trust me when I say it's something I haven't been for a long time.'

'Oh,' she said, touched, but a little sad too.

'Before you came into my life, Ruby, the best I could say about myself was that I was busy. Busy and financially successful. I suppose I got some satisfaction from that. But it's not the same as having someone in your life to come home to, someone you care about.'

Ruby sucked in sharply. Caring was very close to love, but it wasn't quite the same. Was it possible he did love her but couldn't bring himself to say it? They weren't the easiest words to say. She hadn't said she loved him, either. She didn't want to risk spoiling what they had. Which was incredible. He really was a good man. And terribly intelligent. When they'd gone to bed together every night this week, they'd talked endlessly about a wide range of topics before going to sleep. He seemed to know something about everything. He'd travelled all over the world, whereas she had only been to New Zealand. Not that he ever made her feel inferior. He wasn't like that.

'Have I said something I shouldn't?' he asked when she didn't continue with their conversation, her mind having gone off on a tangent.

'No, not at all. I'm happy that I've made you happy.'

He tipped his head to one side as he regarded her closely. 'But have I made you happy, Ruby?'

'Happy?' she repeated, not sure if she would describe herself as truly happy.

She wished...

A wry smile lifted the corner of her mouth. She wished for too much. That was the truth of the matter.

'You make me very happy in bed,' she said somewhat flippantly.

Her answer didn't seem to please him. He frowned for a long moment. It wasn't until he smiled that she finally relaxed.

Ruby picked up her glass of champagne and lifted it in a toast. 'To being happy,' she said, and clinked her glass against his.

'Indeed,' he returned.

A man suddenly appeared by their table, a well-dressed

portly fellow of around sixty who had money written all over him. 'What are you toasting, Sebastian?' he asked. 'And who is this lovely lady you're with?'

Ruby immediately tensed, waiting to hear Sebastian's answer.

'Trust you to come sniffing around, Gregory, when you see a new beauty on the scene. But no, Ruby's not an actor. And not for poaching in any way. She's my girlfriend. My *live-in* girlfriend,' he emphasised. 'Ruby, this is Gregory Bardon, who runs Bardon's casting agency. He's always on the lookout for new talent. Gregory, this is Ruby.'

'Ruby,' the man repeated, taking her hand and lifting it to his lips in an old-fashioned kiss. 'Charmed. You are a lucky dog, Sebastian. Live-in, did you say?'

'I did.'

'Amazing. And there I was, all these years, thinking you might be gay.'

'Really? Whatever gave you that idea?'

'Just a rumour I heard once. Clearly I was wrong. Lovely to have met you, Ruby. Happy Christmas.'

'Same to you too,' Ruby called after him, struggling not to laugh.

'You should see the look on your face,' she said to Sebastian when they were alone again.

He finally saw the funny side and laughed as well.

They had a lovely lunch together, the champagne gorgeous, the food divine, and the trip home on the ferry a lot better than driving. Christmas Eve traffic was always a nightmare. Ruby was glad she'd taken her brothers' presents over to them the night before. They'd had an enjoyable evening together, Oliver coming over to Liam's place so they could exchange gifts. They'd opened them then and there, Ruby wanting the pleasure of giving hers in person. She'd bought her brothers and their partners a very stylish vase each to go with the expensive sheets and towels. The girls had loved everything. Ruby had been just as happy with her own gifts. Now she wouldn't run out of perfume for ages, and she had lots of lovely books to read.

By the time she and Sebastian arrived home, the afternoon had warmed up and Sebastian suggested they have a swim.

'Good idea,' Ruby said.

'You can even wear that dastardly bikini if you like.'

Ruby raised her eyebrows at him. 'Are you sure about that? You might not be able to control yourself.'

'I can always control myself when I know there are better things to come. I'm looking forward to taking you to bed tonight and making love to you for hours.'

Ruby's heart flipped over at his words. Had he really said making love, instead of having sex? Did he mean it or was it just a slip of the tongue?

'Don't you mean have sex for hours?' she couldn't help saying.

'No,' he said, his eyes very serious on her. 'I meant exactly what I said. I want to make love to you, Ruby, because I'm in love with you.'

Ruby decided later that she must have looked like a goldfish with her mouth hanging open and her eyes wide with shock.

'You're in love with me?' she said at last after she'd drawn in several scoops of much-needed air.

'Madly,' he said, smiling as he pulled her into his arms.

'Oh, Lord.'

His smile suddenly faded to a less confident expression. 'Is that good news or bad news?'

She blinked, stunned that he would think him loving her was bad news. But then she recalled the things she'd said to him in the past. She'd actually called him a bastard on one occasion. She'd also said she didn't particularly like him. It was no wonder he was looking a little worried. Even today at the lunch, she'd only said he made her happy in bed, reducing their relationship to little more than sex.

'It's good news,' she said tenderly. 'Very good news. Because I'm madly in love with you too.'

Now it was his mouth's turn to gape open. 'You are? You really are?'

'I really am.'

He beamed down at her like a child on Christmas morning. 'You've no idea how glad I am to hear that. I thought… No, it doesn't matter what I thought. All that matters is that we love each other.'

'Madly,' she added.

'Yes, madly. But also deeply. It's not just lust talking here, Ruby. I really, really love you. *You*, the beautiful, sweet, wonderful person that you are.'

Tears pricked at her eyes. 'I never thought a man would ever love me like that,' she choked out. 'Oh, Sebastian, you've made me so happy.'

'*I've* made *you* happy? You've put me on cloud nine, Ruby, and I don't think I'll ever come down.' He hugged her close, Ruby laying her head against his chest. His heart was thumping behind his ribs, and so was hers. She stayed in the warmth of his embrace for a while before lifting her face to his.

'Could we perhaps skip the swim and just go to bed?' she suggested softly.

Sebastian could not believe the feelings that coursed through him as he lay in bed with Ruby snuggled up next to him. He'd loved Jennifer but what he felt for Ruby seemed so much stronger. It was a for-ever kind of love, with the strength to face whatever problems life would throw at them as a couple.

It was time, he realised, to take the next step. Maybe it

was a little premature but, as Zack said, faint heart never won fair lady.

'Ruby?' he murmured, giving her shoulder a little shake.

'Hmmm?'

'Are you awake?'

She sighed as she rolled onto her back and looked at him. 'I am now.'

'I was going to wait but I can't. I have to ask you now.'

'Ask me what?'

'Will you marry me?'

She sat bolt upright in the bed, the sheet falling off her naked body. She snatched it back up over her breasts, her eyes wide with shock. Sebastian felt his heart sink.

'You don't mean that,' she said. 'You can't. I mean…'

'I do mean it,' he insisted. 'I told you you'd made me break all those rules I was living my life by. They were stupid rules, Ruby. Cowardly rules. Yes, I was devastated when Jennifer died but I think I was more devastated by the way she handled it, pushing me away, not letting me help nurse her. You would never be like that. We'd handle anything life throws at us together. Fight it together.'

By now tears were streaming down Ruby's cheeks. 'That's beautiful, Sebastian,' she choked out. 'And yes, I will marry you. Wherever and whenever you want.'

The joy that exploded in Sebastian's heart was almost impossible for him to describe.

'In that case, as soon as possible, please,' he said, kissing the tears from her face. 'Unless, of course, you want a big fancy wedding.'

'Lord, no. Though I do want a proper bridal gown, and lots and lots of photos. We can have the ceremony here, in the garden.'

'Sounds marvellous. I'll ask Zack to be best man.'

'And my brothers can give me away.'

'Done! Now I just have to go and get something,' he

said, scrambling out of the bed and heading into his walk-in wardrobe. Ruby's heart leapt when he returned with a very small bag, one from a jewellery shop.

Surely not, she thought.

'It took me ages to find the right one,' he said as he produced the ring box and sank down on his knees by the bed, still stark naked.

When he flipped the box open, Ruby stared down at the most beautiful ring she'd ever seen. In the middle of a rose-gold setting was a huge ruby, encircled by diamonds. Quite big diamonds. It must have cost a fortune!

'A perfect ruby for my perfect Ruby,' Sebastian said as he lifted it out and slipped it on her engagement-ring finger.

'Oh, Sebastian, it's stunning. And it fits perfectly. How did you manage that?'

'A combination of luck, my powers of observation and a very experienced jeweller. You really like it, then?'

'I adore it. But, Sebastian, I can't possibly wear it yet. And certainly not tomorrow at your sister's place. Your family will really think things about me now.'

'What kind of things?' he asked as he climbed into bed next to her.

'Well, you know. Like I'm some kind of scheming gold-digger.'

He laughed. '*You?* A gold-digger? Now that's a funny one.'

'I'm serious. After all, we've only known each other a few weeks.'

'Has it really only been that long? It feels like an eternity.'

'I know what you mean. I feel the same way.'

'Trust me when I say my family won't think any such things about you, Ruby darling,' he said as he kissed her tenderly on her forehead, her nose, her cheek. 'My mother will be especially delighted. Now, no more doubts. You will wear your engagement ring tomorrow and that's that.'

'Goodness, you can be forceful when you want to be, Mr Marshall.'

'I can. And you are to call both your brothers tomorrow and let them know as well.'

'They are going to be seriously surprised. I told them I was never getting married.'

'It's a woman's privilege to change her mind.'

'And a man's,' she pointed out.

'True. Now can we stop with the chit-chat and celebrate our engagement as lovers should?'

CHAPTER TWENTY-NINE

'WOW!' SEBASTIAN EXCLAIMED. 'That is one gorgeous dress.'

Ruby preened. 'Someone with taste chose it for me.'

'Someone who knew it would suit you too, especially the colour.'

'It doesn't look too sexy, does it?' she asked, suddenly swamped by her worries over his family's reaction to their engagement.

Sebastian scowled. 'Don't be nervous. You have nothing to worry about.'

Ruby sighed. 'I can't help worrying a bit.'

'Then we'd better get going so we can get the surprise of our engagement over and done with and you can stop worrying.'

'My mother used to call it the heebie-jeebies,' she told him.

He smiled. 'What a wonderful expression. I like the sound of your mother.'

Ruby swallowed. 'She would have liked you too. She liked manly men. She thought Gregory Peck was gorgeous, and you know what? You look a bit like him.'

'I'll take that as a compliment. But I would prefer to be compared with someone a little more current. Are you ready? How do *I* look? Not too casual?'

He was wearing dark blue shorts, a red and navy striped T-shirt and navy loafers.

'You look great,' she complimented. 'And look, we're

colour-coordinated. That red in your T-shirt is the same red as my dress.'

'You're right. We do look good together. Come on. No, wait! Have you rung your brothers?'

Ruby's heart skipped a beat. 'Er…no. I'll do that later, when they're together at the restaurant. That way I only have to make the one call.'

'Good thinking. Okay, let's go.'

Ruby's nerves returned during the relatively short drive to Gloria's. They didn't have to pick up Frieda on the way, as she'd stayed the night before at her daughter's place. When they pulled up outside a house, which Ruby presumed was Gloria's, she sucked in a couple of deep breaths and told herself not to be so silly.

The house, Ruby noted, was rather old. One of those federation homes with dark verandas and stained-glass windows. It was in good condition, however, the front door freshly painted in very fashionable black. The garden was traditional, with lots of rose bushes and hedges.

Two teenage boys burst out of the house before Sebastian and Ruby could get out of the car. They looked about fourteen and sixteen, both with dark hair and blue eyes, like their uncle, confirming Ruby's suspicion that Gloria's blonde hair might not be natural.

'Hi, Unc,' the older one said. 'Happy Christmas. So this is Ruby. Hi, Ruby. Mum was right, Alex. She said the new housekeeper was a looker.'

'Matthew Chambers,' Sebastian said. 'Stop being cheeky.'

'Ruby, this is Matthew and Alexander. My nephews.'

Both boys pulled faces at the use of their full names.

'And this,' he said as he put a loving arm around Ruby, 'is not just my housekeeper. She's your soon-to-be Auntie Ruby.'

The boys were goggle-eyed for a moment, then they dashed inside, yelling out as they went.

'Uncle Sebastian's got engaged,' both of them chorused loudly.

'That's put a cat among the pigeons,' Sebastian muttered as everyone else emerged onto the front veranda, their faces mirroring shock but not displeasure. In fact, when they saw it was Ruby with Sebastian they all looked heartily relieved. Gloria rushed out to the car, grabbing Ruby's left hand and staring down at the ring.

'Oh, my God!' she exclaimed. 'It's true. Wow, this is fantastic.'

Frieda joined them as well, beaming broadly. 'You finally saw sense, Sebastian.'

'Yes, Mum.'

'Welcome to our family, Ruby. I couldn't be more pleased.' And she gave Ruby a hug.

'Thank you, Frieda.'

'Ruby was a bit worried that you might think this all happened a little fast,' Sebastian said.

'Don't be ridiculous,' Frieda replied. 'You're both old enough to know your own minds. When are you getting married? Soon, I hope. I'm not getting any younger, either.'

Sebastian smiled at her. 'We thought in about six weeks. It takes a month to get the licence. Ruby wants to have the ceremony at home, in the garden.'

'Excellent idea,' Gloria jumped in. 'Now, I have to get back to the dinner. Matthew and Alexander, help your uncle bring in the presents. And, Henry,' she directed at the man behind them, who Ruby presumed was her husband, 'take the happy couple inside and get them a drink. We have lots of celebrating to do today.'

And celebrate they did, all Ruby's qualms put to rest by the warmth of her welcome into the family.

Dinner was a very traditional turkey, which was cooked to perfection. Dessert was also traditional—plum pudding and custard. Ruby loved it all because it reminded her of the Christmases they'd had when her mother was alive. It wasn't until they were enjoying coffee and Christmas cake out on the back veranda afterwards that Sebastian reminded her to ring her brothers.

She groaned. 'Do I have to do it today?'

'Yes,' came his firm reply.

Ruby sighed, made her excuses and went inside to where she'd left her handbag on the hall stand. It was with great reluctance that she drew out her phone and brought up Liam's number, her stomach in knots at the thought of how they would react to her news.

'Sis!' he answered straight away. 'We were just talking about you. Merry Christmas, by the way.'

'Same to you,' she said. 'Are you still at the restaurant?'

'Yes. Just. Why?'

'I have something to tell you and Oliver. And the girls too, of course.'

'Sounds serious. I'll put my phone on speaker so that they can all hear.'

'Oh. All right.'

'Out with it. What have you done, sis? Nothing drastic, I hope.'

'Not drastic. No. A bit surprising, though.'

She heard whispering in the background.

'Okay,' Oliver joined in. 'What is it?' Oliver was the more forceful of the twins.

Ruby took a deep breath first. 'Sebastian and I, we... well, we're going to get married.'

Ruby heard various gasps.

'You're not joking, are you?' Oliver said.

'No.'

'Do you love him?' Oliver asked.

'I do. Very much so.'

'He's a lucky man.'

'Does he love you?' Liam piped up.

'He does,' Ruby said without hesitation. 'Madly, he says.'

'Oh, how romantic!' Rachel and Lara exclaimed at exactly the same time. Maybe they were catching that habit from the twins, who often said exactly the same thing at the same time.

'When's the wedding?' Liam and Oliver asked in unison. Ruby smiled. 'Soon.'

'It's not a shotgun wedding, is it?' Oliver demanded to know.

Ruby laughed. 'No, Oliver, it's not.'

'Just thought I should ask. In that case, congrats, sis. As long as you're happy, we're happy.'

'I'm very happy.'

'Yes, we can hear it in your voice.'

They talked on for a little while until Ruby said she had to get back to the others. When she returned to the back veranda, everyone looked at her expectantly.

'All right?' Sebastian asked. 'They were supportive, I hope.'

'Very. They were delighted that I asked them both to give me away on the day.'

'I rang Zack at the hospital whilst you were speaking to your brothers,' Sebastian said. 'Told him the good news. He was thrilled to pieces. Agreed to be best man as well. So that's all done. Now we can settle back and enjoy the rest of Christmas Day.'

It was a grand day full of fun and festivities, the best Christmas either Ruby or Sebastian had had for a long time. But it would not be the last great Christmas, Ruby vowed when it came time to leave.

'Next year,' she told everyone at the door, 'Christmas will be at our house.' And she privately promised herself that there would be a huge tree and lots and lots of lights, even over the front of the house.

CHAPTER THIRTY

Their wedding day, six weeks later...

RUBY SPUN ROUND at the loud knocking on her bedroom door.

'Are you ready yet, Ruby?' Oliver called out. 'It's time.'

Time...

Time to get married. Time to face the kind of future Ruby had never imagined for herself. But falling in love for real made you change your mind about things. Her vow never to trust a man with her happiness had dissipated under the obvious sincerity of Sebastian's love. For he had had to make massive changes, too. Ruby sometimes thought of his first wife, but she wasn't jealous of her, or Sebastian's long-ago love for her. Ruby suspected Jennifer had been an emotionally damaged person, not capable of giving true love in return. She'd hurt Sebastian terribly when she'd pushed him away during her final days, a hurt that had taken years to heal.

But he was all healed now, Ruby thought happily as she hurried over to open the bedroom door.

'Wow, sis,' both her brothers said as one.

'I do look a bit wow, don't I?' She preened, doing a complete turn so they could look at the back of her dress—and her hair—as well as the front.

Her white bridal gown was strapless, with a beaded bodice, a cinched-in waist and a very low back. The skirt was a

full-length fall of shimmering silk that skimmed the floor.
Ruby had decided against a veil, and instead pulled her hair
back and braided it in a loose plait down her back, a circlet
of flowers on her head. The only jewellery she was wearing
besides her engagement ring were the ruby and diamond
earrings Sebastian had presented her with over breakfast
and which had brought her to tears.

Ruby was aware the dress was a little tighter now than at
the first fitting—the result of her being pregnant. Not that
she intended telling her brothers that little piece of news.
They'd accuse her of having a shotgun wedding again. Sebastian knew, of course. But then it had been *his* idea to let
nature take its course when she'd forgotten to take her pill
on Christmas Day. Both of them had been thrilled when
the test had come up positive a fortnight ago, which just
showed how far they'd come. They were already planning
names. Ava for a girl—named after her mother—and Jack
for a boy—named after Sebastian's father.

'Come on,' Oliver urged. 'The celebrant is getting antsy.'

'Don't you mean Sebastian?' Liam said laughingly.

Ruby smoothed her dress before reaching for her bouquet of red and white roses. 'Let's go.'

Once outside the bedroom and in the roomier hallway,
Liam and Oliver linked arms with her, and led her out to
where the wedding was to take place.

Ruby had decided on a simple ceremony on the back
lawn, to be moved inside if it rained. But the day was fine
and clear, and not too hot or humid. She'd been blessed with
the weather because February in Sydney was often stifling.
As it was, the wedding guests would not be uncomfortable
today, sitting outside on the white plastic chairs that had
been set up in rows in front of a portable wooden stage
with an artificial rose arbour decorating it and the obliga-
tory strip of red carpet leading up to it.

Ruby had insisted on the Christmas lights being left up.

The ceremony was scheduled for six o'clock and instead of a fancy sit-down meal for guests, she'd booked the same caterers and DJ they'd had for the Christmas party. The guest list was pretty much the same as well, with a few family extras.

Ruby's heart swelled as she noted there wasn't an empty chair, everyone clearly having turned up. They all had their phones out, snapping photographs. She wanted lots of photos. But not ones taken by an official photographer, just lots of informal happy snaps. Her heart swelled further when she saw Sebastian standing at the end of the red carpet, a huge smile breaking over his handsome face when he saw her. And possibly relief that she'd shown up at last.

All the men in her bridal party were wearing black tuxedos, with red roses in their lapels, matching the red roses in her bouquet. Ruby knew they would look fabulous in their wedding photos, for which she'd already bought frames. Sebastian had been aghast at their number, then had laughed. He knew when he was beaten.

Ruby made her way down the aisle, smiling left and right as she went. She beamed at Georgia, who'd flown up for the wedding but was going back to Melbourne afterwards. For good.

'It's no use,' she'd told Ruby and Sebastian over the phone. 'I won't be coming back at all. I can't live without those kids. I'd miss them too much.' She'd moved in with her sister and taken a job at a nearby hotel where she only worked part-time.

Ruby didn't mind at all. She didn't want a housekeeper. She had Janice and Tom, and that would be enough. When Sebastian had suggested a nanny for after the baby was born, she'd almost choked on the spot. A nanny? No way.

Speaking of Janice and Tom, there they were, grinning at her. She grinned right back, secretly thinking that she should have had the DJ play 'Dancing Queen' at that moment, just like in the movie *Muriel's Wedding*. But perhaps not. Sebastian's family might not be amused.

Ruby moved further down the red carpet, bestowing smiles on all of Sebastian's work colleagues, but reserving her biggest smile for his immediate family, who were now *her* family. There were Gloria and Henry and their boys, sitting alongside Frieda, all looking resplendent. Finally, she looked back at the man she was about to marry, who was standing there impatiently, with his much more patient best friend by his side. Zack winked at her.

What a naughty man he was! Very naughty, according to nurse Susan, who'd shocked everyone by moving into his penthouse with him when he left hospital. Zack pretended he'd hired her as his private nurse, but Ruby had always suspected differently. And she'd been right. Susan was here somewhere in the crowd of guests. Ruby winked back at Zack before shifting her gaze back to Sebastian. What was he thinking at this moment? she wondered.

What a cheeky minx she was, Sebastian thought when he saw Ruby wink at Zack. But a sheer delight in every way. He loved everything about her, especially her down-to-earth nature and her lack of interest in becoming a socialite. She could have had a huge wedding, in a cathedral no less, with a custom-made designer dress, half a dozen bridesmaids and the reception held at some swanky function centre. Instead, she'd insisted on this simple ceremony, with a dress bought off the rack, a cake made by the local bakery, no bridesmaids, and a casual party afterwards with nibbles and finger food. The only thing he'd had a say in was the champagne, and he'd insisted on the very best from France. He'd also put his foot down where the honeymoon was concerned and booked a five-star luxury apartment on Hamilton Island for two weeks. He would have liked to take Ruby away for longer but Harvest Productions was back in full swing and he really needed to be hands-on, especially where *Battle at the Bar* was concerned. The writers of that show could occasionally go off on a dangerous tangent without a close eye being kept on them.

Thinking of close eyes brought Sebastian's gaze back to Ruby. Lord, but she had one lush figure, even more so now that she was expecting. A smile spread across his face at the thought that they were going to have a child together. It was an amazing thought, really, considering that before he met Ruby he hadn't even wanted to get married again. She'd changed him, that was for sure. For the better, according to Zack. Then again, she'd changed Zack too, made him see that he too could commit to one woman and be happy. Apparently, he and Susan were very serious about each other, which pleased Sebastian no end. Zack deserved to be happy.

'You're looking very pleased with yourself,' Ruby whispered after her brothers had unhanded her and returned to their seats.

'I am. I was just thinking what a lucky man I am to be marrying a girl as gorgeous as you. By the way, I love that dress.'

Ruby smiled. 'Oliver and Liam said you'd like it.'

He grinned at her. 'Did they now?'

The celebrant clearing his throat brought them back to the present moment.

'Shall we begin?' he asked quietly.

'Fire away,' Ruby said, loud enough for some of the guests to hear, since they laughed.

It was a happy ceremony. And a quick one. Zack produced the rings on cue and all was over within minutes, and Sebastian kissed her enthusiastically and passionately. Everyone stood up and clapped, with more photos being taken than at Sydney's opening ceremony.

Guests said afterwards it was the best wedding they'd ever been to.

* * *

Ava Frieda Marshall made her entrance into the world by Caesarean section three weeks early, weighing just over two kilos. Despite being small, she was extremely healthy. Jack Henry Marshall followed his sister by only a minute. He was a more robust three kilos, screaming his head off and making his presence known as only boys could. Sebastian and Ruby had known they were expecting twins but they could not have anticipated, however, the rush of love that overwhelmed them both at the actual arrival of their son and daughter. Sebastian cried as he videoed everything, Ruby in tears herself. Frieda blubbered away on a chair in the corner, having almost fainted at one stage. But she recovered quickly when Sebastian put Ava into her arms.

'Oh, what a precious little darling she is.'

Ruby never relented on hiring a nanny but Frieda came to stay for the first couple of months. And she was a great help. After that, Frieda came often. Jack, surprisingly, developed into a cruisy baby, despite his noisy arrival at the hospital. Ava fretted a little with colic for the first few weeks and often would not settle until her father came home to rock her to sleep in his arms. Zack and Susan were godparents at their christening, stunning Sebastian and Ruby when they announced they were expecting a little bundle of their own. They married just before their daughter Delvine, named after Zack's mother, was born. Naturally, Sebastian and Ruby were her godparents. In the years to come, the four adults and three children would often go on holidays together.

Battle at the Bar went on to be the most successful show on Australian TV for a decade, watched all over the world. It was also the winner of many awards, which Ruby displayed around the house along with a plethora of family photos. Ruby eventually achieved her ambition to get a degree in social science, working part-time as a high-school counsellor after her own precious twins started school.

The principal said she was the best counsellor they'd ever had.

* * * * *

MILLS & BOON

Coming next month

HIS STOLEN INNOCENT'S VOW
Marcella Bell

"I can't," she repeated, her voice low and earnest. "I can't, because when I went to him as he lay dying, I looked him in his eye and swore to him that the d'Tierrza line would end with me, that there would be no d'Tierrza children to inherit the lands or title and that I would see to it that the family name was wiped from the face of the earth so that everything he had ever worked for, or cared about, was lost to history, the legacy he cared so much about nothing but dust. I swore to him that I would never marry and never have children, that not a trace of his legacy would be left on this planet."

For a moment, there was a pause, as if the room itself had sucked in a hiss of irritation. The muscles in his neck tensed, then flexed, though he remained otherwise motionless. He blinked as if in slow motion, the movement a sigh, carrying something much deeper than frustration, though no sound came out. Hel's chest squeezed as she merely observed him. She felt like she'd let him down in some monumental way though they'd only just become reacquainted. She struggled to understand why the sensation was so familiar until she recognized the experience of being in the presence of her father.

Then he opened his eyes again, and instead of the cold green disdain her heart expected, they still burned that fascinating warm brown—a heat that was a steady home fire, as comforting as the imaginary family she'd dreamed up as a child—and all of the taut disappointment in the air was gone.

Her vow was a hiccup in his plans. That he had a low tolerance for hiccups was becoming clear. How she knew any of this when he had revealed so little in his reaction, and her mind only now offered up hazy memories of him as a young man, she didn't know.

She offered a shrug and an airy laugh in consolation, mildly embarrassed about the whole thing though she was simultaneously unsure as to exactly why. "Otherwise, you know, I'd be all in. Despite the whole abduction..." Her cheeks were hot, likely bright pink, but it couldn't be helped so she made the joke, anyway, despite the risk that it might bring his eyes to her face, that it might mean their eyes locked again and he stole her breath again.

Of course, that is what happened. And then there was that smile again, the one that said he knew all about the strange mesmerizing power he had over her, and it pleased him.

Whether he was the kind of man who used his power for good or evil had yet to be determined.

Either way, beneath that infuriating smile, deep in his endless brown eyes, was the sharp attunement of a predator locked on its target. "Give me a week." His face may not have changed, but his voice gave him away, a trace of hoarseness, as if his sails had been slashed and the wind slipped through them, threaded it, a strange hint of something Hel might have described as desperation...if it had come from anyone other than him.

"What?" she asked.

"Give me a week to change your mind."

Continue reading
HIS STOLEN INNOCENT'S VOW
Marcella Bell

Available next month
www.millsandboon.co.uk

COMING SOON!

We really hope you enjoyed reading this book.
If you're looking for more romance, be sure to
head to the shops when new books are
available on

Thursday 4th
March

To see which titles are coming soon, please visit
millsandboon.co.uk/nextmonth

LET'S TALK

For exclusive extracts, competitions
and special offers, find us online:

 facebook.com/millsandboon

🐦 @MillsandBoon

📷 @MillsandBoonUK

Get in touch on 01413 063232

MILLS & BOON

THE HEART OF ROMANCE

A ROMANCE FOR EVERY KIND OF READER

MODERN

Prepare to be swept off your feet by sophisticated, sexy and seductive heroes, in some of the world's most glamourous and romantic locations, where power and passion collide.
8 stories per month.

HISTORICAL

Escape with historical heroes from time gone by. Whether your passion is for wicked Regency Rakes, muscled Vikings or rugged Highlanders, awaken the romance of the past.
6 stories per month.

MEDICAL

Set your pulse racing with dedicated, delectable doctors in the high-pressure world of medicine, where emotions run high and passion, comfort and love are the best medicine.
6 stories per month.

True Love

Celebrate true love with tender stories of heartfelt romance, from the rush of falling in love to the joy a new baby can bring, and a focus on the emotional heart of a relationship.
8 stories per month.

Desire

Indulge in secrets and scandal, intense drama and plenty of sizzling hot action with powerful and passionate heroes who have it all: wealth, status, good looks...everything but the right woman.
6 stories per month.

HEROES

Experience all the excitement of a gripping thriller, with an intense romance at its heart. Resourceful, true-to-life women and strong, fearless men face danger and desire - a killer combination!
8 stories per month.

DARE

Sensual love stories featuring smart, sassy heroines you'd want as a best friend, and compelling intense heroes who are worthy of them.
4 stories per month.

To see which titles are coming soon, please visit

millsandboon.co.uk/nextmonth

JOIN US ON SOCIAL MEDIA!

Stay up to date with our latest releases, author news and gossip, special offers and discounts, and all the behind-the-scenes action from Mills & Boon...

 millsandboon

 millsandboonuk

 millsandboon

It might just be true love...